S.R. Atkinson

These books are forever and always
for the young women of Alpine Academy.

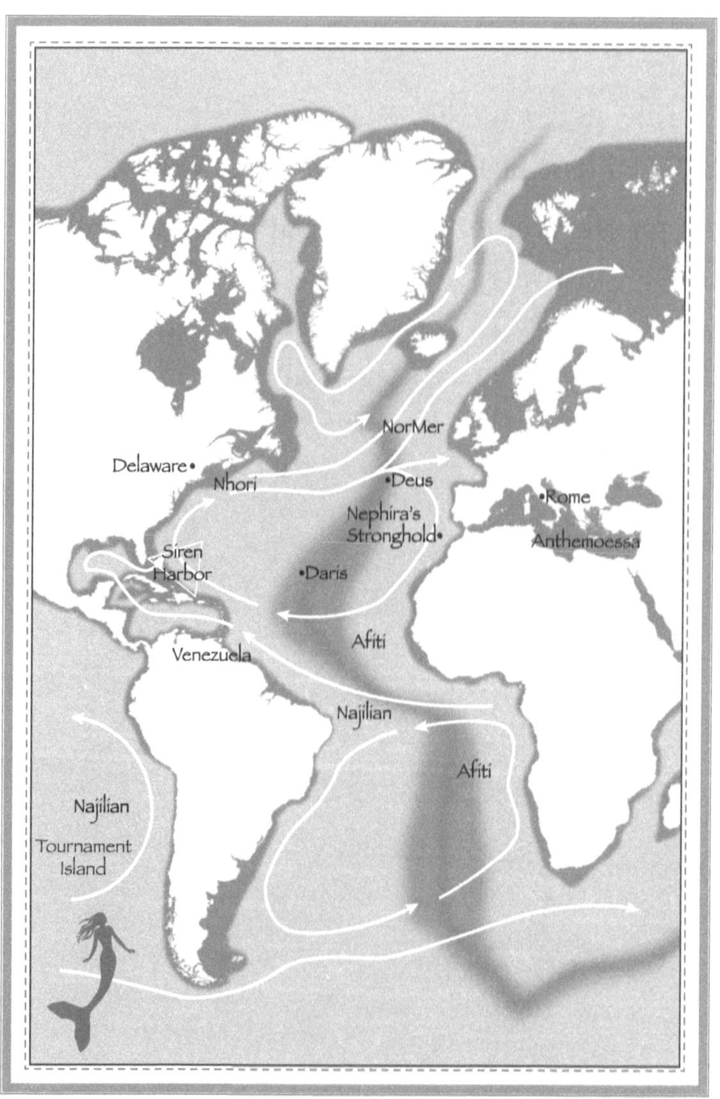
NorMer
Delaware
Nhori
Deus
Rome
Nephira's
Stronghold
Anthemoessa
Siren
Harbor
Daris
Afiti
Venezuela
Najilian
Afiti
Najilian
Tournament
Island

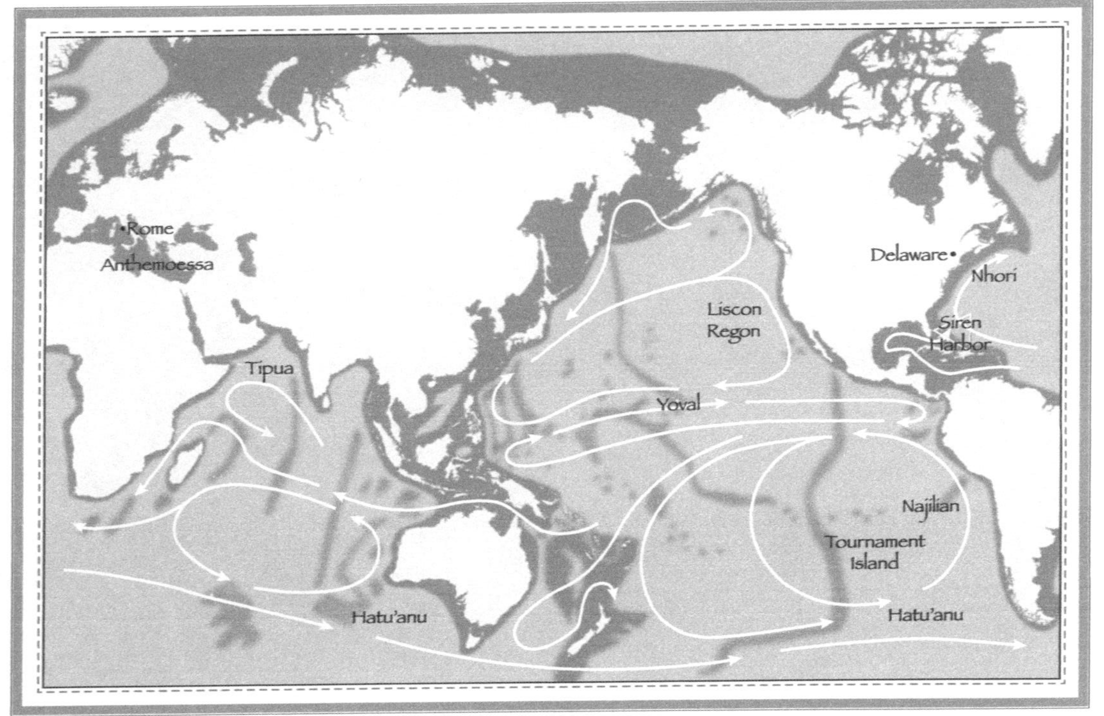
Rome
Anthemoessa
Delaware
Nhori
Liscon Regon
Siren Harbor
Tipua
Yoval
Najilian
Tournament Island
Hatu'anu
Hatu'anu

S.R. Atkinson

Prologue

Sariah
Approximately 667 BCE

Sariah's small cheek was smashed against the white marble floor, her arms crossed over the back of her head, struggling with the lack of oxygen. She lay on her stomach in the large white hallway, flicking the tip of her pink fin against the cool stone. She couldn't stand it anymore, she needed to breathe; her tiny lungs felt like they'd explode.

She hit her whole tail against the ground more forcefully now, trying to distract herself from the crushing weight of asphyxiation. She uncrossed her arms from over her head and beat them against the floor. She balled up her fists and pushed them into her eyes, rubbing vigorously. Would it ever end?

Then it was all over.

Sariah took in a deep lungful of water and relished the tingly feeling that washed over her as oxygen made its way into every corner of her tiny body. She breathed in and out deeply again, enjoying the freedom of easy breathing. She laughed and turned over on her back. Pleased with herself, she looked up at the high white ceiling.

Sucking in yet another deep, expansive breath, Sariah slowly began tapping the tip of her fin against the marble floor to mark off the time.

But before she had even counted to fifteen, the double chamber doors were pushed open wide by two guards. Old Serras began filing out into the hallway, and Sariah sprang up so as to not be lying on the floor in such an undignified manner. Most of the curmudgeons leaving the meeting passed right on by, but the friendlier ones stopped to pay Sariah attention.

"Well, are you not the biggest starfish I have ever seen!" Nhori placed her wrinkled hands on either side of Sariah's face and smooshed gently. "How old are you now, pup?"

"Nine," Sariah said with pride and placed her hands on the side of Nhori's face, tangled amongst her white hair, and squeezed just as the elder had done. It had been a ritual between them for as long as Sariah could remember.

Just then a young dam came up on the side of Nhori and reached out to squeeze Sariah's slight shoulder and tousle her hair.

"Hello, Mereni," Sariah said politely. She liked the new balam, but Mereni was like most bucks and dams her age: they didn't touch each other very often, but they were always squeezing and pinching pups.

"You are just skin and scales, Sariah," Mereni said, giving her another squeeze, this time on her arm. "You need to eat more."

"I am too busy. There is a lot to do as the daughter of Nephira, you know!" She wasn't malnourished, she just lacked any extra plump anywhere on her body. The truth was she was a terrible hunter. She couldn't catch anything, and when she did, it always had too much life in it for her to eat. Even the animals she was allowed, those whose Kus were done with their purpose, she couldn't bring herself to eat. Sariah survived mostly on plants, but not many grew inside the citadel, and she wasn't allowed to go out alone.

Mereni looked like she would respond, but Sariah saw the Serras she had been waiting for emerge from the chamber and she made her leave. "It was so nice to see you, Nhori and Mereni. I hope we may have a dialogue again."

This made Nhori and Mereni send surprised and impressed Kus to each other and the pup.

Swimming away in satisfaction, Sariah was pleased that she was able to show them she was worthy of being Nephira's daughter. She wanted to be polite and strong and smart, to show her mother that she was a good daughter.

She barreled into her parents and gave Phinell three kisses on his right cheek and one on the left. He did the same to her—their secret greeting—and then, sounding a bit startled, said, "Did you wait out here the whole time again?"

She looked a little chagrinned as she admitted that she had and then rushed on to explain, "But I should practice sitting still if I am going to join the meetings!" She didn't think she needed to tell them she actually *didn't* sit very still at all, but she thought the effort was close enough.

This caught Nephira's attention, and she untangled her daughter from Phinell and set her in the water in front of her to look at her directly. Nephira was known for her black skin and scarlet tail, both very beautiful, but neither of those attributes were as lovely as Phinell's coloring, in Sariah's opinion.

She sized her parents up. She was always comparing her skin to theirs and curious about how it was so very different from her older sister's. Phinell's skin was so black it seemed to glow, and his pale ivory tail made it more so. Sariah's own tail looked like a shiny, pink, perfect combination of the two. But the reason it always made her stare extra hard was that even though Sariah knew Phinell wasn't Zitja's father, they shared the same ivory tail.

Curious.

Nephira sent warm, loving beats of her Ku as she spoke. "Sariah, I am worried that you cannot sit through the meetings, but also I worry that they are not appropriate for you. It gets… intense," she said after a pause. "Not everyone agrees about the decisions all the time, and I do not want you to deal with unpleasant things. Sitting in these discussions is so much responsibility for one so young!"

"But Zitja goes to them, and she's only eleven."

"Zitja will be Ocean Mother, and she needs to know what the ocean is really like."

Sariah chewed on her lip. She didn't want to say what she was thinking because it made her sound like a petulant pup, and she was trying to show maturity.

Nephira caught the feelings in Sariah's Ku and answered, "I know you will both be Ocean Mother…" Nephira paused for a moment before she continued. "Zitja has decided, and I think that is fine. Of course I do. I just worry about you. Zitja is… well, she has a different character."

Sariah knew that meant Zitja was stronger. She always had been. And Sariah was weak in her mother's eyes. "It is only because you do not let me see any bad things. I can be strong, too."

As if a gift to Sariah, Phinell sent a strong feeling through his Ku, which Sariah and Nephira both felt. It seemed to change the latter's heart completely. "You are right, my daughter, you shall be at the next meeting… And I am happy for it." She added, not as an afterthought, but with genuine eagerness. "I would truly love both of my daughters to be able to spend more time with me. Now, if you'll excuse me, seal pup, we have to travel with Lorr to the Tipua. We will be back in a couple weeks."

"Mother," Sariah pulled herself out to her full length, "do you not think that Zitja and I should go with you? Because we will be the Ocean Mothers, after all."

Sariah could feel Nephira's love consume her even though there was a trace of humor behind it. Sariah knew her mother was trying not to laugh at her, but she didn't know why.

"Ok, my little seal pup. You have impressed me. You two may come. But!" She held up her hand to stop Sariah before she became too excitable. "You may not come with us now. We have too much serious business to attend. I will have Ro bring you in two days."

Sariah nodded. Ro usually took care of Zitja and Sariah when their parents were gone. He was very nice but rather boring, in Sariah's option. But that did not matter now.

"Thank you!" Sariah squealed and threw her arms around Nephira's neck before they parted ways.

Usually the news of her parents leaving for an extended period of time made Sariah sad, but she was too consumed by all the good news. And two days was nothing compared to the progress she had just made.

As Nephira and Phinell made their way down the hall, Sariah swooped into the chamber where Zitja was waiting for her so they could play Balam Meeting together. She didn't try to stop herself as she careened into her favorite being in the world.

"Did you hear?"

"I did!" Zitja pinched her sister on the tail lovingly. "Now you get to sit through this horrendous thing with me."

"I cannot wait!" Suddenly she remembered the news she had for Zitja, and, as if her mood couldn't get any better, she squealed, "I held it to sixty!"

"Sixty!" Zitja joined Sariah in her enthusiasm. "That is the longest ever!"

"I know. And I was going to do sixty-one the next meeting and sixty-two the next. But now I do not have to. Now I can just come in to the meeting with you."

"Why did you need to do it at all?"

Sariah cocked her head, "I… well I did not *need* to. I just did it to pass the time."

Zitja laughed. She was only two years older, but to Sariah her Ku felt so much more, like she had experienced something that others had not and it left her mature, wise. Jaded. Sariah wasn't sure what it was but figured one day it would all be clear. If it took her whole life, she'd learn what set her sister apart.

"What I am asking is why do you have to sit out here practicing holding your breath?" Zitja clarified. "There is so much else you could do besides lie on the floor waiting."

What Sariah said next was so sincere, so genuine, it tugged at Zitja's heart and left her without comment.

"But Zitja, what would I even do without you?"

It took a full minute for Zitja to think enough to speak. It was true they were always together, and they were the best of friends, but Zitja figured it was because their parents were usually gone, and the other pups didn't like Zitja. Her little sister, on the other hand, did not lack for other pups to play with. Zitja never realized it was such a strong and love-drawn choice where Sariah spent her time.

When she finally pulled herself together, Zitja grabbed her sister by the hand and said, "Come on. You are going to be a part of these meetings soon, so no need to play at them anymore. Besides, you have to eat something. You are skin and scales."

An hour later, Zitja was holding a small, hard, white object in her hand. She looked pleased to show Sariah the discovery. "Father brought some back from his last trip and gave them to all the balams. They are not from this area, but he brought thousands in hopes that they will flourish here. Because they are quite delicious!"

Sariah picked it up and turned it over in her hands. It wasn't smooth, but it was very hard, and it looked beautiful—white with a tint of shimmering gray, and a scalloped edge. She was intrigued.

"What is it?" Sariah asked as she put it halfway in her mouth and bit down.

"No!" Zitja yelled as Sariah cried out at the same time.

"It is too hard!" She rubbed her cheek with a strong fist as if to ease the pain in her teeth and jaw.

"We have to open it. It is called a bivalve, because it is like two doors. The food is inside."

Sariah stared at it. It looked like a flattened circle with no way inside.

Zitja pulled out her small eating knife from her bag. "You have to pry it open."

Sariah made as if to take the knife, but Zitja took the bivalve instead. "No, if you slip you could cut yourself. I will do it for you."

Sariah watched as Zitja struggled to get the tip of the knife into a miniscule slit in the side. Zitja's hand slipped, and the knife slid by the inside of her palm, just missing it.

"Be careful!" Sariah gasped.

"It is so difficult!" Zitja scrunched up her face in thought. "Tata had made it look easy when he opened the little monsters." This made Sariah laugh, and Zitja took note to call more things monsters. She would do anything that made her sister happy.

Zitja nestled the white shell in the sand and placed her knife on the top. She then positioned her tan body so that she was facing the monster at a right angle. She kicked her ivory tail, swimming towards it, pushing her entire body weight upon it. Finally, her knife slipped inside. Once she had the knife well into the slit, she righted herself and twisted the knife so that the two shells popped open.

"See!" Zitja said with pride. "Two little doors. And a special treat for my favorite sister. Feel its Ku."

Sariah stared at the slimy thing. It did not look appetizing, and quite frankly, she didn't want to eat any Kus but had never admitted that to anyone before. She reached out her Ku and tried to connect to the bivalve.

"I do not feel it." She pushed harder. There had never been an animal without one that she knew. "Zitja? I cannot find it."

"That is because it does not have one, little seal. You can eat this without worry. Just like all that kelp you somehow survive on."

Sariah smiled and sent a rush of love towards her sister. "It still looks horrid, but I will try it!"

Just then a shout interrupted them.

"Go back where you came from."

The two pups looked up from the bivalve and stared as four buck pups came upon them.

Zitja looked with disdain and poise at the scowling pup who had spoken. She responded with more maturity than her eleven years. "And where would that be?"

"You are a terrasite!" a different pup sneered at her, pushing Zitja in the shoulder. "Go back to the terra where you belong."

The push sent Zitja crashing into a third pup, bigger than the rest, older than Zitja but not as smart. He pushed her too and said, "You do not belong here with us."

Zitja managed to kick herself above the group of harassers. "I have a tail like you. I have scales, a fin, I breathe water, and my mother is the Ocean's Mother. You tell me how it is that I do not belong here."

The pup that had originally spoken spoke up again, angry this time, as if Zitja's existence was a personal offense.

"Your filthy father is a Crural. You are a filthy demi-Crural. Terrasite."

Sariah couldn't handle all the torment as well as Zitja seemed to. She burst from the sand where she had been sitting, frozen in fear, and came to her big sister's side. "You leave her alone!" She found bravery somewhere in her Ku and looked down on the group from alongside Zitja. "This is not nice of you."

The four tormenters made to move on Nephira's two small daughters, their size and number alone meant to intimidate, but Zitja acted quickly.

She grabbed her tiny sister around the arm and swam away from the group as fast as she could. They pursued. Sariah tried to keep up—at only two years younger she should have been able to—but Sariah was so much smaller than most pups her age. She was over-protected and under-fed. Sheltered from all things harsh, she had never had to swim fast or work hard. She was a frail thing and a slow swimmer.

Zitja readjusted her grip and held Sariah like a nursery pup on her hip and picked up her pace.

She was no match for the bigger, stronger Serras, and they were soon surrounded again. Zitja let go of Sariah and said, still calmly, "Please leave us alone. At least let Sariah go. She has done nothing to offend you."

"Oh sure," the leader of the pack said. "Go on, little Sariah."

"No," Sariah whispered. "Not without Zitja."

But Zitja was pushing her out of the circle of terrorizers. "Just go home, starfish. It is fine. I can handle them."

"But… but I do not want to." Sariah was shaking. "Who are they? Why are they doing this to you?"

Zitja grabbed her little sister by the shoulders and looked at her firmly. "These are just other pups from Daris. They think this is a fun game. They cannot hurt me, but I am afraid they will hurt you, so please go back and find Mother or Father or even Nhori. Ok?"

"But I want to stay with you." Sariah realized then that she would rather stay through the most frightening of events than do anything without her sister.

"Go." Zitja pushed her away from the group, and Sariah had no choice but to slowly swim away. Though she didn't go far or fast, she hoped she could still help her sister somehow.

She looked back over her shoulder as the Serras began throwing rocks at Zitja. Sariah stopped with a hand to her mouth, horrified. How could anyone behave in such a way? She truly had been sheltered from all things harsh.

The awful pups had slings that flung the rocks hard and fast. One after another they pulled rocks from their pouches and flung them through the water, hitting Zitja thoroughly from the tip of her fin to her face. Zitja calmly bore it, trying to reason with them.

Time and time again, Zitja had protected Sariah from the perils of the ocean when their mother was busy with her duties. She looked after the younger pup as if she were much older and wiser than she was. Sometimes Zitja was the only one to remember to make her sister eat, as Sariah didn't think of food as a priority. She could not watch as her sister and protector underwent such torment.

She squared her tiny nine-year-old shoulders and began making her way back to the group. "Leave her alone!" she shouted. "I will get my mother!"

The largest one turned—he had to be at least five years older than Sariah.

"Go away, little guppy!" he yelled as he continued to swing his sling around and around. Then, as if only an afterthought, he flung the rock in Sariah's direction.

It hit her squarely on the cheek. She raised her hand to her face as it burned from the impact.

Zitja exploded.

She screamed in a feral way Sariah had never heard from her before, and the water around her pulsed with an undefined vibration. Zitja lunged at the brute, clawed his face, punched his neck, and slammed her fist into his face. Then she swung her tail tight and fast and hit him across the torso, sending him flying through the water, but she wasn't through. She followed after him and immediately wrapped both her hands around his neck and squeezed. His eyes bulged in panic. He wrestled with her hands, but she was too angry. Her rage gave her strength.

Sariah whispered, "No." She watched in horror as Zitja held the chokehold on the buck until he hung limp in the water. It must have taken ten minutes, but Sariah dared not move. Surely her sister would let go at any moment and the buck pup would swim away. The other three bucks just stared in horror and incredulity along with Sariah. One finally rushed away. Even then Zitja didn't let go. She continued the guttural scream, squeezing her hands and shaking the limp Serra.

Sariah turned and fled.

She had never been afraid of her sister before. She loved Zitja more than any being in the water. She was repulsed by what she had just witnessed and was afraid of what had just happened. But she didn't flee because she was afraid of Zitja. She fled because she didn't want her opinion of her sister to change. Maybe if she went away quickly, she could pretend it hadn't happened. She could deny it in the future.

If Sariah went to their room and forgot about it, then when Zitja arrived she could pretend her sister wasn't a murderer.

Chapter 1

Santiago

Santi flipped the tines of her sai to face outward and spun counterclockwise in a tight circle. She slashed first at her opponent's face, missed, then connected her elbow on the way back to follow the hit. It was effective; he faltered backwards in the water. She continued her tight spin.

Santi would have to be in control if she didn't want to kill him, which she didn't. But had she mastered the kind of control needed?

Doubtful.

As she finished her compact circle, she connected her left heel with his tail where his thigh would be if he were Crural. She was going to finish with her right knee in his ribs, but he caught her. His one massive hand grabbed her knee and flicked her to the side like a mosquito. Santi scowled.

Refocusing, she went in to end it. She'd been working on a new move and kept failing, but she needed to get it right one of these times, and she was determined that this was going to be it.

Santi spread out her toes for maximum traction in the water, kicked her feet fiercely, and dove straight towards her opponent. As he took a short, deadly swipe at her, she parried his swing with the sai in her left hand. She caught his blade between the tines—a move she had mastered long ago—and now tried to finish without injuring herself.

Santi twisted her wrist so quickly and so sharply the force could have broken her wrist; she hoped in the future she would do it well enough to break an opponent's. She felt resistance, as she always had, and then something new. Weightlessness. She had done it. The sword dangled from her sai.

In her possession.

Now she was supposed to flick it away. Flick the sword away and finish her opponent, but she suddenly felt poetic. Or ironic. Or probably just human. The way humans—at least in movies—always needed to put on an extra show of arrogance after they gained control. She sheathed the sai in her right hand and grabbed his sword. Then she turned back on her opponent to finish him off with his own weapon.

He charged at her with a small dagger he had tucked away in the leather strap around his chest, but she was too fast and she pressed the sword to his ribs, just under his left nipple. Right where Grendor had told her.

She stopped, the tip of the sword touching skin, the sai in her other hand poised as backup. She had the control needed. She didn't kill him.

Santi smiled, eyes wide and proud. "I did it!" She dropped the sword and sai. "I killed you. I KILLED you!!"

Amed would have smiled, fatherly and proud, then immediately insist she try it again. But she did not get to spar with Amed anymore and Grendor was much less fatherly and far more friendly.

"Brutal, Santiago." Grendor smiled in approval and clutched the spot where she "stabbed" him. "I thought we were friends."

"Please," she scoffed. "You kill me all the time."

"Seriously, though, Santiago." Grendor paused and pulsed calmness and pride in his Ku at her. His mass of dozens of braids was still floating around his head. "You are doing remarkably well. That was truly a worthy opposition for anyone."

Santi couldn't help being overcome by his praise. "I've practiced every single day since we arrived in Daris. One hundred and twenty-four days of combat practice, to be exact."

Grendor uncharacteristically scrunched up his face at her. "That is quite exact."

She paused, uncertain if sarcasm was appropriate. Though if she weren't sassy right now she would probably scream, "Well… I'm doing literally nothing else."

Darkness passed between them. So much unsaid about Amed's death… about Rogan… hung between them. Finally, Grendor broke through the gloom and inquired, "And Rogan is not doing any better?" His thick braids began to settle on his shoulders, though some of them remained suspended around him, making him look considerably more menacing than he actually was.

Santi shook her head, a gesture she wasn't sure Grendor knew, but he would understand her Ku. What she did not express, what she couldn't say, was that things were not better with Rogan and that the two of them were barely holding onto their Bonding with the edges of their Kus. Did Serras break up? Un-Bond? She didn't know but didn't want to ask or experience it.

With an unnecessary clearing of her throat, a lingering habit from a past life that felt so far away, Santi changed the subject. "It's probably time to go, right?"

Grendor scratched his bushy beard and Santi could tell he was debating whether to press the issue. Probably deciding it wasn't his place, he said, "Shall I accompany you?"

"That won't be necessary. Rogan is-" her entire body went involuntarily rigid. "…There he is now." She felt him coming only moments before he arrived. She smiled and tried to brush off her initial dread, an emotion she was startled to find she felt so deeply when anticipating Rogan's presence.

"Hello, Grendor." Rogan said. Flat, emotionless, unsettlingly calm. He turned his head towards her, though his gaze was distracted. "Santiago, are you ready to go?"

"I am."

Rogan began swimming towards the center of the island. Santi turned to Grendor with as light of a heart as she could muster. "Thank you, Grendor. I appreciate your help."

"Of course." He did not try to lighten his heart. It told her to be sincere with him.

"Kill you tomorrow?" she asked with a smile before turning to follow Rogan.

Santi rushed up to where Rogan was languidly swimming and grabbed him by the hand; swimming ahead, she gently tugged him along. She tried to pretend she was being playful, but the truth was she was afraid if she didn't make him interact, he might not ever be interested in spending time with her. Amphitrite, her turtle friend who had been sleeping while Santi sparred, was now following behind happily, though she kept her distance. Even Amphitrite was feeling a little scared of the darkness that consumed Rogan these days.

Eventually Santi stopped tugging Rogan along, and he took up the duty of pulling her the distance. The trip would take far too long if he didn't take charge of their speed. In the four months they had been at Daris, this was the very trip she had wanted to take with him: travel the city, see it's splendor, visit the hub that was the center of it all, and see the legendary Nephira statue. But she couldn't enjoy it, could barely even see it as they trekked across the city, so consumed was she with Rogan and what she could possibly do to shake him out of his darkness.

Actually shake him, maybe.

After what felt like an eternity of silently swimming, they reached the center of the city. The Troag, they called it, though Santi couldn't imagine why.

She looked at Rogan swimming next to her. Her heart broke. He was so striking: a beautiful, broken buck. She didn't know how to help him. Santi dropped his hand. The contact felt like rejection. She looked to her other side, at the wall that enclosed the Troag.

It wasn't really a wall at all. It was green and lush and leafy. "These look like bushes." She stopped and touched the twelve-foot barrier where Rogan and she were positioned halfway between the top of the greenery and the ground. "Rogan are these hedges?" But he wasn't listening. She continued swimming behind him. "Well, I think this place is pretty cool," she said to Amphitrite, who also seemed distracted.

In over four months—one hundred and twenty-four days, she thought with a smidge of resentment—she hadn't done much exploring at all. Her time had mostly been spent training and managing Rogan's mood. Even her errands of obtaining food, meeting with Grendor, trying to learn the layout around their home, and experiencing their new city consisted of small trips close to their shelter. She had even started going for "swims," as she called them. Much like going for a run, she was working on her swimming skill and endurance. They passed the time well and had improved her physical ability in the water greatly, but she still didn't get anywhere close to the center of the city on these. The building they lived in—the "skyscraper," she called it—was one of the tallest structures, and from their window she could look over the massive, circular city. However, since they lived at the very farthest edge of Daris, the trip to the Troag was a journey that would take her hours alone without Rogan's tail. The trip was daunting, sure, but she also didn't want to explore on her own. It wasn't that she was too nervous to go without him, but she wanted to experience it *with* him.

"It's odd that the street is paved, isn't it?" she continued, just to break the silence, "I mean, Serras will literally never use or need it. Right? Why would they pave it?"

"What?" Rogan stopped and gave her his full attention for what felt like the first time since his father's death.

Santi stammered. She wished she were talking about something other than the road. Why couldn't he have looked at her so earnestly two weeks ago when she had pleaded with him to talk to her about how he was feeling? Or just last night when she had asked him what she could do to help him. But instead she had his full attention as she said, "Oh… the road. I mean… well it's not paved, exactly. That's the wrong word. But… but the stones. I mean why is there a road at all?"

What am I talking about?!

She was so angry with herself. She could feel him drifting back into his shell. She wanted to scream.

"This used to be a Crural city," he responded factually. "Before it sunk."

He was still engaged with her, even making eye contact, so she tried to turn the conversation to something more productive. Possibly get him to talk about something real. Something other that the stupid road. "Is it hard to be here, knowing that your father worked here most of his life?"

Darkness consumed him again.

Santi cursed to herself with all the Crural and the Serra curses she knew.

Too far. Too fast.

She cursed again. His Ku felt heavy in Santi's own, and she wanted to shake him. Or cry with him. She wanted some way of connecting with him like they used to. Rogan's gaze drifted up to the hedges they had been talking about before. He closed his eyes as Santi felt a sharp stabbing in her chest. Then it passed, and Rogan began swimming again.

"It sank?" Santi pushed his hurt and cold Ku aside and tried to keep him in the conversation. Keeping it light this time, she asked, "Is this city another real life Crural myth?" Usually he loved her Crural folklore. It was one of his favorite things to tease her about. She hoped to entice him into a conversation, but he didn't seem to care.

"Rogan?" His shaggy brown hair swayed with the water, but his head didn't turn to look at her. His sharp jawline seemed forever clenched these days, and she missed how his brown eyes used to sparkle with mischief. Now they seemed eternally empty.

Her Ku felt so heavy it weighed uncomfortably in her stomach. She bit her lip to stop it from quivering. After letting out a large breath of water, Santi swam on with Rogan following behind, lost in his own thoughts.

"What do you think, Amphitrite?" Santi said, trying to lighten the mood. Rogan had been endlessly patient with her as she recovered from her kidnapping three years ago. She had gone through her own healing period and often spent time staring off despondently. He had been so good with her; she could do the same for him. "What do you make of Daris, little turtle?" she asked with a light Ku to her friend, who was anything but little.

The city of Daris was beautiful, though the word "beautiful" seemed like a profound understatement. The city was not like anything she had seen before, except maybe in fantasy movies. The entirety of the city was made from white marble and gold. Sometimes the gold was an accent or trim, and sometimes it seemed a part of the marbling in the white. The circular layout only added to the spectacular feeling of the mystery. It reminded her of those small mazes with the shiny silver balls that children got from the dentist. She couldn't decipher the reality of the city—where it had come from, how it came to be at the bottom of the ocean—which made it seem all the more ethereal. It shone brightly through the water for miles, which is why she had been able to see it when she was kidnapped and tied under a whale.

Serras rushed about non-stop. It was truly a bustling city, but it didn't feel crowded or dirty the way cities usually did. A dam with a small pup strapped to her back swooped in front of her and entered a shelter on the ground floor. While the door was open, Santi's curiosity overcame her and she peaked inside. Rogan's small kinship didn't have doors but Daris had a lot of them, much like any Crural neighborhood. As she peeked in the shelter, she noticed that it looked vastly different from Rogan's childhood shelter or the apartment-style home they shared here in Daris. This Serra's home looked much like any Crural home with a woven rug on the marble floor, a few actual chairs made of carved wood, and something hanging on the wall that Santi couldn't make out before the door closed, though she thought it looked a lot like a Crural religious relic.

Santi turned to mention it to Rogan and stopped swimming. He was swimming on his back looking above them at nothing. It felt deliberate, not to swim next to her, facing the same way. Though under water, swimming positions were unimportant, and while it was probably not necessarily rude, it seemed impolite at the very least. She drummed her fingers against her leg. His Ku was churning in turmoil.

What do I do?

"Rogan, I'm excited about this." She settled on honesty in her words and outright false happiness in her tone and Ku. "Are you looking forward to it?" Her pause was short. Maybe she didn't wait long enough for his response, but she was used to the long silences and couldn't bear another one. "Would you please talk to me? I know you're..." She kicked her feet to get in front of him and stopped him. "Rogan," she pled in her Ku, "I know you're grieving and distracted, but I'm..." She decided not to get into the loneliness, the heartache, and the anger. "I'm curious. Please tell me."

"Santiago, it is fine. The ceremony is short and probably not even necessary." He said, his Ku barely present in the conversation. Rogan grabbed her hand and began swimming again.

Not necessary?

Santi was confused, but mostly irritated. How was this ceremony not necessary? It was such a big deal. Something he had looked forward to and discussed with Amed for so long.

Santi hung her head. She felt so blind that she hadn't realized why he was extra tense today. "I'm sure it's hard for you to look forward to this ceremony knowing your father isn't the one leading it now."

"It is hard for me to look forward to most things."

Santi's eyes went wide. That was the most he had said about his father's death since it happened. Right after Amed was killed, Rogan was the one who helped her put it in perspective and see there was hope. But that only lasted a few days. Santi assumed that he'd been able to put his father's death more into perspective while he was still in shock or denial, but ever since they arrived in Daris, Rogan had changed to become the way he was now. She stayed quiet, hoping to encourage more conversation, but nothing followed, and she quickly became resigned to the fact that she had gotten all she would from him today. But if he meant for her to feel placated, she wasn't.

They followed the hedgerow further, and she turned her attention once again to the scenery of the unique city. For a land-walking being like herself, the landscape of the streets and commuting through town at street level was normal. She had never questioned it as a child negotiating through Rogan's small kinship, but it seemed odd in this grand city. With such great distances and so much commotion, traveling on street level seemed an odd thing when one could swim above it.

Major commuting was done high overhead, quickly, efficiently. But for shorter distances, the Serras always swam among the buildings and terrain. She had no one to ask about it so she had to assume for herself that it was probably to give them some semblance of being a part of the place they lived. Like taking the scenic route. It became tiring to swim in open waters all the time, having nothing but water all around, no landmarks or distractions for the eyes and mind. But swimming along this hedgerow with Rogan could be so pleasant an experience… if he'd let it be.

They swam a few more yards until the shrubbery opened in a leafy archway to reveal the Troag packed with Serras, all anxiously waiting. She knew they were all there, had felt the commotion in her Ku and thought about swimming over the hedge several times to take a peek at the Troag—and the famous statue of Nephira she had been dying to see—but she was too focused on Rogan.

The sight of it all left Santi overwhelmed and glad this ceremony was for him and that she could just sit in the crowd fairly anonymously. "Why do they call the center of the city the Troag?" she asked, mostly as a distraction. The crowd was massive, and everyone was clearly adorned in their best wrappings and jewelry with their hair finely ornamented. It made Santi wish she had taken more care instead of throwing on her blue one-piece suit and pulling her hair up in a simple ponytail.

Of course, he didn't respond to her distraction, so she was left to think about how, in a large crowd, she was never quite anonymous. Her Crural legs alone garnered plenty of greetings and questions. Thankfully, she was quite extroverted. Her mother had given her plenty of examples for how to handle a group, and she didn't mind the curiosity of the Serras.

With gusto, Amphitrite broke away from them and made her way into the crowd. Several Serras greeted her with loving pats on the head, making Santi wonder yet again how the giant turtle seemed to be such a mogul in the Serra society.

Even more surprising, a moment later Santi was greeted with a warm embrace by Coral.

"I didn't know you were coming!" said Santiago, pressing her hand against the leather wrappings around Coral's heart, her fingers getting tangled in the layers of beaded necklaces hanging from her delicate neck. "When did you arrive in Daris?"

Coral returned the gesture, then placed her hand over Rogan's heart to greet him as she said, "Just this morning. I would not miss this, my dear."

The three of them sat in reverent silence for a moment. It was the first time they had all been together since the HaruVivo. The stark absence of an important member of their family made Santi bite her lips and blink rapidly to avoid crying. She wanted to say something, but nothing would suffice. She hoped Tizz would arrive soon, though that might make Amed's absence all the more stark.

As if reading her mind, Coral sighed happily as she said, "Tizz should be here very soon. All of the Daristor groups have arrived for the ceremony except hers. Maybe we should go out and greet her?"

"Oh, lets do!" Santi said, relishing Coral's upbeat mood after living so long in gloom.

"You two should do that," Rogan said, engaged but distracted. "There is still over an hour before we start, so there is plenty of time, but I have to join the others."

"Of course," Coral said, as if realizing for the first time that he had a purpose here other than a family reunion. "Santi and I will go."

Rogan said goodbye to his mother, and to Santi's surprise and delight, he leaned over and kissed her and said, "Thank you for being here. Please find a space in front when you get back."

Santi could barely respond, "I will," through her shock before she watched his gorgeous blue tail swim away from her.

"Shall we?" Coral said, but at that same moment Grendor was at her side and the greetings began again.

"May I talk with you for a moment?" Grendor asked. "I need to discuss the ceremony with you."

"Certainly," Coral responded before Santi could reply.

Santi gave a small shrug and said, "I'm going to go out and meet Tizz still, I think. I'd like to see a bit more of the city anyway, since there is time."

"Very well," Grendor said, a moment of confusion sparking in his Ku. "Are you sure you would not like to discuss this with us?"

"No, thank you. I think I'd rather spend the time exploring a bit. Calm my nerves a little."

"If you are certain," Grendor said and bade her farewell.

Santi turned to leave and wondered why Grendor's usually calming presence had made her so anxious all of a sudden. She felt she could not get away fast enough and was only happy to go out of the city for a moment of peace. As she was making her way back through the hedgerow, Amphitrite joined her and Santi laughed. "You have a sense for adventure, don't you? Well I'm sorry to disappoint, but we aren't going anywhere fun right now." And then as an afterthought, she added, "Well, for you, anyway. You've seen this whole city before. Maybe you can be my tour guide."

Santi made her way down a street heading towards the grand archway into the city. She didn't need directions because it could be seen from anywhere in Daris.

At one point, she stopped swimming and planted her feet firmly on the cobblestone street and walked for a few steps, wondering what this place was like when it was above water. She kicked off and began swimming again. Even with her slow legs, swimming was twenty times faster than walking underwater, which was an utterly unrealistic way to get around.

Calling the Troag the city center was a misnomer, and Santi knew it or else she would never have ventured out on her own. Calling it the "center" was more of a description of its relevance than its location. Traveling from the actual geographic center of Daris to the front archway would take her far too long in the short amount of time she had. The Troag was off-center by quite a bit, located much more closely to the entrance gate than the heart of the island.

In no time at all, she arrived at Nephira's Citadel, which was directly between the Troag and Daris' entrance. It was another place she knew how to get to without having to ask for directions. It was like a small castle, grand and impressive, the only landmark besides the archway she could make out from her skyscraper apartment. She had noticed it as she swam by earlier and wondered if she would ever have the pleasure of going inside this building someday. Sentinel Headquarters was in part of it, for one thing, so maybe someday soon this building would be a part of her everyday life.

A few minutes later, Santi stood on the sandy floor beneath an enormous archway, gazing up. The portico, it was called, was the highest point in the whole city, wide enough for a whale to swim through, and so tall she could barely see the top from where she stood.

"What needed to pass through here when they built this? Dinosaurs?" Santi scoffed and then smiled at Amphitrite. "When do you think this city was built? Rogan said it sank. You know what that means, right?" Santi wiggled her eyebrows a couple times at the large reptile. "Yeah, you know."

In response, Amphitrite began swimming through the arch, away from Daris.

Santi followed after her. "What? You think I'm wrong?" Santi was tired of feeling ignored—even by a turtle that wasn't actually disregarding her—and she mumbled to herself irritably. "Well I think it's the Lost City of Atlantis."

Santi followed behind Amphitrite as they casually swam around with no direction. Outside the walls of the city the ocean floor was cleared of most of the vegetation. Kelp, coral, and small fish flourished in the area, which made it beautiful and teeming with life, but the area was free from the usual tall plants and ocean matter that often obstructed sight in the water. Santi remembered Rogan telling her they kept the area around the city cleared so that enemies couldn't hide outside the city.

Santi swam directly away from Daris, inspecting all the plants and feeling surprised by the variety of life she was seeing. She was sure there were more plants and animals undiscovered by Crurals than they even knew. Bright oranges, purples, blues, and pinks filled her vision as far as she could see. "It's so beautiful, isn't it?" She looked over her shoulder for Amphitrite but couldn't see the turtle. Santi's shoulders sagged, but she continued swimming.

Headed out towards the open ocean, leaving the city behind her, Santi felt the physical manifestation of her internal isolation. She swam low to the ground, the foliage becoming a blur of bright colors below her. She turned herself over, staring up to the surface. She could see the sun shining, a dancing yellow, fuzzy ball above. She took a deep breath, closed her eyes, and tried to shake it all off. She couldn't believe it had been almost three years since she had decided to step back in the water and find Rogan. Such a short amount of time, yet things had changed so much since then. She had experienced both the happiest and saddest time of her life in the last three years.

Opening her eyes, she turned herself back over to look at the beautiful flowers again. Maybe she could plant some of these in her apartment. She hadn't done anything to make it feel like a home, and it might help them both to feel better.

Suddenly, the ground dropped away and Santi floated above a black abyss. There was nothing to be seen under her feet, and a chill ran through her body. It wasn't as much a fear of heights as a fear of unknown terrors lurking in the depths that caused goosebumps to cover her body, and she quickly kicked herself back until there was ground beneath her again.

Lowering herself to stand on the island floor, Santi scanned the cliff as far to the left and right as she could see. It wasn't a gradual decline like the coastal shelf Rogan's kinship sat on; it was a severe and drastic drop with nothing but blackness for miles below. She had been in this kind of water before, but never alone. "What is this place?" she asked no one, and no one responded. The silence spurred her to find Amphitrite.

Santi pushed out her Ku through the island as far as she could reach and found the big turtle around the side of the city. She started making her way towards her friend, scanning the ocean behind her once more. She knew she was safe. She didn't feel anything for miles in any direction except the bustling inside the city, but that didn't stop the chills she felt. The ocean could be majestic… and also very unnerving.

When she finally reached Amphitrite, the animal was digging at the bottom of a giant cage where a large chain lay staked to the ground. The green swirly pattern of her shell became mesmerizing as the turtle flittered around the cage trying to find an access point. The cage was completely empty save for some dark red, spikey balls.

"What is this?" Santi said, cocking her head. The cage was wide enough for several Serras but very short. As she stood beside it, it only went up to her knees. The holes in the cage were very small, much like chicken wire—not even big enough to stick a hand through, except the metal mesh was very strong and thick.

Amphitrite was digging at the side of the cage, trying to get to the small plants inside.

"Amphitrite, stop!" The turtle did not stop. "This must be a trap for some sort of animal." This gave Santi another little shiver. What was this large that would need to be trapped? And so close to Daris?

Santi grabbed Amphitrite by the shell around her neck and pulled her away. "You would fit perfectly inside this cage, so stop messing with it. I don't know how it works, but I don't want to find out either."

Just then Amphitrite turned her attention towards the open ocean, her head perked up as if listening for something. Then she took off in that direction.

"The attention span of a squirrel, I swear," Santi muttered before pushing out her Ku to see what had gotten the large sea-squirrel's attention.

Santi didn't have to push her Ku out far before she found what she was looking for, connected Kus, and exclaimed, "Finally!"

"What do you mean, finally?" came a sassy, smooth voice back at her. "We are early."

"I mean finally, today. I've been out here waiting." This wasn't necessarily true. Santi hadn't felt like she was waiting at all, but it seemed appropriate to do a little ribbing.

Amphitrite and a teal tailed Serra dam with sprawling blond hair swooped down on her. Tizz and Santi embraced like the adoring sisters they were.

"Well, I am back now. And I will be here a while, so we can have some fun!" Tizz's brown eyes sparkled the way Rogan's used to. Santi smiled. Amaratizz was a near clone of Coral: teal tail, light skin, blond hair. But those eyes… Those were Amed and Rogan's eyes: dark, mischievous, full of fun and wisdom.

"I've missed you so much, Tizz. It wasn't until this very moment that I realized how lonely I've been." Santi sighed and released her tight grip to look Tizz in the eye but still held her shoulders. "I've been talking to the turtle like a person for weeks now. It's not healthy." As if offended by being called "the turtle," Amphitrite bumped into her side, showing her ever-present devotion.

Confusion passed over the younger girl's Ku and Santi could feel Tizz really searching their connection. "Why are you lonely? What is my brother doing?"

Santi paused, not sure what to say or how to say it. What was the appropriate amount of loaded information to share with a sixteen-year-old? But then, sixteen-year-olds were typically smarter and more aware of the world than adults gave them credit for, so she decided to be honest. "Nothing. That is to say he's really not *doing* anything. He is struggling." But then as if she felt she needed to defend her Bondmate, she added, "It's only been four months, so..."

"That is true." Amaratizz said slowly, her own Ku was filled with grief and sadness.

"It hurts," Santi said. "My sadness and disappointment physically hurt. In my stomach, in my heart, in my entire being. I feel consumed by darkness. But for Rogan it's worse." There was a moment of silence as they both immersed themselves in their thoughts. Then Santi said, "You seem to be doing better than he is. How are you moving on with life?"

Tizz was stoic, calm, and levelheaded when she said, "We know my father well. He would want it that way." Tizz took a deep breath. "If what I feel from you is a fraction of what Rogan is feeling, our father would not want that. Not at all."

Santi only nodded. She thought the same way often but didn't think it was her place to say so to her grieving Bondmate.

"And now that Daristor is back, we are celebrating. We are going to have some fun. Plus, there is the tournoi de jeux!"

Santi cocked her head to the side. "The what?" Santi said and laughed.

The two of them started to make their way back towards the portico where the rest of Amaratizz's group was entering the city. "What is this… thing?" She didn't trust herself with the French word.

Tizz chewed on her index fingernail as she thought. "The tournoi de jeux. It means 'Tournament of Games.' It's a stupid name. We all hate it. We just call it the Tournament."

"Oh!" Santi exclaimed. "The Dwattle Tournament! Yes, I know what it is. I've heard about it before and always wanted to see it." She thought for a moment about all the times growing up that Rogan had mentioned it and wanted to take her, but how she couldn't possibly explain away a week's absence to her mother.

"That gives me an excellent idea," Tizz said as they entered the arch into the city. "We should make a team! That will be *just* the thing Rogan needs."

"Knowing him, I don't think so." Santi side-eyed Tizz. "Maybe before, but not now." She raised an eyebrow, though Tizz couldn't see. They were swimming side by side as Santi looked once again at the beautiful flowers on the floor below her and Tizz looked up at the surface, arms out to her side as if she was embracing the ocean. It reminded her earlier of Rogan when he was swimming "upside down" next to her. She realized the configuration wasn't rude, just Rogan.

She tried to push Rogan's gloom out of her mind and focus on the matter at hand. "If you can talk him into it, though. Yes, you're right. It might be just the thing he needs."

"We can talk to him about our team after the ceremony," Tiz said more joyfully than the moment warranted.

"We?" Santi raised her eyebrows high. "As in you and me? I don't think so."

"Well, a team needs four players, but yes, we should be two of those players. And Rogan should be the third."

"Convincing Rogan to play will be harder than convincing me to play."

"So, I have convinced you then? Great! And I have an idea for our fourth."

"No. No, that's not what I'm saying. I don't think I should play. You know I'm not good at Dwattle. And my legs are always such a hindrance in these types of things." But Santi knew she was going to do it. Amaratizz had a way of getting people to do exactly what she wanted. She wasn't manipulative or conniving, she just oozed so much charm there was no way to say no.

Tizz halted her swim so quickly Santi had to backtrack to align herself face-to-face. "I thought we were past this," Amaratizz chided, flicking the shiny teal tail at Santi's legs in an agitated motion. "In your nuntiums, you tell me how well training is going and how you are finally feeling ready to fight in this 'war,' when it is time. Grendor says you are doing great. And you are always saying how you feel more and more like a Serra and how you want to stop being treated like just a Crural who happens to live underwater. Well, this is your perfect opportunity to put your kelp where your Ku lies."

At this, Santi burst out laughing. "Ok, I've been thoroughly chastised and convinced. Let's tell Rogan we're entering this turno du ju."

Chapter 2

Yemri
Approximately 640 BCE

"May I present to you," Nhori said from Nephira's dais, "your new Ocean Mother: Yemri of the Afiti, daughter of Sariah and Tope, granddaughter to the Great Nephira. May she bless us and guide us as her mothers before her."

All attention turned from Nhori to Yemri as she made her way to the front of the room to take her place on the dais. She had prepared for this. Her father had made sure she knew what to expect and what to say so she would feel comfortable when the time came. As she reached the front and turned around to face the multitude, she was overcome with a deep understanding. She didn't think she could ever feel comfortable as Ocean Mother. Something about it was wrong.

How was she going to lead the entire ocean when she didn't feel she was the right one for the duty?

The room was packed. It was filled to the brink of bursting, yet still couldn't accommodate the thousands of Serras who had traveled from afar to see her. Hundreds of eager Serras were outside the building, having arrived after it was already full. Thousands more were on the island outside the barrier who could not be granted admittance into the city because it was at capacity. Yemri decided her first Ocean Motherly duty would be to greet them and make sure they knew she appreciated them making the trip. A small flicker of pride washed through her Ku. She could do this. She could be a nine-year-old mother of the ocean. There was nothing wrong. It would be fine.

It will be fine, she told herself again for reassurance. I *will be fine*.

She made sure to push fear aside and fill her Ku with warmth, welcoming, and confidence.

"My fellow Serra," Yemri began, with a boldness in her Ku that she mustered at the last moment and a steadiness to her voice she had practiced for days. "I am here before you today, humble but happy. I am young and have a lot to learn, but I hope you will all help me to learn to be the Ocean Mother you need."

She had thought about this. About what she'd do. From the moment Nephira died three weeks ago, she had planned and plotted how to get out of becoming the next Ocean Mother. Immediately after Nephira's death the Cor had been called together. Yemri told them she could not possibly lead. With wisdom beyond her years, she told them it was foolish to put a pup in charge. They claimed her resistance was an excellent example of exactly why she would be so good.

Shortly afterward, she learned she would need to speak to everyone—the entire ocean if possible, in large groups—to build their confidence in her. She knew right away that she could not possibly cultivate trust as Ocean Mother if she wasn't honest about the fact that she had a lot to learn. Tope suggested she ask them to help her learn, thus gaining their support for her through her humility.

"Together," she continued. She wanted to wrap up quickly and get on with meeting everyone one-on-one. She felt that was more important, and it was a skill she could handle. "We can make this ocean a marvelous and harmonious place. A world we are happy to raise our pups in."

The last part had been Nhori's idea. She was constantly reminding everyone that Serras needed to rebuild their numbers after the devastation the Sirens had caused, though Yemri felt bizarre talking about pups when she wasn't even finished with her own hegira and had only received her chest coverings last year.

Her age didn't seem to faze the crowd. As soon as she stopped talking they broke into shouts and waved their arms in excitement.

Fools.

She immediately swam away from the dais, wanting the terrifying public speaking portion to be over with. She made her way towards the closest Serra, a small brown-skinned buck holding his tiny pup asleep in his arms, treading next to his petite Bondmate.

"Thank you for coming," she said to him. "Your support means everything to me."

"It is our honor to be here. We have come all the way from the Najilian to meet you, Ocean Mother."

"Then I am truly honored by your sacrifice. Tell me, what can I do for you?"

"Oh no!" the dam spoke up, alarmed. "We are not here to ask anything of you."

"But I insist. You have come all this way. Surely you require something?"

"Mother," the buck spoke. He was nearly three times her age, and she felt foolish to be called mother by him. "We wish only to look upon your illustrious tail and meet you in person."

Yemri did well at hiding the cringe she felt run through her. *Not this again,* she thought to herself but brushed it off and said, "Then I am happy not to disappoint you." She gave her tail a little wiggle that set off the family into a chorus of "Oooos" and "Aaaaahs"

"Mother," the dam spoke this time. Her voice was high, almost squeaky, possibly from nerves. "It is everything we heard it would be. I do not know the word in your language but in our kinship we call it *arco iris.*"

"That is lovely sounding." Yemri mustered a smile, gave the pup a gentle pat on the head, and moved on to the next group awaiting her attention.

Luckily, most Serras had not waited around for her greetings, and she was able to make it through the remainder of those waiting rather quickly. Finally she was speaking with the last Serra, an elderly buck with brown leathery skin, a crooked back, and nearly no teeth left in his mouth.

He seemed to have been waiting for her rather impatiently as he said, "Mother." The word dripping with acerbity—he was, after all, old enough to be her grandfather. "I hope you can handle the needs of the ocean."

"I will do my best," she answered with all the calm and confidence she could muster. "It is all I can do."

He turned his back on her and swam away.

"Waited an hour for that, did he?" Nhori was at her side. "Do not pay attention to him. Some of the followers of Maato… well." Nhori, not being one to speak ill of others, left the sentence dangling. "Your best is all that you can do. And we will help you as best we can."

Yemri did not understand the depth of trouble Maato had caused in the past, but her mind was not on that at the moment.

"Is it too late to have someone else be the Ocean Mother?"

"It is too late," Nhori answered. "Come, I will accompany you outside the walls of Daris to meet the Serras who could not enter."

They swam through swarms of Serras within the city that wanted to meet her, but Nhori ushered them away saying Yemri would make time for them in the days to come and to enjoy their accommodations. Those outside of the city were sleeping on the sand and couldn't stay long.

Yemri saw the archway before her pointing towards the surface of the ocean. Its lovely white-gold arc looked inviting and alluring. It seemed odd that it was in fact a barrier between the city and the ocean. As she looked through the opening, she saw the swarm of Serras on the other side. Yemri faltered in her swim and stopped her tail's motion in one halting jolt.

Nhori continued swimming a few strokes before she noticed Yemri had fallen behind. The older dam turned back to the pup and put her arm around her shoulder, ushering her forward. "There is no better time to get used to this than now, on your first day."

Yemri's stomach flopped over inside her gut, and she feared she might lose control of her faculties. "Is this something I will get used to?"

"I will always be honest with you, Yemri, as I was with your grandmother. You won't always like what I have to say."

Yemri indicated for her to continue.

"You may never get used to it. Possibly it is not in your disposition. You are much more like your mother than you are your father or Nephira. The two of them handle these situations easily. Sariah was always more… well, she was more like you."

Yemri understood. Introverted. Although she was young, she knew the difference between her mother and father. Yemri would just have to fight against her nature if she wanted to be successful.

Tope was at her other side then, offering his silent support. Kicking their tails forward, the three of them headed through the archway. Once they broke the barrier the scene was worse than she had expected, part of her view having been blocked by the walls. Before her was a throng of Serras so thick and deep she could not see the ground, the sky, or the distance behind the crowd. There didn't seem to be water between the Serras to breathe, let alone keep them all afloat.

There must be over a million Serras out here. Though she really had no concept of what a million would look like. Nephira would know. Sariah might even know what a crowd like this was like, as she had been training diligently to be Ocean Mother since Zitja's transformation left her as the sole beneficiary of the title. Yemri, though, had still been allowed to be a child playing with her little brother until her mother's death almost a month ago.

She closed her eyes. She hadn't really been allowed to mourn her mother, and now was not the time either. She controlled her breath and tried to steady her heart. It was impossible. She opened her eyes and pressed on.

The next few hours were a blur. The entire ordeal felt like an arduous swirl of activity and inactivity. She barely moved from her spot yet she was exhausted as if she had swum the length of the ocean. Yemri addressed the crowd as a whole and spoke to them at length, hoping that would suffice many of the visiting Serras so she would have fewer to meet one-on-one. The very thing she had thought she wanted only hours ago now seemed too daunting. Somehow, now it appeared speaking with large groups was preferable.

Luckily, she guessed correctly, and after making her speech to the crowd, half of the group left to make the journey home, though half of a giant crowd was still a large number for her to meet. Yemri found herself yawning by the time she was coming to the end of the evening. She could finally see through the water, and it was darkness all around.

"We were not supposed to come," a tanned, emaciated, leathery skinned dam said, clutching a small pup by the hand. She had the Ku of a dam about Sariah's age, but the appearance of one twice as old. "As you know, the Maato is very strict but we had to see you. I had to show my daughter that, though she is young, there is hope for her still."

Yemri stared at the dam, who glowed a light pink around her skin, her pale blue tail flicking nervously as she spoke. Yemri was confused. This dam appeared genuinely afraid of Yemri.

No, not afraid of me...

"I just want her to know... well, I have already said. I... I should not bother you." The emaciated dam was hesitant and unsure as she finished her thought. "I just wanted her to see you. That is all." She indicated towards the pup, whose scales were still up to her shoulders and her skin brown like her mothers, but unlike her mother's, the pup's skin was soft and supple. It made Yemri wonder what would cause the mother to acquire such rough skin.

Yemri wanted to respond but was still trying to make sense of what the dam was saying or how to assure her that she shouldn't be afraid when suddenly they were interrupted.

"You were not to come here!" The voice was angry. Yemri could feel the wrath without a Ku's connection. She had not known someone could express their feelings without a Ku. Yemri looked around. She wanted to connect, to find out who it was.

But the dam was looking frightened, and the pink glow around her was turning a sickly yellow. Yemri didn't understand what was happening.

The leathery-skinned dam rushed on. "We must go now. Thank you for meeting us, Yemri. This is truly the greatest thing that has happened in my life."

And just that quickly the dam swam away, dark hair streaming behind her. The child clutched protectively to her mother's bosom looked back at Yemri with a sad expression that Yemri could not understand.

Yemri held the dam in her sight to find out where she was going and whom she was afraid of when she suddenly saw the buck burst through the crowd. He was the old buck without teeth, fierce and angry. The same buck who had challenged Yemri in Nephira's—her—chamber. He grabbed the Serra dam by the hair roughly, and Yemri quickly connected to him so she could overhear their conversation, even though she knew it was wrong of her to do so.

"You will regret this insolence, Moira." He continued to hold her hair as he hauled her swiftly away from the crowd.

Nhori called attention to a Sentinel nearby and sent him after the couple without even a word—merely a flick of her wrist and a knowing look, and the Sentinel was off after them. Yemri wondered if she could ever gain such authority and command. Even more, she wondered what was going on and how she would ever learn and understand it all.

Yemri held on to the retreating Serras' Kus as long as she could, but neither of them spoke, and she was only aware of the ever-present fear and hatred Moira felt. Finally their Kus popped out of her range, and just like that, they were gone from her awareness.

Yemri looked to Nhori to explain. She began to ask but faltered and just said, "Maato changed to a Siren long ago. What does he have to do with anything anymore?"

The older dam answered regretfully. Her creased pink skin still looked so fresh and youthful despite the wrinkles. "I wish I could shelter you from all these things, Yemri. I wish you could stay a pup for longer, but alas, that will not do you any good." She paused, appearing to be marshaling her thoughts and the right words to use. The crowd around them was so thin now only a handful of families waited to greet the new ocean mother.

Nhori sighed. "Maato's influences on the Hatu'anu clan were devastating. Originally, one kinship made up the entire clan. Twenty years ago they split into two; one followed his beliefs, the other raged against him. The kinship that fought against Maato's beliefs flourished, multiplied, and split again a few years later. They are the current Hatu'anu clan.

"In that kinship, however, there was dissension again, and a large group left the clan to form another group. They threw off the language Nephira brought down and created a society unlike any other in the ocean.

"The original followers of Maato, however—the one that buck belongs to—are so controversial. They had to go into hiding because Nephira and your father were constantly trying to get them in line. Their kinship had more transformations into Sirens than any other in the ocean when Nephira's curse hit. Their ways are not like ours."

Yemri was confused. Nhori was speaking as though she was delivering terrible news that she was trying to protect Yermi from, yet she was saying almost nothing. Yemri could not make sense of how terrible things were in the Maato because this information did not sound terrible. She would have to ask her father if Nhori continued to be evasive.

"In fact," Nhori continued, "they have to continue moving around the ocean because they must hide for fear of being stopped. Which is why I am quite surprised that one came here today, and why I sent the Sentinels after him."

"Stopped how? And why?"

Nhori looked like she wouldn't answer, then simply said, "Their treatment of dams is abhorrent. They are regarded more as property than Serra. The dam pups are raised to be servants, and the men are either raised to follow the Maato way or are kicked out of the clan very young, often dying from neglect."

"We have to stop them!" Yemri's innocent heart felt dirty. Seeing the dam so emaciated, knowing that her daughter was due for the same fate, left Yemri feeling sick. She saw the energy around her arms shift from its usual yellow to a slight brown in her revulsion.

Nhori didn't say anything but Yemri got the feeling the older dam was not in disagreement, though she was filled with hesitance. "There is much you will feel powerless about in your position, small Yemri, but you will learn to do what you can and forget what you cannot."

Yemri did not like this answer, but she stayed quiet for now. She would think about this and do something. She surely would not forget about it.

Nhori shook it off and said, "First things first, Yemri. You have a few more Serras to greet."

Yemri looked at the crowd awaiting her and felt as though speaking with them seemed so unimportant in light of all she had just learned.

Two days later, Yemri was sitting in what was now her chamber feeling like she could never command this room as well as her grandmother. She was practicing sounding and acting like an Ocean Mother in public, even if in private she was riddled with doubt. Luckily this was just a meeting of the Cor. She could manage to address six other people, especially since two of them were Nhori and her father. She felt confident going into the conference that she could handle herself.

"I think," she said not sounding as confident as she would have liked, "we should begin by welcoming the new Balam for the NorMer clan?" She looked to her father, who sent an encouraging tick of his Ku to her before she proceeded. "Freydis, welcome." Though Yemri did not feel it was her place to welcome someone who took their position at the same time Yemri had.

Freydis was a mid-aged dam with a striking chin and cheekbones, strong and fierce in her demeanor, wearing a furry stole that was necessary in the cold northern waters.

"Thank you." Her Ku was not unpleasant, but it wasn't warm and inviting either. "I hope to do the best I can for my clan."

Yemri noted that the glow she put off was a warm red and that brought her comfort, remembering the warm red glow that followed Nephira around.

"I want to start right away by talking about the Maato," Yemri said. It was the only thing she had conviction about at the moment. Well, that and not being Ocean Mother, but only one of those was within her control. "Something has to be done about them! They are terrible."

Tope spoke up, knowing Yemri was worried about having support on the matter. "I agree. They cannot live underwater and treat their fellow being so abhorrently. I think we can easily send a scouting party out to find them. Once we do, a visit to the kinship is in order. They have been out of the Ocean Mother's eye for far too long."

Just then, Freydis spoke up and drew the attention of the group. "Ocean Mother!" she sounded enthusiastic, which made Yemri relax. She had felt the resistance from the rest of the group about this idea. She was glad Freydis, at least, seemed eager on the matter of the Maato.

"I have finally placed the thing of which your tail reminds me."

"My… my tail?" Yemri looked down and wished she could hide her tail under her sitting cushion.

"The people on the land have a word for it: *sateenkaari*. I do not know what you would call it here. You know, that thing in the sky? You have seen it before?"

"No." Yemri was irritated. "I have not seen anything in the sky before. Now, about the Maato."

"Oh, yes!" Efren, the Balam for the Tipua exclaimed, dark green eyes full of excitement. "I do know the thing you are referring to. I do not know the name. I will find out for you, Yemri."

He paused in a way that led Yemri to believe he wanted her to say, "Thank you." Once she complied, he rushed on.

"I have only seen it once. Remarkable! Just like your unique tail."

Muleki spoke up. "Let us get back on track, please," he said, smiling at Yemri. Nephira had always trusted and relied upon Muleki. It seemed to Yemri that she had an ally in him as well. "We have to make some moves on Zitja. I think we can capture her. If we can do that then we can finally kill her. End her torment in the water."

Yemri leaned back on her cushion. Somehow she had lost control of the meeting.

Did I ever have control?

Would she ever? She balled up her fists at her sides and tried to remain poised through her fury.

The meeting passed without her saying another word, not because of obstinacy on her part but because the entire meeting changed from topic to topic and resolution of problems without her input. She was unneeded in the proceedings, and she felt the sting of obscurity. How could she ever lead the world at nine years old and without wanting the responsibility in the first place?

The last thought she pushed aside because it would do her no good to harbor it.

Towards the end of the meeting she was about to interject her agenda again—the Maato—a topic she felt strongly about, when someone burst through the double doors, flinging them wide open.

"Ocean Mother Yemri," said a commanding buck with a crooked nose that she didn't know. He was one of her father's friends, a Sentinel. "We have captured Zitja. She is in our custody outside the island."

Chapter 3

Santiago

After Amaratizz initiated what had to be the ocean's first adorable and awkward three-Serra embrace, Coral leaned back and said, "My daughters are back together. Amed would be happy."

Santi nearly burst into tears but managed to maintain her composure. She wondered how Coral and Tizz seemed to be moving on so well while Rogan was stuck in despondency. She wanted to ask how they were doing it and how she could help Rogan, but Tizz interrupted her thoughts with a jovial, "Mother, Santiago and I are going to do the Tournament."

Coral visibly beamed as she said, "I knew one day you and Rogan would do it. You used to talk about it as pups all the time." She shifted her gaze to Santi as she said, "Good luck being on a team with those two. I doubt you will get to touch a dwattle at all."

Santi threw up her hands and said, "Fine by me!"

"Who will be your fourth?" Coral asked.

But before Santi or Tizz could answer, Grendor swam up to the group and extended cheerful, warm amicuses all around. Then he turned, all business, and asked, "Santi, how many Serras do you think you can hold in your Ku?"

"Oh, um… I don't… The most I've ever done is maybe a hundred. Probably less. Yes… definitely less. Why?"

Grendor scanned the crowd, musing. "That is not going to be sufficient."

Santi looked around, puzzled. The Troag was packed with what looked like every inhabitant of Daris. Maybe more. They filled the city center entirely; head over tails, several Serras high, they were packed in the water up towards the surface, and at every break in the hedges they filed out into the city. The statue of Nephira—looking as regal as Santi had imagined—shone brightly in the center of the thick crowd. It made sense that others would come to the city for this event, including the parents or friends of those taking part. It only happened once a year, and it was a big deal. Though why did holding the Kus of the throng matter to her? She wasn't participating in the Auditus Ceremony.

Santi's eyes went wide in panic. She wouldn't be participating in this ceremony, would she?

Amed's plan had been to train her to fight so that when the time came for the Sentinels to attack the Siren lair *en masse*, she would be ready. It was why she had taken training so seriously since their arrival. But she wasn't actually a Sentinel at the moment. She hadn't been allowed to train with them or partake in strategy discussions or even learn any of the lessons from the beginning of training. Krell was doing things his way since taking over from Amed, so why would she be a part of the Auditus? Especially since she was already deaf from her kidnapping?

The center remained relatively clear around the statue, and she could see Krell, authoritative and confident, commanding the Serras around him with gestures and aggressive finger pointing. The Serras then took off to do his bidding. He looked very regal. His dark orange tail had a leather strap around his hip holding a short sword. Around the base of his tail—where Rogan wore their Bonding Simul—Krell had a little knife. On his chest, he wore a small leather vest that Santi thought would look absurd anywhere else, but on him it looked like a uniform. Even the way he wore his hair very short where most Serras left it long screamed authority.

She gazed wide-eyed back at Grendor. "Am I going to have to connect to them?"

"I was hoping you would be able to. I should have known you would not have practice with so many. Let me see what I can do to make sure everyone will be able to hear you." Grendor swam away, leaving Santi to wonder what he was talking about.

Santi looked at Coral and Tizz. "Everyone will hear *me*?"

Coral's white-blue eyes widened, "Did they not tell you?" She looked at Santi with compassion. "When Grendor came to speak to us earlier, he needed to speak to you as well and assumed that was why you wanted to leave the city to greet Amaratizz. Why you did not want to stay and discuss things with us. That you were nervous."

Santi's heart thumped like a hummingbird. She never had a problem with public speaking; her year as president of the community outreach club in high school gave her frequent opportunities to lose that fear. But why would she need to speak to an entire city's worth of Serras at the Auditus Ceremony? This was for Rogan and his class of fellow graduates from the Sentinel Opus Training. She squinted her eyes. "What do I need to do?"

Coral swam closer to Santi and took her hair out of the ponytail it had been sloppily swept up in and began an elaborate plait that started on one side of her head moving towards the other. "I believe they want you to address the crowd. You know, say some words of encouragement."

"A… about Rogan? Or the deafening ceremony? That-" She was about to say that it didn't make sense when Coral answered.

"Santiago, they want you to say something about being the Heir." Her Ku was calm, but Santi could feel the pain behind it. "Until six months ago, everyone thought Amed would kill Zitja. Possibly Rogan or even peaceful Amaratizz could have done it, but they all believed it would be Amed. Faith was shattered when he died, but as word spread that it is actually you…" She let the last go unsaid.

The bottom of Santi's stomach dropped. "I need to pee."

"Oh, you will be fine." Tizz said with a wave of her hand.

Santi suddenly had to go very badly. "No. No, I really need to go and…"

"You do not." Tizz said firmly but gently. "You always say that when you are nervous. Hey!" Tizz said, getting Santi's attention, which had been darting all over the crowd, taking in the size of it. "Hey, Santiago. You will be great. You are always a charmer."

Santi pursed her lips. She wasn't so sure about that, but she did feel bolstered by Tizz's confidence in her.

"Ok, we have got it worked out!" Grendor said, swooping in and guiding her towards Nephira's statue. Coral followed suit, hands still working furiously in Santi's hair. "I want you to connect with the most immediate Serras around you. I will connect with the rest and repeat your words to them."

"Like… some sort of translator."

"Um, sure, like a translator."

Santi nodded. It didn't help her feel better about speaking—and her feelings of betrayal for not knowing she would need a speech prepared—but at least she didn't have to worry about connecting to hundreds of Serras.

Coral finished Santi's hair, resulting in a braided halo around her head. Santi thought of it as a crown of her own hair, and it gave her a little courage to address the horde. Her courage might be a result of the hair-crown, or she could be in denial. They wouldn't really make her address a city's worth of Serras without preparation, right?

Coral admired her handiwork and said, "You look lovely! Everyone is here to support you and the graduates." And then, as an afterthought, she pulled off the pearls and beads from around her neck and placed them around Santi's. "The mood is nothing but supportive and encouraging. Nothing can go wrong!"

Somehow, Santi thought it could.

In a wave of calm that was not her own, Santi felt a new connection in her Ku. It was startling and comforting at the same time. It was gentle and inviting, yet powerful and demanded attention; it was a Ku unlike any she had felt before. It left her feeling humbled and emboldened at once. Then a sonorous voice filled up her being and she turned to the center of the crowd to find out to whom the voice belonged.

"Welcome, everyone, and thank you for coming!" The speaker was an elderly Serra dam with a sleek purple tail and pink, wrinkly skin. She looked extremely thin and frail. She wore an oversized white fur stole that Santi thought was to keep her warm from lack of any body fat whatsoever.

The first time Rogan had handed her a wet blanket for warmth, she laughed, but the layer did help remarkably well, even if it was constantly soaked. Santi assumed this stole had the same effect, though it also made her look both elegant and extra fragile. But through all her frailty, the elder dam still commanded respect. She looked like a loveable grandmother with the demanding presence of a dragon. Santi knew who this dam was.

"That's Yazi?" she asked Coral, though she did not need her confirmation.

Coral nodded, and Santi looked on in astonishment, her own worries forgotten. She never thought she would have the honor of beholding the Ocean Mother. Yet here she was, just yards away. Santi soaked it all in and forgot everything as she let the comforting presence of Yazi's powerful Ku fill her.

"This is a momentous day," Yazi addressed the multitude with poise. "Our system of capable, dependable, and formidable Sentinels will add sixty new members to their ranks today. Every one of them brilliantly ready to protect our lives." Yazi grew silent and waves of hands shot up in the water and swayed back and forth followed by a few cheers from Serras that Santi could hear through their connection with her. Santi looked at Coral, to her left, who also had her hands in the air, gently swaying. Santi was puzzled for only a moment but realized it was like clapping. She had seen it before when she was younger but never realized the significance.

"And…" Yazi paused and Santi could almost feel the old woman's smile. "We have the true Heir, finally among us."

The crowd's attention was suddenly on Santiago, and hundreds of Serras connected to her and cheered. She was overwhelmed again. Now the throng of Serras waving their hands excitedly was for her.

Santi threw her hands up as well. She waved her arms, letting the crowd know she was very happy to be of service. Maybe she could say something short and encouraging. Wasn't that her duty? The reason she wanted Amed to train her in the first place? She had decided to do all she could for the ocean. Santiago let herself get carried away by the positivity flowing through the crowd. She wondered if Rogan could hear from wherever he was at this moment and what must he be thinking about Yazi's proclamation that the Heir was *finally* among them?

She was so wrapped up in her thoughts of Rogan that she barely noticed when Yazi turned, looked directly at her and held out her right hand. "I present to you Santiago, the one we did not even know we were seeking. Our Heir."

Grendor gave her a gentle nudge on her back and Santi glided towards Yazi's outstretched hand. In the half a minute it took to swim to the Ocean Mother, it felt like hours passed. Every eye watched her graceless kicks as she clumsily propelled herself forward. There was nothing about her that looked elegant. Nothing about her flailing arms or flopping legs helped her to exude confidence before the crowd. The swimming practice didn't matter. The fact that she was mostly imagining her lack of grace didn't matter. All Santiago felt was her lack of tail and the same out-of-place feeling she had worked so hard to overcome. She felt instantly inferior in her position as Heir, and she knew that everyone could sense it.

Finally, she reached Yazi and the old woman placed her hand on Santi's heart. Santi returned the gesture, her hand getting lost in the furry stole. She couldn't believe she was touching the actual Ocean Mother. She felt the years of wisdom and confidence flow from the matriarch into her body, filling her with a confidence she would never have found on her own. Then the slightest flicker of a glow crossed the Mother's knowing face and she gestured towards the crowd.

Emboldened by Yazi's presence Santi took a moment to connect to the most immediate Serras and hold as many as she could. When she felt at capacity, she looked at Grendor and he nodded.

"I am so happy to be here with you." She paused. In the minutes she had to prepare something to say she had come up with several more clever opening lines, but it would seem her mind chose the lamest possible way to greet the multitude. "That is to say, I've been a part of the Serra world almost my entire life. I began my adventures here as a small child, and I grew up among some of the most wonderful influences, having amazing experiences." She felt like she was losing a grasp on what she wanted to say, and she wished there had been a way to write things down underwater. She could have thought up some bullet points to cover while Coral braided her hair at least. As it was, she was lost in the details of things she should say. Santi decided to skip to the crux of her message. "I love many and I also lost many in this ocean, and I feel the sting of the Sirens. Since learning about my heritage and the destiny that awaits, I have no other goals but to stand with you in defeating Zitja and all that follow her."

Santi was finally getting on a roll. She didn't know where she was going with this, but now that she was speaking her nerves had left her. Suddenly, every hand in the crowd flew up into the water and she was taken aback. She was saying exactly what they wanted to hear. That was a relief. She would just continue this path until a natural stopping point came around and hope she had been a good motivator.

"I have been training! I am working diligently and vow to work as hard as I can to become a Sentinel so that one day-"

But she stopped as Krell put his left arm around her shoulders firmly and the other he raised to the crowd to calm them.

Santi felt deflated. She was finally speaking coherently, and now she was being silenced.

It took Krell a few moments before he could quiet the cheers and calls of encouragement for Santiago. When he felt the attention was focused on him, he began in a tone so serious it seemed counterintuitive to the mood in the water. Santi found she couldn't focus on the words he was saying because she had a terrifying, sinking feeling in her stomach, and the hold he had on her shoulder was beginning to hurt.

Krell's Ku was severe. It was deadly, and there was no place in it for Santi's desires. She knew that immediately. Santiago also got the feeling that she was not as important as Zitja's death, and Krell would do whatever it took to obtain it. Santi pushed her own thoughts aside and focused for the first time on his words. What she heard made her blood run cold through her veins.

"Now that we have our secret weapon we will move out at once."

Arms flew into the air and a deafening cheer ran through her heart. Every Serra in the crowd had connected to her since she started speaking, and the noise was overwhelming. She wished she could press her hands to her ears to shut it out.

Krell's fingers on her shoulder tightened even more, and he held her close. She realized he was slowly pulling her away from the limelight. She looked up at him as he smiled to the crowd. Suddenly she didn't get the impression her goal to be a Sentinel was in the plans. He was probably not going to even let her fight. But she had to! She was the only one who could kill Zitja. What was he playing at? And why was she beginning to feel like his trophy? A talisman to be propped up and used?

Looking out into the crowd realization struck her: that was all she was to every one of them.

She was ushered, in a daze, to Coral's side—right in the front, just as Rogan had requested. She was still reeling from the abruptness of it all when the graduates swam into the Troag. As they entered in a line, she was glad for their front row position. Rogan looked stunning. They all did, but she only had eyes for him. Santi wasn't the only one who had had a makeover in their time apart. Rogan was now wearing his weapons. Two short swords peaked up over his shoulders, and their leather holsters crossed his chest in the center. She had seen him wear this a thousand times before, but it never ceased to make her completely lusty for him. Another leather strap joined the ensemble now, right under his pecks, across his ribcage with a small dagger positioned just under his left arm. She had seen this before on Amed, and her inspection of the other graduates revealed that each of them had the same weaponry.

She did not understand the significance of it or the rest of his wardrobe additions, so Coral explained. "He is wearing Amed's *stithos*, the dagger on his chest." She pointed to her own ribcage, to the spot where Rogan wore the knife, and Santi recalled hearing the word before. "I saved it for him. That was one of the things Grendor needed from me earlier. All graduates of the Sentinel training get one, though not all of them choose to wear it on duty. They do not have to, of course, but I do not see why they would not want an extra weapon." She shrugged in a very Crural way, and Santiago smiled.

Santi was glad Rogan got to wear something that had been so important to his father, but she wondered if that only made this day all the more difficult for him. She was about to ask about the rest of the embellishments when Coral continued.

"The stíthos signifies keeping your Ku protected above all else while performing such a demanding Opus. Killing—well, all the things that Sentinels are required to do—goes against every belief Serras are raised to value. They have to learn to communicate HaruKu, to fight HaruKu, to lie at times, and to fight to the death if needed. The stíthos is a reminder that protecting their Ku from evil influences should be their top priority. The irony is that that very knife will often be the thing used to kill their opponent before they are killed themselves." Coral was quiet for a moment as she listened to Krell rallying the crowd, Santi could not seem to hear him through her intense focus on Coral. The lessons never stopped from this dam, and Santi would soak them up as long as she lived.

A flicker of irritation passed Coral's Ku as well, and Santi did not have to ask to know it was directed at Krell. He was projecting the impression of a warrior into the Ku of the crowd. Santi was sure that when Amed led this ceremony, that was not the case. She imagined it was that of protector more than anything else. Finally, Coral continued describing Rogan's attire.

"The leather strap around his neck symbolizes honesty. Though he might be required to tell lies during his post, he is not to believe them. The leather strap around his forehead represents trust. Though he will often be HaruKu in battle, he is to trust that his fellow Serras are there for him should he falter. The leather strap around his tail symbolizes strength, that his tail shall not fail to get him out of danger. It also reminds him to willingly go wherever he is needed."

Coral paused for a moment to allow Santi to take it all in. The strap around his tail was just below his coverings, where his thigh would be if he had legs. She noticed another small dagger tied to that as well. She found it odd that the strap around his neck would represent telling the truth—something that made sense if he spoke, but was really double symbolism since he did not use his voice to communicate. The leather strap around his head was nothing but attractive to her. His hair was pulled up behind his head in a new way she liked, and the strap wound around his head underneath the mess of hair in the back. Maybe she could get him to wear that more often.

When Coral didn't say more and only looked at her knowingly, Santi blushed, realizing she should stop ogling her Bondmate and pay attention. It was a good twenty minutes after Santi had been ushered to Coral's side, and the Auditus Ceremony was underway, before Santi felt herself relaxing. Coral's explanation had served as a very effective, calming distraction. It also helped that Coral and Tizz seemed to rally around her for moral support. They knew what Amed had planned and how hard Santi had worked. They tread on either side like her personal cheering section. Santi leaned into Coral like she would have her own mother and hooked her arm through Coral's.

Santiago hoped the crowd would not remember that Krell had most certainly brushed her aside in a very visible manner. Coral rested her hand on Santi's and gave it a little squeeze.

Instead of dwelling on the humiliation Krell had heaped on her—as well as his very suspect motives for her future—Santi turned her attention to Rogan and the others. She couldn't help but feel a sense of longing. She missed him. True, they had been together every day since their Bonding, but their Bonding Celebration was also the same day as Amed's death. Nothing had been right since.

As Krell was speaking, the graduates lined up next to one another, and Santi found she still couldn't pay attention. Everything about Krell filled her with rage. Most of it was unwarranted as she hadn't had many interactions with him; much of it, however, was fully deserved. It brought her some peace, however, to know that she was not alone in the matter.

While sparring with Grendor that morning, she had asked how he was dealing with the changes since Amed's death. The darkness from his Ku had mingled with the darkness in her own as he told her, "Ocean Mother Yazi choosing Krell as Sentinel Commander over me was a blow I am learning to accept. Krell removing me from second-in-command is not."

Though Grendor wasn't able to spar with her most days, when he did they often used their sessions as a time to talk about things. Grendor said the distraction was good for her. She relied more on instinct to fight while she was talking. Then, in a real fight, her mind wouldn't be pulled in different directions, and she would be all the better for it.

Santi was shocked by Grendor's revelation. She didn't know the hierarchy or plan of succession in the Sentinel ranks, but even Coral said it was strange the way it had happened. Apparently, Krell had removed almost all of the highest-ranking Sentinels and replaced them with others, presumably those who were close to him. Rogan also found it suspicious based on what Amed had shared with him about how the sentinels operated. Rogan didn't know what Krell's ultimate plan was that motivated him to remove all of Amed's bucks in preference to his own.

When Santi remarked that it all sounded "very fishy," it was not received with the levity she was trying to bring to the situation. Levity was Rogan's department. Not anymore, apparently.

Focus came back to her eyes and mind; it was Rogan's turn. She had almost missed it in her daze and frustration. She looked at him and nearly swooned. Bad mood or no, he still cut an impressive figure. He'd been swimming great lengths, sparring, and training since he was a child; every inch of him was toned and solid. His shoulders were nearly twice as wide as she was, and when he wrapped her up in his embrace, she was completely sheltered from the world. Even during this horrible time for them, she didn't feel any less for him. He was calm and sure, handsome and sturdy, and she was almost desperately in love with him. She just needed to figure out how to help him through.

The Sentinel who would now be Rogan's direct superior—she could remember his name if she thought hard: Strong? Gron? String?—swam up to his side, hands clasped behind his back. An assistant followed him carrying a tray of long spikes.

Rogan's superior plucked up a fresh spike and pointed it towards the surface high above. It was about a foot long, shining silver, with a point at one end and a handle in the other.

Santi quickly connected to the buck and shook her head, irritated with herself for missing so much of the ceremony by not even being connecting to the right Serra to listen to.

"Rogan," he said, "you have chosen a noble path, and Ocean Mother Yazi and the Serras in every clan thank you for your sacrifice. Are you willing to protect your fellows, even accepting death if required, to bring safety to our waters?"

"Yes, of course," Rogan answered with equal parts stoicism and composure. So much stiffer than he had ever been. More serious. Dangerous.

"And are you ready to have your hearing taken from you so that you may do your duty to the best of your ability, giving up the option for hearing in the future, and all its benefits?"

Rogan nodded, which made Santi smile. Serras didn't nod. Serras didn't use much body language at all because the Ku's penetrating sensation expressed far more emotion than gestures or facial expressions ever could. It was nice to see that he was still influenced by their relationship, even if he couldn't be interested in speaking to her lately.

Realizing his error, he suddenly answered, "Yes. Yes, I do." His jaw muscles clenched and unclenched.

Sing? Sangria?? ...Sangrin! Santi finally remembered his name.

Sangrin moved his hand up the shaft of the spike and held his fingers at the red line around the middle that indicated the depth it would be stabbed into her Bondmate's ear.

He plunged the spike into Rogan's head up to his fingers.

It wasn't actually his head, Santi knew, but someone stabbing the man she loved in the ear look remarkably like being stabbed in the head. Santi clutched at her heart as Rogan's pain pushed at her. The assembly would feel a hint of his pain—though he hid it well, remaining composed through it all—but Santi, as his Bondmate, felt the true pain of the wound. She swore she could feel a small pierce in her ear. It was how she had been able to be so patient with him lately, even she wanted to smack him in the face. His heart was in such pain that possibly this stab in the ears would be a relief from that, if only because of its distracting effects.

Sangrin went around to the other side and repeated the terrible operation on her love's other ear before turning and moving on to the next new Sentinel. A small amount of blood floated out of Rogan's ear and disappeared in the water. Each buck and dam took the pain just as stoically as Rogan had until Sangrin and the other direct superiors were finished with their new recruits.

Finally, the gruesome business of deafening perfectly healthy, strong Serras was finished. Santi imagined what it must be like now. She remembered how she used to hear the rush of water around her at all times, where now there was silence; the occasional sounds of dolphins and disturbances in the water, where all she heard now was her own thoughts. Her deafness had happened slowly over months, so she couldn't imagine how startling it would be for such a sudden change to occur.

Ocean Mother Yazi came back to the forefront and spoke to the crowd. Once again Santi felt a wave of calm strength fill her up.

"Thank you, new Sentinels, for your sacrifice and dedication to the betterment, protection, and care of our ocean. You are truly doing Nephira's own work throughout these waters. It is a scary business to be out here in the world today, never knowing where evil may be lurking, never knowing if your family is safe, if your homes are secure, whether things will be the same for you tomorrow as they are today. It is frightening and uncertain. I wish this were not our plight. My greatest desire is to be better than this as a whole. As an ocean." She paused for a long moment, and the waters around her pulsed with love. Was it emanating from her, Santi wondered, or towards her from the adoration of the crowd?

"With the addition of these dedicated bucks and dams to the ranks, we add not only additional strength in numbers, but hope: hope that we will one day see the better day we are fighting for."

Everything was powerfully still for a moment as everyone waited for her to say more. *Wanted* her to say more. When she didn't, the assembly burst into euphoric cheers, arms waving wildly through the water.

Just as the feeling of finality was taking hold of the crowd and it seemed time to go about their business, Yazi added, "Before you begin celebrating, Krell wishes to speak to you about our time-honored tradition of the Tournoi de Jeux." This was received with another wave of hands and excess of cheering. Santi knew that the tournament was something the ocean looked forward to and smiled to see just how much joy it brought to everyone. It only made sense that Yazi would remind everyone of it now while spirits were already so high.

Krell pushed himself to the front of everyone's attention at Nephira's statue. He kicked his large burnt-orange tail with haughtiness and rose so that he cast a shadow on the statue of the greatest Ocean Mother in history. Santiago felt a cold chill replace the warmth Yazi had left behind.

"I must insist," Krell spoke, his thin lips pursing in a tight line on his brown face as the multitude stilled to listen, "that everyone make the necessary preparations to attend the Tournoi de Jeux. We have a wonderful surprise included this year." Krell turned and looked Santi right in the eye as he said, "Is that not correct, Santiago?"

Her eyes went wide, and she straightened, looking out at the crowd and then back to Krell and Yazi. All eyes were upon her. There was nothing she could do but nod. Krell began to speak, and attention was turned once again to him.

Santi looked at Tizz and said, "How does he know?"

Tizz was wide-eyed as well and sent just as much confusion back to Santi's Ku as she had received from her sister.

Krell ended the ceremony, and a wave of cheers rang out through the crowd. The graduates were leaving the podium to find their families, and Tizz flipped on to her back casually to pet the underside of Amphitrite's belly.

"You don't seem concerned with Krell's big announcement. You know what he's thinking?" Santi cleared her lungs, trying to focus on her new problem.

"Oh sure," Amaratizz said nonchalantly. "We had the unfortunate pleasure of spending a lot of time with him when he was my father's general." Tizz turned and lounged on her side and gave Santi a little punch in the shoulder. "He probably just wants a big spectacle from his Heir during the tournament. Better get those kickers in line."

Santi pursed her lips. Rogan always called her legs her kickers, and she used to frequently lament about how they would never get in line when she needed them to.

Just as the crowd dispersed, Rogan rejoined their group. Santiago looked to Rogan for clarification, but she could feel his Ku was finally filled with new emotions besides grief and sorrow; he was just as confused as Santi.

"What did that mean?" Rogan asked but she couldn't tell him about their plans to play in the tournament at this moment. When she had to convince him to play, she would need more time to do it right. For now, she merely shrugged as if she didn't know. It would not do to rush it. His mood was too volatile, so she would need to be gentle about the suggestion.

From the corner of her eye Santi saw Krell swimming towards her. The floor of her stomach dropped out of her body.

Before she could think of anything to say to Rogan, Krell was there, asking to speak to her.

"Let me be honest with you, Santiago." Krell jumped right in and she sucked in a deep breath and held it. "Amed was reckless to fill your head with ideas that you could be a Sentinel. Do not deny it: you are not capable."

She stared at him, fighting to keep her face neutral and not scowl at him. All she could do was give a small nod so that he would get on with his point. She could feel Rogan's Ku had a hint of defensiveness in her honor, but he said nothing, both of them wanting to hear Krell's reasoning.

"The tournament will be well planned and controlled. You will be fine. In the meantime," he leaned in close, looking down on her both physically and metaphorically, "do not disappoint me."

He left.

Santi let out her breath. She shuddered. "What did that mean?"

Chapter 4

Yemri

Yemri pushed herself off her seat and exclaimed, "I cannot believe it!" Zitja, captured already! She was elated. This would make her time as Ocean Mother that much easier and she'd be remembered forever as the Mother who got rid of the Sirens. She looked around the room. Everyone was glowing a bright pink and bursting with excitement in their Kus.

The sentinel that interrupted the meeting continued. "What shall we do with her? She is just outside the city, but we cannot bring her in because she will not pass the enchantment."

Yemri thought fast; this was a pivotal decision, her first big act as Ocean Mother.

Before she could come to a conclusion, Tope spoke up. "Take her to the Afiti, to Nephira's old stronghold. There are dungeons there that will keep her secure until we decide what to do with her."

"Yes, Tope."

"I will meet you there," the Sentinel answered and turned and rushed out of the meeting.

"This is great news for us," Tope said to the Cor. "With this, we will be able to get control of the Siren problem. I am going to leave at once. Muleki, you will come with me?"

"Of course."

With that Tope and Muleki left the chamber hot on the tail of the Sentinel before them.

Freydis, Nanti'ouato, and Efren all began talking at once, making plans and decisions together. Nhori gave many opinions and instructions until finally they reached an agreement about who would do what. All the while, Yemri watched with eyes wide and voice silent. Freydis, Nanti, and Efren bustled out of the meeting, leaving Nhori looking at Yemri with a far off look in her eye.

"This is a wonderful moment, is it not?"

"Mmmmm," was all Yemri could manage to mumble.

"You know, Efren and Freydis are right. Your tail does remind me of that sky anomaly. I have only seen it once from a brutal storm in the middle of the Atlantis Ocean," she muttered to herself as she floated out of the hall. "Beautiful. Very beautiful."

Yemri looked around the now empty and hollow cavity of the bright white room. In the last two minutes, so much information and activity had swirled around her like a hurricane while she sat peacefully in the eye of it.

She felt very young.

It was weird to Yemri not to be told what to do. She had been Ocean Mother for three days and she found she was always waiting to be told what to do next or where to be, but she was the one who was supposed to make those kinds of decisions. She thought about going to her chambers or finding her brother to play with, but that didn't seem right. What would her mother do? Sariah would probably do what she was told, as well. Yemri sighed, missing her mother to a heartbreaking extent. Sariah had never had her time to rule, and thus Yemri did not have her as an example.

What would Nephira do?

Still, she wasn't sure. But one thing was certain: she would not sit in her chamber while everyone else dealt with Zitja. She would make sure things were taken care of the way she wanted them.

I am the Ocean Mother. I get to decide what is done with Zitja.

Although she hadn't yet made up her mind about what to do with Zitja, she rushed from the great hall and shot through the water out of the citadel. Her personal guards followed a short distance behind, but as she swam, she started to feel she was making a spectacle. Her urgency might bring alarm to the Serras who watched as she fled from the city. She was conflicted between making sure nothing happened in her absence and looking regal. Yemri slowed her pace and projected calmness from her Ku. There was so much to be aware of as Ocean Mother, so much to be cautious about that she had never thought of before.

Serras were looking at her as she passed. Some looked up in alarm, others curiosity. Whatever the feeling, she read one thing loud and clear.

She was causing panic.

She slowed down her pace a bit more. It seemed as if days passed before she made the arduous trek through the city to the portcullis. When she passed underneath the white-gold grandeur of the arc and out of the enchantment's protection, she was also away from the curious onlookers. Yemri quickened her pace once again until she swam upon a group of Sentinels all surrounding one lone Siren.

They were poking at her with the butts of their spears and brandishing swords and other weapons. One punched her in the stomach, and Zitja, still young and poised despite the hideous transformation, doubled over and let out a scream in the water. Yemri realized she would eventually need her ears to be deafened, just in case. That would be a wise thing for an Ocean Mother to do. She was proud of herself for having the idea.

Just then, a Sentinel got everyone's attention. Smiling cockily, he said, "Let me try!" before he took his long knife and stabbed it into Zitja's chest. Yemri was shocked; they were just going to kill her right now? It made sense, but why were they toying with her so? Yemri was sickened.

Zitja let out a bloodcurdling scream at the same time Yemri screamed in horror at the sight. However, no one seemed to hear Yemri or acknowledge she was even there.

Zitja was barely glowing a faint orange, a color of halo Yemri had never seen before. And as the buck pulled out the knife revealing Zitja's chest completely blemish-free, the buck made a gesture to indicate he knew that would happen and he was showing off for the others.

After the pain passed and she was revealed to be uninjured, Zitja glowed darker and darker orange. Yemri was confused by this dark burnt orange color but reasoned she was usually confused by the colors Serras emitted.

Zitja yelled, "Only my family members can kill me, I told you!" She looked haughty, proud. Invincible.

Yemri listened to what the bucks were saying to Zitja, but the language they used was not suitable for children to overhear.

She spoke loudly and with authority. "Stop!" She was appalled at the sentinels' abhorrent behavior. Yemri had been sheltered from such language and actions in her short life, and she felt repulsed to see it now, no matter who was on the receiving end.

They stopped, much to Yemri's relief.

But then she didn't quite know what to do next. Everyone waited and watched as Yemri took stock. She felt strangely confused by Zitja and all that she was. The Siren Queen. The terror of the ocean. An aunt she had never met. Beloved sister and best friend of Yemri's mother until the very end, yet also her mother's killer. Sariah had never spoken of her sister with anything other than adoration. But as Yemri looked at Zitja now, she didn't know what to think. By all accounts, Zitja was supposed to be hideous with her white skin, black tail, sharp teeth, and strange eyes. But instead she was oddly beautiful. Her loosely curled hair flowed around her in all directions, a wraithlike halo. Her faint orange glow, still so mysterious, left Yemri curious. Zitja's one arm wasn't disturbing to Yemri like it was to others because she had heard the tragic story of how Yemri's own father had accidentally cut it off. He regretted it deeply, even now.

The thing that most troubled Yemri was on top of Zitja's head.

No one had told Yemri about this little detail before and now it left her feeling a strange conflict between Zitja's dark, curly head and the gorgeous item that nestled on top. Poised high and proud on her head was a crown of shells, pearls, and gems. It was stunning. It was majestic. She truly looked like a queen. It made Zitja look like everything the Serras told themselves she wasn't, like a ruler of the ocean. It was both impressive and arrogant, beautiful and terrifying.

When Yemri looked into Zitja's face, she could not believe the expression she saw. The Siren Queen was shocked, utterly and completely surprised by Yemri's presence. But just as quickly as the expression flashed across her face, it was gone again.

Yemri did not know what to do next, but before she could think, Zitja spoke to her. "I can see Sariah in you, tiny pup."

Yemri stiffened. She had never met a Siren before—seen plenty of them, sure, but never met one—let alone heard one speak. She hadn't realized they could speak, and since she couldn't feel a Ku in Zitja, she hadn't thought it was possible.

Yemri didn't respond, but Zitja continued. "You look just like her when she was little. She hasn't been gone long now. You must miss her as much as I do."

This pierced like a knife into Yemri's heart. She thought she actually felt a physical pain. How dare Zitja talk about Sariah's death when she was the one that caused it? On the other hand, Yemri yearned to hear more about her mother. Tope hadn't known Sariah when she was a pup, and he couldn't tell Yemri anything about her. She was frozen between fear and curiosity.

"What is your name?" Zitja asked with almost a purr. "I did not know I had a niece." She shook her head and smirked. "I did not know I had any family members left."

This hit Yemri the hardest of all. Zitja was her aunt, her blood and scales. Yemri had only ever thought of her as a horrible entity that needed to be stopped. She stared at the Siren Queen hard, and she also saw a bit of her mother staring back through Zitja's eyes. This terrified her more than anything else.

"Where is my father?" she asked the bucks with a shaky voice.

Someone gestured behind Yemri and she turned to see him deep in conversation with Muleki. She wanted to connect to them to know what they were talking about but knew that would be wrong for her to do, even as Ocean Mother. She couldn't start dropping eaves just because she was angry. She turned to the Sentinels. Her Sentinels. "Do not harm her. Do not touch her. Wait here until I return."

She turned and swam to her father. As she got closer, she could see both her father and Muleki were each surrounded by a fierce red halo so bold she was surprised it didn't light up the entire Atlantis a bright red. That color, Yemri knew, was anger. She might not understand what these colors were or why she saw them, but one thing she knew: whenever either of her parents glowed red, she always avoided them.

Not today.

Muleki and Tope were startled when she swam up to them and halted their conversation as soon as she connected with them. "Yemri, what are you doing here?" Muleki asked.

She felt her own glow turn red to match theirs. "Should I not be?" she asked with all the authority she could muster.

"That is not what I meant, of course," Muleki said with a forced meekness that belied the still red glow around him. "Only that it is dangerous out here with so many Sirens in the water. And with Zitja right there."

"There are always Sirens in the water." She was trying on a boldness she'd never worn before. It did not feel like herself, but might prove useful. "What were you talking about? What are you planning to do with her?" Yemri didn't know if she felt protective of Zitja, and she was confused by her own confliction. To have Zitja talk so fondly about her mother shook her to the core. Zitja was a threat. She had killed her mother and grandmother, Yemri knew this. Possibly her feelings had nothing to do with Zitja at all, and the overwhelming sensation that she wasn't welcome here despite her authority as Ocean Mother made her suddenly angry. Unsettled by her irritation at her father and Muleki, Yemri focused on asserting her authority. "Why are you arguing?"

"We are not—" Muleki began, obviously trying to misdirect, but Tope cut him off.

"We were discussing what is to be done with Zitja. Muleki feels we need to kill her right away. I feel, well, it does not matter what I feel. He is right. We need to kill her right now."

This clearly startled Muleki, and his fiery Ku rapidly reverted from angry red to his usual green glow. He looked pleased but humble.

Muleki nodded to a buck at his side, who presented a short sword. Muleki took it and handed it to Yemri. "She says she can only be killed by a member of her family. We have tried to kill her and found that none of us can. She must be telling the truth."

Yemri gathered the sword in her hands without thinking. If what they were saying was correct, she had no other option.

She had been waiting to be told what to do, and she told herself she felt better not having to make any decisions. But as she held the sword her hands began to shake.

Muleki placed a hand on her back and pressed gently. Yemri felt herself being pushed through the water towards Zitja.

When Tope said she needed to be killed right now, he meant *right now*. Muleki was not going to wait around for Yemri to process the reality of her situation. She kicked her tail to stabilize herself as Muleki let go of her back. The sword was too heavy for her, and she sank in the water. Her whole body was shaking as she lifted the sword.

"Wh... where?" She hoisted the sword as best she could. "Where do I put it?" Yemri asked without bravado, her voice betraying her fear to everyone watching.

To Muleki's credit, he looked ashamed as he pointed to a spot on Zitja's chest at the base of her leather wrappings, just to the left of center.

Yemri lifted the short sword in two unstable hands. The sword, though it was short, was longer than her arms and heavier than her entire body. She held the point in the spot where Muleki had indicated, and Yemri saw the glow around her arms fade away completely. Her whole body shook. She pressed on the sword, but it only resulted in pushing herself backwards in the water. Zitja thrashed and threw the sword off of her. Yemri's entire body began shaking so badly the sword slipped and fell from her hands.

As it plummeted in the dark water below, everyone looked around for a brief moment before a Sentinel dove to retrieve it. When he returned, he handed the sword back to Muleki, not to Yemri. He looked at her with pity in his eyes and regret in his Ku.

Muleki handed the sword back to Yemri. She could barely lift it. Her fear left her weak, and the audience made her uncomfortable and upset. She again pressed the sword to the indicated spot, and Zitja held completely still as if she, too, were curious about whether Yemri could do it.

Yemri knew she'd have to swim hard to be able to get the weapon to break skin. Her arms weren't strong enough on their own, though she doubted she was strong enough at all. But was that the real reason she couldn't do it, Yemri wondered.

As if reading her mind, Zitja spoke to her calmly, almost amused. "Little pup, are you strong enough for murder?"

Yemri understood. "Strong enough" wasn't just a question about her physical ability.

Yemri didn't know.

She kicked her tail and pressed again. The blade didn't even break through the leather.

Muleki got the attention of two Sentinels and said, "Help her push the blade in."

Yemri nearly vomited.

"Enough of this!" Tope yelled. "Stop. Just stop this right now. She is a pup. She cannot be asked to do such things."

Yemri dropped the blade again, and this time no one retrieved it as it sank into the depths. She turned to her father, and he ushered her away muttering quietly and privately, "I am so sorry, Yemri. I am so sorry."

"I wish mother was here," she said, feeling so forlorn it cut through her heart deeply.

"I know she is proud of you."

But Yemri knew that Sariah would not be proud of her. Even after death—even after death at Zitja's hands—she knew her mother would not want her sister to be killed. Yemri did not know how she would be able to do it.

"I just wish she was Ocean Mother instead of me. It is not fair that she did not get her turn."

Yemri looked at her father. She cocked her head slightly. He had lost the angry red glow from his confrontation with Muleki and the horrible position he had put his daughter in, but at the mention of Sariah, his glow changed from his usual purple to a muddy brown. Yemri immediately felt responsible for his sadness and tried to remedy it. "I will do my very best for her." She straightened. "I can do it!"

"Shhhh," he cooed. "Not now." He smiled fondly at her, his purple haze slowly returning, though a dark shadow still filled his Ku.

Just then, Muleki rushed to their side, actual regret in his Ku. "Ocean Mother Yemri, that was… well, I am sorry. It was too much to ask of a pup. I forgot myself."

Yemri said nothing. She wanted to be coddled and cared for in this moment. She was still shaking and upset, but still she knew her authority had been damaged. She would have a hard time getting anyone to listen to her after she had embarrassed herself so much. She unwound herself from her father's embrace. She was still shaking, but she spoke as calmly as she could. "I am sorry. I was not strong enough."

She agreed with Zitja. She didn't know what kind of strength it was she was lacking.

Muleki wasn't overly emotional. A Balam and Sentinel Commander through and through, he asked the obvious. "What do we do with her now?"

Yemri knew she needed a good idea to make up for her failings just now, but she didn't have a single thought in her head.

"We are going to have to go back to my original idea," Tope said forcefully. "Take her to Nephira's old stronghold in the Afiti." Then he looked at Yemri and his gaze passed to Muleki deliberately as he said with irritation, "This is the very thing we were arguing about when you arrived, Yemri. Whether to take Zitja there or have you kill her now."

"As I said before, this is not a permanent solution," Muleki rebutted. "Sirens know of it, and we can not keep it as secure as we once did."

"Not a permanent solution, no," Tope agreed. "But as I said before, Yemri is too young to do this now. Give her time."

Yemri did not think she would ever be up for it after what she had just experienced, but couldn't bring herself to say so. They were still expecting it from her. She thought hard. She had to come up with something long term or she would just have to kill Zitja eventually, a thought that sickened her.

Everyone looked silently at each other, angry at the situation and wracking their brains for a solution.

When it came to her, Yemri was so excited to finally have an idea that she blurted, "Put her in a cell! I know there are plenty of them inside. The Crurals were fond of… what are they called?"

"Prison," her father responded helpfully but begrudgingly. Yemri knew what he thought of her idea of permanent imprisonment without asking.

"Mother," Muleki interjected. It was as weird for the sixty-year-old buck to call her "mother" as it was for her to hear it. "Zitja cannot pass through the enchantment."

Yemri was annoyed at herself for not remembering. She would need to be smarter with her commands in the future.

"Then we must build her a permanent and hidden prison," she said, knowing she wasn't being helpful at solving the problem.

"Where?" Muleki asked. He kept the disdain out of his voice but not his Ku.

"Under the city," Tope said, and both Yemri and Muleki looked at him. "The island of Daris shoots deep into the ocean. We can tunnel through the rock and create a cavern for her. With bars. Does that suit both of you?"

"It does," Yemri said gratefully. Hopefully, that would hold Zitja for at least ten more years. Maybe then she'd be ready to handle killing her.

"I suppose it will work," Muleki conceded. "At least we have removed their queen from them, and possibly that will be enough. And it is a place that does not now exist. If we can keep it a secret… Yes it could work for a while." He turned to send out the orders.

Yemri stopped him before he left and said, "Stop the Sentinels from hurting her. They keep punching and stabbing her. They do not need to do that." She knew she sounded like a stupid pup. She *was* a stupid pup to him, she could feel it.

He only responded, "Very well," and left her still shaking in the water.

She looked at her father. "Mother would not tolerate treating her sister like that," Yemri said with the first conviction she had ever felt in her whole life. "Even after the transformation. Even with the murder and chaos Zitja has caused, do you know mother still loved her? She talked to me all the time about her older sister. She loved Zitja. Father, she loved her very much, even to the very end."

That left Tope in stunned silence. Yemri was surprised to think she might have caught him off guard by this knowledge, that she had revealed something to him he never knew before. Yemri was pleased to finally know something he didn't.

"I know," Tope said in a whisper. "Sariah always spoke to me about changing Zitja back. She did not know how, but she was determined to make it so. I did not know she spoke to you about it."

Yemri was crestfallen. At nine, there wasn't anything she could know that anyone else wouldn't. How was she supposed to lead with absolutely zero wisdom?

Tope gestured towards Zitja, and the two of them made their way like ghosts through the water. Yemri followed behind her father feeling like she would rather hide for the rest of her life than continue what she was doing. She kicked her tail slowly but steadily, letting herself feel secure in the monotony of the back and forth. She looked at the broad black back of her father and his dark brown tail, so unlike her own. Everyone always asked her how she had gotten such a tail when her father's tail was so dull and her mother's so pale. But Yemri didn't find her father's brown tail dull. Sure, it was brown, but it was also rich and dark, with a glossy shine that not many others had. She found herself getting angry on his behalf. But if she were honest, it was just to distract herself. She was just angry.

When they returned to the group, the Sentinels were tying Zitja securely to a palanquin, about to leave for the Afiti. The two of them stared at their Siren kin. Tope spoke clearly to Yemri with a connection to Zitja, Muleki, and the Sentinels around them so that all could hear. "Yemri is too young for this task right now." Her father spoke calmly. His Ku was filled with a protective love, and his glow began to return to the purple it usually had. "But Muleki is right. To make the ocean safe, something must be done." He was gently overriding her, trying to publicly tell her that Sariah's desires didn't matter, that she would have to kill her aunt when the time came. She was frustrated, but didn't know what to do. No one had thought to teach her how to lead; they all thought she still had so much time. Now Tope was taking over, and she was left to listen to his decisions. "Zyler is still young," Tope concluded. "We must think of those still being raised in these waters. When the time comes, we will take care of this. You can all rest assured." Instead of comforting her, he was saving face in front of everyone watching.

At the mention of her brother, Yemri stiffened. She had always felt protective of the tiny pup even though their age difference was small. She knew Tope was using Zyler to manipulate her feelings, and she was upset that he would do such a thing.

Before anyone made any decisions to overrule her, Yemri spoke to the highest-ranking Sentinel she could find. She had to have the last word, and she was sure that was the right thing for the Ocean Mother to do. "Find a way to secure Zitja while we travel. Put her in chains or a cage or whatever you can." And just in case Muleki did not bother to spread her message, she added, "And do not harm her!"

The Sentinels looked to Tope for confirmation. It wasn't until he sent confirmation through his Ku that they began to follow Yemri's instructions.

They left slowly and with confusion. Yemri's instructions meant nothing. Zitja was already secure, but they made themselves busy.

When Yemri was alone with her father again, she turned on him.

"Father." Yemri was resolved. "You have to stop telling me what to do in front of everyone. You have to stop allowing everyone to look to you for confirmation in each matter. I do not know what I am supposed to say or do. I am nine years old." She was upset in a way she couldn't define. "I already cannot get anyone to take me seriously—

especially when they think my father has to have the final say in everything I decide."

Apparently, anger made her confident. It gave her the authority she was going to need to get through this duty. Yemri would need to stay angry to pull off this role.

Tope looked like he wanted to argue. His Ku became guarded and hostile, but then he stopped and responded with the same love and concern he had shown her before. "You are right."

"Tata, I need your help," Yemri said, placing her hand on his heart, "and I am going to need you for a long time. But… but maybe you should not help me. Maybe I need to figure it out. Or… or at least when others are watching, I will be the Ocean Mother and you be the Balam for the Afiti and not my tata." He would always be her Tata, and when they were alone, maybe she could still feel like the pup she was. "Please?" Her hands were shaking when she was finished. This was not the way she was raised to speak to her parents.

"Of course." He scooped up her hands in both of his. "If you continue to be this brave, you will not need me at all."

"That is not even a little bit true." She took a deep breath. Finished with what she needed to discuss with her father, Yemri bolstered her bravery again and powered through all she had to tell Tope, the Balam for the Afiti. "It feels wrong to kill Zitja. I know that we must… but must we?" She sounded so young and stupid, even to her own ears, but she was so shaken by her first attempt to kill Zitja, she didn't know if she could ever try again. "What I mean is, is there not another way? What about reversing the curse? Or imprisoning all the Sirens? Must we kill her?"

He sighed, and his Ku was irritated. "We must. It is truly the only option." Tope let go of her hands but said no more.

It had been two days in the open water and Yemri was growing restless. There were only a few palanquins, and the rest of the sentinels swam on their own volition, so the company was going quickly—but not quick enough. She was glad that at least she didn't have to swim the whole way like some of the others did. Regardless, she insisted they all travel together because she was still worried harm would come to Zitja if left alone with the Sentinels and Muleki. They would torture Zitja despite her childlike wishes, she was sure. How many times had they stabbed her before Yemri arrived on the scene, trying to kill her, everyone failing but causing Zitja great pain in the process?

"It is just that Zitja does not seem evil to me," Yemri said to her father as they traveled behind Zitja in their palanquin, a massive shell that held Yemri, Tope, and Zyler all comfortably. A large plank across the top formed a bench to sit on, and the front end was tied with seaweed ropes to a team of dolphins.

"Why in Nephira's blue ocean would you think that?" Tope was shocked and didn't hide it, though he was as gentle with her as her age dictated.

"I just know some things. Things other people do not."

He gave her his full attention and placed a hand lovingly on her shoulder. "What are you talking about?"

"I have to tell you something strange," Yemri said after a pause.

"Strange?" he asked gently, Zyler curled up in his arms, sleeping soundly. He shifted in his seat to look at Yemri while they spoke, doing his best not to disturb his small son. "What do you have to tell me that is strange, daughter?"

"I have only told one Serra, another pup I used to play with when I was little." She shook her head. 'When she was little' was only last year. She seemed to have aged a few decades since then. "I told her and she mocked me. That is how I learned it was strange. I never told anyone else."

"What is it?" He squeezed Zyler tighter and looked anxiously at Yemri.

"I see a glow around everyone. A colorful one. It is different for everyone, and it will change depending on how they are feeling. I know it sounds so weird, and I thought everyone else could see the colors, but no. Is it something wrong with my eyes?" She was rushing to say everything she had thought on the matter over the years. When she finally stopped, Tope was calm.

"I wondered if you could see the penumbra."

"Penumbra?"

"It is called different things in different places: *ôré, émanation, gepräge*, auras."

"So it is not strange?"

"Strange, no. Unique, yes. Your mother could see them. It was one of the things about her that made her such a wonderful Serra. She could see things others could not and knew things about a Serra whether their Kus reveal it or not. It is a gift, Yemri. Use it to your advantage."

They were both quiet for a moment and then Tope asked cautiously, "Is this why you think that Zitja does not seem evil?"

Yemri sent a cautious affirmative through their Kus' connection. "I do not know what the pe… pen-um-bra," she stumbled over the word, "the penumbra means, but I have gotten a lot of clues over time. For example, when someone is glowing dark red they are very angry, but that is only an emotion. Sometimes a Serra is just naturally a light red, but that is not related to their emotions, it is just who they are. That does not seem to make any sense. And every single brand new pup is bright white, but that fades to a light blue and then eventually turns into the color that they are. I watched it with Zyler." She indicated her peaceful little brother asleep in her father's arms. "He is turning a violet color like yours."

Tope chuckled so quickly and fiercely that Zyler squirmed, opened his eyes, and then sat up. "Your mother always called me Roxo. I guess it means purple in a language from a kinship she visited as a pup. Or maybe she was just teasing me. Though, I never knew Sariah to tease anyone. "

Yemri thought for a moment and then she confessed, "I do not know what it means, the red penumbra, but I have seen it enough to know that it is bad and it should be feared and avoided."

"That makes sense to me."

Zyler was awake now and trying to climb out of the palanquin. Tope wrestled with him playfully for a bit and then Zyler got bored and started climbing around Yemri. His tail was pointing towards the sky, fin wide above them like an umbrella as his hands crawled around her face and pulled on her hair.

"Yemri!" Zyler said with unwarranted enthusiasm.

She grabbed him and pulled him in for a squeeze and kissed his chubby pup cheeks. "Zyler!" she returned the enthusiasm.

"Tata," Yemri said, deciding definitively that when they were alone she still wanted him to be her Tata and not the Balam, an advisor, and instructor. Besides, playing with her brother made her feel very much like the pup she was. "All the Sirens are red. All the time. But Zitja is not."

"Maybe…" Tope mused, "maybe she is not inherently evil, but that does not necessarily mean she is not evil. She is evil in action. And what are we but the accumulation of our actions?"

Yemri did not know the word "accumulation," but she got the idea. If one acts evil, does that not make them evil? "But would that not change her penumbra?"

"I do not know, my pup."

"I do not know, either." She looked up ahead to where Zitja was bound with ropes and guarded all around her palanquin. She was radiating red at the moment, but that only happened, Yemri noticed, once she was tied up. But Yemri did not fault her for her anger at the situation.

Zyler escaped over the side of the palanquin, and Tope reached out a long arm and scooped him back up without even looking. His attention was on a Sentinel streaming towards them.

"Ocean Mother!" The Sentinel swam up to their palanquin recklessly, jostling it in the water. "Nephira's stronghold is overrun with Sirens."

"They are looking for Zitja." Yemri was thinking quickly about what to do. The Sentinel, though he spoke as if he were addressing her, looked at her father the entire time and seemed to be waiting for his instructions. She needed to be decisive. "Stop!" She yelled to the procession, and one by one the palanquins and their guards and charioteers brought the group to a hold. Muleki joined them, along with the Sentinel commander. Yemri chastised herself for not knowing his name. That is something she should know. She added it to the growing list of things she needed to do better. And it was only her first week.

When they were assembled, she said, "We need to turn around. We have to take Zitja somewhere else."

"Where would that be?" the commander challenged.

"Think of something!" she retorted. She was feeling tired and cranky. She looked longingly at Zyler who was curling up eating some seaweed, oblivious to responsibility. "We also need to get the Sirens out of Nephira's Stronghold. That belongs to her!"

Muleki looked like he might argue. But she wanted to get her way for once, the way he did when he gave orders. So she squared her shoulders, lengthened her body and tail to their full extent, and said with authority, "Round up as many Sirens as you can and take them prisoner along with Zitja."

No one moved the way they had when Tope gave instructions in her chamber or the way the Sentinels scrambled to follow Muleki's orders outside of Daris just days ago. She resisted the urge to thrash her tail and throw her fists like Zyler did when he didn't get his way. She just stared at them, Ku resolute.

Muleki turned and instructed, "Pangor, assemble the Sentinels to storm the stronghold. We will attack in the morning. Instructions are to take prisoners, not kill."

The Sentinel commander turned to follow out the instructions, and Yemri took note that his name was Pangor.

Tope called a dam over and instructed her, "Head back to Daris ahead of us. Take the dolphins from Zitja's palanquin and add them to your own. Increase the number of graggers working on the tunnels underneath Daris. We will need a room to keep Zitja." He added quickly but with a tinge of pain at having to say it, "And a larger chamber to hold a significant number of Sirens."

The dam's eyes went wide, but she did not argue and immediately began unhooking the dolphins from Zitja's palanquin.

Tope then turned to his daughter and handed over the sleeping pup, still covered in scales up to his chest. "You will have to be in charge of your brother for the time being, Ocean Mother." He was irritated with her, and Yemri breathed deeply to remain calm. "I will go with Muleki to find a safe place to keep Zitja for now."

Yemri collected her now sleeping brother from Tope and he left her. She told her charioteer to take her back to Daris, and he turned the dolphins back the way they came. She felt completely exhausted and wanted to curl up and sleep in her shell. But she didn't want everyone to see, so she sat as stoically as she could, though she was shrouded in forlorn misery. She wondered how she could possibly be doing such a terrible job already.

Chapter 5

Santiago

With the ceremony over and Krell's ominous instructions pushed to the background, Rogan and Tizz reunited and the family was together again. With reverent Kus, they all greeted each other, placing hands on hearts and hugs for Santi. Even Rogan lingered in an embrace with his Bondmate for a moment. This was the scene Santi had pictured hours before. This was what was left of their family. Santi would have felt like an outsider in this moment except for the complete inclusion she felt in the others' Kus. It made Santi miss her own mother.

A few weeks ago, Celia was underwater being ushered around the ocean by Grendor, looking for their relatives. Celia's mother had been a Serra; surely they still had kin alive. Hopefully she would find them, and her tiny family would grow instantaneously. Celia wasn't under water anymore. She had to go back to work, and Grendor needed to return for the ceremony, but Santi hoped she'd receive a nuntium soon with an update and information about when her mother might be back.

For now, she let herself absorb the peace she felt being back together with her Serra family.

"Santiago, I need to go talk to-" Tizz made a general wave in the direction of her Daristor class. "I will see you tonight. I love you." And off she went in a blaze of energy before Santi could respond.

The mood broken, Rogan got back to the business he needed to be doing. "I have to finish up here. I will meet you at home tonight, Santiago." He pulled her in tightly and kissed her on the forehead. Santi was nervous about making the long swim all the way home by herself, but she didn't want to feel so helpless, so she breezily answered, "Of course! See you tonight!" before he released her and swam after the rest of the recent graduates.

"Santiago, I need to go get settled, and I have some things to gather. Would you like to come with me?" Coral asked considerately.

"Oh no, it's fine. I'm finally at the Troag, I'm going to look around a little."

Coral smiled lovingly and squeezed Santi on the arm before she left as well.

Santi looked around to see virtual emptiness in the city center, which, only hours ago, had been bustling. Even Amphitrite was nowhere to be seen. That turtle had a busier agenda than any person Santi knew. Now the Troag seemed almost eerie in its echoing emptiness.

Santi looked up at Nephira's marble stoic face and scrunched up her lips. "What are we going to do, Ocean Mother?" Santi asked, then laughed. "Talking to animals and objects that can't talk back is my new hobby, apparently." Her voice was light. Santiago was learning to be the jokester in Rogan's absence. It didn't really fit. She had always taken things too seriously. Maybe this was a good time to learn a new skill.

Then suddenly she scowled.

"But I wouldn't have to if someone else would listen to me." Santi kicked her feet off the ground and swam towards the sunshine above. As she left Daris in the depths, she focused on the light. The four months since Amed's death had been very hard as Santi worked through her grief while also trying to hold Rogan together and train to fight as well. And now Krell seemed to be making his own plans that did not involve anything Santi had been preparing for. It felt like things were unraveling.

The truth was, things had probably been unraveling for longer than she realized.

Finally, her face broke through the surface of the water and the sun was hot on her skin. Santi expelled the water from her lungs and breathed in a deep breath of air. She repeated the process before she relaxed and tread water, breathing freely. It had been nearly a year since she had been above water, and the air felt so thin it was almost unbreathable. It reminded her of a passage from her abuela's journal about how she felt that the air was making her weaker.

An unconscious frown crossed her face. Santi sighed and kicked herself back to float on her back. "How do I fix this?" She bit her lips and wiggled her toes. "What would Nephira do? What would Abuela Carmen do? What would my mom do?" Santi closed her eyes and felt the sun warm up her body. It was an incredibly hot day, and Santi soaked it in. She turned to see a little Amphitrite head poke through the surface next to her face. She looked at her faithful pet and asked, "What would Amed do?" She focused her eyes with determination.

When Santi was about eleven, she joined Rogan and Tizz when Amed took them to learn which plants were edible and which were not. After digging up some squished potato-like roots he called corms and putting them in their basket for dinner, Amed thought for a moment before digging up a handful more and plopping them into the basket as well. "I'm going to take these to Flora," he said with such a deliberate tone even Santi knew it was for Rogan's benefit. Rogan had been in a grumpy mood all day and she was sure this was Amed's way of getting to the bottom of it.

"But you hate Flora!" Tizz answered, and even Santi agreed.

"I absolutely do not hate Flora," Amed responded genuinely.

Amaratizz, not realizing this lesson was directed at Rogan but helpfully facilitating the discussion said, "But you are always arguing with her."

"I know, and that is probably my fault. We both have very strong personalities and want what is best for the kinship. So we clash most of the time. But nothing she wants is wrong, and neither are the things I want, so we have to come to common ground. I was very angry with her earlier, so I will bring her these corms and make amends."

When no one said anything, Amed sent a pointed pulse through his Ku and Rogan finally answered. "Fine! I will talk to Sully." Santi was glad to learn the reason for his moodiness. The two bucks were always getting into small arguments. "But I am not bringing him corms. They taste like dirt."

Amed lightly chuckled. "That is fine. But bring him something as a peace offering." Then he added with another laugh, "We are having corms for dinner so do not tell your mother you think her food tastes like dirt."

Santi opened her eyes and sighed at the memory. Amed faced things head on with grace, charm, and a peace offering. She nodded her head slowly. It couldn't hurt.

The seaweed wrappings on the very top of her chest dried slightly in the extreme heat, and Santi splashed water across them. Seaweed was strong and sturdy as long as it stayed wet, but as soon as it dried it began to crumble, and Santi thought it wouldn't do for her to go back to Daris topless. With one last deep breath of salty air and sunshine, Santi flipped forward and dove back under the surface. Amed's system was to make a plan and address it head on. As much as it terrified her, and as much as she preferred to be told what to do and go along with plans, it was time for her to be the one making the plans now.

She had to speak with Krell.

But first, she had to help her Bondmate. Amed was stronger because of Coral, and Santi would never be whole with half her heart in such agony.

Feet kicking up towards the surface, arms pushing towards the ocean floor, Santi felt motivated like she hadn't since Amed's death. With fresh air and perspective, Santiago

Scout Morales Williams of the Nhori was going to fight for what she knew was right, for what she deserved. She still didn't know how to help Rogan, but she was sure that answer would come to her. She kicked quicker, feeling light. A smile spread across her face. The city of Daris seemed brighter than it had before. Amphitrite dove with her, feeling the burst of enthusiasm spark Santi to life. The turtle zipped around Santi and then took off northward, leaving Santi laughing at the reptile's short attention span.

As she neared the city, she took in the sight of it all. Not often did one look at a city from above. It reminded her of the helicopter tour of New York she had taken with her mother as a child. Serras bustled about their business. Some swam with determination higher above the city, others strolled leisurely through the city, a part of the commotion. The buildings were white and gold, and all around the city were smatterings of greenery. Sparkling Serra tails and brightly colored fish created a gorgeous rainbow of colors, the most beautiful sight Santi had ever seen. As if in a dream, she drifted farther from the surface and towards her home.

Santi swept her arm in front of her to propel herself forward when a bolt of pain shot through her fingers and up her arm. She screamed in agony and surprise. Before she could process what had happened, the rest of her body crashed into the invisible barrier, causing her entire right side pain. She was immediately halted in the water, crumpled upon herself as if she'd run into an invisible glass door.

"What?" Santi said incredulously and furrowed her brow. She held her right wrist in her left like a baby. Her fingers throbbed. She let out a groan that was mostly a growl, and the remaining air in her lungs seeped out in little bubbles.

Tentatively, Santi reached out with her uninjured hand and touched the barrier. "What is this?" she asked with irritation. She could see the tops of the buildings roughly ten feet from where she floated in the water above. She slid her feet down to stand on the obstacle and began walking. She found herself headed in the direction of her home towards the back of the city when suddenly it dawned on her.

"The enchantment!" She nearly laughed at her own foolishness. "Oh, Nephira."

Santi stood on top of the city, blocked by the ancient enchantment that kept the city safe from Sirens. Santi was suddenly very aware that anyone could look above the city and see a silly Crural girl standing above them and trying to break in. She kicked off quickly and swam to the closest side of the city. Her home was far away towards the other side of the city, and walking across the enchanted dome just wouldn't do. In fact, it would be quite humiliating, and she wouldn't know how to get in once she got there anyway. "You are an idiot, Santi," she chastised herself.

"So… how do I get in?"

As she swam towards the outer wall of the city, Santi thought hard. She had come and gone several times. Earlier today, she was outside to greet Tizz, and then they had come back in with no problem. As Santi landed in the sand on the far right side, near the back of Daris, it came to her. "The entrance is the only way into the city."

Santi looked towards the gate. It stood high above the rest of the wall, jutting majestically towards the surface. She rolled her eyes; it was very far away. She wasn't at the back of the city but almost as far from the entrance as she could get. Once she reached the entrance, she would have to go back nearly this far to the other end of the city to reach her shelter. Her legs and arms already felt a little tired just thinking about it. And where was Amphitrite when she needed her? Santi thought about calling her pet, but honestly, it felt rude to call upon her friend every time she needed to get somewhere quickly. A little exercise wouldn't hurt her. Daris really was a huge city, even for someone with a tail, but especially for her stupid legs.

"Let's go," she said with resignation to no one and pushed herself into motion. There was nowhere for her to be today. Or any day for that matter. She had plenty of time to get home. From where she started at the outer perimeter of the city, it would take her over half an hour to swim the distance. At the thought, her motivation started to wane.

As she swam, Santi slid her hand along the wall. The marble was nearly seamless and in perfect condition even after being under water for so long. In the distance she saw a Sentinel on guard, swimming in the opposite direction. She wondered if he might give her trouble for any reason. Maybe it was a little suspicious for her to be outside the walls so far from the entrance. Then again, Serras weren't restricted in their movement around the ocean or the city.

I can go wherever I want, right?

It was difficult with her being a Crural who felt so at home under the water. Not everyone thought she belonged, but for the most part she never had any problems.

The Sentinel turned and looked at her but didn't move. She kept swimming, trying to be natural.

I've worked so hard to feel like I belong.

But in a big city she didn't always feel the warm inclusion that she had in the small kinship, where everyone had known her since she was a child.

However, there was just *a ceremony that I was a part of....*

Santi reached her Ku out quickly and connected to the Sentinel, then waved her arm high over her head. "Hello!" she said warmly. If he was going to be suspicious of her activities, she was going to power through with confidence and kindness.

"Hello, Santiago," he said calmly and with reserve but not without warmth.

She did not know him, so she kept swimming. Their Kus disconnected and Santi looked back over her shoulder and saw him turn back to scanning the ocean. She didn't mean to, but she let out a little sigh of relief. Since Amed's passing, she has felt on edge with Krell and the Sentinels, not sure where she stood. But it was becoming ever clearer that wherever she stood was no longer in the same place as before.

She turned her gaze out in front of her just in time to see that she was about to run into a school of stingrays feeding on shrimp. The plan she needed came to her instantly. Santi swooped down and began gathering shrimp while a memory washed over her, and she was struck with the answer for how to help Rogan.

~

Santi's first experience with crying under water occurred when she was eleven. She had been diving down the tunnel towards Rogan's kinship choking on water and tears as she transitioned to breathing water. She sobbed hard and sucked water in and out of her mouth in awkward gulps. She coughed and choked on the water as her diaphragm quivered. Though she was under water, she was still crying noisily. Her fists were in balls, making swimming inefficient. She just wanted to be in Coral's arms and tell her how awful her own mother was. Coral would make her feel better. This wasn't the first time she had swum to her surrogate mother for comfort when she felt like Celia failed her.

Santi broke through the entrance to Rogan's shelter, and Rogan popped up from the cushion he was sitting on.

"Santiago! What is wrong?" He swam to her quickly and gathered her in an embrace that was both brotherly and concerned.

"Where is your mother?" Santi was glad she didn't need her voice to speak; she didn't think it would work. "I need her."

"She is not here. Everyone is in the next kinship." Rogan indicated southward towards their neighboring kinship over two miles away. "What is the matter? Can I help?"

Santi sobbed harder. "I don't think so. I need Coral."

Rogan held Santi tighter and pulled her down to the cushion where they could sit together. He allowed her to cry without asking questions or having expectations from her. He just held her while she cried for as long as she needed.

Finally, Santi righted herself, all out of tears. "Thank you, Rogan. I… I think I needed that." He didn't reply, only looked at her with concern. "My mom only cares about her job. She says she has important clients at her company that were going to leave if she didn't convince them to stay. So

110

she missed my play. I didn't even want to do it in the first place!" Santi's pain radiated through their Kus and the water around them. Her anger from before the big cry returning with a vengeance. She had cried herself out, adding extra saltiness to the ocean water in the shelter. "My mom convinced me to do the stupid play, probably so that I'd be busy after school and she wouldn't have to deal with me. And tonight was closing night! She didn't make it to *any* of the performances."

Santi's anger covered the pain she felt but it was still simmering away down there, strong and devastating. "She doesn't even care about me. She cares about her job and making money. That's it."

"No, Santiago, do not say that. Your mother loves you."

"You don't know. You've never met her."

Rogan was silent. Thirteen was a difficult age for knowing how to comfort someone. He wracked his brain.

At long last he said, "I have an idea." He grabbed her hand and pulled her gently out of the shelter and towards the far end of the kinship to the community garden. When they reached the garden, Rogan hovered above the plants with his head and arms buried among the foliage and his tail sticking up in the water above him. The sight made Santi giggle a little and already she was starting to feel better.

Rogan rooted around in the greenery, and every once in a while, he plucked something off of a leaf and held it in his palm. After doing this five or six times, Santi couldn't stand the suspense anymore and she joined him in the search.

"What are we looking for?" She asked, interested in the hunt.

Rogan held out a hand that was nearly twice the size of hers, "These."

Santi gave a little squeak and pushed away from him. "Ew! You're picking bugs?"

Rogan laughed. "These are shrimp." His eyes twinkled at her.

Santi wrinkled her forehead and leaned over his hand to see. They were small, only the size of a dime, and all legs and antenna. "I don't think I've ever seen one with its head and… well… moving." Her brow unfurled, and she squished her lips from side to side thinking. "Shrimp are like ocean cockroaches."

"I do not know what a cockroach is," Rogan said, looking at the little creatures, "but these are good to eat."

Santi only nodded. Up until this moment she had liked shrimp, but now she wasn't sure if she could ever eat them again. "So are we eating shrimp? Is that your idea?"

"No," Rogan replied, and Santi relaxed. "Just find some more and stop asking questions." He flicked his dark blue tail ever so softly, yet he moved quickly back to scour the floor. How did he move so easily and gracefully without hardly any effort at all?

When they had a few handfuls of shrimp, Santi shivered as their skinny legs flailed about, wiggling in her loose grip. Rogan pulled her to the outskirts of the kinship, and paused just on the border of the last shelters. Santi looked around. It was just open ocean with the usual plants and animals going about their business. She was about to ask questions again when she noticed Rogan's Ku was searching for something. She remained quiet and respected the process.

She didn't always have to talk and interrupt, a lesson her mother was always trying to teach her.

This was the first time she had actually used her Ku as a tool for awareness of her surroundings. Of course she felt what Serras were feeling when she was connected to them for communication, but never before had she thought about the other possibilities.

She sat quietly, connected to Rogan's Ku, and felt him search their surroundings for what he was looking for. It was as if through her connection to him she could see what he saw—so to speak—but to a lesser extent. She sat by him quietly as she felt his attention move through the water around them. She was so intensely focused on the determined feeling in his Ku that as soon as he found what he was looking for, she felt it too. Once she knew where he was focused, she pushed her Ku there and connected to the objects.

"Stingrays?" she asked.

He looked at her, startled for only a moment, then his face lit up. "They are like—what was that thing you had? Puppies?"

She cocked her head doubtfully. "They're like puppies?"

In response Rogan called to them. "Ayy-ooo." He grabbed her hand and pulled her towards them. It only took a moment because as soon as he called, they swarmed Rogan and Santiago, swimming all around and rubbing up against them.

"You've done this before!" She squealed as they tickled her face and legs as they slid smoothly against her skin.

"They know I bring food when I come." To demonstrate, he held out his handful of shrimp, and the stingrays flurried around him, snatching up the sea bugs and rubbing against Rogan as thanks.

Santi held out her hands magnanimously and was gratified when they swarmed her just as exuberantly. Santi reached out her hand and felt the smooth but tough skin on a large ray. It felt much like a dolphin's, but even softer. Like self-propelled silk sliding against her fingertips. She let out a laugh that gurgled in the water but lit up her and Rogan's Kus.

Santi grabbed a smaller stingray by both fins and twirled around. Then she pulled it in for a hug, forgetting her anger at her mother for the moment.

~

With her ratty old bag slung over her shoulder, full of wriggling shrimp, Santi picked up her pace to get inside Daris. She felt bursting with love for Rogan and determination pounding anew in her chest. She knew this would work.

Chapter 6

Yemri

"Are you ready?" Pangor asked, remarkably gently.

Yemri sent an assenting beat through her Ku without speaking or even opening her eyes. She knew she would need to work on her bravery if she were going to lead the ocean, but for now—only three months into her reign—she wasn't ready to be brave in this moment.

Her father held her hand and she squeezed it tightly as Pangor held her earlobe securely between his two thick fingers and pressed the tip of a long, thin piece of metal into her ear. He pushed until there was a pop. Yemri screamed out in pain. It felt as if the metal stick were a giant sword going through her entire head. Then, as Pangor turned and twisted the handle, Yemri could hear crunching, and more pain washed over her body making her feel weak. A dizzy wave washed over her and she felt light and tingly.

Pangor moved to the other side while Yemri kept her eyes scrunched tightly shut, gripping her father's hand as if it could save her. Thankfully Pangor didn't ask if she was ready again because she might have said no. Pangor thrust the stick into her ear once more and Yemri filled the water around them with her scream. This time with the sickening crunch of him slaughtering her inner ear, Yemri feared she would be sick in the water.

As if a gift from Nephira herself, Pangor said, "I am finished, Mother. And the pain should dull to a throbbing soon. It is not so bad."

Yemri opened her eyes, but when she saw her blood dissolving in the water around her, she wished she hadn't. "Thank you, Pangor," she squeaked out. She still felt lightheaded but also she was impressed. "All Sentinels have had this done to them?"

"Yes, Ocean Mother Yemri. They could not do their job otherwise. Hearing is the only thing that makes us susceptible to the Song."

"This sacrifice needs to be rewarded," Yemri said with conviction. She thought about making it mandatory so that no one would be susceptible to the Song, but it felt wrong to take away Serras' free will. What if they loved hearing dolphins sing, or what about Serras whose opus it was to learn the languages of the Crurals? No, they should choose to do it, she decided, and that made her want to make a big deal out of the choice.

She felt a pulse pass between Pangor and Tope. She knew they wouldn't be so improper as to speak about her in her presence but the unsaid felt just as hurtful.

Finally Pangor spoke, "Of course, of course. What would you like? We can give you anything you think will make you feel better."

She saw her own penumbra glow red and she knew they felt it in her Ku. She would need to guard her emotions better. Yemri calmed herself before she spoke and cleansed the irritation and sarcasm from her voice. "I do not mean for myself. I mean for the Sentinels. The deafening should be a ceremony. It should be praised and applauded."

Tope spoke up then, perhaps trying to reverse the perception of naiveté she was having on Pangor. "This little thing does not need a whole ceremony. It is just a necessity."

This made Yemri dig in her fin. All of her decisions went this way so far. Everyone argued and no one thought she ever had any good ideas. "They are doing bodily harm and damage. It is painful and permanent. And," she emphasized firmly, "they are doing it all by choice. They deserve a ceremony and we shall do that for all new Sentinels."

Again the two older bucks paused and passed a tick between them. Finally Pangor loosened his shoulders and defenses. "It will be done, Mother."

"Now," Yemri pushed herself up from the stone bench she had been sitting on, "I am going to see Zitja."

"Yemri-" her father started, but she cut him off.

"I will be safe now. Her Song cannot harm me, and she is safely in her new prison." With that she turned and left the two to inevitably discuss her senseless ideas in her absence.

Yemri made her way under the portcullis and took a sharp right along the periphery wall. It was decided that for the under-island tunnels and chambers to be effective, no one could know about them save those who must. As it were, only she, Tope, Muleki, Pangor, and the graggers who made the tunnels knew. Her guards would have to follow, and now they would know as well, but they were sworn to secrecy in every aspect of their position, so they posed no threat.

Yemri entered the crude tunnel entrance and passed through the small opening until it expanded into a longer, wider passageway. The larger portion she entered, however, was still only a few Serra lengths tall and wide. Graggers were still working, and eventually it would be wider, with more off-shooting tunnels and caverns. For now, it was a tiny bit claustrophobic as the walls were still so tight all around. Bioluminescent bacteria had been planted on the walls and were growing, albeit weakly. It didn't seem to be thriving in its new environment, but it was enough to light her way.

She stayed close to the walls and the meager light from the bioluminescent bacteria, passing through a cavern opening on her right where graggers were working on making space for future needs. The tunnel she was following bent to the right before bending back and straightening out again.

Pangor had taken her on a brief tour four days ago so she knew where she was going. He had refused, however, to take her near Zitja, choosing only to point out the way when Yemri asked. It irritated Yemri that she was expected to rule—wasn't even allowed to abdicate—yet they protected her from her job at every turn.

When she got to the area of the cavern where Zitja was tucked away, the tunnel opened up after she passed through a smaller hole in the rock. She floated into the large area and looked around for her aunt, her guards following closely behind.

Yemri wished she could be alone for once in her life. What harm could come to her down here? It was spooky, for sure, but everything dangerous was supposedly locked up tightly—the entire reason for hollowing out the island in the first place. Not that she didn't like her guards; they were just ever-present. The smaller dam guard, Tammin, was serious, poised, and professional. She was a fierce fighter and kept her head shaved so that her hair didn't get in the way of her work. Yemri appreciated her and trusted her, but she wasn't fond of her company. The large buck, Forcer, on the other hand had been her guard since before she was Ocean Mother. He was genial and quirky. He had a scar on his cheek after protecting Yemri as a pup from a spear directed at her father. She trusted Forcer and she liked his company, but since becoming Ocean Mother both her guards stuck close to her always. It got tiring.

The round, open cavern had smaller outlets on the sides. Yemri propelled herself to the first opening on the left, where a barred gate had been inserted into the rock. She marked her approval in her mind and went up to investigate. The chamber was empty. She reached out and touched the cool polished metal and took a hold of it. With a firm hand, she pushed and pulled, shaking it with all her strength. It was very strong and secure. It would do well for whatever they chose to put in there in the future.

She leaned in to see how big the space inside was, but it was so dark in the chamber she couldn't see well. She pressed her face to the bars and looked through. If it weren't for the faint red ruddiness, Yemri would not have been able to see the bluish-white silhouettes all along the walls. She shoved herself back from the bars, startled to realize there were people in there. A cold chill washed over her as she absorbed the information. Chained all around the room were white-skinned Serras, haloed in dark red. She knew she had ordered this to happen, but she almost didn't expect her orders to have been followed. And no one had told her. Pangor had only said that Nephira's Stronghold had been secured once again and that Zitja was under the island. But here she was faced with dozens of Sirens all caged in a cavity together.

The room was suddenly freezing. Eeriness flooded her awareness. Yemri realized just how foolish it had been to come down here alone. She felt a Siren floating behind her, breathing water onto her neck, though she knew that couldn't be true. Not only were the Sirens all locked behind these bars, but they were each chained to the walls.

Regardless, she looked over her shoulder, just in case. She thought she saw something and whipped herself fully around. Nothing was there, as logically, she knew nothing would be. Her guards had given her space—just a little—so she couldn't see them in the darkness but she felt their presence near. She breathed out a relieved sigh just as something grabbed her by the arm and pulled her backwards against the bars. Another white hand reached through and grabbed her other arm, pinning her tightly.

Yemri kicked her tail and flailed her arms wildly. She clawed madly at the hands on her upper arms, but she was much too weak to fight off a full-grown Siren. Panic wracked her entire being, muddling her thinking, and she flailed helplessly against the iron-strong grip.

120

Her guards sprung from their positions and hurtled themselves to their Ocean Mother's rescue. Though it felt like forever, Yemri was released from the Siren's grasp as quickly as she had been taken into it.

Powerful and quick, Tammin raised her staff, turned it deftly, and plunged it between the bars directly into the head of the Siren holding Yemri captive. Yemri was freed instantly and turned to see the unconscious Siren floating to the rocky floor of the carved out room. Yemri told herself to be regal and to thank her guard. She turned, placed her hand on her own heart, and said, "Thank you, Tammin. I owe you my life."

Tammin merely placed her own hand on her heart and returned to her post. This was routine for her. Tammin had been assigned to Yemri because she had been one of Nephira's guards and knew the perils of the position. Yemri breathed hard and pressed her hands to her stomach as she turned back to look at the Siren on the ground. At this moment, Yemri wanted her mother. She knew it was such a pup thing to want, but she couldn't help herself.

As she watched, the unconscious Siren stirred. Yemri kicked herself away from the bars to create distance. She would not be caught unaware again. The Siren sat up and reached a hand through the bars again, only this time it was different. The Siren buck looked desperate, sad, like he was pleading for help.

Was that why he had grabbed her? Did he want something? Or was he actually menacing now? She could not feel his Ku, could not sense his intentions. And she didn't understand facial expressions at all. He continued to reach out a hand that Yemri noticed only now was illuminated by a slight orange halo.

Finally, he spoke. "Ocean Mother." It was quiet, a gentle dolphin song in her Ku. Like an echo of a voice. "Ocean Mother, there is a mistake."

Before Yemri could decide what she would reply—or if she would reply at all—Tammin was at her side, ready to fight off the Siren once more. "Come, Mother Yemri, I think it's best we be quick and leave the caves."

Yemri could only follow along. Sometimes it was nice to be told what to do and not have to think about what she should do or what was right, just follow where she was led.

Thankfully, Tammin did not lead Yemri out of the tunnels, which was what Yemri expected. Instead, the stoic Sentinel led Yemri to her desired destination: Zitja's prison.

Facing Zitja's bars, Yemri hesitated to look inside. Fear washed over her. She could still feel the imprint of the other Siren's hands on her arms. She glanced at Tammin and Forcer waiting for her to finish her self-imposed mission so they could all leave. With them close by, she felt safe enough to proceed. She looked inside and saw Zitja lying on the floor, seemingly asleep. This gave Yemri a moment to take stock of her aunt.

Zitja looked like the other Sirens with her black tail and arm scales contrasting both fearsomely and stunningly against her white skin. Her penumbra was the same as the Siren Yemri had just encountered, the two of them the only burnt-orangish auras she had ever seen. Zitja's head was laid on her stump-arm, and the other lay gingerly along her flank, making her look quite whole. Zitja's hair looked exactly like

122

Sariah's had, black, curly, and long; though Zitja's curls hung loose where Sariah's had been much tighter. Sleeping peacefully like this, with her eyes and mouth closed, Yemri thought Zitja looked quite lovely.

And just like that the illusion was shattered. Zitja's fierce black eyes shot open. She saw Yemri and sprang towards the bars, sharp teeth bared. Yemri was startled but managed to keep her composure as, this time, she had not ventured close enough to the bars to be reached. She was proud of herself for at least learning something from her last encounter.

When Zitja realized she could not stretch her good arm far enough to reach Yemri, she stopped immediately, as if she too wished to appear as composed and regal as possible. In this way, the two rulers faced each other quietly and suspiciously for a time.

Finally Yemri spoke, trying to take the quiver out of her voice. "Zitja, you know that I am Yemri, Sariah's daughter. I am..." She intended to say more—had a small speech prepared, in fact—but as she paused to slow the frightened pounding of her heart, Zitja interrupted.

"So, you are here to kill me and be done with it then?"

Yemri was confused. Surely Zitja would know—no matter how desperately they wanted her dead—that they would not send a tiny child to kill her, alone, after what happened last time she tried. "No. No, I am not here to k… kill you." She hated that she was showing fear. She just wanted to say her little speech and leave.

Zitja's smile was mocking. "Oh, so you would rather I live forever to terrorize your ocean."

It was not a question. It was a statement so confusing Yemri forgot she was trying to be diplomatic. "What?" she asked, just as a nine-year-old who had no idea what was going on would.

"If you do not kill me, I shall live forever. And if I live forever, I promise to terrorize this ocean forever."

"How? How can you live forever?"

"You truly were not sent here to kill me?"

"No." Yemri was so confused. "I know I have to kill you but…" She wanted to say "but what do you mean 'live forever?'" but she already felt so stupid for having come. What hadn't she been told? What wasn't making sense?

Everything, Yemri told herself. *Nothing made sense to her, ever.*

"You are the only one who can kill me now that I have killed my father."

Again, Yemri was confused. Phinell had died long before Yemri was even born, but she knew the story. Everyone knew the story. Zitja had been turned into a Siren, killed her father, became the Siren queen, and then killed Sariah and, later, Nephira. But what she did not know was why Yemri would be the only one to kill Zitja. "But Phine--"

"Think, pup. You know Phinell is not my father." Yemri was silent, but she did remember. She knew that Zitja was actually the daughter of the king of the Crurals, Tullus.

Zitja saw understanding dawn on Yemri's face and she proceeded. "Your grandmother cursed me twice in my life: once to be what I am now, and again that only my flesh and blood could kill me. I have killed every one of my family members but you. So I dare you to try."

"There is my brother, too!" Yemri said defiantly, but the look on Zitja's face let her know she had made a terrible mistake. Yemri kicked herself further back from the bars in alarm. Yemri and Zyler had been born long after the transformation of the Sirens. Zitja would not have known about their existence, but now Yemri had revealed the existence of her pup-brother.

Blood pumped through her in an angry panic. Would there be no end to the mistakes she made? Yemri slowly backed her way towards the tunnel entrance, wringing her hands and breathing in shallow gulps.

"Or you can change me back, my darling niece," Zitja called after Yemri's receding form.

Yemri turned and fled.

But the tunnel was long, and by the time she reached the wide-open part of the cavern Yemri had slowed her pace to think. Did she possess the ability to change Zitja back, just as she was the only one who possessed the ability to kill her? Had she just placed her itsy brother in danger? Was she eventually going to have to kill Zitja to set the ocean free from her brutality? Would permanent imprisonment not be enough? And nagging in the back of her mind at all times was the question of whether she could possibly make a good Ocean Mother. Yemri placed her face in her hands and agonized about all she had learned in her brief encounter with Zitja. She had so much to think about that she did not realize for a moment that she had stopped swimming and was floating, her face in her hands, across from the cavern full of Sirens.

Yemri righted herself instantly and pulled her body to its full length. She looked back at her guards. Tammin, at least, was doing her best to look interested in the handy-work the graggers had done on the tunnel wall. Forcer was staring straight at her, as if he wanted to scoop her up and protect her like he had when she was a baby.

Yemri's shoulders sank with her embarrassment. She closed her eyes, took a deep breath, and began swimming towards the exit again.

"Ocean Mother, there is a mistake!" came a call from the cavern. The Siren was looking at her, pleading once again. The Siren who had attacked her, though still in his chains, was pressing himself to the bars.

"What is the mistake?" she asked kindly—though she did not know where the kindness had come from. It just seemed wrong to treat this buck as any other Siren when he was clearly so desperate.

"I am not supposed to be here."

But before Yemri could ask what he meant or why he thought he shouldn't be, something horrible and bewildering began to happen.

The Siren had only a moment to look at Yemri with genuine fear in his eyes before throwing his head back and screaming with such a guttural sound that Yemri heard it with her Ku despite it being an actual sound. She was shocked but couldn't look away, her curiosity gluing her eyes to the howling beast. He was thrashing around and flinging his arms and tail against the floor, walls, and bars as far as his chain would allow. The chain around his waist held him to within a small radius, but it was enough to give him the freedom to thrash.

After the initial shock had worn off, Yemri began to grow irritated. Was this Siren trying to trick her into something? Maybe he hoped her sympathy for his pain would cause her to release him? She was suspicious of his motivation, but she felt in his Ku that his pain was sincere. He was hurting both in his mind and his body. Something serious was happening.

That was when she realized something astounding.

He has a Ku?

Yemri moved closer to the bars to get a better look. She had never felt a Siren's Ku before. As she watched, the inky blackness of his tail turned to grey, and his translucent skin pinked up. His eyes softened, and his teeth rounded. His angry red glow changed slowly to a muddy brown. Finally, he lay on the ground of the cavern, a look of total defeat and exhaustion on his face, the face of a Serra buck.

At once the other Sirens comprehended the difference in him, and those nearest to him lunged on their chains to attack him. They grabbed his chain to pull him closer. The episode had taken so much energy that the buck did not even fight back but allowed them to punch and claw at him.

"Get him out of there!" Yemri shouted to her guards.

"Mother, I do not think--" Tammin began, but Yemri cut her off.

"Do it!" she yelled, knowing there wasn't much time.

Forcer opened the bars, and he and Tammin pulled the transformed Serra out of the grasp of the Sirens. While Tammin unlocked the chains at the wrist and tail of the Serra, Forcer grappled with the three Sirens within reach. Chains restricted the Sirens, but they were still able to put up a good fight. Forcer Pushed them off, punched with his fists, and smacked them away with his tail. He knew Yemri didn't want them killed, but they were becoming overwhelming for him. Just as he was pulling out his stíthos, Tammin pulled the transformed Serra out of the cage and Forcer retreated. All three of them were exhausted as they emerged from the cell.

Once the bars were relocked and secure behind them, Tammin and Forcer held the limp Serra between them and looked at Yemri for further instruction.

"Take him to Daris." She almost asked as if it were a question. Hopefully her father would know what to do. She hoped she hadn't made another mistake.

Chapter 7

Santiago

Rogan of the Nhori, son of Amed and Coral, newest member of the Sentinels was a sight to behold. His broad back and shoulders flexed and tensed beneath the crossed holster straps as he unsheathed his blades. He swung one blade after the other through the water. His powerful muscles swept the swords deftly around to attack his opponent in swift, precise motions. He was laser focused.

Rogan's sparring partner was someone Santi didn't know, but it could have been Zitja herself for all Santi cared; she only had eyes for Rogan. Rogan struck at his opponent, first with one blade, then the other. The dam he fought only had one short sword to Rogan's two. Though she did have a small shield, she could barely keep up. He struck at her again, and she parried with her sword. He struck at her other side and she barely moved her shield in time. The shield was small, only about the size of a dinner plate and punched through with several small round holes to reduce water resistance. It served to cover her unprotected side from attack, because attack Rogan did. He beat on her with a deftness that made Santi's temperature rise. When had he gotten so good? Had he always been so sleek in the water, smooth in his form, and powerful with his hits? He probably had been, but the times he'd been near her in a fight, she had always been entangled in her own brawl. Rogan struck again and again until his opponent was rendered incapacitated.

Santi remembered that furious passion. He'd unleashed it on her several times, though not on the sparring field. She missed his unbridled hunger immensely and hoped his sorrow wouldn't take it away from him permanently.

As soon as Rogan's opponent had been incapacitated, the sparring immediately came to a halt. Each placed their right hands on the right shoulder of the other and then broke apart.

Santiago cocked her head from her vantage point watching above.

Some sort of salute?

Once done, the two opponents turned to each other, smiles breaking across their faces, and they reopened their Kus. No harm done, and no hard feelings.

Santi sighed.

She would give anything to get to train with them. Krell had not agreed to let her. Now she knew why, at least. He had no intention of letting her become a Sentinel. Fine. The only practice she could get was any that Grendor or Rogan would give her, but Rogan didn't really have much interest in swinging swords at his Bondmate. It wasn't that he didn't support her doing it, he just didn't want her to be at the other side of his blades.

If what she was left with was to watch him train and pick up tips that she could practice on her own, then that was she would do. Santi spent as much time as she could lingering high above the sandy floor of the sparring pits. She had originally found it odd that they brought in sand for the floor when the fighting took place above it in the water—this is until she saw a trainee get hit so hard into the ground he left a trail in his wake. She realized then that everything served a purpose, from the round sand circles to the six-foot hedges around each of the five pits that set the sparring boundaries.

Rogan's blue tail swung in a wide but tight arc, slamming his next opponent across the face and shocking him so fiercely that Rogan was able to pull him into a tight embrace around the chest, constricting his breathing.

Santi's heart pounded more intensely in her chest. Watching him train often had the distracting disadvantage of making her want to run right home with him. Sadly, Rogan's frame of mind had kept them from any such exciting activities lately.

That didn't stop her from watching as he used his strength to dominate his opponents again and again. She got lost in the stretch of his muscles, the flex of his tail, the intensity in his eyes. It was the only time he didn't seem so sad to be a part of the world.

"Santiago, I am glad to find you here."

Santi startled. So focused had she been on Rogan that she had not noticed Krell's approach. How long had he been there? How much could he feel from her Ku? Her face flushed in embarrassment as she tried to remind herself that she was Bound to Rogan. She could lust after him all she wanted.

"Krell. Hello." They tread water above the large sparring pit. It was easier to see—and stay out of the way—from above the fighting but now she regretted being so visible in the center of the Sentinel epicenter of activity. This wasn't the Sentinel building, where Krell and his generals held strategy meetings and other important business, but the sparring pits were always active. This was where the Sentinels chose to go whether it was their assigned practice time or not. It was a hub of commotion at all times. Deep down, she probably knew she'd run into Krell if she hung around here. Maybe, she mused, she was even hoping she would.

Santi was thinking like Amed now, and Amed would confront Krell.

She was going to confront Krell. She wished she had a peace offering, but try as she might, she had not thought of anything she could bring him. Cold confrontation would have to do.

"You are aware of the tournament coming up."

Santi had to physically restrain her eyes from rolling. The tournament that was announced at the ceremony just this morning? The same one in which he had announced she was going to be playing a mysterious role? The Tournoi de Jeux Tizz had decided they would make a team for? Yes, she was familiar with it.

"Yes, of course," she answered. "In fact, I was thinking we would enter. You know, just the amateur contest, just for fun."

Krell's pinched face lit up as much as she had ever seen, which wasn't much. "I am glad to hear this. I was going to suggest that very thing. It will be good for the Serras of the ocean to see you taking part in a favorite custom. We want them rooting for you."

Now Santi was irritated. She didn't feel like doing anything he wanted her to do. "Well, I'm only thinking about it still. Nothing decided. I have to convince Rogan to join, of course. He doesn't seem in the mood for games."

"He cannot say no to me. I will tell him to create a team with you."

"No!" Then she calmed her tone. "No, that's fine." She did not want Rogan to start being ordered to spend time with her. She wanted him to play and have fun of his own free will or not do it at all. Santi put her hand on the strap of her tiny grey bag that crossed her chest. She could feel the little shrimp moving around inside. She hoped her idea would cheer Rogan up, and then she would ask him about the tournament. Getting Krell involved would not be helpful to their situation. "I'm sure I can convince him. You can count on it."

"I am glad to hear. You have to play." Krell made the statement with such energy in his Ku that Santi felt it as a threat, was sure it was meant to be a threat. "Just a few weeks until the tournament, so start practicing now. I want your team to go far in the tournament."

Santi cocked her head. "Isn't the amateur portion only one day of the tournament? I can't go much farther than that."

"Yes, of course I do not expect you to play with the experts. But I expect you to do very well in the amateur contest."

Santi squinted her eyes, but said nothing more on that matter. "Speaking of practicing, I'm wondering when I can start training with the Sentinels. I want to be prepared whenever it is time to attack the Sirens. I don't want to fail."

Something shot through Krell's Ku that Santi could not identify. It was calculating and zealous, an eerie combo of certainty and dismissal. "You will not fail, Santiago. But you will also not be training with the Sentinels."

Santi felt utterly deflated. She had expected this from him, but hearing this decision so abruptly... Whatever faux-confidence she was holding on to at the beginning of this encounter with Krell was well out of her grasp now. He turned away from her to leave, and Santi panicked. She knew she was unlikely to get an audience with him again so easily. "What should I be doing, then, if not becoming a Sentinel? I feel rather useless around here."

"It does not much matter."

"But surely I must have some way to contribute. I must do… something?"

"Then go see Tillop at the Opus Complex. But focus on the tournament for now." And with that, he swished away in his stupid leather vest.

Santi grumbled. She looked back down to where Rogan was unbuckling his swords from his back and packing his things away to leave. She had no idea what Krell meant about Tillop or the Opus complex. For that matter, she didn't know much concerning the tournament, either.

She sure did a good job confronting Krell, she thought ruefully.

"Rogan, I have an idea," Santi said as she slashed at him with her sai. Her heart wasn't in it, and she knew his wasn't either. But he had offered to train with her after she told him what Krell had said, and it was the first time since Amed's death that he had shown interest in doing anything with her, so she had jumped at the opportunity. The bag of shrimp would just have to wait.

"What is it?" He lifted his blade and parried her blow effortlessly.

She had become a fairly competent opponent, but she was not trying hard, and swipe after swipe, he flicked her away like a fly. "Well it's not really my idea. It's Tizz's. We were thinking we should join the amateur contest in the tournament." She made her Ku feel light, as if it didn't matter whether he was interested or not because it was a silly thing. Telling him about the pressure from Krell would not help him be interested.

"Oh, that is a great idea," Rogan responded.

"You think so?" Santi's heart soared.

"Yes!" he said with actual interest. "I think you have the skill and ability to do just fine. Plus, you have been working very hard to be a Serra. I think this is a good opportunity to do something challenging."

"That's what I was thinking too." Santi smiled. "I think this is a great way to really be a part of the ocean. You know what I mean?"

Rogan smiled approvingly, and the usual faraway look in his eyes wasn't present as he said, "So who else is on the team? You need four."

"Tizz said she has an idea for the fourth person. I'm not sure who it is though."

Rogan was silent for a moment. He stopped sparring with her before slowly saying, "So you intend for me to be the third." It wasn't a question.

Santi's eyes went wide. "Yes, I'm sorry, I thought… well, that's what I meant this whole time. Maybe I didn't explain it well." She felt him losing the enthusiasm he had about the tournament—which wasn't much to begin with. "I thought it would be fun to do it together.

"I am not really interested in it."

"I totally understand that. I do. It's just, this is really important to me. I really want to immerse myself down here and show everyone that I truly am one of you all."

"Yes, I agree. I think you should do it. But you will have to find another Serra for the team."

"Rogan, you have been so impossible lately. Can't you just do this thing with me?" She didn't mean to raise her tone, but she was loud, and her Ku was hostile. "I have been really patient with you, but I need this from you now."

"Santi you are being very selfish." As heated as Santi was getting, Rogan was doing the opposite. He grew colder and more detached.

"*You* are being selfish, Rogan." She didn't mean it, but she couldn't stop. Krell's threat to get involved loomed over her. "Can't you just do this one thing for me? I've let you grieve in peace, but it's been so long now."

Rogan was angry now, too. "It has not been long at all."

Santi agreed with him, but she was in the middle of an emotional avalanche. "We are newly Bound, Rogan. This sadness and anger and almost *no* talking has been our entire relationship. I've been patient, but you aren't even trying."

Rogan looked at Santi in a way he never had before. He was hurt. She had hurt him. "I am trying." He said, and he sheathed his swords. He gathered up his things and swam away, no longer angry. Worse, he left hurt and disappointed that she had turned on him.

The regret Santi felt was instant and all consuming. All the tension in her body released, and the sais in her hands hung loosely by her side. Santi let herself sink into the sand by her bag.

Three rogue shrimp had crawled out, and Santi rounded them up and put them back. "I really messed that up." Her shoulders slumped.

Just like I did with Krell earlier.

Her ambition to make Amed proud of her by handling this the way he would have was not going well. She slung her bag over her shoulder and followed after Rogan.

As Santi swam up to her and Rogan's shelter on the twelfth floor of their marble high-rise apartment, she felt two other Kus in the room and balled up her fists. Not in the mood for company, Santi swooped in through a giant square in the front room that she was sure had been a window at one point—if this city had really once been above water as the legend said—and tried to remove the gloom from her Ku.

Immediately, any harsh feelings were forgotten as Santi gathered her mother up in a tight embrace. All the anger, loneliness, and frustration of the past four months slipped off of Santi's shoulders and on to her mother. It was the relief from burden only a mother could offer, and it was exactly what Santi needed. Santi connected her Ku to the familiar buzzing that was Celia's constantly moving energy and nearly sighed with the relief of having her mom back under water. "What are you doing here, Mommi?" She squeezed her again and then released suddenly. "And… how?"

"Grendor sent a nuntium asking me to come," Celia said, and her thick Spanish accent washed over Santi's heart comfortably. "He has a lead to our family! And also, he told me about the tournament, of course! If joo are playing, I am watching." The enthusiasm was a little too forced on Celia's part, and Santi wondered if she was trying to make up for missing so many of Santi's plays, games, and events in her childhood.

Santi was surprised, but she shouldn't be, she thought. Growing up as Celia's child, Santi knew her mother always had a pulse on everything going on with her. Always. "But how did you know we were playing?"

"Grendor told me las' month."

"Last month? But…" She looked at Grendor. "How did you know last month? Tizz and I just talked about it today… and Rogan…" She gestured to her Bondmate but she wasn't sure she wanted to get into it right now. She felt her anger welling up again and she pushed it down.

Instead, she turned back and said, "I'm glad, Mommi, but how did you get all the way here?" For their Bonding

Celebration, Celia had flown to Delaware, and Santi had met her at the little cove and brought her down to the kinship. But Daris was so far away from her home in California.

"Grendor set it all up." Celia smiled at Grendor. "I tol' him when I could get away from work, and he had Serras waiting at de shore to bring me here."

Santi looked at Grendor who was floating in the water next to Rogan and decided to finally address the issue.

"I'm curious." She forced nonchalance into her Ku. "I only learned of the tournament today and decided to play. It was Tizz's idea." Santi was surprised to feel the shock in Grendor's Ku. "How did you know that we would be playing?" He must have known that Krell required her to play. Maybe bringing her mom here was part of the plan? She couldn't let herself believe that Grendor was working with Krell to manipulate her. Not Grendor, too!

Grendor's startlement was genuine, however. "Krell told me a while ago you were playing. I had no reason to doubt him. I had no idea this was new to you."

Santi felt conflicted. She wanted to press him more, but also knew that he could be valuable in convincing Rogan to play, something that was apparently already set in stone as far as Krell was concerned.

"Tizz has a third, but we just need one more." She looked at Rogan pointedly. "And Rogan says he won't play, but without Rogan I don't really want to play either."

This had the desired effect from Grendor, though surprisingly Celia scowled.

"You must play, Rogan!" Grendor said. "I am sure Santi could use your skill. The two of you with Tizz could go very far in the tournament."

Grendor's use of Krell's exact phrase to 'go far in the tournament' told Santi that Grendor did know about Krell's plans and that her participation in this event clearly had an important agenda behind it.

"I told Santi I do not wish to participate." Rogan looked at her with what Santi could have sworn was hatred, though his Ku held nothing but love for her. "But I told her she should still play without me."

"I don't want to play without you, Rogan. So…" she looked at her mom, knowing her next statement would get Celia to jump into the cause to sway Rogan to play. "So, I guess we won't play. We will still go watch though, right?"

Before Rogan could respond, Grendor shouted, "No!" with such force Santi could see Rogan was surprised. "Santi, you must play," Grendor insisted, even as he toned his eagerness down and turned to Rogan with a steady determination in his Ku. "I do hope you will reconsider."

Rogan's eyes shifted from Grendor's meaningful gaze to Celia's confused stare and rested on Santi's face. Santi felt upset. She was abruptly aware that at some point she had crossed her arms. She felt like a child digging in her heels to get her way, but she couldn't seem to stop herself. If she had to play, so did he, and it was best if he chose it before Krell ordered him to. Though, if she were honest with herself, she didn't feel much like playing anymore, and she hated how this was all unfolding with Rogan. A diplomat she was not.

"Fine," Rogan said quietly. "I will play in the tournament. If it will make you happy, Santi."

Relief washed over her. Santi leapt through the water and wrapped her arms around Rogan's shoulders and kissed him on the cheek. "Yes, it will make me very happy. Thank you, Rogan." Though she did not feel happy, the relief would have to be a reasonable substitute.

Rogan sighed heavily and wrapped his arms around her. "Good, I love it when you are happy." He kissed her gently on the forehead and released her from the embrace.

Santi felt lighter, though not by a lot. She felt guilty that she had gotten her way but also that it was not *her* way at all. It was Krell who had gotten his way today.

The room felt tense, and Santi wanted to shift the mood as she looked around at everyone treading water in her living room, but she didn't know where to go from here.

Luckily, Grendor broke the tension by saying, "I am going back to headquarters now. Celia, I will see you later?"

She nodded but said nothing as Rogan added, "Grendor is going to introduce me to the Sentinels in his squad. I have been assigned under him."

"That's great!" Santi cheered with a clap of her hands. Grendor was the closest thing to a best friend Amed had had besides Coral. "That will be nice for you. Nice for you both."

They simply nodded at her. "Santi. Celia," Grendor said by way of goodbye. Rogan kissed her quickly and bade Celia farewell before followed behind Grendor.

"That was weird." Santi looked at her mother. "Right?"

Santi saw the look in Celia's eyes before she recognized the feeling in her Ku. She had seen that look a million times in her childhood. Her mother was upset with her. Santi scanned back through their encounter and knew it could be for several different reasons, but she wasn't sure exactly which one was the cause.

Chapter 8

Santiago

Santi tore her eyes from her mother and looked around the room as she tried to figure out how she'd made Celia angry. She'd rather try to make amends before they even got into it. When she was young, the lectures seemed to go on forever, but she found if she could apologize before Celia got on a roll, she could stop it before it started. In this moment, however, she wasn't sure what she had done wrong.

Her home wasn't very inviting, with no drinks to offer her guests or seating for more than three people. It was also completely void of any personal items, as Santi kept waiting for Rogan to be interested in making it cozy together. The walls were melancholy, the floor bare and cold. It was all so unlike any Serra dwelling she'd ever been in. She could have welcomed everyone better, had them all sit down, at least. She sighed; this empty, sterile space was an indicator of how much her and Rogan's lives felt like they were on hold. She knew she could have done better to be more hospitable, but that didn't really seem like what the lecture would be about. And she was certain one was coming. She felt ridiculous. She was nearly twenty-one, Bound, living in almost a different world than Celia; yet here she was, about to be lectured from her mother as if she were fourteen again. She had no idea what she had done wrong, so she made eye contact and waited.

Mother and daughter looked at each other for a moment before Celia sighed and gestured to the high-backed wooden seat that served as a couch—it was the only furniture in the whole room because it came with the apartment. Santi followed and sat stiffly on the board, noting that some cushions would be necessary.

Santi held her breath and felt her defenses rise as Celia began, "Santee, joo did not tell me things were so bad. Jor nuntiums say Rogan is not healing well but this, this is not like joo two at all."

Santi breathed out the breath she was holding. It felt like a breath she had been holding for four months. She didn't know why she hadn't thought to talk to her mom about this before. She figured she could handle everything herself. She should have known Celia would know how to help.

"It is bad." Santi crumpled against her mom as she rushed on. "I don't know what to do. Rogan won't talk to me, and his grief is consuming him. How do I help him? How do I snap him out of it?"

Celia pushed Santi upright and stared. Her Ku was filled with that buzzing energy as usual, but irritation was hiding in the background of it all. Finally, she said, "Well, that is not really what I mean. I cannot help joo know how to help him besides with patience and love. What I can tell joo though, is that joo were not being fair to him just now."

Santi felt her defenses rising again. "What do you mean, being fair? I wasn't unfair."

"Santee, joo used Grendor to get your way, tried to manipulate everyone to get what you wanted. Joo are habing a marriage argument and joo shouldn't habe put us in the middle." Celia was calm, reasonable. It made Santi feel less calm.

"We aren't having any sort of 'marriage argument,'" she said with irritation.

"Sorry, Bond argument."

"That's not what I mean. I'm saying I didn't put you in the middle of an argument. We aren't arguing. Rogan didn't want to do the tournament, but he needs to. I knew that you and Grendor could convince him. So I just presented the discussion for the group."

"But it was not a discussion for a group. I think he already told joo no, correct?"

"Yes, but I was right, and he's going to do it now."

"He said he wouldn't do it, Santiago Scout Morales. And joo used *us* to manipulate him."

"I did not!" Santi was angry. She would never manipulate Rogan. "I just… I just knew that Rogan needed to play and that… that Grendor could convince him." As she spoke the words, she knew Celia was right. That was even worse. "And maybe that you would, too." Santi let out a throaty growl. "Yes, ok, fine. I see that I manipulated the situation, but you make it sound so terrible. I was just doing what I had to do because..." But she didn't want to get into

144

Krell with her mother. There was too much to explain and too much she didn't want to think about. She deflated like a popped balloon. It would have been so much easier if they were in the middle one of Celia's lectures, like when she was a kid.

Celia was still calm and compassionate when she said, "It wasn't fair to do that to us, but I'm not mad. I'm worried. Joo seem bery unhappy, and joo and Rogan aren't being a team. Joo two usually habe a way of working together that no one understands. Like jor own language. The two of joo are best friends; joo habe to get back to that place."

Santi nodded. Celia was right, but it was hard to shake off the anger.

"I know, mom." She sighed and flopped her head against the back of the wooden sofa, looking at the ceiling. "I know, but I don't know how! It's very hard. This teamwork stuff... it's so new. It's so tricky! You were lucky."

"Why am I lucky?"

"You had the luxury of making all the decisions your whole life and then just taking me along with your plans. You didn't have to be a team. You just got to have your own way."

"Tha's a low blow, Santi." Celia stood up and looked directly at her daughter with hurt in her eyes. "I learned to be a teammate for jears before joo were born. And I would rather have had all the struggles in a normal marriage than have been without jor father, if I had de choice."

Santi's eyes went wide, and she was momentarily distracted from her own plight. Celia had never brought up

Santi's father in conversation before. Santi always had to be the one to try to pry information out.

"Not having him in our lives," Celia continued, "to love *and* to fight with was far worse than trying to get him to do something he didn't want to do just so that I could have my way. Joo are an adult now." She pointed an accusing finger at Santi, and that hurt more than the words. Her voice was calm, almost hurt as she said, "Just think about jor team, jor common goal, and Rogan's feelings first. I know you will do the right thing for him." Then she added, with a feeling of total exhaustion that washed over them both, "I think I'd better sleep. I've been traveling for three days to get here, and I barely slept along the way."

Santi led her down the hall and showed her to their spare room. She gestured to the sad little bed in the corner. "Thank you for giving me so much to think about. I was worried you were going to lecture me."

"I'm pretty sure I did." Celia smiled as she nestled into the down cushion under a thick blue blanket. "Abuelo taught me how to lecture adult children without them knowing you were lecturing them. It was my first try. We both have a lot to learn." She yawned and closed her eyes as she said, "How did I do?"

"You did great, Mom." Santi nodded. She was going to say more but she felt Celia's Ku drift away, and she knew her mother was asleep. "You gave me a lot to think about." She grinned and, since Celia was asleep, she added, "And I'm really annoyed that you were right. I love you."

As she drifted down the hall, her head and heart were full to bursting. She pushed herself out the front window high above the city. Her mother was right, and she had been an

146

incredible jerk to them all. Suddenly, she was embarrassed to have acted in such a way in front of Grendor. She kept swimming, completely overwhelmed with a commotion of thoughts, trying to leave her embarrassment behind her. Above all, she was distracted by something her mother had said. This was only the third time in Santi's life that she could recall her mother ever mentioning her father. She wanted to know more.

Santi was left looking down on the city from above, alone and unsure what to do next. She wasn't sure what to do in the next few days or weeks, let alone at this very moment. She looked back at her high-rise building jutting up towards the surface and thought about going back in, or maybe going out and finding items to make it homier. Maybe she would find Coral and get her artistic eye to help. All she knew was she was too restless to hold still.

She felt uncomfortable with her interactions today and wanted to calm her agitation. There was nothing she could do in this moment to make things better, but she also couldn't do *nothing*. She fidgeted and looked around. Had she really made no friends in all this time? Overcome with homesickness for the small kinship where she had known everyone, Santi decided she had to be better. She had to make a life. She kicked her feet in irritation again. Her heart and head buzzing with pent up emotion. She and Rogan lived in one of three buildings allocated for young, un-established, or visiting Serras. If they were to make a permanent home in Daris, or if Rogan were a high-ranking Sentinel, they would be moved into a larger shelter in a more desirable area of the city. As it was, Santi and Rogan's shelter was in the furthest corner of the city, near the outer wall. It was truly too far to go anywhere on her own unless she had plenty of energy and time.

She laughed. Those were two things she had in abundance at the moment.

"I guess I'll go to the Opus Complex," she mused out loud. "Visit this Tillop guy."

And make some friends so I can stop talking to myself.

She didn't know where The Opus Complex was but figured the downtown area was a good place to start. Santi sighed and closed her eyes to muster the motivation for the long trek and then began swimming.

Daris was laid out in a giant circle. The Nephira statue was the center of the Troag and bordered by a three hundred foot circumference of the tall green hedges she had seen earlier. That was all near the front of Daris by the portico. Around that were tall buildings that housed the city officials; the citadel was in this areas. Krell and the Sentinel's headquarters were in the citadel, along with Ocean Mother Yazi's chambers, where she held council. Santi wasn't sure if Yazi's actual home was located in the citadel as well, but she knew smaller apartments were available for each of the Balams when they came to the city for business.

The city continued on in circular rings from the citadel. The front of the city was the portico and the end of the enchanted wall, but further behind the buildings surrounding the Troag were the smaller and shorter homes for Daris locals. Other homes were scattered around the city, along with schools, gardens, healing centers, crisis centers—though Santi had yet to learn what that meant—and hundreds and hundreds of other buildings that made up the inner

148

workings of the city. She hadn't learned much about the city but what she'd picked up from various conversations. She was impressed that she retained the information. One of the buildings closest to the Troag was surely the Opus Center. The closer to the heart of Daris, the more important the buildings were. She could ask once she got there.

Santi swam just above the buildings. Below her, Serras traveled along the streets and between the buildings when they weren't going very far, but she had too far to go to wind through them. She watched as a Serra woman popped out of her shelter with a pup in her arms, enter her neighbor's shelter, and then emerge without the pup and head off in another direction. Small errands were happening in the city below her, just like in any other city in the world.

The commotion high above her—the space for fast-moving longer commutes—Santi deliberately avoided. Though she hadn't done much exploring in her time here, she had learned how the commute process worked, and she was no match for the speeds Serras reached high overhead.

On the outskirts by her home there wasn't much traffic, but she knew the closer she got to the center the more hectic it would be. She had learned earlier that the enchantment created an invisible dome-like barrier along the top of Daris, but just underneath, Serras traveled in a highway type fashion. Dolphins, giant tuna, and even a few Orcas were used for commuting across the vast city. Most travelers, however, were swimming at top speeds on their own power. Rogan had said some used their daily commute for exercise, which Santi thought was an excellent use of time. She liked riding her bike across the large campus between classes but hated arriving sweaty. She definitely appreciated the convenience of Serras using their commute for exercise and not needing to shower once arriving at their destination. In fact, not needing to bathe was a definite perk of living in the ocean. That had probably freed up three hours a week for her—five if she factored in the hassle of blow-drying her hair—though, as of yet, she wasn't filling that time with anything useful.

Regardless of the benefits, Santi knew the fast-paced highway overhead was no place for her to travel. It was far too quick for her. She would just have to take her time traversing the middle waters all the way to the Troag, where she could ask about Tillop and the Opus Center.

Before she had gone even a quarter of the way to the city center, with miles still ahead of her, a Serra buck appeared at her side with a bundle of seaweed in his arms.

"Hulloo, Santiago. Amicus." He placed his hand on his own heart, a gesture to show respect for her personal space, as they did not know each other and had not been introduced by friends. "My name is Merrek."

Before she could be surprised that he knew her name, Santi reminded herself that she had just been the focal point of a giant ceremony, and her legs gave her away to anyone who had heard about her. "Amicus," she said, placing her hand on her heart. It was customary that, now that they had been introduced, they would place their hands on each other's heart. For the time being, she appreciated the boundary for their first meeting as strangers.

"I noticed you swimming, Bab. Where are you headed?" he asked, his blond ponytail bobbing with his head.

If she were on land, she would have been skeptical about his question, but she felt no ill intent in his Ku. "I'm going to the Troag. Well, I think I am, anyway. But ultimately, I don't know if that's my final destination. Maybe you can direct me. I'm looking for the Opus Complex."

A large smile broke across Merrek's face. "Are you choosing an opus? Or being assigned? We've been wondering if you would stay here permanently. If you're getting an opus, then that means you will be."

Santi felt extremely welcomed by Merrek's enthusiasm, but his litany of questions felt overwhelming, especially as she didn't know any of the answers. Above all, she was feeling uncomfortable with his familiarity and suspicious as to why he had stopped her in the first place. "Well, one thing at a time, I guess." She could feel his Ku was so eager and gentle, and she didn't want to be rude, but she wasn't quite sure why he had struck up a conversation in first place. "First I need to get there. Then I'll learn what my options are. I'm afraid I don't know much about how such a large city functions. So, I'll just be on my way."

She began to swim again when he said, "That's great! I will take you, Bab." Merrek began unwinding the seaweed in his arms.

She stopped. "You will... take me?"

"Yes, Santiago. You will get there very fast. I am the fastest courier in Daris."

"Courier?" Santi felt like she knew nothing of Daris. It was so different from Rogan's small kinship.

"This is my opus. I travel the city most of the day looking for those too weak or tired or burdened with too much to carry, and I take them to their destination." He shook out the seaweed he was holding, and to Santi's astonishment, it unfolded into a large woven seat. She'd seen contraptions like this plenty of times, but usually a dolphin or other such animal pulled them, not another Serra. "Not to say you are too weak or tired, of course. Go ahead and have a seat. It would truly be my honor to take you wherever you need!"

Santi was overcome with his kindness. "I know this is your job, but you really don't have to take me. I'll make it there. Eventually." She laughed and shook her head at herself.

"Nonsense! Sit, Bab. Sit!"

For the first time Santi noticed he had an accent. His r's had a bit of a roll, and his a's were short. "Bab" sounded so quick, almost like "Bub." She hadn't met many Serras outside of Rogan's kinship, and she didn't really go out and mingle here in Daris, so she hadn't realized that there might be different dialects, accents, and languages. Santi made her way to the bottom of his sling, which hung just above the roof of a short building. "I just sit on this part?" She placed her bottom on the wide seat made of tiny shells all tied together, which made the seat firm yet flexible, and held on to the ropes that Merrek had fastened around his waist. She felt like she was sitting in a giant swing.

"Just like that. And keep holding on, Santi. Can I call you Santi? I heard someone call you that and it sounded so fun."

She had to laugh. "No one has ever called my name fun before."

"Serras always call each other by their whole names, but I've met six Crurals now—more than any of my friends—and I noticed you seem to shorten each other's names. I like it."

And Santi liked Merrek.

He reminded her of a young, bright-eyed, Wayne, her Crural-loving friend from Rogan's kinship. "I would love it if you called me Santi."

With that, he began pulling her up into the busy traffic in the higher water. She was nervous at first but once he entered the stream of commuters, Merrek took off, proving how fast he truly was.

Santi's basket lifted through the water, and she realized why the ropes attached to the basket were so long. Santi traveled behind and slightly below Merrek as he kicked his tail ferociously. The long ropes allowed his tail a full range of movement. He was probably a faster swimmer than Rogan, even carrying her weight.

The traffic chaos grew as they got closer to the Troag. More and more Serras wove in and out among one another. "How does no one run into each other?"

He was silent for a moment before responding. "I never thought about it before. I imagine if we were HaruKu, everyone would be careening into everyone else, wouldn't they?"

Having an outlet for her curiosity was too much to pass up, so she unleashed the questions Rogan had been too distracted to answer. "Why do they call it the Troag?"

"It is a pet name for the center of Daris around Nephira's statue," he responded cheerfully, "like a nickname for the area."

"Hmmm," she mused. "I like that." She nodded to herself, but quickly thought of more questions. "But why? What does it mean?"

He looked back at her for a moment, and she worried he was annoyed with her questions. Not everyone enjoyed her weird Crural inquiries as much as Rogan did.

Or used to.

Merrek turned back to focus on his path and finally said, tone light and friendly, "It used to be a longer name, but over the years it got shortened. That was long before my time, though, and I do not know what it used to be called. I was trying to remember, Bab, but I do not."

"And what is 'Bab?'" Santi had long gotten over being embarrassed by her lack of Serra knowledge. Merrek's friendly nature allowed her the freedom to ask questions like a child would, uninhibited by self-preservation.

"Where I come from, it is a term of respect."

Santi nodded. "Where are you from, Bab?" She tested the new word, but he gave a polite grimace that let her know the word wasn't for her to use in this situation. That was fine. She'd rather have a better grasp of its meaning before using it. She made a small cough in her throat and added quickly, "I've never heard your accent before, Merrek."

"What is an accent?" he asked in return.

"The way you speak differently than I do."

"Ah, I am from the NorMer clan. That is just how we speak, Bab."

"Oh! I know nothing about the NorMer, but I hope to go there someday," Santiago said with genuine interest. To pass the time, she said, "Tell me about it."

He was silent, and Santi began to worry her question was ridiculous. It was such an open question to ask someone, and how did someone just tell you about where they're from? But a moment later, Merrek jumped right in. "Well, I guess I will start at the beginning, Bab. NorMer was made when the Nhori Clan became too big and needed to split. It is named for Nhori, the first Balam of the Nhori, and Mereni, the first Balam of the NorMer after they split. NorMer. See?"

"Fascinating. I never knew!"

"NorMer is the most *chimba* of the Clans, you know. Do you know the word *chimba*?"

"I do," Santi said, and then thought he would like to add a Crural word to his lexicon. "On land, we would say, 'cool.'"

"Chimba, Bab. I mean, cool." She felt him mull it over for a minute before he continued. "The NorMer is the most cooool of the clans. We are the ones who breed and raise the Cryptids. Very important work we do up there."

"Very!" Santi agreed, thinking of her giant friend she had named Nessy. "You know, that fits right in with Crural lore about Loch Ness Monsters."

"Ah, Bab, you must tell me the Crural legends about us!"

"One day, Merrek, but please tell me more about the NorMer."

"Well, well." He seemed to be thinking about the most impressive thing he could tell her. She felt his Ku and could almost see his brain churning for the best piece of information to share. Finally, he exclaimed, "Oh, did you know the NorMer holds many valuable secrets to the ocean? Nhori was a great Balam during the time of Nephira, and she tucked secrets away in the vaults there."

"Wow, Merrek that is interesting! What kinds of secrets?"

Merrek seemed to deflate at this question. "There is a legend of the Byblio of Nephira that holds all the secrets. But…" He was dejected now. "I do not know, Bab. We all have a lot of pride in this little fact, but it means nothing. No one knows any more about these mysteries than the fact that they exist." He seemed overly disappointed in himself for not knowing her answers and changed the subject. "And your… accent. That is from? The only Crural place I know is Ireland. My Kinship was fifty miles or so from there, but we weren't really by any land at all."

"I'm from Delaware. That's in North America." When she didn't sense any acknowledgement, she added, "Right next to the Nhori."

"Oh yes. I went to the Nhori during Daristor. But we did not talk about the land very much because I always knew I wanted to live in Daris. It is so far from any land that I did not have to take Crural lessons. When I change opuses when I am older, I might need to learn about Crural things depending on what opus I pick then."

"You won't do this opus always?" Santi was intrigued by everything that involved opuses. She really only knew about being a Sentinel like Amed, a magister or artisan like Coral, and the few others she had learned in the kinship.

"No no, Bab. I am eighteen now and a strong Dwattle player. But in maybe ten years, I will not be nearly as fast or as strong, and I do not think Serras would like their Courier to be pulling them along slower than they could swim themselves."

"You're a Dwattle player? Like, professionally?"

"Sure, Bab. Being a courier is excellent training for playing Dwattle. I hear you will be playing in the amateur contest."

Now Santi was surprised. "Word travels fast around here, huh?"

"I would hate you to feel concerned about your privacy. It is nothing like that, Bab. Amaratizz is a friend of mine. Wait! I mean Amara? Is that what you call her?"

"Actually, I call her Tizz."

"Yes, amazing! Tizz." He seemed to be swirling the word around in his brain. "Tizz. Brilliant, Santi. That is brilliant."

Just then, Merrek took a sudden lurch downward and Santi held on tighter to the ropes. "It is just right there. Do you see that round white building?"

They both gave a small chuckle. She could tell which one he was referring to because it was markedly rounder than anything in the area, but they were *all* white buildings.

Santi hoped to see more of Merrek. It was nice spending time with someone so silly. He reminded her of Rogan.

"Right, sure," Santi tittered. "That white building by the white building next to that white building."

"Yes, that is the one!"

When they arrived, Tillop was with another Serra. His office was on the ground floor with his front door leading straight to the street, so Santi found a bench outside to wait. She sat down and looked around. It looked like any other city, except without the garbage, panhandlers, or street traffic. Plenty of Serras bustled about, along with fish and an occasional animal. It wasn't very sunny above the water, but that never seemed to affect the brightness of the city. It was as if it put off its own glow. She smiled to herself as Merrek sat down next to her.

"I will wait with you," Merrek announced.

Although she would like him to wait with her very much she said, "You don't have to. I'm sure you have to get back to work."

"This is part of my work. You will need me to take you wherever Tillop sends you. I am yours for as long as you need me."

Santi thought about all the taxis she had taken and how they were so expensive that paying them to wait while you ran your errands was preposterous. "Do… well, I don't know how to ask this but, do I need to pay you or something?"

He was nearly exuberant when he said, "Crurals are so strange!"

"Interesting response."

"I have only couriered two Crurals before you, and both of them asked about paying me! It is only because of them that I even understood your question. It seems you would know by now that we do not pay for things. We work for them. Couriering is how I earn my home and other services." Santi nodded. She knew Serras had a barter system of sorts, but it was so relaxed. It was far from *quid pro quo*, and she was unused to the magnanimousness of the system. "And today you are going to get an opus, and that is how you will 'pay' for my services whenever you need them."

Santi nodded again. She still had a lot to learn, but every time she was made aware of something new, her love of the Serra world grew. "Ok, I have another question for you."

"Please ask me," he said, looking her in the eye. "I cannot wait to answer."

But she didn't get to ask.

Merrek and Santiago only knew something was wrong by a wave of commotion rolling through the surrounding Serras. Their Kus were simultaneously filled with a surge of dread, panic, and an indefinable need to flee. Heads on a swivel, they both scanned the area with their eyes and Kus. Santi couldn't see the source of the panic, but she saw the result. A hum was spread through the water. Everyone in the vicinity was zooming around frantically. It was a buzzing chaos with no discernable direction. Santi stood on the cobblestone street at attention while Merrek sprang through the water, both of them looking around and pushing out their Kus wide. Santi reached out and connected to as many Serras as she could. "What's happening?" she asked at random.

She heard a woman scream. Then another Serra in the distance shouted, "Zitja!" but that didn't make any sense.

"Zitja can't enter the city," she confirmed with Merrek. "Right? The… the enchantment?" But he wasn't paying attention. He was frozen, staring off into the distance, positioned so that Santi could only see his back. "Merrek?" she asked again, panic rising in her own voice. He didn't respond, so she kicked her feet off the floor to the side so she could see around him, to know what was causing this undeniable fear to rise up in her throat.

She swam around Merrek just as the monstrous Siren queen shot through the crowd directly towards her. Santi pushed herself backwards in the water, but she was far too slow.

Zitja was swimming full speed and was on top of Santi in a moment, grabbing her around the neck. Zitja's jagged teeth were bared as she began to squeeze.

Merrek sprang on Zitja's back to try and help, but she flung him off like a cockroach. She leaned in close to Santi so their faces were inches apart, and Santi remembered the last time she had been this close to Zitja, this close to death. In this same suffocating choke-hold in the cave. Santi was reminded of her putrid breath that smelled of decay. Her memory flashed back to being trapped on that shelf above water, held captive by the Sirens for days before one day opening her eyes to find Zitja in her face, hand on her throat, ready to kill her. She still had dreams about her kidnapping and the horrific things she saw at the hands of the Sirens. It all came back to her, and her fight-or-flight instinct vanished. She froze.

But back then, Santi had been helpless and clumsy in the water.

That was three years ago.

Santi tucked her chin, reached up with her left hand, and grabbed Zitja's left wrist. Her only wrist. Then Santiago Scout Morales gathered all her courage and called upon her training to initiate a series of smooth, flawless moves. She raised her right hand, palm open, and slammed it into Zitja's forearm, shaking her grip looser, then immediately turned in a tight circle to her left, freeing herself. She continued the motion, twisting Zitja's arm as she ducked underneath and ended behind Zitja, pinning Zitja's only arm behind her back.

In a move she had perfected with Grendor long ago, Santi used the only advantage she had over Serra or Siren and wrapped her legs around Zitja's waist from behind. As much as Zitja kicked her tail, Santi remained on her back like a bull rider, holding on to her arm.

Zitja flipped herself onto the ocean floor, landing hard on Santi, which knocked her loose. Santi knew she should have held on better, that no matter what Zitja did, Santi's only advantage was when she held on with her legs. But she just wasn't strong enough, and as Santi released her hold on Zitja's arm, Zitja immediately turned and clawed at Santi's face and neck. Santi pushed herself off the floor and shifted to Zitja's armless side and tried to repin her arm, but Zitja was much too strong and quick. She would not fall for the same trick twice. The only option left for Santi was to kick her legs against Zitja's tail and give herself some space from the assault. Wishing she had her sais with her, Santi righted herself in the water and sprang into a defensive position. Zitja let out a shriek that reverberated through the water and began barreling down on Santi. In a heartbeat, Zitja was back on Santi, pinning her to the cobblestone street. Zitja was quick, but luckily, so was help.

Swarming them at full speed, what looked like the entire Sentinel army led by Grendor swept in. They were upon Zitja in moments, ripping her off of Santi, and carting her away.

"Santiago," Grendor called from far to her left, where he was busy with the other sentinels tying Zitja's arm to her body with ropes. "Are you all right?"

Santi sat up, dazed. She spoke as she assessed her body. "Yes. Yes, I think I'm fine."

Rogan swooped down on her and gathered her in his arms. "Santiago. Santiago, are you all right?"

She felt excessively cold and very tired. She couldn't answer, only nod. Others were asking her questions and assessing her scratches. Everyone was fussing and chattering. They all had questions. Accolades. Gasps of disbelief and worry. There were too many Serras all asking questions and remarking in anger, confusion, and disbelief.

After binding Zitja, in chains the Sentinels hauled her away, and Grendor came to her side on the ground. "Your neck, it is cut." He turned to the healer working on a wound on Santi's hip from the cobblestones. "Take care of her neck. Santiago, do you feel all right?"

"Should we take her to the healing center?" Rogan asked the healer. The small dam wasn't listening to Rogan's questions, though, because she was asking Santi question after question, looking in her eyes, touching her neck and back. So many questions bombarded Santi, but she didn't answer any of them.

Santi had a question of her own. "How did Zitja get in?"

Chapter 9

Santiago

The chaos that ensued between Santi being attacked by Zitja and the Sentinels ushering her into Krell's chamber left Santi's head spinning so much she couldn't hear what Krell was telling her. Or she didn't think she understood him correctly, at the very least.

"So, you want me to kill Zitja?" she said, trying not to sound incredulous. "I thought that was always the plan. I don't understand how what you are saying is different from what Amed wanted for me."

Rogan squeezed her hand supportively from where he sat next to her at the oval table. Krell's "office"—for lack of a better word—including the table, chairs, and walls were just as white as the rest of the city, but somehow it seemed dark. Whether it was the presence that Krell put off or Santi's own mood, the room was dim and the luminescent bacteria put off a faint blue haze unlike the usual effective brightening.

"Yes, Santi," Krell agreed, though somehow it didn't feel like agreement. "You will kill Zitja just like you have been training for. But unlike Amed's reckless plan to make you a Sentinel, I will make sure you do not fail." He adjusted his asinine vest as though it held its own authority. "We cannot risk your life in the middle of a battle. Zitja is secure and you will swiftly and safely end her existence."

"So, she will be, like, tied up?" Santi questioned.

"Oh, most definitely."

"Ok. Yes, that makes sense." She nodded, it felt wrong to kill anything that was defenseless, but since Zitja had proved for thousands of years that she was anything but, this plan made as much sense as any. She nodded again. Ready. "Ok, let's get this over with." She felt a little excited. The culmination of thousands of years of bloody conflict, her kidnaping, all her training, it was all coming together. "I can't believe this will all be over now. Just like that."

Touching the scratch on her neck where Zitja had injured her, Santi felt motivated. The cut wasn't as bad as everyone had initially thought, but the mere fact that it was there reminded Santi of who they were dealing with. She let out a laugh that was more from nerves than humor. "No one will believe it. After so long and it will just be over like that." She was getting herself ready. Pumping herself up. It was going to be gruesome and uncomfortable, to say the least, to murder someone who was tied up. But that was what she was here for. What she had agreed to. "Seems unreal."

"Ah, yes," Krell said in a way that made Santi's stomach flip over. "That is precisely the problem. That is the reason we are not going to do it now."

This time Rogan actually laughed out loud. "Then when?"

Krell had a mysterious look in his eye and a dangerous feeling in his Ku. "Picture this, Santiago. Day one of the tournament, your team wins while the ocean watches your prowess and skill. You are our hero with legs. The excitement builds all day until it crescendos in the ultimate match for the Dwattle championship. Everyone is full of excitement, and then we bring Zitja out. Bound to a stake. You will truly be our hero then."

Santi sat back in her seat. She clutched her stomach, which suddenly ached tremendously. "And I will just kill her?" She was revolted and nauseous. "For everyone to see?"

"So that there is no doubt Zitja is no longer a threat," Rogan added with the same revulsion.

"Exactly." Krell was extremely pleased with himself. "It will make an excellent spectacle for the end of the tournament. A big show to the entire ocean of Serras that Zitja is gone." He nodded, then pointed a finger at her as if he was letting her in on a secret. "This was always the plan for you." He looked deliberately at Rogan. "The reason you two *must* be in the Tournoi de Jeux."

He leaned over the table conspiratorially as if he were blessing them with more secrets. "We were set to raid the Siren lair in just two days' time to obtain Zitja. She just happened to make things easier by coming to us. We are going to show the ocean that Zitja is no longer a threat and we brought her down. The tournament finale is a perfect showcase to let them see they are safe and protected by us."

Santi didn't respond. She couldn't respond. She and Rogan were clutching hands as if they could save each other from this atrocity.

Luckily, Rogan spoke up, fierceness radiating from him, "Why do we not just do this now? I hardly think a spectacle is what anyone wants—not the Serras of the ocean, and certainly not Santiago."

Krell barely let Rogan finish before he interrupted, "No. They need to see this."

Narrowing her eyes Santi, added snidely, "Why don't we just post a video online? I'm sure it'll go viral."

He ignored her sarcastic question, knowing he had no idea what she was talking about, and said brusquely, "You are free to go now. I have other engagements. We will travel to the tournament together next week."

With that they were ushered out by his assistant.

It wasn't until they were outside in the open water, looking at each other in disbelief, that Santi spoke up. "This is really strange, right? I mean, this is what I'm here for, but I thought it would be more... dignified. That's not the right word but that's why I've become a fighter. This way seems so..." She couldn't think of the right word. There didn't seem to be any English words to describe it.

"I want you to be safe," Rogan said, clasping her hands. "Staying out of battle is optimal for me, so I should really like this plan. But, Santiago." He paused, disgusted. Santi didn't need him to proceed to know what he felt but he did anyway. "This is vile. To make a show of murder, even if it is Zitja, that feels wrong."

"I agree." She took a long breath. "Rogan, I can do this, and I will if it's truly the only way. But… but it can't possibly be the only way."

Rogan slashed his sword down at his opponent's neck halting the blow just before it became fatal. Santi exuberantly fist-pumped in her mind. Rogan had beaten the last three of his sparring opponents in a rather dramatic and quite unequivocally winning fashion. Things had been better between them since Krell's nasty revelation the day before. The Zitja attack on Santi and then their unity against Krell was working in their favor, and Santi had hope that Rogan was reaching a turning point in his grief.

Last night they had actually talked like old times. Granted, it was all about how they were disgusted with Krell and how Amed would never put anyone—especially not Santi—in such an uncomfortable position. But it was a start. At least they were talking.

"Every time, Rogan," Rogan's opponent said, "but one day I will beat the invincible son of Amed."

Rogan looked unblinkingly at his opponent and friend. He chewed his lip and sheathed his swords. "Thanks, Warg," was all he finally said.

Warg looked overhead where Santi was watching and said with a laugh, "It is so precious that your new Bondmate cannot be away from you for a second."

Santi, from her vantage point above the sparring field, straightened her back and looked away instinctively.

"What?" Rogan demanded, more of a challenge than a question.

Warg nodded his head in Santi's direction. "She always watches you spar. Wants to make sure you are safe." He was teasing Rogan, but Santi felt Rogan's Ku and knew he was not taking the ribbing well.

"Santi is not what you should concern yourself with, Warg. You should be worried about how in a battle with Sirens you would be dead ten times over, if your sparring with me is any indication."

Warg nodded and put up his hands in supplication. Santi breathed a small sigh. She had worried a bit that she was annoying when she watched the practice but was glad to hear Rogan stick up for her.

"Goodnight, Rogan." Warg said amicably. The two placed their hands on each other's shoulders. "I will see you tomorrow, and we will see who will be dead ten times over."

The two friends laughed, gathered their things, and went their separate ways. Rogan made his way over to Santi, and the two of them began traveling homeward in silence. Hoping to rekindle the intimacy of last night, she asked as casually as she could, "How was sparring practice today?"

"You saw." He said no more.

She did. It was a stupid question, but she was trying. Santi thought she might actually punch her Bondmate, the love of her entire life, in the face.

They swam on silently for a moment longer before Santi—anger boiling out of her every pore—finally just wanted to have out with it, "Rogan, I'm just concerned—"

"I am concerned, too."

"Ok, great!" she responded with barely suppressed rage. "What are you concerned about? I want to know."

"You."

Santi recoiled as if she had been slapped. "Me?"

"I am concerned that you do not have a purpose to your day. To your life. What are you doing for yourself and the underwater world for the long term?"

Santi was offended to her core. In their entire friendship, love, and Bonding, Santi had never wanted any harm done to Rogan. Now she wanted to punch him for the second time in only a matter of minutes.

"Are you kidding me?"

He looked truly confused, as if the Rogan who used to joke around all the time had never existed at all, and this new version of him had no concept of kidding. "Why would I joke about this?" His tone was calm, not angry, but his words still hurt. "Since we got here, you have done nothing but watch me train or practice yourself. Krell told you days ago that you are not going to be fighting." Santi just looked at him incredulously. "So find a way to contribute."

Santi realized that if he had been on her side, he would have joked with Warg about her hanging around, but instead he shut his friend down in a rather rude manner. And now he was berating her. His defense of her just a moment ago had meant nothing. He was just saving face for his friend. That thought hurt her the most.

He was embarrassed of her.

Maybe, at another time, she might have felt bad about herself, but she didn't now. She was angry. Furious. "It's like you don't know anything about me at all. Or you've forgotten everything."

She clenched her fists. She had been patient long enough. "Rogan, you aren't mad at me. You are mad at your friend for teasing you about me. But the Rogan I know would

169

have given as good as he got and enjoyed the banter. I have tried to help you through this, and I was patient while you moped around and lost interest in life. But now you're growing mean, and hard, and… and you're being a jerk!" She wanted to say worse. A handful of insulting epithets ran through her mind, but she imagined what her mom would say about name-calling one's own Bondmate and decided "jerk" would have to be sufficient. She was supposed to be lifetime teammates with him?

It was too hard.

"I am truly sorry your father died. He was a father to me too, you know. And your sister. And how about you don't forget what he was to your mother. But you don't see them floating around in a sullen daze being mean to the people they love. Do you still want to be Bound to me? Because it sure doesn't seem like you do, and I will be damned if I'm going to chase after you forever hoping that you'll love me again."

In her Ku, she felt that hit him hard—she had always felt love from him, even through the worst of it—but she didn't care. She kind of wanted to hurt him a little. "I'm going to go see your mother. You go ahead and find me when you've pulled your head out of the sand."

And with more cursing ready on her tongue, Santi turned and swam away. He would have to come find her if he cared to speak to her again because she was done trying.

After three hours of studiously learning the Serra form of knitting—which used four needles, two strands of wool, and an intricately tight weave to keep one warm in all waters—Santi was no more proficient at the task than she had been before, though her mood was markedly lighter.

"It feels like too much to hold in my fingers," Santi proclaimed without frustration. "Your fingers glide from needle to needle effortlessly. How long did it take you to learn this?"

Without pausing in her knitting, Coral looked up at Santi and replied, "I've been doing this since I was so small the…" She lifted up the needle and corrected Santi, "*Iskir* really didn't fit in my hands. You'll get the hang of it in no time, and you'll be able to trade them to Wilfie next time he's in Daris."

Santi snorted, which did not produce a satisfying sound in water, "Wilfie is the only mercatera that would take them, and only because of his love for *your* work."

Santi hadn't known where Coral was living in Daris, but she found the guests shelters quickly after only asking one passing Serra where a guest to the city might stay. She was directed to a large building a few rings out from the Troag, protruding high towards the sky. After being barraged with questions about what Santi called a "free hotel," Coral took Santi to the city repository to get a supply of yarn. Coral explained that was her way of contributing to Daris while she stayed in the city.

Coral had sensed that the notion of contributing was a sore spot with Santi and had reassured her—without prying—that Santi was contributing in other ways. However, that sparked thoughts she didn't want to think. Thoughts about how Krell felt she was contributing, for instance. But Santi was starting to feel like she was getting all of Rogan's credit for his hard work and she was merely living for free. Coral on the other hand was making shawls for Daristor.

"So after you make these shawls, um, cloaks?" She wasn't sure what they were called; they were like capes with sleeves. "Ponchos?"

"*Takki*," Coral corrected. "It is another word taken from Crurals. In fact, the design is nearly identical to the Crural takki. Just a few modifications to make it more underwater-friendly."

"Right," Santi nodded. "So after you make the takki," she stumbled with the strange accent of the word, "you will take these where?" To distract herself—and Coral from asking too many questions about why she showed up in a foul mood unannounced—Santi had asked approximately five million questions since her arrival.

Coral chewed on her lip a moment, and Santi could tell her Bond-mother was going to turn this question into a lesson. One Santi was glad for. She hoped it would be long.

"As part of the Ocean Convergence," Coral began, "every Serra must give to the greater society as a whole. This you know. It is why everyone has an opus or contributes in some way. Technically, I studied as an artisan until my children were born, and I stayed with them as a magister—as all parents do until their youngest is sent to Daristor—and then I resumed my practice beautifying the ocean through my art."

Santi's mind couldn't help wandering a bit as Coral spoke about her art. She had learned last year about Amed's Crural hippy mother and Artisan father. No wonder Amed had loved Coral's creative beauty so much.

"Now that I am doing more traveling," Coral's heart gave a pulse that held a hint of pain, since the reason she traveled so much was because she no longer had a home with Amed, "I am not able to participate in the Ocean Convergence as much as I did when I had a workspace and my supplies, so now I contribute wherever I am staying for the community space I am in."

"I see." Santi nodded. She was somewhat familiar with the Ocean Convergence and the community trading system in general.

"But to answer your question more specifically, after I have finished these takki, I will take them to the Daris Convergence Facility." Coral worked her small lips back and forth a moment and her ice-blue eyes went back to her work as she counted and made sure she was weaving correctly.

Santi took a moment to notice how little Rogan resembled her with his dark skin, hair, and eyes. It was as if Rogan was his father's son and Tizz, with her blond hair and light features, was definitely her mother's daughter. The siblings had the look of two completely different families.

"Every big city has a convergence facility," Coral continued. "Our little kinship did not need one because we all managed well together, but as soon as the bartering breaks down, a facility is created to organize the exchanging.

"So when I am done with these takki, I will take them there and then receive another assignment. These takki are going to the Daristor group for their travel to the NorMer clan. I got the wool from the facility, as well, but they were running low, so my next assignment may very well be to spin more raw wool." Coral gave a Crural-like shrug. "It is not fun work, but it is a way I can contribute until I move on from here."

"Where do you get wool from?" Santi looked at the knitting in her hands and realized she hadn't even thought to wonder where it came from.

Coral laughed as she said, "We trade for it. Many of the Mercaturas and Thaeds work together to trade with Crurals."

Santi nodded. Trade with Crurals was the obvious answer. She asked, "And where are you moving to next?" Santi loved the idea of traveling the entire ocean and learning all about the different clans and kinships, a dream maybe she could fulfill one day after her duties with Zitja were finished. That sudden reminder of her grisly duty made her stomach turn.

"Well, the tournament, of course, but after that-"

Both women dropped their weaving as they felt the presence of two Serras reaching out to them. Santi's heart twisted. It had to be Rogan. They were going to set things straight now, and relief washed over her. She had said what she needed to say and left it in his hands, but if she were honest with herself, she would do anything to make it all better right now. She'd forgive him immediately just for seeking her out. She reached out and connected to the two approaching Serras.

Her heart sank when the connection revealed it was not Rogan coming to make amends. But just as sudden as her disappointment was her joy. Swimming into the small apartment were Celia and Grendor. It always made her heart happy when they were together. How did they not see they cared for each other? It was possible their feelings for each other were only platonic, but it seemed like there could be much more if they would allow it.

After everyone made their greetings, Grendor shared their news with quiet elation.

"Celia and I are here to make our farewells. Before heading to the tournament, we are going to make a detour to the Afiti, as that is where our sources say your family may be." He gestured with his hand at Celia and Santi. "We have learned that your Abuela Carmen had a brother, and we want to follow that lead."

"That's wonderful!" Santi said, turning to her mother.

Celia nodded, a massive smile spread across her face. "We are trying not to get our hopes up, but it is exciting!"

"But before we go," Grendor interrupted, "Coral, I must speak to you alone, if you will." His Ku reverted from the lightness of his announcement to a sense of business.

"Of course." Coral freed up her hands and pushed herself off her seat.

Santi set down her weaving to leave, but Coral stopped her, waving her hand at Santi. "Grendor and I will swim outside. I need to go get more wool because I did not pick up enough. Will you swim that direction with me, Grendor?" Coral put her weaving in the basket full of yarn, and she and Grendor took their leave.

Santi gestured towards the wall lined with limply stuffed round pillows—the guest accommodations were very meagerly furnished—and said, "Please have a seat, Mommi. Shall I teach you to knit while we wait?"

"Thank joo, Santee, but I already know how to knit."

Santi looked at her mom in surprise but then brushed it off ruefully. Of course Celia knew how to knit. She knew everything. Santi didn't bring up the fact that this was a different kind of knitting because she was sure she couldn't teach anyone anyway. She looked back down at her work and tried to sound casual as she said, "So, Grendor is being very helpful."

"Oh jes, he's been very great," Celia answered matter-of-factly.

Santi, not getting the reaction from her mother that she wanted, looked up quickly and said, "Mom! I really hate to sound like a twelve-year-old but, well, I think he likes you."

Celia's Ku fluttered for only a moment before Santi felt her deliberately shut it down.

"What?" Santi felt exasperated at her mother's stubbornness. "Why do you always do this? You care about him. I know it. And he obviously cares about you or he wouldn't be your personal guide around the ocean for months. Pursue it! Why are you hanging on to Filipe so hard? Move on already."

"Santiago Scout Morales, don't speak about things joo don't understand."

"I understand as much as you'll let me," Santi retorted heatedly. The anger she was suppressing about Rogan flared up. "You married him when you were eighteen, and by the time you were twenty he was dead and you were pregnant with me. Unless you explain more than that, I have to think that twenty-one years of mourning is long enough."

"Santiago, joo are about the same age I was. If Rogan died now, would joo feel better in twenty years?"

Santi wanted to immediately and fiercely rebut the statement by arguing that Bonding was so much more than
176

marriage, but she knew Celia was a deep soul. Ku or no Ku, if she felt a similar connection with Filipe, then Santi would respect it. Just the thought of Rogan's death caused any remaining anger and resentment to flee from her heart. When she was finished here, she would seek him out and make things right between them no matter what it took on her part.

"You're right. I'm sorry. But would you please help me understand? My entire life you've told me nothing about my father. You haven't dated, and you haven't let me ask questions. No more, Mommi." Santi was resolute. "Tell me."

Celia was silent. Unreadable.

Santi wanted to push, but she didn't know which direction to push. Pleading? Stern? Desperate? Kids usually knew how to get what they wanted from their parents, but Celia was always so unpredictable in her responses.

She waited and slowly started to feel Celia's heart softening. Santi didn't breathe for fear she would spook the truth away, never to hear the story.

Finally, Celia whispered so quietly that, were they not connected through their Kus, Santi wouldn't have heard. "I just have so much guilt about the whole situation."

"Tell me. Then maybe you can let it go." Santi wasn't sure what emotion she felt more: desire to help her mom move on, or curiosity about her father.

"Ok, I'll tell joo."

Santi's heart fluttered and her stomach flipped over upon itself. This was the one thing she had wanted her whole life: to know the truth about the man she knew only as Filipe, her father who had died before she was born.

~

1997

"Filipe! Aren't you going to stand up for yourself?" Celia shouted in Spanish. Having lived in the states for only a year, she still didn't feel very confident speaking English, even though Spanish provoked angry Americans even more. "Stand up for me?"

The belligerent drunkard squared his shoulders. "Get back here you lazy Mexican!" he shouted as he stepped forward, swaying on his feet ever so slightly.

Filipe and Celia had been at a restaurant celebrating the news of Celia's pregnancy. They were lost in their joy for so long the restaurant turned into a nightclub around them before they got up to leave. That was when a man, entitled, racist, and far too plastered to function, began to pick a fight with Felipe with no provocation.

The Filipe Celia married would have knocked the accoster unconscious and then apologized for not giving Celia a turn to punch him herself. It infuriated her that he was acting so weak.

They continued to head for the door as the man shouted behind them.

"Filipe, don't let him get away with this."

Filipe held her hand gently and ushered her away from the man. "Celia, we aren't going to fight with him." He spoke in English, hoping the man would overhear and calm down.

Celia didn't care about such things and responded in Spanish. "You have to do something. He can't treat us like this. We did nothing wrong."

"Exactly," Felipe said calmly. "He's only angry because he's drunk. We do not need to get into a fight tonight."

Celia sighed but began to calm down when the man stumbled closer and pushed Felipe in the chest with both hands, causing Felipe to stumble backwards into another man, who yelled angrily, "Watch out, man!"

By way of response, Filipe grabbed Celia and turned, rushing her towards the door.

Seeing the opportunity for a fight fleeing before his drunken eyes, the first bully shouted obscenities before he punched Filipe in the back of the head, knocking him sprawling onto the street. Celia let out a small growl before lunging at the man.

She was barely able to let loose one weak punch into the air at her husband's attacker because Filipe was back on his feet pulling Celia away.

"Celia! The baby!"

Her hand went to her mouth and her eyes shot wide, already rimmed with tears of regret. "I forgot! I forgot!"

"We aren't in Venezuela anymore. You can't go around attacking everyone who tries to goad you into a fight, my love." He began pulling her quickly down the street, talking calmly, trying to remain composed. "Our visas are only temporary. We have to walk the line if we want to stay permanently. These people will find any reason to get us sent back. Any reason."

"You're right. You're right. I'm so sorry," she agreed, still dazed that she could forget she was pregnant. Though she only learned of it this morning, she felt forgetting

her own baby was surely a sign she was going to be a terrible mother.

The streets were dark. The sun had set long ago, and the air was chilly. There were plenty of people on the streets enjoying the evening. Filipe and Celia tried to appear calm, minding their business. But that did not stop the tall, blonde aggressor from following them down the street, shouting horrible things at Celia.

Finally the man reached out and grabbed Filipe's shoulder, flipping him around. He was so drunk that he fumbled the knife he was holding in his other hand, and it sliced Celia on the upper arm, drawing blood.

Without thinking, Filipe pounded his fist into the man's face, and he went down like a stone, unconscious. This was not Filipe's first fistfight.

But it would turn out to be his last.

~

"It was out of our hands after that," Celia sighed. She looked down and played with a loose string floating from the cushion on which she was sitting. "There were witnesses all up and down the street who saw Filipe throw the first punch—the only punch, as it turned out. He was taken to jail where I could not get in to see him, and within the week he was sent to Mexico without a trial."

"But he wasn't Mexican!" Santi furrowed her brow.

Celia looked up and scoffed, "Do joo think that mattered? No trial. No word to me. Nothing. The local government did not actually get Immigration involved. We were living in Arizona then. The police there… well, they handle things their own way."

Santi covered her mouth with her hands unconsciously.

"It was so stupid. So unnecessary. The man barely cut me, and I was completely fine." She paused and took a deep breath before she continued. "Though, if you had told me that at the time, I would not have cared. I would have wanted Felipe to lay him out just like he did. That day changed a lot for me. I used to be such a hothead."

Santi shook her head, "I just… I just can't believe this."

"He called me when he arrived in Mexico and told me he was safe and was working on how to get home. I was relieved, of course, but there was still so much that could go wrong. It would be hard for him to get back without his visa and ID and things, so I asked where I could send them to him, but we were cut off.

"That was the last time we spoke, and I just had to wait."

"Did you ever find out what happened to him?"

Santi felt pain rip through her mother's chest. Celia hung her head in shame. "Aye." She put her head in her hands and cried. The connection of their Kus allowed Celia to tell her story while she sobbed. "Right after you were born, someone called and told me. I 'ave known all this time, but I thought joo were better not knowing." Celia continued crying, and Santi didn't know if she planned to tell her or not. Santi wasn't actually sure if she wanted to know. She waited quietly for whatever her mom chose to do.

"I wish I did not know what happened." Celia paused again, and Santi waited.

"Jor father tried to sneak back with some coyotes smuggling Mexicans over the border. I don' know how he got the money, and I don' know how long it took him to try to come back. He neber called those eight months, so I just kept going back and forth about what might have happened. Either he managed it all very quickly and didn't have time to call, or things were so bad for him that he couldn't call me. I used to wrack my brain sometimes to think about how terrible it must have been for him to neber call. And then sometimes I thought he might have moved on. Settled down in Mexico and had a new family. I was horrible for thinking this. What happened to him was terrible. I imagine it still, sometimes. I think I deserve the punishment of thinking about how much he suffered."

"Mommi, what happened?"

"Five men were crammed into the trunk of a car to cross the border. The man who called said that it was worse than a nightmare. They were in there for three days. There wasn't any food, and they each only had one water bottle. All of them had to relieve themselves at some point, and some of the men vomited. I am so angry because Filipe was allowed to be in this country, but I had his papers with me. If only I could have gotten them to him!"

Celia was overcome with emotion again, but Santi sensed underlying anger beneath the sadness and also the conflict that anger caused her. Santi began to understand why her mother had never let go of Filipe after all this time.

"By the time they made it to Texas, only one man in the trunk was still alive. The rest had died of suffocation or starvation or dehydration. Four men died just trying to get back home. The man who lived found the families of each of the dead men to tell them what happened. Aye, aye, aye."

Celia put her face in her hands and shook her head. "The last thing I said to him was that he should stick up for me. I thought him weak. What's the most hard for me is that I was thinking worse than that." Celia's pause was heavy with guilt, but she looked up at her daughter and went on. "I was thinking that he was not a man for not fighting. Him walking away and acting like… acting like… well, it was so terrible the things I thought. And then I neber saw him again."

With the knowledge of her father fresh on her mind, Santi wanted to do nothing else but find Rogan and set things straight. He was the only person she wanted to share this discovery with, and she wanted to show him she could support him no matter what he was going through. It could always be worse. Her talk with her mother really put things into perspective. If she had to keep being patient with his grief, she would. At least he was alive. They could come out the other side of this.

As soon as her mother and Grendor left for the Afiti, Santi took off to find Rogan, but as she was headed home, Merrek swooped down upon her from the highway overhead. "Santi! I am here to give you a ride."

"Oh, Merrek!" Santi nearly swooned at the offer not to have to swim the distance back home. "Thank you so much."

He unraveled the sling, and she took her position in the seat before Merrek shot straight up towards the sun and joined the commotion of Serras cruising next to them.

"Merrek, wait!" Santi exclaimed after she had been carted along behind his swift moving tail for a few minutes. "My shelter is back that way." She craned around in her seat to make sure she wasn't just confused. It was entirely possible that she had become disoriented.

"I am not taking you home, Bab."

His Ku felt pure and innocent of malintent, but her Crural instincts kicked in, and she thought about jumping off her seat and heading for help. "Where are you taking me, Merrek?"

"It is a surprise." She felt a twinkle in his Ku. He was up to something, but it was more mischievous than devious.

She pushed down fears of being kidnapped again—was it considered kidnapping when you were a grown woman?—and figured she could probably take him if she needed to. "Ok then," she said hesitantly, though she kept her guard up.

Merrek swam at top speed, cruising over the city. He had picked her up near the Troag, and at the pace he was setting they would reach the outer wall in less than ten minutes. This far edge of Daris, near the back, was where she had been when she accidentally breached the enchantment and had had to make her way back to the portico. It was far and remote. A chill washed over her. The buildings and community of the city were growing sparse. A few seconds later and nothing was below them but a bare patch of sea floor.

"Seriously, Merrek, where are we going?" She realized that no matter how fond of him she was or that he was three years younger, he was stronger and faster and she did not actually know him well.

"Almost there now, Bab." He was nonchalant.

Santi's stomach flipped over. This was eerily familiar. Memories she had buried deep came flooding back to her, of Sully pulling her out into the open ocean and keeping her captive for days. She had trusted him then, too.

Chapter 10

Yemri

When Yemri returned to the citadel after seeing the retransformed Serra, she was so preoccupied that at first she didn't hear the Sentinel speaking to her.

"You… found *them*?" She asked, trying to catch up.

His Ku beat strong and proud as he said, "After that Maato buck confronted you and fled with the dam in his grip, after your induction, remember? Nhori sent me after them. I decided rather than confront him, it would be more valuable if I followed them. I found them, Mother Yemri."

Yemri's eyes went wide. Then she got to work setting up a plan.

The journey took three days, and Yemri was worried the Maato might leave their hiding spot and find another before she and the Sentinels arrived.

"Father," Yemri said just before climbing out of the chariot at their destination, "if the Maato are what you say they are, then I have to be seen as an authority figure. If I am just a dam pup then I will not be able to accomplish anything. It will already be very hard."

Tope helped her out of her seat and they made their way through the open ocean. He was thoughtful but not brooding as he looked around at the hulking guards and Sentinels they had brought with them.

Tope breathed deeply and, for the second time in as many days, said, "You are right. I am sorry I continue to forget your fragile position."

Before leaving for the Maato, Muleki, Tope, and Pangor had all discussed and debated whether to wait or to leave immediately. None of them took seriously Yemri's order to leave straightaway and spent precious hours discussing whether the Maato was even a priority at the moment.

Tope was resolute now when he said, "Debating and disagreeing with Nephira was part of the process to ensure all sides were being viewed fairly. It is not what you need from me, I know."

No more was said on the matter as their convoy made its way through a narrow opening into a tunnel hewn out of solid rock wall. Once they emerged through the channel, they were presented with thick wild plants growing up to the surface. And heat!

The heat was unlike anything Yemri had ever experienced. Like swimming on the sun. The weeds were so dense vision was impossible from floor to sky. Yemri pushed out her Ku and found the area littered with Serras. "Stop!"

she commanded. Though she wasn't sure if she made the decision out of fear or strategy.

It turned out she did not need to decide because through the weeds appeared dozens of stout Serra bucks armed with long spears. They surrounded Yemri's group, who were all still funneling through the small opening in the rocks. Those at Yemri's side pulled out their weapons.

"No one enters the Maato encampment," a tan buck with a smashed-looking face commanded. "Turn around now."

"Who is in charge here?" Yemri demanded.

The smash-faced buck addressed Pangor, who was the closest in proximity. "Turn around now or we will have no choice but to use force against you."

"This is your Ocean Mother," Tope responded to the Maato buck who appeared to be in charge. "I think you had best answer her."

None of the Maato bucks responded, but it was clear they were discussing what to do amongst themselves without allowing Yemri's party to hear. An extremely insolent act.

That's when Yemri realized they were not using their Kus to communicate. Remaining HaruKu was enormously offensive, though, strictly speaking, there was no law against it.

"You may follow us," Smash-face said, "but only a few of you may come. Your army must wait outside the encampment." As an aftherthought, he added, "Our space within the ramparts is much too small for a large group. You must understand. There wouldn't be space to swim if you all entered the boundaries."

Pangor, as was his right as Sentinel Commander, made the decision on whether this was satisfactory to the protection of their group. "Our army—as you call them—will wait outside the periphery, but there will be ten of us coming into your kinship. I will not negotiate this number."

"Yes. Yes, whatever you need. No harm will come to you." Smash-face was trying to be cordial now for a reason Yemri did not understand. She hoped she would pick up on the politics of it all in time.

Quickly, Pangor addressed his bucks and chose four Sentinels to accompany Yemri's two personal guards as well as himself, the two Balams, and Yemri. Once it was decided, the group of ten followed behind the Maato bucks through the brush. In only a few feet, they had broken through the concealing barrier of sea grass, which parted to reveal a ghastly sight.

Yemri nearly stopped swimming, but Tope ushered her along, teaching her a valuable lesson in concealing her feelings.

The rock gorge they had entered through was the only passage into and out of the Maato encampment, and a barrier of the rocks enclosed the encampment fully. No one would find the kinship unless they knew where they were going. Even Crurals would not find this place because the entire kinship was nestled against a towering volcanic island, completely uninhabited.

"This place is really hidden," Yemri said to the bucks around her.

"It's almost scary how well positioned they are to remain secluded," Muleki agreed.

But neither the position of this faction of Serras nor the nearly unbearable heat was what had repulsed Yemri upon seeing the kinship. The conditions of the small settlement disturbed her deeply and confirmed the necessity of her intervention.

Smash-face was right when he said there wouldn't be room for the entirety of Yemri's party; the capacity of their kinship was small. It was so uncomfortably small and barren that Yemri could see every single Serra by taking a quick scan of the area. There were about fifty or sixty bucks, all well fed. The dams outnumbered them by more than double, and all were so thin they weren't much more than skin stretched over bone. The Bucks lounged and talked, eating and playing games while the dams worked. They wove baskets and prepared food, took care of children, and hauled rocks. No vegetation was in sight once they passed through the kelp in the front meant to conceal their whereabouts. It was a barren wasteland with a brown sandy bottom and smothered with muggy hot water from the volcano.

Yemri noticed something else that made her stomach flip over. She couldn't feel a single Ku, and every penumbra was a murky reddish grey, a color she had never seen before but knew instantly was not good. There wasn't a single bit of wildlife to be seen within the walls, a feat nearly impossible to achieve as the ocean belonged just as much to the fish and animals as it did to them. It was a despicable and unjust place; that much Yemri would feel even if she didn't have a Ku.

Their group was ushered to a corner of the encampment and taken into a cavern in the side of the volcano. The tunnel immediately took a dive downward, and they felt relief from the ever-pressing heat. Finally, the tunnel leveled off and opened up into a large cavern lit by a flurry of bioluminescent fish swimming about the room. Yemri had never seen fish used as lighting, but it seemed to be an effective—albeit cruel way—to make these fish do their bidding.

The chamber was cool, bright, and comfortable. In the center sat an overly corpulent Serra, the size of whom she had never seen before, as swimming and daily labor did not allow one to gain weight in such excess. He was propped up on a plethora of cushions while being doted on by several underfed dams. The stark contrast in appearance between them and him was repulsive.

Yemri was becoming more upset. This was a lot to take in at such a young age.

Smash-face turned to the obese buck and said, "This is Maatis, son of Maato, and ruler of the Maato Serras. He will hear you only as long as he wishes to and then you will leave without complaint. For every moment you stay while you are unwelcome, we will kill a dam as punishment for your defiance."

Maatis sat up slightly in his seat, though Yemri wasn't sure if it was because he didn't want to sit up further or couldn't. "Hemrin, who have you brought me and why have they been allowed here?" He sounded angry, but Yemri didn't think there was much he could do about his anger in his state.

"We have come to--" Yemri began but Smash-face—Hemrin—cut her off.

"Apparently, this pup is the Ocean Mother. They would like to talk to you." Hemrin said.

Yemri felt uneasy. She had never spoken to someone who was HaruKu before, and the feeling was like speaking to a rock. But it didn't matter; before she spoke again Maatis addressed Pangor who had an air of authority about him. "How did you find us?"

Yemri did not wait to allow Pangor to speak and instead she addressed Maatis. "That is irrelevant to the matter at hand, Maatis." Then she launched into the speech Tope had helped her prepare on the way over. "We have come to discuss your kinship's compliance with the societal agreements Serras undertake as part of our oceanic cohabitation." She was glad Maatis was HaruKu so that he was not aware of the pride she felt at having remembered all the big words. That would not help her authority in the matter, even if he couldn't feel it. She tried to rein it in nonetheless.

Maatis did not break eye contact with Pangor as he said, "Hemrin, you know we do not allow outsiders to enter our kinship."

After which Hemrin finished addressing Pangor himself. "They tend to... disturb our ways."

Yemri was livid, but she was trying to work on her poise and control. "Your ways are precisely why we are here."

Hemrin spoke for Maatis, and his tone was polite but carried an undertone of threat. "Again, I must ask, how did you find us?"

They were speaking in an absurd circle, Yemri to Maatis, Maatis to Hemrin, Hemrin to Pangor. To his credit, Pangor said nothing while Maatis stared at him firmly. As silence began to fill the cavern, Yemri began to grow more

192

uncomfortable. She wished she could ask someone what to do, but that would ruin everything she was trying to accomplish.

"Your treatment of the dams of your kinship is unacceptable," Yemri continued. "We have come to discuss your compliance with Serra tenets. You are not in compliance with the Oceanic Cohabitation Societal Agreements." She was just repeating herself now with the words rearranged but she didn't know what to say. She couldn't move on to the next part in her speech until she got some response from Maatis on any matter other than how they were found.

Seeing he would get no reply from Pangor, he turned his attention to Tope, who floated at the head of the group, hand on the hilt of his short sword. "We do not allow outsiders to be armed in our kinship. Well," he laughed as though it were incredibly funny, "we do not allow outsiders at all, now do we?" He was positively jovial as the dams around him nodded and cowered in agreement with his joke. "We have let you keep yours in good faith so that we can converse amicably, but we will have to ask you to leave if you continue to posture so aggressively."

Tope removed his hand from the hilt but did not relax a single muscle.

"Now, we cannot offer you any food, I am afraid, as we are a meager kinship. Nor can we offer you a place to rest, as we do not have the room, as you could see on your way down. We are small and pathetic, not worth your time. So I am afraid you will have to go without anything from us."

"We are not leaving here without the dams and pups," Yemri nearly shouted. She had forgotten the rest of what she had practiced to say in a diplomatic manner and now had no control as her anger took over. "We will take them all with us and throw you in prison."

Finally, as if a shrimp had crawled on his arm unwantedly and he had to face it, Maatis looked at Yemri for the first time. "My dear little pup, you have the most beautiful tail. Does she not?" He looked at the dams around him for agreement, for which he was immediately rewarded. "You are truly a pretty little thing, and we would welcome you into our kinship gladly if you would like to stay.

"Now," he said turning his attention back to Tope. "I am afraid I will have to ask you to leave. Our kinship has been badly mistreated, which is why my father split the clan. HaruKu is the only way to survive in this world, and you would rather we live as the OnaKu. That clan is the one you should trouble yourself with." He nodded vigorously as if in agreement with himself about the seriousness of the problem. "They have blatantly defied Ocean Mother Nephira and her cause. Now, again, I must ask that you leave."

"We are not leaving until--"

Maatis looked from Tope to Hemrin who, without hesitation or consultation, pulled his knife from the sheath at his waist and stabbed the nearest dam in the back, just under her ribs.

As if knowing her duty, she didn't cry out as she suffered.

Nearly all of the bucks who had been up above in the rest of the kinship filed through the tunnel and into the now-cramped cave.

"I will ask you once more before killing another dam—though I really cannot spare many more, so I hope you will comply—to leave our kinship at once and do not return."

Yemri put up her hands as if to stop it from happening herself. "Yes, of course we will leave."

She turned to go but Pangor said, "Mother, we can take this pathetic group. We are all well trained and we outnumber them easily."

Before she could respond, Tope answered him, "Our Ocean Mother has said we will leave before more harm is done, and we shall."

Pangor nodded, though begrudgingly, and the group funneled out of the tunnel into the pressing heat.

As they made their way across the desert, Yemri wanted to shout to all the dams to follow them, but the bucks had all taken up arms and were pouring out of the tunnel after them. The women would not be able to leave without many casualties.

After they had breached the gorge and arrived on the other side of the wall where the water was cool once again, the sentinels broke into a confusion of disagreement.

"As Commander of the Sentinels I am telling you, Tope, you are not the one to make this decision."

"Now. Now!" Muleki spoke up for the first time. "I will not allow you to speak to a Balam this way." Muleki was the unofficial leader of the Sentinels and acted as their representation and leader even over the Sentinel Commander. "Tope was responding to an order from our Ocean Mother. Whether you agree with it or not is beside the point." More gently, he turned to Yemri and said, "Now, Mother Yemri, I think it is safe to say that this meeting did not go well. As, I am sure, you expected."

She had not expected that. She thought she could reason with Maatis.

Stupid.

"But all is not lost," Muleki went on. "We will storm in after they have let their guard down and take them by force." He turned to Pangor with authority in his voice. "I think we wait until night when they will be asleep and less on guard. It will be--"

"No!" Yemri shouted. "We are leaving…" She felt completely panicked. "If we attack…" She wrung her hands. How to make such a decision? "If we attack so many dams and pups will be killed. That… that is not what we want to do! We have to… um… persuade Maatis to change their ways or imprison him and his followers. But we cannot risk hurting anyone."

"Hurting anyone?" Pangor scoffed. "This-" he gestured behind him, but she couldn't hear him because Muleki started yelling about something too. Yemri wanted to run and hide under her sleeping cushion. Finally, Tope's voice prevailed, "She has made her decision. We will go back to Daris now."

Pangor swam away in a fiery huff and Muleki looked as if his head would burst. Slowly, he too swam away and the Sentinels waiting began to leave the perimeter.

Once Yemri and Tope were back on their palanquin, Yemri turned to her father and said, "Thank you. You know, for following my command. It helps me so much. Hopefully I can gain control over the others soon enough."

Tope did not look at her. His Ku was hard as he said, "I am not sure why you wanted to come here if you did not want anything to be done once we arrived."

Yemri deflated in her seat. What did she want them to do? She hadn't had any foresight going into this expedition and didn't have a plan when things went poorly. What had she expected, indeed?

Chapter 11

Santiago

Up ahead was the wall, a towering white barrier between the safety of the city and the unprotected ocean. They were swimming high enough above the top of the city at this point that they would exit the protection dome before they reached the wall. If they broke through the enchantment, Santi was much less likely to be able to swim for help. Her heart pounded in her chest and she felt sweat prickle from her body contrasting the warm water around her. She felt shaky and irrational as memories came back to her that mirrored this situation far too closely. Sully had invoked this very same panic three years ago after she had known and trusted him her entire childhood.

"No!" Santi shouted.

She had been through too much to allow herself to get into danger the same way twice. "I'm not doing this Merrek."

Santi grabbed hold of the straps that connected her seat to Merrek's waist and began pushing herself out of the seat.

"Wait, Santi we are almost there."

But Santiago didn't reply. She pushed her bottom off the seat and kicked away, detangling herself from his ropes and pushing herself back in the opposite direction. Merrek swam a few more strokes before stopping to look back at her. They both tread water looking at each other. Santi's eyes and Ku were full of fire, a challenge to Merreck to take her where she didn't want to go. Merrek's face was sheer confusion.

"Santiago." He began swimming towards her but stopped when she kicked herself backwards and put up her hands in a defensive motion. "Bab, I would never hurt you."

She didn't say anything. She was debating pulling her sai out of its holster on her thigh.

"It is only that… I was told not to say anything. It is a surprise, but… but I will tell you if it will make you feel better."

She squinted at him without loosening her defenses. "You'd better tell me."

"It is Rogan."

This made Santi stop squinting and drop her hands from their fight-ready position, but she was still skeptical. She pushed out her Ku further but didn't feel him anywhere. "Where is he?"

"He is outside the city."

"I can't feel him," she said haughtily.

He cocked his head at her. "I know." His face was blank in typical Serra fashion, so Santi searched his Ku. The uncertain confusion she was getting from him was genuine and wholesome. He truly did not understand why she was upset with him. "The barrier, Bab. You cannot reach your Ku through it, nor from the outside in."

Santi let her guard down and felt foolish. "I'm sorry, Merrek. You have been nothing but helpful." She hung her head.

"No need to be embarrassed, Bab. I heard what you have been through." His NorMer accent was remarkably pronounced in that moment. He wound up the sling. "Come, I will swim next to you and make sure no harm befalls you. But you are in charge. Ok, Bab?"

Santi nodded, ashamed. She felt silly as they began their slow swim to the wall, but it did make her feel better.

Luckily, they were already close to the wall, and in no time at all they were soaring over the top of it and out of the protection of the enchantment. They dove to the ground and there was Rogan, waiting amongst the brush beyond the clearing. He had set out a blanket like they used to do when they were kids sitting on the bank of their cove. She used to pronounce the word "pic-lic" when she was small, and although she had learned to pronounce it right by the time she met Rogan, they still called it that as their own joke.

As soon as Santi saw Rogan, Merrek smiled at her, "Have a lovely evening, Bab. I will see you in two days." Excitement filled his Ku. "I have requested to be part of the team that takes you to the tournament!" With that he turned and made his way towards the front of the city, to the giant archway that would grant him access back into Daris.

Santi floated to the ground and connected to her Bondmate. Rogan sprang up from the island floor and gathered her in a smothering hug. His broad shoulders and massive arm span could wrap up her entire body twice over. Often when he was exuberant with his embrace like this, it was overwhelming. But this time, it was exactly what she needed.

Rogan pulled her down to sit with him in the sand and she started, "Rogan I-"

But he pushed her out of his tight embrace and held up both hands to hush her. She felt his Ku, like the sun trying to shine through a dirty window. "No, you do not need to say anything. You have done all the talking for months, and that is not fair. You relax and I will do the talking." He reached out and held her hand as he continued. "I have been terrible," he said earnestly.

She was torn between the apology she planned to make and agreeing with him that he had been terrible. She was about to say something when he continued. "Please, just let me."

She did as he said, and it felt good to relax and listen. He seized up her other hand in his and squeezed them tightly as if he could replace the months of lost affection by sheer strength. They sat on the blue blanket that had been on their guest bed, small plants and flowers waving around them in the gentle current. "I have been terrible to you. I am sad, sure, but so are you. I am mad, I am hurt, I am so very uncertain about who I am anymore, but none of that is because of you. In fact, most of those things are solved because of you." He reached forward and held her face in his hands. He kissed her quickly, as if unsure it would be well received and it was best to make it swift.

He pushed away from her and maneuvered into an awkward position she had never seen any Serra perform.

From his torso to his waist he held himself vertical but was bent into what looked like a very awkward curve. He made a giant 'J' shape with his fin splayed out behind him. It looked uncomfortable and, Santi thought, unsettling. His tail did not have joints in it to make a right angle like she assumed he was trying to do. "Rogan what are you doing?"

He smiled with a look that showed the old Rogan peeking out. "I am here on my knees asking you to forgive me."

At that she laughed out loud, mouth open wide, head thrown back. She had taught him about typical Crural proposals after they were Bound, which led to a big discussion about knees and how often they were used for gestures and symbolism for Crurals. She laughed again and shook her head. He remembered her telling him about groveling and begging.

She looked at him and nodded. He was doing a pretty good job.

He looked behind him and leaned backwards to reach for something hidden in the weeds but then stopped and turned back around. Gathering her hands back up he said, "I am so, so sorry for what I have put you through. Please tell me you can eventually forgive me? I will wait as long as you need."

Without hesitation Santi sighed and said quietly, "I forgave you already, Rogan. And I have already forgiven you for anything else you may do in the future. That's how much I love you. There is nothing you will do that I wont forgive."

With that confession, the dirty window was wiped clean and the sunshine spilled through the clear, beautiful glass that was Rogan's Ku. Santi almost felt pushed backwards by his outpouring of love for her.

He unwound himself from the awkward "kneeling" position and pulled her onto his lap sitting on the blanket once more. They kissed fervently, and she finally breathed a cleansing sigh that had been trapped in her lungs since Amed's death. The tightness in her chest released. She genuinely felt happier than she had in months.

"Oh Santiago!" Rogan exclaimed. He was visibly startled, giving a little jump. "I did not know just how miserable I had become until just now when I felt the darkness in your Ku leave. That darkness... you were carrying it on my behalf."

She did feel lighter. Brighter. Rogan had let go of the darkness that was holding him back which allowed her to let go of it too. She felt a freedom that she had not felt since they were celebrating their Bonding.

"What caused this sudden change?" she asked as she tightened her grip around his neck. She settled into him and rested her head on his shoulder right where it belonged. "I was awful to you earlier." She sat up straight again. "I mean, I don't think I regret yelling at you." She laughed because it was true; yelling at him *had* felt really nice. "I truly wanted to say those things, but I could have delivered my message much better. Surely, my chastisement was not the right method to snap you out of this." She shook her head. "I am so sorry for the awful way I spoke to you earlier. I wasn't fair."

"You were fair to say how you felt. And I needed to hear the truth of my behavior. But you are right, it was not *how* you said it, but *what* you said was important. And as soon as I returned home I found this." He removed her from his lap and leaned back, reaching out an arm to retrieve something from the weeds. He brought his hand back clutching her ugly tattered gray bag. He reached inside and pulled out a handful of shrimp. "How long have you been trying to take me to the stingrays?"

"I only collected those yesterday after the ceremony."

"One day or twenty, the fact that you could not get me to listen to you and realize you were trying to do something nice…" He shook his head. "It is unacceptable."

"Rogan, you are mourning. I understand. You are angry with Zitja, with me, with… well… the world, probably."

"Santiago, I thank you for your understanding. But no. You have been wonderful for four months. The fact that you lost your patience with me only yesterday is remarkable. I think I can find it in myself to grieve without being an unbearable buck to be around."

Santi only nodded. She definitely agreed that it should be possible at this point. But what did she know? She could not judge his grief now just as she had tried not to before.

"But I must correct you." Rogan's Ku was serious. "Through all of this, I was never mad at you. I love you more than anyone or anything I have ever loved. You are everything to me. Why would I have been mad at you?"

Santi scrunched up her face. That didn't seem right. "Because your father is not the heir,'" she said the title with derision, "because you and your sister are not. And Amed died because of that. Because I am the reason for all of this."

Rogan looked genuinely shocked. "No. No of course not! Are you blaming yourself for his death?"

Irritation was growing in her chest but she pushed it down. They were finally making amends, and she didn't need to go getting hot again. She removed herself from his lap anyway so that she could look at him as she answered, "No, Rogan. I don't blame myself. I might have in the beginning, but I've had time to deal with it and think about what your father would say on the matter." She couldn't help it, she felt her voice and her temperature rising. She was glad she wasn't sitting on his lap anymore but had her own seat to stand her ground, "But Rogan, if you haven't been blaming me all this time, why have you been so horribly nasty to me?"

He didn't say anything, but his Ku was buzzing in her chest. It looked to Santi as if Rogan were scanning back through all their interaction the past four months for accuracy of her statement. Was he trying to find falsehood in what she had said? She felt their argument welling up in full force. She pictured the silence ensuing for months more to come, and she was about to take the question back when he finally spoke.

He looked at her intently with his deep brown eyes and she could feel his Ku was full of regret but also shock. "I did not realize I had been so bad to you."

That confession only made her angry but she responded calmly, "I find it hard to believe you didn't notice."

"No, you are right. I knew I was angry, I knew I was not responding to things appropriately. It was like I was a volcano of rage and every little thing made me erupt. I knew that but I had not realized I was erupting so often. Nor had I realized you were at the brunt of so much of it. I thought for the most part I was erupting at the other Sentinels in training with me. Though I can see now that being dismissive and quiet to you is not much better."

She nodded. She knew the feeling. "It's like your anger is a bucket. Usually that bucket is empty and any time something makes you mad it just fills up the bucket. But you were so angry about the loss of your father that any little thing made it overflow instead of just fill up."

Rogan smiled and said, "I love you, little Crural, and I get what you are saying but I do not know what a bucket is."

Santi laughed and scrunched up her face, "A basket then."

"Yes. Yes I was an overflowing basket of rage."

"I can agree to that!"

It was nice to laugh together, but she still didn't feel satisfied. It was months of anger from him and she was having a hard time just letting it go. "I still don't understand why. Why are you so angry? That's surely a step in the grieving process you should have gotten over by now. Right?"

"I think I had! Which is the frustrating part. Remember two months ago when I was gone for a week with the Sentinels to Tipua? I felt like I had really accepted things. The duty we were on resulted in no action and plenty of alone time guarding a kinship from what turned out to be nothing. It gave me plenty of time to ponder by myself. I honestly felt better!" He breathed in deeply and then released all of the water as he said, "But as soon as I returned, our troop met with Krell and everything was ruined. I was back to anger and distraction."

"Well I can't say I blame you there. He makes everyone's rage basket overflow."

Rogan gave a throaty noise of agreement and said, "Something is going on there. He is doing something mysterious that goes deeper that anyone realizes."

"Amen to that."

"Amen?"

She found that she held no anger for him anymore and instead she wanted to be his teammate again, to solve the mysterious Krell problem like they might have chased an elusive octopus into a cave long ago. Santi leaned over and kissed him passionately. If there were not Sentinels always patrolling the city walls she would have done more. When they finally pulled apart, Rogan grinned like the little boy she had met almost fifteen years ago. "Thank you for making me this pic-lic. It's wonderful."

He kissed her again and said, "Shall we go feed some slippery animals?"

The nostalgia, love, and relief washed over her and she began to cry.

"What is wrong? What did I do?" Rogan was truly puzzled.

"I'm just so glad you're back, Rogan." She flung her arms around his neck. "I felt so alone and I am so scared. I need you on my team. Krell is making me do this terrible thing, but all I could think is how I wish I could talk to you about it. You'll know what we should do."

He hugged her back tightly, smiling on his face and in his Ku. "I have no idea what we should do."

After thoroughly making up and getting reacquainted, the couple lay together on their soft sleeping cushion wrapped in a fuzzy gray blanket. At least Santi assumed it would be fuzzy if it were on land. Underwater and fully saturated, however, it was just soft and thick. When she first saw the blanket she had assumed it was not a Serra-made item. The stitching was so tight and perfect, it looked like the work of a sewing machine. Soon after, she watched a dam sewing while they both waited at the nuntium outpost for a jellyfish to become available and discovered that they could do very excellent, precise work by hand. In that moment, Santi stopped doubting the Serras' craftsmanship abilities.

"I know I have to kill Zitja," Santi said from the crook of Rogan's shoulder, where she was wrapped in his arms. "I'll do it, and I'm ready for it, and I've trained all this time to do just that! But do we agree that doing it as a tournament finale is really… well, for lack of a better word, it's gross! Isn't it?"

"It is definitely gross. But you are right; there are many better words. I will just say that it is repulsive for Krell to want to turn it into a show like this. There has to be more to it than just letting everyone see her die. What does that accomplish besides verification, which I think the ocean would believe if they were told she's dead? You know what I mean? They would not doubt it if they heard the news. No one needs to actually see it happen. Do you agree?"

Santi was silent. She was too distracted to answer his question about the significance behind the spectacle because she was only worried about her part in the it. "Besides," she said with exasperation, "I can't stand the anticipation." She wiggled a little as she wrestled with the thought. "This could have been over with yesterday, Rogan! Yesterday. Today we could just be enjoying this wonderful moment in our bed, but instead all I can think about is committing murder on stage."

"Stage?"

"I don't know." She waved her hand back and forth in the water. "I keep picturing it like a theatre but I know that's not right. I just figure if I can picture it, I can control it. Do it my way. But none of it is my way!"

"Ok, so then let us do it your way."

"I think it's too late for that. My way would have been in battle alongside your father."

Instead of crumpling within himself like he previously would have done, Rogan allowed Santi to share the sorrow in his Ku with him. He said, "I agree, but since you cannot do it in battle, what else could we do?"

"We should have just gone straight to her cell yesterday as we left the citadel. Though I don't know where to find her. Do you think the citadel's walls are too thick to find Zitja with our Kus?"

"Zitja doesn't have a Ku. Sirens are nearly impossible to feel with them."

"Right," Santi said, feeling dejected. "So I wouldn't have even known where to find her."

"But I know where she is."

"Of course! Well, that's what we should have done. I think that would be my way, if I had a say in all of this. Just be done with it. The waiting is making my stomach churn."

Rogan pushed himself up on his elbow to look at her, making her head slide down to the pillow underneath. "Why do we not do it your way?"

"It's too late. We already didn't." Then her eyes went wide and she sat up. "But we could!"

"We can. It is late."

"Everyone will have already gone except the necessary Sentinels."

"Zitja is still tied in chains and locked in a cell." Rogan pushed himself out of bed.

Santi crawled over the covers and began putting on her sturdiest one-piece swimsuit—the green one with long sleeves and a higher neckline that prevented any embarrassing slips when she sparred. "We can be done with all the anxiety tonight!"

Santi could feel that Rogan had the same frenetic energy as she did as they peered into the chest against their bedroom wall.

"Are you sure you want to do this?" Rogan asked as he picked up a pile of weapons and holsters from the chest.

Santi had to restrain herself from frantic laughter. "No."

He untangled the various leather straps and handed Santi her portion of the weaponry. "Great, at least we are in agreement."

Santi took her sais and began fastening the straps around her thighs. The sais were a gift from Amed, and a few months after he'd given them her, the holsters had arrived via delivery Orca from Coral. Coral had made them herself, and she had included a nuntium assuring Santi that now Coral and Amed would be with her during her hardest times. As Santiago buckled the last strap around her waist, securing the garter-looking holster on her hips, she had to wonder whose idea this was. In their usual fashion, they had hyped

210

themselves up for an adventure without knowing how it started.

Rogan fastened the last clasp across his broad chest so that four straps and buckles crossed in a double 'X' on his breastbone, the handles of the short swords peeking above his shoulders. "Ready?"

She appraised him. He looked a force to be reckoned with. Full of adrenaline and anticipation, she suddenly wondered how much extra time they had. "Well…" She winked at him.

"After," Rogan nodded, grabbing her hand pulling her out of the bedroom. They made no stops as they sped down the short hallway and out the large, square window in the front room.

He pulled her directly upwards to the usually bustling Serra highway. At this time of night, it was almost completely deserted. Daris didn't really have a nightlife scene, though there were places close to the Troag where one could find plenty of shenanigans to get into late into the night. They knew they would be least noticed high above the city with darkness as their cover.

When they got to the citadel, they dropped down directly on the roof. As crime wasn't really an issue in the Serra communities—and especially in Daris—they didn't have to worry about guards outside the building. Once they went inside, their presence might raise suspicious, and—though Rogan was a Sentinel and well within his rights to be there—they might have some explaining to do. They prepared for this on the way over; it would be up to Santi to do the lying. Rogan hadn't reached mastery of his genuine, honest, Serra Ku quite yet. It was part of Sentinel training but would take years for him to be able to be convincingly deceitful. Santi's Crural Ku, on the other hand, was well accustomed to telling believable lies.

"No turning back now," Santi said stoically.

"We can turn back at any time," Rogan said with genuine concern. "We have done nothing but swim to the Troag."

She could tell he was gearing up to reassure her more fervently that she could change her mind, so she said quickly, "It's just a thing people say!" She looked at him firmly. "I think this was your idea, so let's just proceed before I chicken out."

Rogan's mood lightened exactly where Santi needed it to be. "This was not my idea. You cannot blame it on me."

"Well, it wasn't mine."

"Perfect," Rogan nodded. "Then we clearly are not to blame if this goes wrong."

Since making up, they had both been in a manic state of euphoria. Every joke was extra-funny, every kiss extra-zealous, every decision extra agreed-upon. As if to make up for the terrible feelings of the past, their every interaction was saccharin and over-the-top.

Santi flung her arms around Rogan's neck and kissed him firmly on the mouth. "Glad to have you back. I need you."

Rogan gripped both of her shoulders tightly and looked her in the eyes. He took a deep breath in and let it out quickly, resolved. The look they shared said they were back to the beginning, all hard feelings washed away. It also a look that said *"we're really stupid, why are we doing this?"*

212

Rogan nodded one quick nod, and Santi responded in kind. Then he grabbed her and pushed her off the roof.

Santi laughed as she floated next to the building. "Your concept of gravity is broken." She placed a finger next to her eye. "But I appreciate the gesture." One last moment of levity before things got serious.

They dove down to the ground floor and entered the building through the main entrance. The Citadel was one of only a few other important buildings that weren't open at every window. To keep things orderly, this building had only one entrance and exit. Just inside the doorway was a large atrium that opened up to half a dozen floors of balconies. Low to the ground, in the middle of it all, two Sentinels stood guard. Rogan and Santi's goal: don't kill either of them. If possible, try not to even have to fight them. But Rogan and Santi knew that they would fight or kill if need be to get to Zitja. They decided that, ultimately, her death tonight was most important.

Santi and Rogan swam inside and stopped directly in front of the two Sentinels.

"Tyyvek!" Rogan proclaimed too enthusiastically. "It is great to see you tonight. I did not know you had already gained a position."

Luckily, Tyyvek showed no sense of suspicion in his Ku as he responded with a prideful nod. "I was assigned just two days ago. So far, it is an uneventful position, but a good one to prove myself."

"Congratulations! You will be guarding the perimeter in no time."

It could not be felt in his Ku, but Santi knew Rogan held a small jealousy. He was more qualified, a better fighter, and exceptionally trained, yet Krell found every excuse to hold Rogan back from gaining an actual position with the Sentinels.

"Well," Santi interjected, "Rogan has just left some things in the training room. Sorry to bother you both so late in the night. We will be only a moment."

"Of course!" Tyyvek answered, unaccustomed to being lied to. It was almost too easy. Stupid, honest Serras. Santi had to squelch a pang of guilt rising in her gut so as not to be discovered.

She and Rogan started their glide beyond the two sentries, up past the first balcony, when the other Sentinel spoke firmly. "Why are you wearing your weapons to retrieve an item? And why did you need to come in the middle of the night? Rogan?"

Rogan was so quick Santi didn't even have time to react before one blade was unsheathed and Rogan had knocked the butt of the handgrip on the base of Tyyvek's skull, rendering him unconscious immediately. At the same time, Rogan's tail flashed through the air and struck the other Sentinel across the face. Both guards floated limply to the marble floor. Rogan righted himself, chest heaving, ready for a fight should either of them have remained conscious.

Santi stared at him wide-eyed. His speed was almost impossible. And the whole thing was probably unnecessary, as she would have thought of a lie quickly enough.

"That was hot," she smirked, and he re-sheathed his sword.

Lifting one shoulder in a gesture he had picked up from her, he replied nonchalantly, "This is a very novice position to be assigned to. Who in the city is going to break into the citadel when it houses Sentinel Headquarters?"

"Give yourself credit. They have still been through training. Though they probably should have been a better match for you."

"Do not get too smug, the next ones will be. Come on, let us hurry before these two come back to their senses."

He grabbed her hand and pulled her swiftly up the center of the atrium. They arrived on the sixth floor in no time, sailing over the balcony. Santi wanted to make a joke about how much easier that was than taking the stairs, but her stomach was in knots. Now that Rogan was back, she'd leave the jokes to him to break tension. Her role had always been to absorb the tension and dwell on it. She did that now as they turned to the left, made their way down a long corridor, and arrived at their purpose.

Santiago Scout Morales couldn't speak; in fact, she thought it was more likely she'd vomit.

Grateful she didn't have to open her mouth to communicate, Santi said, "Rogan, will it be worth it if you have to kill them?"

But he couldn't answer. The sentinels on this floor had been alerted to their presence as soon as they felt Santi's and Rogan's Kus. They also knew what Santi and Rogan had done to the Sentinels downstairs, and they were armed and making their way towards them.

"Rogan and Santiago," said a broad chested middle-aged buck firmly. "Why have you come here?"

Santi was ready with her lie, though she didn't know if she could regain composure enough to say what they had practiced. "We... we've been assigned. We are here to relieve you and take over your post for the evening because…"

"No, you are not," retorted a small but menacing dam who carried one hooked blade and she began charging at the pair. These were not novice Sentinels and they would not be tricked by lies or caught off guard by Rogan's speed.

Rogan squared his shoulders and unsheathed both of his blades, his shoulder muscles contracting sharply, and swung his swords in one tight circle at each side before charging the two guards. If this went poorly—and even if it went well, she presumed—Rogan's opus as a Sentinel would be at risk. After tonight, his and Santiago's imprisonment was likely. What would happen to them? They hadn't really bothered to think of the consequences, though their conviction that they were doing the right thing was strong.

Rogan parried a blow from each of the Sentinels, but they came at him again and again, and he was being backed down the corridor. Rogan twisted his lower body to strike the dam with his tail, but she caught him by his simul, the symbol of his Bonding, and stopped his blow. She grabbed the thin wire, pulled his tail, and flung him away from her, ripping and destroying the simul along with it.

They had truly wanted to kill no Serras; Santi felt the shift as Rogan's anger overcame his compunction not to kill. He responded with a fury she had seen only a few times, each of them when Santi's life was at risk. Rogan immediately stabbed the buck, the lesser of the two threats, through the shoulder of his sword-wielding arm and once in the hip, deep enough to stop him swimming. Then Rogan focused his attention on the dam. She was quick, relentless, and skilled. It was only because Rogan had trained with his father since he was a small child that he was able to keep up with her.

Her Ku was closed off tight, and she was intensely focused on the fight, which she fought like a mercenary. Each swipe of her curved blade landed exactly where she intended. Some Rogan caught, and some hit their mark. Rogan was now bleeding from his right shoulder and his left hip, and a large cut on his tail was clearly causing him trouble. But he fought on, landing a few blows himself.

Finally, Santi snapped herself out of her shocked torpor and pulled her sais off her thighs. Quickly, she kicked off the wall towards Rogan.

Without opening his Ku to give himself a disadvantage in the fight, Rogan shouted to Santi, "No! Just go. I will give you time. Just do what we came to do."

Santi followed his instructions without hesitation. She sheathed her sais and dove to the limp and bleeding buck on the polished floor. He had lost a lot of blood and was weak, but he still reached for his sword with his uninjured arm. Santi saw the pouch on his belt immediately and dove for it. She didn't have much time as he began sliding his way along the floor towards where his sword had fallen. She grabbed the pouch and yanked hard and fast, but the leather straps were too strong to break. The buck punched at her, but she kicked his arm away and stayed out of reach. She grabbed her sai and sliced through the leather thong, freeing the bag.

Suddenly, Rogan's back was pressed against her side, smashing her to the floor as he protected her with his body. The Serra dam's blade curved through the air and sliced the leather of the straps on his chest. It caught on the buckle, which saved Rogan's life, and gave him a moment to cross his blades over the top of the dam's wrist. He was still pressing on Santi, and she wasn't sure if she should remain still to support him or move on with her task. Rogan flexed with all the power in his massive back, shoulders, and biceps, and, using his swords like a giant pair of scissors, cut his opponent's hand off succinctly.

"Santi, hurry!"

Pouch in hand, Santiago kicked off the floor, freeing herself from Rogan's weight, and made her way swiftly down the hall. Santi had not learned how to communicate HaruKu, though she didn't know what she would say if she did. *Be safe? I love you? Please don't die right now because that would not be cool?*

Santi made her way down the hall until she reached the end and turned right. This was the hallway they had come for. Bars lined both walls as far as she could see, separating the free world from captivity. She made her way slowly down the deserted corridor, looking in every cell. What had once been white marble on the walls and ceilings of each cell had grown dark and dingy from neglect. A grey-green film covered the walls and floor. In the corners, the ocean's current had washed in rubbish and debris, where it had been trapped it for years. The desolation was eerie. The floors Santi floated above were caked with settled residue and layers of dirt, weeds, and littered with Crural junk.

Finally, Santi reached the end of the hall and found what she was looking for.

The floor was just as filthy in this cell, save a small semi-circle where the bars had been opened recently and pushed all the rubbish aside. The walls were gray and dingy except where the mildew had been rubbed away by hand

218

marks and signs of struggle. Besides the debris, there was nothing in the cell except a small cot. On that cot, Santi could see nothing but a lump in the shadow wrapped in chains.

Santi took a deep breath and closed her eyes for one single count, then squared her shoulders and pulled a key out of the leather pouch she had taken from the guard. She jammed it in the rusty lock and turned until she felt a small click. The lock was so stiff that if someone else hadn't opened it recently, it would have been impossible for her to unlock it now.

She swung the gate open and gingerly used the bar to propel herself inside until she glided over the threshold and stopped in the middle of the cell. She turned to her left and settled her feet on the ground, standing beside the cot on the cold dirty floor, looking down on the bound figure of Zitja.

Even chained to a bed inside a prison cell, Zitja looked fearsome. Zitja's very being challenged Santi. Though everything was in Santi's favor, she still felt terribly daunted by the fierce ocean queen lying sheathed in chains.

Santi slowly reached down with her right hand and gripped the handle of her sai, but otherwise didn't move. She didn't know how much time she had or how long Rogan could hold off the dam, but she did not feel like she could move any faster. The business of murdering was new to her, and she felt her hands begin to shake.

She unsheathed her sai and assessed the prisoner. Zitja showed no fear. She was at Santi's mercy, and yet she was completely composed. Santi scanned the area over the Siren's heart, but thick chains were wound around her chest several layers deep. Santi wondered how they didn't crush Zitja's ribs with their weight. As it was, Santi would not be able to stab the right spot on the body to make it a quick death.

Santi assessed her options. The chains only spanned from stomach to shoulder, so there was enough of the Siren's body exposed to injure, but a death like that would be long and horrible—for both of them—and it wasn't something Santi thought she could deal with.

She reached down and tried to pull the shackles away to reveal Zitja's heart, but they were incredibly tight, and she only succeeded in pinching her fingers between the chains.

She pulled her hand back in pain and clasped her fingers in a fist to try to dull the sharp throb. There was no way she could get access through the chains, so she weighed her other possibilities. Gutting Zitja was not something Santi had the stomach for. Cutting her wrist was an option, but that would be incredibly slow and disgusting, and if she were caught early enough, they could save Zitja and follow through with the plan. Santi's eyes roamed upwards and settled on Zitja's thin white neck. She grimaced and leaned in closer.

Zitja showed no sign of response besides following Santi with her eyes. She seemed to understand the decision Santi had made and lay poised for the assault. Santi placed the edge of her long middle tine against the Siren's cool, translucent skin. They both took a deep breath.

Cutting off Zitja's head entirely would be impossible with such a small weapon. Even with a large weapon it was a feat of strength Santi didn't think she possessed. She would just have to settle for slicing her neck ear to ear. A shiver went through her body at the thought, goose bumps breaking out on her skin, and a wave of nausea at the thought of that amount of blood nearly overwhelmed her. Santi licked her lips. She shifted from foot to foot. She pressed the sai against Zitja's neck harder and then pulled it away. She put it against the vulnerable slender neck once more. And then Santi made a giant mistake. She made the mistake that every cliché villain in movies had warned her about: Santi looked into the villain's eyes and saw them staring back at her.

They were eyes. Eyes just like any other pair, studious, intelligent, full of depth. It made Santi wonder what Zitja was thinking in this moment. It was the absolute wrong thing to wonder.

Santi slipped the sai back into its holster and went to the gate. She retrieved the keys and made her way over to the bed.

She knew she was being an idiot, and if she were watching herself in a movie she'd be screaming at the screen. *Don't be stupid,* she told herself. But in movies you couldn't feel what was happening to the character, and the only thing Santi could do right now was feel. She imagined following through with what she had just been contemplating. She would slice Zitja's throat, it would have to be deep, blood would pour out, and Zitja's head would roll back on the part that remained intact. Santi couldn't do it. She had killed before, twice. They were performed in the heat of battle to save her or Rogan's life.

She still thought about them.

She could not go through the rest of her life thinking about this, thinking about slicing the neck of anyone, Zitja or not. That would haunt her, and Santi was still so haunted from the other trauma she had experienced in her life. She could not add this image to them.

Crouching over the padlock, Santi decidedly did not think about what she was about to do. She stuck the key in and paused, looking at the open cell door behind her. Santi got back up and closed the gate with a loud bang. It wouldn't do for Zitja to escape now; one of them was going to have to kill the other in this cell. It might be so much easier to live with if Santi had to fight for it. She was ready to fight for it.

Santi crouched over the padlock again and turned the key without thought, already determined. She was going to have to let Zitja free in order to kill her in a way Santi could live with for the rest of her life. She pulled the top layer of chain off Zitja's chest and let it fall heavily on the floor. As if in slow motion, Santi pulled her sai out once again, cut the ropes that bound Zitja's one arm to her side, then pushed herself backwards, floating in the middle of the small cell, leaving the rest of the escaping for Zitja to do herself.

The Siren queen appraised Santiago expressionlessly. Very slowly, she pulled her hands free of the cut rope and began unwinding the chains from around her body. As she pulled the heavy metal off her arm and chest Santi saw deep red marks and scratches where the chains had cut her.

Zitja, finally freed from captivity, pushed herself up to meet Santi face to face. She did it all very slowly, deliberately, as if calculating what trickery Santi must be planning. Because surely Santi wouldn't be so foolish to just set Zitja free without some other scheme.

Santi had no such other scheme.

She suddenly felt very foolish. Where was her head when she let Zitja get free of the chains? She could have just removed them and left the rope tying her arm down. Santi knew how much damage Zitja could do with that one hand.

Santi touched her neck gingerly where Zitja had scratched her. It was healing up just fine. No need to add more damage to Santi's already beat up body.

Santi pulled out her other sai and positioned herself, ready for a fight. She didn't feel even a little bad about being armed while Zitja was not. Zitja could do plenty with no weapon and one arm as it was. Santi clutched the sais tighter, though not so tight that it would make her fight worse than having a loose grip. Santi had already made so many absolutely reckless mistakes, she wouldn't add any more to the list.

Neither of them moved. Santi didn't dare open her Ku, and yet the cell was heavy with calm. That calm did not come from Santi. Her heart was pounding loudly in her ears, the only sound in the entire ocean at the moment.

The beating of Santi's heart felt excessively loud. Could Zitja hear it or was Santi just in a panic? As still neither of them moved, Santi continued to appraise the dam. Zitja was supposed to be the very first *demi*—half Serra, half Crural. Nephira had had dark black skin, and Santi knew that Zitja should actually have much darker skin than Santi, but that wasn't apparent now. As a Siren, Zitja's skin was so white it was nearly see-through. *Zitja must look completely different now than how she once did*, Santi mused distractedly. She found herself wondering what such a transformation must be like, how angry Zitja must be. Surely Santi would be livid for having her life cursed the way Zitja's had been.

As if to illustrate her anger, her desire to kill all Serras because of a motivation Santi only now began to understand, Zitja's gaze shifted to Santi's weapons and reached out her hand.

Slowly, ever so slowly, Zitja reached out her one clawed hand to grab Santi's wrist. If the grip had been strong and threatening, Santi would have fought immediately and fiercely. But it wasn't, and that threw Santi off completely. Zitja held Santi by the wrist so gently it could have been a friendly gesture. It left Santi feeling confused. Confused and surprisingly curious. The two women stared at each other, neither breaking eye contact, neither moving a muscle.

Zitja lifted Santi's arm and brought it to her own chest, exactly where Santi had tried to reach through the chains only moments ago. The Siren's pale, white hand pulled Santi's darker tan arm towards her, and a moment later, the longest tine broke Zitja's skin. She bared her sharp teeth in pain but did not break eye contact and did not stop pressing the sai into her body.

Zitja pulled the sai into her until the two prongs on the sides also broke skin. She let out a ferocious scream and pulled on Santi's arm until her hand hit Zitja's chest. The sai was fully immersed up to the hilt.

Santi had never touched a Siren before. Zitja's skin was warm and soft and felt like any other Serra or Crural. Warm red blood seeped over Santiago's hand into the water around them.

Fear, confusion, and a mysterious bit of sadness began to consume Santi then, and she tried to pull her arm away, but Zitja held on. They both waited.

Then, just as slowly, Zitja reversed the process letting out another cry of pain as the curved side prongs scraped their way out of her body.

Santi stared aghast as the wounds healed instantly—almost around the sai's tines and they exited Zitja's body. When the long center tine finally broke free of Zitja's skin and was revealed to be in perfect condition, only then did her face no longer grimace in pain, and she let go of Santi's wrist. The only indication of emotion on Zitja's face was a slight scowl on her brow. She looked once again impassive, almost bored.

Time finally caught up to Santi in a sudden rush, and swiftly things seemed to happen in double time. The cell door burst open and Krell shouted, "Santiago, not yet!"

She looked at her hand, poised with the sai against Zitja's chest as if she were about to plunge it into Zitja's heart. Except now Santi knew she could not harm Zitja. Neither woman fought as the sentinels rushed into the cell and grabbed them. Santi was roughly ushered out while Zitja was once again wrapped in her chains.

They carted Santiago down the hall—no doubt to Krell's chambers for punishment—but she didn't resist. When they reached the stairway, she saw Rogan held at bay, badly injured, but no longer resisting. Only then did she open up her Ku and reach out to him.

"I couldn't do it," she said in defeat.

"It is ok, Santiago," he reassured her. "You are too good of a person for this."

"No. Rogan, I couldn't do it." The Sentinels pulled her down the stairwell, out of sight of Rogan, and she spoke in hurried desperation. "And Zitja knew I wouldn't be able to!"

Chapter 12

Santiago

"This is nonsense," Santi said to no one, as she couldn't get anyone to talk to her. "Honestly, this isn't necessary." She growled in frustration and turned to Rogan, but he was in the same position she was.

"We are coming," Rogan said firmly, with just as much irritation. "Regardless of what you think, we *are* coming."

Krell had not believed Santi when she said she didn't have the ability to kill Zitja. Instead, he chose to believe she was a lying, or worse, weak, unable to dispose herself of her selfish Crural nature. So, although Santi had fully planned on going to the tournament and was looking forward to playing in the amateur contest, she was now being escorted there under guard. She and Rogan were nominally Kell's special guests to the event so that it didn't appear to the Serra population that their hero and heir was a prisoner.

They had both been under guard all night before being escorted to the tournament by a throng of Sentinels, who had apparently been instructed not to speak to them.

Rogan took a calming breath. "Let us view this trip as Krell is trying to present it." Rogan reached out and grabbed her balled fist in both of his hands, trying to calm her. "It is just two days under guard to the tournament grounds, and after that, Krell has promised us freedom around the grounds."

They were surrounded by Sentinels and Serras all gathering in the Troag to travel together. The tournament grounds were set up in the deep middle ocean of the Pacific in a rarely traveled territory unpopulated by Serras. The trip could be dangerous so there was safety in traveling together. The tournament was next week, but every day one large group would leave together to allow tournament participants to arrive and get prepared. Krell was taking them in the first group because it was nearly impossible for them to get into trouble out in the middle of the ocean. He didn't want the Heir and son of the ocean's hero to appear to be imprisoned, so he would only give them freedom once they arrived. Thus, a grand caravan was escorting them to their own personal Alcatraz.

They shared a look that held a collection of conversations they had leading up to this moment. In summary: uncertainty.

"As Krell has presented it," Santi almost laughed, "an honor! Resulting in our freedom at the end of the tournament."

"Our freedom, *if* you follow through on doing what you have proven not to be able to do." Rogan tried to ease the tension. "What a fun challenge." Though other bucks and dams packed around them tightly as they waited at the Troag, they connected only to each other to speak. In such a situation, it wasn't considered rude not to connect to everyone. They were all having their own conversations as well.

Now she breathed a sigh of relief and her shoulders unclenched for the first time since deciding to break into Zitja's cell. "I've thought about that and, well, fine! I will play Krell's game. I'll be proud and eager to kill Zitja in front of everyone. When they see that I cannot, he'll have to believe me."

Rogan wrinkled his nose. "It still feels…"

While he struggled for the right word, Santi knew exactly how it felt. "Gross." She had decided that long ago. She shivered. "It feels really gross. There is something wrong with Krell."

"Come on. We are ready," a stern Sentinel finally said to them. All around, Serras began to make last-minute preparations, gathering their bags and small children for the journey. Santi picked up her usual old bag and left the heavier bag for Rogan to manage. Everyone swam together to the arch to exit the city, where various rides had been arranged. Santi was sure Merrek would be there to take someone else on the journey. She sent word to the courier network saying that she wouldn't be able to travel with him, as she was Krell's personal guest. He had responded with a personal nuntium expressing sorrow for the lost honor of couriering her and hopes that he could take her around the tournament grounds any time she needed him.

When they exited the city, Santi was taken aback by the scene, and for the briefest of moments forgot the predicament they were in. She nearly laughed at the absurdity before her.

"Rogan!" She grabbed his hand in pure joy. "This is phenomenal."

Rogan nodded, slightly impressed himself. "Wayne would be beside himself with joy."

It reminded Santi vividly of the last time she was truly surprised and taken aback by something in the Serra world.

~

Santi pressed a hand to the starfish on her cheek. The physical wounds Zitja had caused were almost healed. The Healer said they could take the starfish off her cheeks in a couple of days and let the salt water do the rest of the work. The emotional wounds—the nightmares, day panic, and jumpiness—would take more time to heal. That's why Rogan was whisking her away now.

"This will take your mind off of everything," he had crooned over her in the weeks after returning from her kidnapping ordeal with the Sirens. He had doted on and coddled her so much before she had to go back to college that she was uncomfortable.

"I'm ok. Really!" she assured him, sitting awkwardly in his massive embrace while he swam swiftly but easily out of the kinship. "You really don't have to do anything special."

"Ok, so pretend I am doing this for me." A hint of a smile crossed his smirking lips. "The louriers never come to our tiny kinship. Never in my twenty years of life have they even come so close."

"Why not?"

"They do not think we would be a big enough crowd. They want it to be worth the trip, you know? When they decided to come to Kaifee's kinship, we all agreed that we would show them that small kinships can draw a big crowd just like the large ones."

"What is Kaifee's kinship? Is that, like, the name of the kinship?"

"Kaifee is the kinship's ambassador to the Nhori Balam. The kinships do not have names themselves, but we refer to them by their ambassador."

"Oh, fascinating." Santi thought it was a lot like how Serra's didn't have last names but rather referred to everyone by their parentage or where they were from. "So then you live in Amed's kinship?"

Rogan looked down at where she sat in his arms, finally relaxed by the conversation. His eyes were scrunched, and his nose wrinkled, making his expression seem very Crural and very charming. And extra cute.

"No…?" he answered as a question, but she could tell it wasn't a question about who their kinships ambassador was, it was more a question of why she would think such a thing. "You know my father is the Sentinel Captain. He is not an ambassador."

"Right, of course." Santi pursed her mouth and swayed back and forth as she spoke. "I think I still view him as I did when I was a child. I thought he was like the king of the ocean or something."

At this, Rogan laughed so firmly he jostled her in his arms. "I think I remember you saying as much when we were young."

"That sounds like me," she nodded.

He laughed again. It was a nice laugh, hearty and completely innocent, the kind of laugh that only comes from a person not weighed down by any pressing thoughts or feelings. She hoped to get back to that point herself, but for now she was very aware that she was just lucky to be alive.

"Ok, so what kinship do you live in? Who is your ambassador?"

"Her name is Delany. She is wonderful, though quite meddlesome."

"I don't think I know her."

"She definitely knows you. You have met, of course, but you may not remember."

Santi nodded in thought. The name didn't ring a bell, but she was sure she'd remember her Ku and face if she saw her again. "So when will we be at Kaifee's kinship?"

Rogan made a general indication with his shoulder. "We are here."

Santi looked around. It was not set up like Rogan's kinship—Delany's kinship—with obvious homes, a kinship square for gathering, a community garden, and Serras all swimming about interacting with each other. This looked like the ocean floor, nothing more. Sand, rocks, fish and animals, plants, and fairly shallow water was all Santi could see. It made her realize that besides one trip to the Nhori Sariahdiem celebration and then the Siren lair, Rogan's kinship was all she knew of Serra life. Her travels as an adult were limited, and everything felt unfamiliar. She knew almost nothing. She found herself looking forward to going back to college in a few weeks. She felt a little homesick in the moment and looked forward to the comfort of the familiar.

When nothing kinship-like materialized, she said, "Ummmm, there's nothing here."

Rogan chuckled to himself as he gently disentangled her from his arms and took her by the hand for her to swim of her own volition. He pointed to the shore just in sight of where they were. "The land here is very close, and Crurals are constantly in these waters."

At this, Santi laughed as hard as Rogan had earlier. "I would think so! If my bearings are correct, we are at Rehoboth beach. It's a popular destination. I imagine the Crurals would be like ants at a picnic here."

Rogan made an indistinguishable noise, as if what she said corroborated his experience with the Crural ant. She still wasn't sure, however, how they were at the kinship. She was about to ask when their leisurely swim took a sharp dive and Rogan let go of her hand.

"Ok, follow me. It is tight." He then slid into a slit in the rocky bottom of the ocean shelf. It looked like nothing, as if he disappeared into the rock, into a crevice that was just barely wide enough for his broad shoulders to fit through easily. Santi slid in with plenty of room to spare and slowed down as her eyes adjusted to the complete darkness. Rogan, sensing her hesitation, flicked his tail directly in front of her outstretched hands that were groping to find orientation. "Just hold on to me. Do not worry. It is safe, though it can be startling your first time down."

Santi grabbed ahold of his tail, right at the junction where the end of the tail met the top of the wide expanse of fin. This was only the second time that she could remember that she had touched his tail and was again surprised that it wasn't slimy like a fish. Santi smiled to herself remembering what he said to her when they were children: "That is because I am not, in fact, a fish" She held on as her eyes slowly adjusted and Rogan continued to dive slowly between the two walls of rocks.

A dedicated Crural might be able to find the path they were taking, but Santi figured the kinship had safeguards in place to ensure they were never found. As her pupils dilated larger and larger, she could see that the path they took seemed fairly innocuous, as if they were merely taking a stroll through a narrow chasm. After they dove about ten feet and Santi noticed a slight increase of light, Rogan stopped and gestured towards a stone wall. "After you."

She scowled at him, knowing she was being messed with. Rogan smiled and said, "It is merely a trick of light and shadow. Swim directly forward."

It had been eleven years since they met, and they had only been reunited for a little over a week, and yet if there was anyone she would blindly trust, it was Rogan. Santi swam forward. As she reached the place where she would run directly into the floor of the tunnel, Santiago kicked forward without hesitation and passed right through.

Once on the other side of the opening, Santi smiled, shocked, and turned to look up at Rogan. As she did, her new perspective combined with the barely visible light from the top of the chasm. Santi could see that the cavern opening was actually very large. She chuckled; it was large enough for three of her to fit in sideways. She smiled delightedly and gestured Rogan to follow and exclaimed, "Such a carefully placed opening to keep out unwanted Crurals. So clever!"

Rogan swam abreast of her and said, "It is a good thing you are wanted then." He took her hand led the way.

It wasn't like they had never held hands. One of them was always pulling the other along, but this time… this time she wanted it to mean something. She thought it might.

When they reached the end of the tunnel, they took two sharp right turns and swam through a small, dark gap into a bright, massive, lively kinship. From her vantage point high above, Santi could take in the whole scene. Built entirely within the cave, the kinship was an area of about a square mile. Santi did some quick math and figured the entire kinship was about four miles around the perimeter of the cave. Having only Rogan's small kinship for comparison made this kinship seem like a bustling metropolis.

As they made their descent towards the floor of the cavern, Santi was completely distracted as they passed home after home carved out and built directly into the walls. Rogan nearly had to pull her along as she gawked and dawdled, taking in all the wonderfully new sights but contributing in no way to progressing their journey. She knew it was not proper, but she couldn't help looking inside the wide openings of each shelter. Many were empty as the inhabitants were already down on the floor amongst the crowd, but every once in a while, she passed a home with a family inside. In one, a mother was getting her pups ready for the show; in

234

another an old Serra dam sat in a comfy looking chaise lounge next to a younger dam, the pair deep in conversation. Each dwelling was uniquely decorated and comfortably welcoming. Rogan made a noise to suggest Santi was peeping more than decorum allowed.

She focused her examination instead on the approaching kinship floor. They had nearly reached the bottom at this point, and Santi could see that this was definitely more city-like than Rogan's kinship. Suddenly Santi wanted to see every kinship in every clan in the ocean. "Are all the kinships so different?" she asked in awe. "So different and remarkable?" She gestured with her free hand to the giant cave and continued without waiting for an answer. "The homes here are all in the walls of the cave, and the rest of it is on the floor. Kind of like a downtown area." She laughed. "Literally!"

Rogan disregarded most of what she was saying, used to her Crural comparisons, and placed his arm around her shoulders in a way he never had before. "They are all quite different. I would love to take you all over the ocean and show you."

Santi looked up at him as a flutter ran through her stomach. She wanted to kiss him. She wanted to stop swimming and kiss him hard, even though everyone from the city could see them from below. But they hadn't taken that step in their relationship, and Santi wasn't sure how to make it happen.

But her Ku betrayed her.

Rogan stopped swimming and pulled her firmly towards him, wrapping his arm around her waist. Then he kissed her soundly, deliberately, and without question about his intentions.

Santi forgot everything about Kaifee's kinship below, the shelters all around them, and the ocean in general as she sank deep into their kiss. She placed her hands on his waist, feeling the solidness of his sizable muscles in her small hands before sliding them up to his back. Their kiss lasted only a moment, but it was heavy with implications of more to come.

Suddenly, he pulled away. Santi hadn't had her Ku open to the activity around her, and she didn't know what had grabbed his attention. He looked at her with pure joy in his eyes before saying, "They are starting now."

Santi gave him one nod before they began swimming again. They settled down into the very center of the city. It was set up with rows of seating in a circular amphitheater with a raised dais in the center. "Theater in the round!" Santi clasped her hands together as they took their seats on stone benches. "I love it!"

The play began and they were well into the story before Santi realized she hadn't been paying attention in the slightest. Her mind was so preoccupied. After being underwater nearly a month now, things were moving along almost as if she belonged. She was going back to college in a few weeks, but she had been enjoying every moment of her time underwater.

Rogan sat next to her, watching the stage, consumed by the entertainment in front of him, but all she could think was how warm his arm pressing against hers was in contrast to the water around them. Even the scales on his forearm were warm, smooth, firm, and comforting. Santi wanted to kiss him again.

Now is not the time.

Her hand moved up to touch the starfish on her right cheek as she marveled for the millionth time that she had lived through her encounter with Sully and the Sirens. She only hoped her face wouldn't be too scarred. Just then, Rogan reached up and took her hand gently off her face, kissed the back of her hand quickly, then held it on his lap. He was constantly telling her not to worry about her face, that she was beautiful no matter how the scratches healed. She wondered what their future might hold. After she was finished with college, after Rogan decided where his future was going, anything could happen.

Abruptly Santi's attention was drawn to the stage. A beautiful young Serra dam arrived on the scene. She floated down from the "backstage" area, which was a large black canopy suspended above the stage where all the louriers went when they weren't performing. The dam's tail was the most elaborate and gorgeous thing Santi had ever seen. It was a rainbow of colors, every color imaginable swirling around her tail and arm scales. Santi leaned forward. The costume tail had been made of scraps of cloth that looked to be tied around the lourier's own tail so that the rainbow of colors all moved independently in the water. Santi watched the scene, rapt with interest, but realized she was too far into the play without understanding what was happening.

"Rogan?" She closed her Ku off to the performers so she wouldn't interrupt them and just held his Ku in hers. "Why are they being so mean to that small Serra?" She was aghast as the other performers on the stage threw rocks at the pup. However old the player was, she was clearly portraying a pup. "Who is she?"

Rogan didn't seem concerned that she didn't know who the character was and must have felt her attention was not on the play. Maybe he was even distracted by some of the same thoughts that were keeping her distracted. He responded patiently, "That is Ocean Mother Yemri. She was the most beautiful Serra ever to swim the ocean. However, she was an awful Mother, selfish, foolish, and greedy. She was known for her rainbow tail, unparalleled beauty, and for almost single-handedly ruining the ocean during her reign."

"What did she do?" Santi was fascinated. She knew the name Yemri from her lessons as a child but could only remember that she was Sariah's daughter.

"She abandoned the ocean. Left her reign to hide in a cave while Sirens attacked and killed everyone. She left no leadership, no guidance, and no hope of recovery. It was because of her that the Ocean Mother title is not passed down from mother to daughter. The Balams had to find someone to take her place. She was truly terrible."

"That's awful! How could someone in such an important position be so selfish? Just... just run away like that?"

She thought it over as she watched the entertainer on stage. A cavern began caving in on all of the other louriers. The Serras were shouting and crying about the tunnel collapse and someone said, "Where is the Ocean Mother? Why will she not help us?"

The lourier playing Yemri, now represented as an adult, fled the stage.

"Help us, Ocean Mother Yemri, help!" a small pup was crying out. But Yemri remained offstage as everyone on stage was crushed to death.

Santi found her mind drifting again, and she missed the lesson the play was portraying while she sat, deep in thought. Yemri was young when Nephira died and left her in charge of the ocean. Maybe she wasn't suited for such a large responsibility at such a young age, but surely she must have gotten the hang of it eventually. The dam in the play was an adult; clearly Yemri was the Ocean Mother for many years before she ran away.

She didn't learn in all that time?

When the play was over, Santi was left feeling awestruck by the experience and bewildered by the story. She didn't want to leave Kaifee's kinship unless it was to see other new and amazing sights under the ocean. She wanted to learn it all, see everything, and experience the entire ocean. She looked forward to being able to come back and see even more on her next visit.

~

Now Santi completely understood Yemri's decision to abandon her impossible responsibilities. She put her hand to her cheek, remembering the scratches Zitja had inflicted, glad there was barely a noticeable scar.

But unlike Yemri, I am going to follow through no matter how hard it is.

Watching the louriers was the first time Santiago was truly awestruck by a sight under the ocean—besides the mere existence of mermaids in general—this was the second.

Santi stared wide-eyed as a line of Serras, ready to start the journey to the tournament grounds, swam off the edge of the Daris Island towards a massive blue whale. They boarded two buses fixed end to end and tethered beneath the massive animal. The first bus in line was a yellow school bus, whose wheels, windows, and entire front end were missing. The nose of the next bus was fixed right up against the back of the school bus, *Chicago Transit Authority* emblazoned along the side above an advertisement for a romantic comedy Santi hadn't seen.

This had Santi on the edge of laughter.

But what she saw next made it all spill out. A family of four cruised past her, towed along by two swift sharks as parents and children sat snugly inside of a bathtub.

"Rogan!" Santi was fit to burst with joy. "This is hilarious!" She couldn't even take in all that was going on around here. "Amazing! Ridiculous! Absurd! More adjectives I can't even think of!" She held on to his arm for leverage as she twisted and turned on the spot. There were the traditional modes of transportation: seaweed slings tied to dolphins and massive shells holding two or three Serras fixed behind sharks or dolphins; and off towards the left edge of the island, Santi saw a queue of couriers loading old, young, and less-abled Serras into their slings. Santi knew Merrek must be amongst them, but she didn't have a chance to spot him before she was jostled roughly on the back by the throng of people coming behind them.

"Excuse me," came a gruff voice. "Please keep moving."

The area had started to thin out as everyone began the caravan towards the tournament grounds, led by the lumbering blue whale and his harnessed busses. Santi, Rogan, and their group of guards swam off the edge of the island and made their way towards their mode of transportation. Santi was almost giddy to find out how they would be traveling. In what unique contraption were they going to spend the next two days of travel?

What she saw did not disappoint. She saw a small green Volkswagen Beetle. It was an old model from sometime in the sixties, Santi guessed. The glass of the windows had been removed and in its place were four different flags, probably taken from shipwrecked vessels. Santi could only see the flags from Greece, Portugal, and a red, yellow, and green flag she didn't recognize. The fourth window was covered by something she was sure wasn't a country's flag but an important piece of fabric nonetheless. The front and back windows were left open to allow the water to move through the vehicle without dragging. Santi laughed. "We're going to be traveling in a bug. This is awesome."

But that wasn't even the most impressive part. Fashioned to the front of the Beetle were ten giant fish, each double the length of a man and nearly four times as large, secured in two rows of five each. It looked like a dog-sled team for some sort of underwater Olympic event. Santi couldn't help but squeal. "Are those marlins?" She clapped her hands together.

"I do not remember their actual names, let alone what you would call them on land, but we call them pace fish. They are the fastest in the ocean. I actually cannot believe they are giving us the honor of traveling this way."

"What do you mean?" Santi cocked her head to the side.

"These fish are different. Dolphins and sharks and other… what do you call them?" Rogan thought quietly for a way to explain. "We call them KuCores. They are more like you and I than fish."

"Oh, mammals!" Santi said, "Like whales and seals and such."

"Yes, exactly. Mammals. We can connect and ask permission. We have an arrangement and a respect for one another. The average fish, we do not. These marlins? They are more like servants. They do not have an understanding of the role they are playing or the help they are providing. In return they ask for nothing, and generally we give them no services in return as we do with mammals. It is generally frowned upon to use them for couriering."

"I am surprised they would have us traveling this way, then," Santi said. "Why do you think that is?"

"We will arrive the soonest. These fish are the fastest in the ocean. We will arrive before the rest of the convoy."

Santi rolled the information around in her mind as one of her guards opened the door for her. "Have a good trip, Santiago," the buck smiled at her.

"Thank you." Santi nodded towards him.

Since Krell was put in charge, Santi seemed to run into an increasing number of power-hungry, more-brawn-than-brains type of Sentinel, but the opus was still full of genuine Serras who hadn't lost their impeccably polite upbringing. Santi was used to the latter from her early experiences with Amed and was glad to see she held no prejudices against them despite her more recent experiences with some meathead Sentinels.

Santi and Rogan entered the vehicle to find that it had been completely hollowed out of everything that made it a car and was transformed into a remarkable and comfortable space. The entirety of the interior had been padded and upholstered so that it looked almost like a small padded room. The four side windows weren't even recognizable as the walls were covered with a wave of blue silk, save for a small seam where the door closed tightly. On the floor of the car was a donut shaped seating bolster that ran around the perimeter. When the door shut, the interior looked seamless, save for the open front and back windows.

"I guess being a prisoner is not so bad after all," Rogan said, pulling her in and squeezing her tightly.

Santi nodded agreement and nestled into him.

Just as they were settling onto the cushion and resting against the back wall of the car, the door opened to the right of them one more time.

Krell entered the cozy blue bubble and the illusion burst. He settled himself onto the bolster directly across from them, his back to the marlins. Now their view would be Krell's scowling mug the entire journey.

Rogan curled up his fin and Krell pulled his in tight, as well, so that neither of them looked particularly comfortable. As soon as the door shut again, the marlins began their journey, taking off swiftly and gliding the entire vehicle smoothly into the open ocean.

"This must be your personal traveling vessel," Santi guessed.

Krell looked up from the jellyfish in his hands as if just noticing them. "It is."

Rogan looked at her, a newfound bond of solidarity formed between them. "Well, that answers that," he said. Krell was the reason the marlins were put to work when it was frowned upon; Krell didn't care about flouting convention.

Krell resumed what he was doing, paying them no more attention. Santi stifled a chuckle as Krell connected to the jellyfish—turning it a glowing blue—put his message inside, and sent it off through the front window before absorbing himself with something from his satchel. It was all very Crural of him to ignore the people in the car with him and instead send messages and do work.

How similar Crurals are to the worst Serras.

Santi mentally shriveled in upon herself. Two days in Krell's company was not something she found desirable in the slightest. What would they even talk about? Or were they all going to pretend the other didn't exist for the entire journey?

Suddenly, Santi sat up straight. If they had to be his guests, then she was going to make the most of this undivided audience until she got what she wanted from him or they were kicked out and forced to travel by other means.

She leaned forward. "Krell," Santi said by way of launching into verbal battle.

"Hmmmm," was all he responded, though he looked at her impassively.

"Though you fail to believe that I cannot kill Zitja, fine, you will see. But I have to ask why we do not just imprison her?"

"She is in our captivity now."

She was annoyed, knowing he was going to be difficult through the entirety of this conversation.

"You know what I mean. Why don't we just keep her in prison? For eternity? She is the only Siren with the

244

inability to be killed. With her in captivity, we can be rid of the Siren problem. If the rest were killed, she would be the only Siren left, and we will have her in confinement."

Krell merely looked at Rogan in a way that suggested he should get his dam in line. Santi scowled further. Crural or Serra, some men always thought women should be tamed.

Rogan only stared in defiance. Santi appreciated that he said nothing even more than if he had defended her. This was a battle she wanted to have, and Rogan's interjection—even at her defense—would further illustrate to Krell that she was only capable because Rogan allowed it.

"Zitja has been in captivity before," Krell sighed in exasperation.

The only indication that Rogan was even listening was a slight tightening of his muscles. Santi was surprised to realize that Rogan didn't know this fact about Zitja.

"In fact," Krell continued, more interested now in the conversation once he saw that he had information Santi did not and he could put her in her place. "Zitja was imprisoned at the old fortress in Nephira's original stronghold." He paused and then said deliberately, "For two hundred years." He looked smug. "You see how well that worked."

This had the effect Krell was hoping for. Santi was thoroughly surprised and sufficiently silenced.

"Sirens are still transforming through the ancient curse." He pointed a nasty accusing finger at her. "You need to do your duty. Kill Zitja. Dissolve the curse."

She wanted to lunge at him. She thought might kill him. "I cannot kill Zitja, and even if I could, how do you know that would dissolve the curse?" For a moment she had forgotten that Serras were still being transformed by the curse, but how did anyone know that killing Zitja would also break the curse? They all thought she could kill Zitja, and that turned out to be wrong, too. "I bet you a million bucks that will not work!" she exclaimed.

Krell was truly stunned by this outburst, but not for the reason Santi wanted him to be. "Why would I need a million bucks?" He looked at Rogan in a way that showed genuine confusion.

Santi rolled her eyes and looked at Rogan, who was equally as confused. With no concept of currency, minimal understanding of gambling, and no notion of the slang for money, it sounded to them like Santi was offering Krell a million Serra men to prove her point. She sighed and sat back against the padding and closed her eyes.

Santi closed off her Ku and remained motionless. Without giving off any sign that she was doing anything other than pouting about losing the argument, Santi very gently connected just to Rogan. "Don't move. Don't react as though we are communicating at all. We are doing this my way now, and forget about Serra courtesy."

A flutter in his Ku was the only indication he made to show he was in agreement. Santi leaned away from Rogan, curled up against the other door. The padding was comfortable, and she curled up as though she would go to sleep, defeated and exhausted from her encounter with Krell. She hoped he was convinced of his victory.

"We have to do something," Santi said. "Krell is literally blind with power. The truth means nothing, and reason is beyond him." Santi thought for a moment, completely still. "Rogan? Where is Yazi in these decisions? Why does it seem as though Krell has taken over?"

Rogan was motionless beside her, their only contact being where their hips touched. "I have been worrying the same thing as of late. I have an honest fear that he has usurped the ocean from her."

Chapter 13

Yemri

Yemri ran her hand down the naked white bone that reached high into the water above her. The Ular—a name for the few types of whales Serras have relationships with—had been dead somewhere from seven months to a year. Yemri wasn't exactly sure how long it took for the fish, crabs, and other scavengers to clean the flesh off a whale, but Loramn, the head Horp, said now was the time to harvest the bones. Any longer and the same vultures that cleaned the bones would begin to literally eat them, and then they would become too weak to be useful.

"How will you get these back to Daris, Loramn?" Yemri asked, still awed at the impressive size of the bones. She imagined all the possible items the graggers could build with these.

When Loramn didn't answer right away, Yemri looked at him. His Ku felt sheepish, and he wrung his hands as if he wouldn't answer. Finally he said, "Well, they are very large and heavy, you see.... And from here in the Hatu'anu it will take a while to get to Daris. So... We... we have to tie them beneath an ular. To travel the distance."

"Oh!" Yemri squeaked. "That is grimly ironic."

"Indeed, Mother."

At that moment, Nanti'ouato arrived at her side looking remarkably frail. Yemri wasn't sure who was older, Nanti or Nhori—though sometimes Yemri thought Nhori was immortal—but either way, the two dams were older than most Serras in the ocean.

"Nanti'ouato, thank you for letting us harvest these bones from your clan. I know you have rights to them first, and I am sure you could use them for your ever growing population."

"It is fine," Nanti said genuinely. "True, it is a rare opportunity that we are able to find them but Daris and Tipua are in need, and we are happy to help. I believe the NorMer have staked a claim to some of the smaller tail bones, as well." She looked at the giant array of stark white pillars still forming a neat skeleton, thinking.

"Nanti'ouato?"

"IImmm?" She was looking at the bones longingly, and Yemri worried she truly did need them but was acquiescing to Yemri's authority. Yemri shrugged. It was probably about time, though she still felt awkward. "I have a question for you before everyone arrives for our council meeting."

Nanti looked at Yemri seriously and kindly. "Of course, how may I help? Though, I must tell you, almost everyone is already here. We are just waiting for Efren."

"Oh, excellent. I would like to get started." Yemri said, but in truth, she didn't want to get started as much as she wanted to get finished. Leading meetings of the Cor was not something she enjoyed.

But what do I enjoy nowadays?

"This will be quick, I think. I was just wondering what the OnaKu is? Maatis mentioned it."

"Muleki is the one to ask about that."

Yemri decidedly did not want to ask Muleki about anything. He wasn't easy to talk to, and she was tired of appearing uninformed in front of him. She had chosen to ask Nanti specifically because Nanti was very kind. Besides, Yemri had thought OnaKu was from Hatu'anu.

"And why should I ask Muleki about it?"

"OnaKu is a kinship in his clan. He will have more specific information."

Yemri wondered how to press the issue without seeming pushy. "Oh," she said sounding casual. "I do not need specifics, exactly, I do not even know what the OnaKu is enough to ask specifics."

"I can help you then," Nanti said kindly, and Yemri breathed a relaxed sigh. "It roughly means Only Ku or With One Ku. It is a kinship that did not learn the language. They broke off from Hatu'anu right after Maatis' death and have moved to the borders of Najilian." Nanti turned to Yemri as she warmed to the topic, her eyes and Ku earnest. "They kept with the old ways. Only Kus. No words."

Yemri was immediately interested. "I thought Nephira said that everyone had to learn the language? You allowed them not to, why?"

"This happened in between Maato's death and my appointment as balam. They went to the Najilian to seek approval and protection from Muleki. They were extremely fearful about the direction the Hatu'anu was taking during Maato's time. Muleki gave them special permission, and Nephira agreed. She felt preserving our history in that way was important."

For some reason, Yemri was filled with excitement. She couldn't put her finger on it, but she knew this was important. It seemed she would have to speak to Muleki about this after all. "I cannot believe I have not heard of them before."

"The clan stays rather private about it so there is no intrusion from outsiders and therefore, no language brought in. Although those in OnaKu are free to roam the ocean and many of them do speak the languages, they still refrain from speaking about where they are from."

Yemri thought for a moment. "I like that, for the preservation, but it seems like the Maato with their secrecy. I do not like that."

"Pup!" Nanti looked at her, shocked, "I am sorry. I mean, Mother. OnaKu is the farthest thing from the Maato you will ever find!" Nanti's Ku was filled with an unidentifiable peace. To Yemri, it was like the warmth of lying in bed with her mother early in the morning.

Had that all just come from the thought of OnaKu?
Yemri had to go there.

"It is fine, Nanti'ouato. Just a few months ago you were calling me pup. And I am a pup, after all. Anyway," she rushed on, feeling awkward and not wanting to talk about it anymore, "I will ask Muleki. It seems I have a lot to ask everyone about."

Nanti placed her hand on Yemri's heart. "You will get there. Do not be discouraged. Even the great Nephira had her struggles and felt like a failure, and her mother, I hate to admit, was worse in the beginning."

"That may be true, but Nephira is known as the greatest Ocean Mother we have ever had. It is hard to be in her wake."

"But she got there. And so shall you. And your daughter, and then hers afterwards."

Yemri blanched. She had not thought about having a daughter. In her entire nine years of life, she had never thought about her future in that manner. It was a topic she hadn't considered, but she knew she was still too young to think about it now.

Do I even want to have children?

"Efren!" Yemri exclaimed, happy for the reprieve from her thoughts and the intense conversation. "Welcome! We are happy to see you."

After greetings were exchanged, and Efren and his companions were settled, Nanti gestured away from the carcass back towards the kinship. "I suggest we have the meeting just a few miles away." She smirked in a knowing way that lit up her face. "It will be fitting that since we are having this meeting in the Hatu'anu to collect the ular bones, we should hold our meeting at Yoval."

Yemri did not know what Yoval was, but everyone else seemed to appreciate the significance. Yemri wondered if she would ever know what anything was or if her entire reign would be spent trying to figure everything out.

A mile swim wasn't a long one, but Yemri figured they might as well not waste the time. Once they started making their way, Yemri jumped into her agenda, "I have learned something startling and I am not quite sure what we should do about it."

It took a moment for the balams to stop talking amongst themselves and turn their attention to Yemri. They swam in a rather tight group with Nanti leading the way at the front, Yemri on her left side. Tope and Freydis swam above the group, and Muleki, Efren—the new balam for Tipua—and Nhori brought up the rear. On both sides of Yemri and Nanti were Yemri's personal guards, Tammin and Forcer, with the balam's personal sentinels surrounding the entire group. In all, they made for a substantial group, and Yemri hoped whatever Yoval was it was large enough for them all.

When she felt the attention of the balams, Yemri revealed her new knowledge. "I have spoken with Zitja."

"What!" came Tope's voice booming in her Ku from above. "Who…" but he trailed off and Yemri knew he had been going to ask who gave permission for such a dangerous visit before remembering that Yemri didn't need to ask for permission anymore.

"She told me about Nephira's final curse."

"What do you mean, *final* curse?" Freydis asked, and Yemri was pleased that for once someone else was playing catch up.

"It appears that when Nephira went to speak to Zitja that final time, before her death, Nephira cursed Zitja once more."

"Oh, Nephira!" Nhori said. Yemri knew that the two old dams had been good friends, and it was probably comforting to hear something new about someone she cared about, even if that information was a taint on her character. That Nephira would curse her own daughter twice must have been surprising.

"What was the curse?" Efren asked.

Yemri enjoyed the last moment of actually knowing more than these older, wiser, and smarter Serras before she said, "Only a member of Zitja's family—blood family," she added specifically for Tope, who was Zitja's brother in Bonding only, "will be able to kill her."

There was a small gasp from Freydis, but Nhori spoke quietly, "That answers some questions I have been presented with from Sentinels." She mused on that piece of information for a bit.

Yemri was tempted to ask what questions the Sentinels had been asking, but she would have to do so later because she still had more to reveal. "She has killed Tullus, so it appears that I and Zyler are the only blood relations left."

"I cannot believe this," Efren said. "What remarkable and ghastly news."

"We already learned this," Muleki said with a touch of exasperation.

"What?" Efren asked, shocked, and Freydis echoed Efren's surprise.

Muleki had the decency to look embarrassed as he amended, "I mean we just learned of it when Zitja was captured. We learned that Yemri has to be the one to kill her." He became adamant. "It has been my position since then that Yemri needs to be done with her right way. It should already be finished." Then as if embarrassed again for his determination to have a small pup kill someone he added, "It will be great for your reputation as a new and young Ocean Mother to finally end the Sirens once and for all."

Yemri took in a deep breath. "There is still a little more," Yemri said meekly. The next bit of information sounded ludicrous, and she wasn't even sure she believed Zitja or if the balams would believe her. "Zitja said that she will live forever."

"What do you mean?" Nhori asked. "You said that you can kill her."

"What I mean is that she will not die of old age or anything like we will. If I do not kill her, she will never die."

She didn't believe what she was about to say but she also knew it wasn't good that she was constantly disagreeing with Muleki, so she said, "You are right, Muleki. I need to kill her soon. It is the only answer."

This seemed to throw him off guard. She felt his Ku falter as the defensiveness he was building slipped away. She turned over her shoulder to look at him. His penumbra was glowing a pleasant blue. In fact, they all were. The news had brightened everyone's spirits. It seemed to be the answer they were waiting for. Only Yemri felt uneasy about it. Murder was a tough shell to swallow as a nine-year-old.

When she looked forward again, she was startled, immediately halting her strokes. Her tail hit Efren in the face.

"I am sorry!" she said to him then began her swim again as she asked, astonished, "What is that?"

Nanti smiled, pleased that Yemri was impressed. "That is Yoval."

Yemri had traveled the entire ocean many times over with her mother and Nephira so she assumed that during her years of visiting clans she had seen everything under the surface.

She was wrong.

Yoval was unique, massive, and breathtaking. There was nothing but open water all around, save for a massive boulder protruding from the depths. Set on top of the large boulder was a stark white circle of curved whale rib bones. The bottom of the rib—the thicker part—curved out towards them and rested on top of the rock. The rib then made a dramatic curve inward before the final bend of the bone jutted the same direction as the bottom, with the tips peaking above the water.

"It must look like the sun if you looked down on it from above," Yemri said thinking of the pointed spears protruding in a circle.

Nhori chuckled. "It is a good thing the Crurals cannot fly or we would be given away."

"Thank Nephira their legs keep them firmly on the land," Efren said, equally entranced by the sight.

As they swam closer, Yemri could see the small, tightly woven thongs of leather that tied one bone to the next. The weaving was so secure, so precise, that Yoval was a safe and well-built edifice.

"Why was this built? Because of the Sirens?" Yemri asked, thinking that it must have taken more than twenty years just to gather the materials.

"Over a hundred years ago, this area lived in harmony with the sharks." Nanti paused as if to tease and warn the group. "This is a heavily shark infested area!" She gave a small smile and proceeded with her explanation. "At first it started as a small wall against one side of the boulder resting on the ground down there." Nanti gestured to the earth at the bottom of the boulder.

Yemri looked at the ocean floor beneath them. It was far below, just breaching the darkness.

"It was hard to live in the depths—these were primitive times you know, before the use of the illuminating bacteria we have today—and the cold was not unlivable, but it was unpleasant. And then they were blessed with a rare opportunity."

They swam closer to Yoval until they were only a few strokes from the great white wall. Yemri wanted to touch the incredible wall when they were close enough.

Everyone was entranced by Nanti's story. "An ular made its final resting place right by Yoval—of course that was before it was named, and kinships did not usually have a name—and they felt it was a sign to expand and move closer to the surface. After that, it only took a few more trips to other fallen ulars over the years to complete the circle."

Yemri knew how rare it was for a whale to land in its final resting place high enough that Serras could scavenge its skeleton. Usually they perished in wide-open oceans and fell to depths to which even the bravest Serras dared not venture.

When they finally reached the gates, Yemri asked, "So what keeps them from being scavenged upon? Like the bones we are taking now? If they sit there longer, they will become too weak to build with."

"We keep the scavengers away. Our horps' only job is to keep this fortification intact and clear of anything that would do it harm."

Yemri sent Nanti a pleasant beat of her Ku and examined the circular wall closely. The bottom and top portion of five of the ribs had been cut before they bent so that when the gate opened, the curves would not run into each other at the sides. It was a massive doorway in the middle of the otherwise flawless wall. As the large party arrived, the bone gates slowly swung open. When it was close, Yemri stuck out her hand and felt the gate's smooth, hard, yet porous bone slide along her fingers. Nothing was getting through that wasn't invited.

Nanti finished her explanation. "When the Sirens became an ever-present threat, they fortified the perimeter with Sentries."

"So Sentinels are on permanent watch here?" Muleki asked, and it seemed strange to Yemri that he wouldn't know something like this, considering he was unofficially in charge of the Sentinels.

"Not Sentinels," Nanti'ouato replied. "Sentries that are members of the kinship and have trained themselves."

"Interesting," Muleki mused, and Yemri wondered what he could possibly be thinking. Was he applauding their ingenuity or irritated that they had trained themselves?

When they emerged through the gateway, Yemri was caught off guard once again. Kinships were always made into the natural geography of the land. Shelters were made out of driftwood and twine, caverns and weeds, and occasionally carved out of cliff sides or built into the bay. Even the arrangement the Maatis lived in did not suffer much Serra disturbance aside from cleared brush. It was wholly unheard of to *create* an entire kinship. Even the tunnels and caverns she had dug out of the bottom of the island of Daris was an innovative concept that some thought would not work. Looking around Yoval gave her many ideas about all the possibilities that were open to them.

Yoval was made entirely of carved and engineered stone structures. Massive square pieces had been stacked on top of one another to create small shelters, grand buildings, and even decorative art throughout the kinship. Some were built right up against the whalebone, the gray stone contrasting pleasantly with the white whale bone wall. And all of it was neatly situated and organized inside the bone circle that did not seem large enough to contain it all. It was a veritable city made of stone, hidden in the shelter of ular bone.

It made Yemri wonder why, after the discovery of Daris, no one had tried to create cities or kinships like it since? Were those types of materials not available under water? Surely stone was, as well as the knowledge to build with it. She was bursting with the idea of building more from it, but she didn't know what.

They situated their group on benches in the exposed water in the middle of the kinship. The benches were arranged in a circle, carved elaborately with scenes of Serras building Yoval. The bench Yemri chose was adorned with a scene of the building of the gates and inlaid with gemstones.

She ran her fingers over the groove between rock and gem, from smooth to rough and back again. Maybe she could leave Daris and the responsibilities of Rule and live here.

The Cor sat in the circle on their benches, with the guards and Sentinels hanging back, looking more relaxed inside the walls of Yoval than they had been only minutes ago in the open water. Everyone was quiet and looked anxious to begin. Yemri felt the urgency to get the meeting over with and hoped it would begin soon, too.

Suddenly, she sat up straight and focused her attention. "Amicus," she said, placing her hand on her heart. She had forgotten that it was up to her to begin the proceedings.

After everyone had returned the gesture, she began, unsure of how one would typically start, since this was only her second meeting and the last one had sort of started on its own. Uncertain whether she was supposed to give some sort of welcome or official commencement, she jumped right in. "We must do something about the Maato. The things I saw were horrid. I know I made a mistake when we were there before, but I was worried about the safety of the dams and pups. Upon reflection, though, my conviction that they are not slaves to be used as the bucks see fit makes me realize we have to do whatever we can. I have been thinking, and I believe it is best that all the bucks have some sort of… What is the thing that Nephira did for the rebels she turned into Sirens?"

"A trial?" Tope answered. He presented it as a question, but they had already discussed this and the trial had been his suggestion.

"Yes!" She was angry for forgetting the word. She had practiced her whole speech and forgot the last word! "A trial for all of the bucks in the Maato. Especially Maatis. And the dams and pups will be freed."

"That is all well and good, Mother," Muleki said with less impatience than she expected. His Ku exuded no hostility and his penumbra was a calm blue. She felt a small wave of victory. She would have to be sure to agree with him more often because it made *him* more agreeable.

"But we had this opportunity already and you chose to leave without action. I cannot guarantee when—or if—we will be able to find them again," Muleki continued.

"I have to agree," Freydis said. "They will be hard to find. Harder now, probably. However, I am with you. Their treatment of dams is deplorable. The NorMer has taken in a young dam that escaped. Her stories of their treatment are reprehensible. I will not repeat them here."

Yemri did not know about this. She sat up a little straighter, bolstered by the support she was receiving for a change. "So we are agreed that we will find them again? That we will bring them to justice."

"I think it is a worthy cause," Tope said with fierceness. "I think seeing it all ourselves has changed minds. It was easy to ignore when the information was merely rumors and stories, but experiencing the horror myself has convinced me. It will be a challenge, but if we spread the word throughout the clans to be on the lookout for them, the strength of the multitude will get it done."

Yemri smiled widely—something she could not remember doing in a very long time—and breathed out.

"This will be good for our people. If we can bring them to justice, it will change the course of our history."

The mood around the circle was positive and electric. For once it seemed that they all agreed on a course of action and a solution to a problem.

"And after you kill Zitja," Muleki added, "you will be revered for the rest of time!"

Suddenly Yemri's heart sank. She thought she could do better than just killing Zitja, in truth. She had big—secret, but big—ideas after seeing the Siren in the caves transform back into a Serra. She looked up at the open skies above her to the sun shining down on them and breathed deeply.

The feeling of foreboding only intensified when Freydis added, "They will remember you for the wonderful things you have done for the ocean, truly," if she had stopped there Yermi might have been encourage, but she added something that made all of Yemri's possible enthusiasm turn bitter in her mouth, "and your uniquely beautiful tail!"

Chapter 14

Yemri

After Freydis' comment about Yemri's tail being so beautiful, the other balams joined in the fervor. It seemed she had rallied the group so thoroughly to her cause to get the Maato that they were all in the spirit to compliment and encourage her.

"I have seen the thing in the sky before, above the water, that looks just like your tail!" Nhori said. "Beautiful!" she said emphatically. Yemri was crushed; she thought of all Serras, at least Nhori would understand. "You can only see one because of a storm, but they are worth the trip up to the surface to see, for certain."

"What are the other items of business?" Yemri asked, changing the subject. "We should finish so that we can enjoy the beauty of Yoval." They quieted down and Yemri proceeded. "I had an idea after watching the Siren change back into a Serra. Maybe this is the way to go for Zitja. Maybe we can change them all back."

Nanti breathed water in and out slowly. They all knew about the changed Siren and were equally curious, but she could feel they were skeptical about having any control over it. "I am afraid anything KuVis-related is out of the question at this point," Nanti said. Yemri was too young to know a time when the water was teeming with KuVis—the energy that created power and magic, the magic that had put the curse on the Sirens and the enchantment on Daris. "Nephira and I tried to reverse the curse many times." Yemri could feel Nhori's Ku pulsing agreement, though if anyone could find Vis left in the ocean, it would be her.

Freydis made a sound of agreement. "Vis is gone. No point in trying to reclaim what is lost when there is so much more to be done."

"This thing you want to do is impossible," Muleki agreed. "But do not worry. Once Zitja is dead, your legacy will be peace and beauty instead of fear and war."

Suddenly Efren burst out, "Upinde mvua!"

Everyone looked at him.

He laughed at his folly and added, "I have been thinking about it since we last met, Yemri. It just came to me. That is what the people call it where I'm from. Before I was Balam, I was a Thaed. I spent so much time on land that I've seen several of them firsthand. Very beautiful."

Everyone agreed and spent just a tick too long looking at her tail. Yemri shifted uncomfortably, but before she could say anything, Tope brought the conversation around to follow up on old business from the Afiti.

Yemri sighed in relief at his distraction. She looked at her tail and wondered if every color in existence was contained in her shimmery scales. If she shifted or turned, there seemed to be more colors than before. It was a beautiful tail. Unique and mesmerizing.

She hated it.

Looking up into the blue sky above with the sun shining down, Yemri wished she were anywhere other than were she was, or who she was, doing the things she was doing. In that moment, she decided she would go see OnaKu. If nothing else, at least she would have a little quiet for a moment.

The next morning, Yemri was on her hard seat again, being ushered through the ocean. OnaKu was on the way from Yoval to Daris with only a minor detour, and as she sat in her palanquin being conveyed behind a team of dolphins, she sent out orders. "Pangor, have the retransformed Serra put in a chamber as a guest," she said, "and be sure that he is treated well."

Pangor looked at her from his swimming position next to her palanquin, hesitated a moment at the absurd request, then said, "Of course, Ocean Mother." And he quickened his stride to outpace the caravan so he would arrive at Daris before them.

"Your guest? Treated well?" Tope asked from beside her on the long bench fashioned into her giant clamshell.

"Well, yes." Yemri looked at him with confidence. "If I am going to find out how he changed back, I will need him to be comfortable and know that I am on his side. If he is treated badly, he will not want to share with me."

Tope looked at her with a pride in his eyes she had never seen before. "That is a very wise thing to do."

Yemri sat back and beamed bright blue.

The trip to OnaKu was long, but Yemri was glad they were making the short detour because the trip to Daris was much longer, and Yemri's bottom was getting tired of sitting on the hard plank. Maybe she would add a cushion for future long trips. Maybe she could reinvent the entire palanquin. Maybe enclose it and make it more comfortable for the long trips an Ocean Mother was endlessly taking.

Maybe she would revolutionize everything.

"Father, I have a lot of ideas. I want to be known for more than just my unique tail."

"I know, and you will. You have great ideas." He squinted his eyes at her. "You just have to be smarter about carrying them out, I think."

Yemri knew he was right, but it was hard when she and everyone around her second-guessed her every decision.

"We are here," Forcer said as the procession stopped.

Yemri looked around, but nothing stood out to her as a kinship. The grasses were high around them but not particularly dense. She could see between the blades of grass and thick stalks of plants. Small fish swam by, and sand and rocks covered the floor. It was lackluster in its uniqueness, and Yemri found herself feeling disappointed by the innocuousness of it all.

Muleki had accompanied them—feeling protective of his clan—and floated to her left side, Tope at her right, the guards and Sentinels treading in the background. None of

266

them moved, and Yemri stared at the forest of greenery in front of her. She was about to ask what they were waiting for when a small, old, and frail buck wove his way through the shrubbery and paused before them.

He was bent over, as if the weight of the ocean on his shoulders was too much to bear, and his tail was small and lifeless, though his Ku was the purest and most innocent Yemri had ever met. His penumbra glowed a bright light blue.

When he spoke, it was quietly and with such a gentle lilt to it that Yemri felt more at ease than she had since she was a pup just aware of her Ku. "Amicus," he said like the movement of the current, strong but quiet and nearly undetectable. "We are so happy to be blessed with the presence of our Ocean Mother. Thank you for coming."

"Amicus," the group responded, placing their hands over their own hearts.

Yemri added further, "Thank you for allowing us to come."

"I am Toc, the keeper of OnaKu. All that I ask is that you do not speak within the borders of our kinship. That is our only rule. But you will find that being HaruLingua will give you intuition for decorum, so do not worry if you are unsure of our ways." Toc went on, his little speech sounding rehearsed, as if he'd said it a thousand times before. "Many of us do speak your language and know the ways of the rest of the ocean, though a great many of us also have never left these borders from birth. We are allowed to speak if we wish, but not here. If you can agree to this, you are welcomed friends in perpetuity."

"We agree." Yemri spoke for the group, and the frail buck gestured them into the throng.

As Yemri followed, she watched Toc swim. Even while horizontal, he still had a curvature to his spine that made it impossible to see where he was going. As if old age had brought his head and fin closer to the ocean floor with the weight of the water. Yemri closed her eyes and followed behind with her Ku, trying to truly experience OnaKu with her whole heart. She felt him and each blade of kelp as she wove her way inside, already shedding off the troubles of the rest of the ocean.

Once through the forestry, Yemri was overcome with peace and tranquility so profound she felt as if her Ku were radiating warm sunshine through her body. Nothing seemed to matter, and all thoughts were forgotten. Yemri opened her eyes and sucked in her breath at the beauty of it all. The ocean floor was beautiful coral, anemones, sea whips, and fish of every shape and color: reds, oranges, blues, and purples created by both plants and animals. All this sat on a bed of green, surrounded from the outside by dozens of feet of tall kelp. It was gorgeous. Though not unlike other places Yemri had seen before, the addition of the complete peace and hundreds of Serras with open, honest, and compassionate Kus was a combination of marvel she hadn't experienced.

All around her, Serras went about their business. Pups played with the fish, hid amongst the coral, and slept in their mothers' arms. Dams and bucks carted large baskets filled with food or textiles or rocks and coral, took care of their young, and sat in silent meditation. Yemri saw middle-aged bucks sitting on the sand weaving colorful strands into large pieces of cloth. And through it all, every Serra glowed with a light, bright blue Ku.

She had learned this penumbra represented a Ku that was at its most content. She and her group all began to change from their usual aura coloring to the lighter—though not quite as bright—blue as the kinship members. Yemri had never seen so much of the same peaceful color in one place before. She never wanted to leave.

But she had to. They only had a short time to spare as they had no official business in OnaKu and had only detoured for Yemri's curiosity. So she would make the most of their short time and meet as many Serras of OnaKu as she could.

As if reading her mind—or maybe this was what a more in-touch Ku was like—a middle-aged dam with white hair greeted Yemri. Yemri noticed it was odd because her hair was not gray from old age but merely colorless on its own accord. It contrasted her brown skin—much lighter than Yemri's, but darker than Pangor's light pink skin—marvelously. The dam placed a hand on Yemri's heart. When Yemri returned the gesture, placing her hand over the leather band around the dam's chest, she almost said "amicus" out loud. She caught herself in time, but the dam could still sense the near *faux pas* and placed her other hand on Yemri's shoulder for reassurance. Yemri felt her Ku bursting with the acceptance coming from the dam. She was surprised to know immediately what emotion the white haired Serra was trying to convey. Yemri was not being judged for her near mistake, nor was she upset that Yemri almost broke their most sacred rule. She looked into the face of the dam. It was unreadable and expressionless as most Serras features were, but the love that radiated from her was remarkable.

Another Serra swam up to the two of them and placed his hand on Yemri's heart. She returned the gesture and noticed a large jagged scar across his chest that had healed poorly. She wanted to ask but did not know how to convey her thoughts. It did not matter because as she was thinking of how to communicate, she was flooded with thoughts of her mother. Why Yemri thought of her, she did not know, only that the feeling in her Ku was exactly the same as she used to feel in her mother's presence.

Sariah was gentle and pure and had the only white penumbra Yemri had ever seen in her life besides those of newborn pups. The purity and tenderness that radiated from Sariah at all times was exactly how Yemri's own Ku felt now. Just as quickly as she was reminded of her mother, she felt sad. But it wasn't her own sadness at the loss of her mother, it was being given to her. She looked into the older buck's eyes. He was sorry for the loss of Sariah. He was telling Yemri that he was sorry she had lost her mother, that he grieved for Sariah and for Yemri as well. She felt sorrow as if her heart was nestled in the back of their spine, low in the belly. She felt that sorrow, but she wasn't sad. It was just a message. Then it was gone, and she felt as light and happy as she had upon first arriving.

She tried to thank him. She wanted to thank them both for their kindness but didn't know how to express it. How had they done that? Made her know what they were feeling?

How did she express a thought?

Then she realized she had it right the first time. She was not expressing thoughts. She was expressing *feelings*. She filled her Ku up with the feeling of gratitude. Her stomach felt like it was full of air and would float away from her appreciative heart. When she had it just right, she sent it to them both, and they accepted it.

Yemri could have sat in that feeling forever. Did she really have to leave this place?

Just then, a buck with hair the color of fresh lava before it hits the water greeted her. He met her eagerly by placing his hand on her heart and when she returned the gesture, she felt a pounding in her chest so hard she thought she would burst with the happiness emanating from it. No, she realized. The happiness was not coming from her, it was coming from him. And then she realized further that although it felt like happiness, that was not quite correct. It was much more a feeling of eagerness. It was pride. He was very proud of something. She could feel him sending another emotion her way, but she could not identify it. It was a deeper pride than any she had felt before, but she didn't understand what it meant.

When the lava-haired buck reached out his hand, she took it immediately. She wanted to see whatever it was he was so proud of.

He took her to a cluster of coral that had grown very tall and wide. They swooped inside the purple and orange archway of the rocks, and what Yemri saw inside made her immediately understand the feeling she had received from him.

The reason Yemri had not understood the message he was trying to convey was because she had never experienced

271

the feeling on her own accord. She couldn't understand the meaning of the second-hand emotion without ever feeling it first-hand. This buck was proud of his family, of his Bondmate, and the product of their love.

Sitting on a massive cushion in the main chamber of their shelter was a small dam with yellow hair, and in her arms lay a sleeping pup. The pup was brand new to the world, and her purple scales still reached all the way to her neck. Yemri could see wisps of the bright orange hair, the same color as her father's. All around her glowed a bright white aura. The pup was placed gently into Yemri's arms, and she felt she better perch on the floor to stabilize herself. With tail tucked to the side, she sat on her bottom and stared intently at the small thing. The bundle was precious and valuable, and she hadn't held such a small pup since the day her brother was born three years ago.

She wasn't sure how long she stayed in their shelter, passing feelings between them like stories. The mother told Yemri about the difficult birth and how they thought they had almost lost their pup, but a dam in their kinship came and saved the tiny pup just in time. Through their stories, Yemri recognized Serras she knew by the feelings put into her Ku. The dam that came to help with the delivery was someone Yemri did not know, but Muleki had come right after the birth to offer congratulations. When the flame-haired father shared this, Yemri recognized Muleki's Ku by the passing of feelings. Muleki had a feeling of hardness and intimidation wrapped around tenderness and genuine care for others.

In this way, Yemri learned that each Ku was unique in a way she had not before realized, and that the OnaKu referred to each other by simply sharing the individual feeling of each Serra's Ku. She was fascinated.

She left their shelter and met with many more Serras, each of whom told her a story of their own in this same slow expression of feelings. She didn't always grasp their message, and she assumed, like the newborn pup, that her lack of understanding was because she could not empathize with them. Her lack of experience in speaking purely through Kus created a hole in her ability to understand others' hardships and victories.

Before she was ready, Tope found her playing with a group of pups and held out his hand for her to go. She didn't want to. She wanted to stay in OnaKu for the rest of her life. She wanted to live in the peace she found in her Ku, in the quietness, and in the small, personal interactions. But she pushed herself up off the sand and followed him through the crowd while they expressed their farewells.

When they reached the border of the kinship, Yemri looked through the forest of kelp and grasses with a heavy heart. Muleki led their group out, and as Tope was disappearing in the stalks, Yemri looked back one last time. The kinship was again going about their business, and Yemri watched everyday life pass for just a moment longer.

As she turned to leave, a remarkable penumbra caught the corner of her eye. She looked harder to see if it was possibly the newborn pup, but it wasn't. The outline was much too large as it made its way across the open field in the corner of the kinship. The pup was probably Yemri's age, with brown hair flowing down to her tail. Yemri wanted to meet her.

It was remarkable that someone that age still had a pure white Ku. Yemri instinctively began making her way towards the pup, but something caught her hand.

She turned to see her father kindly urging her out. She knew they had to go. Being Ocean Mother carried too much responsibility for her to waste her time. She had already spent a whole day here when she should have been headed to Daris to handle all her obligations there.

Yemri made her way through the outskirts of the kinship and back into the palanquin. No words were passed as Muleki and his Sentinels went their way, and Yemri, Tope, and her guards went theirs. Yemri sensed that no one wanted to speak and lose the delicious calm that had settled into each of them.

As they made their way home, Yemri pondered something that was tickling her mind. The OnaKu "spoke" of other Serras by sharing the feeling that Serra emitted in his or her Ku. It had been so clear to Yemri when Serras wanted to tell her about Sariah and Muleki. Those two gave others the same feeling in their Kus that they did in hers. Her mother's was a gentle grace and Muleki's confident tenderness. Every Serra that referred to either of these two shared the exact same feelings.

Yemri wondered what feeling she left in others' Kus. She hoped it was what an Ocean Mother should feel like.

Chapter 15

Yemri

By the time she reached Daris, the calming effect of OnaKu had vanished and was replaced by the overwhelming weight of her responsibilities. Not a fair trade, Yemri thought. But she eventually convinced herself it was better. In OnaKu, she only felt concern for the one person she was interacting with at the time she was with them. She wanted to help that Serra and their plight. With such deep connection to her heart, she saw only what was right in front of her. But outside of OnaKu, she didn't have to be so present and feel so deeply; she relied less on her heart and more on the words spoken to her. They came quick and effortlessly, all those words. It presented the ocean as a whole, and she worried about the greater good. She hadn't decided yet which was the *best* way to go through life, but she knew which way she *had* to.

Her first item of business was meeting with her guest to find out how he had broken the curse and how she could apply that to Zitja so that she could avoid having to kill her aunt. The entire Cor wanted to meet him and ask him questions, but Yemri thought that would be too overwhelming. Besides, whenever the Cor was around, she felt like just a pup and was all too aware of her mistakes. So as much as they all insisted they should come, Yemri insisted she go alone with just her guards to keep her safe.

She swam up to the room where the retransformed Serra was housed and paused. Two guards stood sentry on either side of the door. She assumed they were going to give her a hard time about going in, but they opened the door immediately upon her arrival. She scolded herself. She was the Ocean Mother. Of course they were going to let her in. As she glided into the room, she wondered when she would start expecting that Serras would yield to her authority instead of presume they were going to oppose her at every move. Besides, the guards were there to keep this Serra buck from leaving, not others from entering.

"Welcome, Ocean Mother," The blonde, medium-built Serra said. "Amicus."

He was friendly and looked so much like any other Serra—with no apparent residual side effects from his time as a Siren—that Yemri nearly forgot her manners as she stared at him just a moment too long. He had a grey tail, however, and she wondered if that might have been a result of the retransformation, though she'd have to do more research to be sure.

"Amicus," she said when she regained her composure. "And your name is?"

276

"Dorio," he responded eagerly. "Thank you for seeing me!"

Yemri was tempted to feel suspicious of his eagerness, but his Ku was genuinely earnest.

As she followed him to the back corner of his room, she was glad to see that he had been treated like a guest in her citadel, though his room was the most meager of accommodations. The sleeping cushion in the center was large enough to sleep on comfortably and was raised up on wooden planks so that it wasn't so close to the cold marble of the floor, but it didn't have grand pillars at each corner like hers, or even wood around the sides to keep the cushion from slipping around with the current. The walls were bare white marble, unlike most rooms, which usually had planted flowers or artwork adorning them, the floors, and the ceilings. The stark bareness left the room feeling rather impersonal. It looked just like what one could expect for a guest who was really a prisoner, Yemri mused.

She sat upon a crude stone lump—smooth on top and bottom—one of two that stood near a matching table. Though they were primitive, Yemri thought they actually looked quite lovely as a set.

"Would you like anything?" he offered genially, indicating the table, where a basket sat in the middle with a cage covering the top. Sitting inside were some carrots, apples, taro, and rolls of seaweed. A few grapes and smaller scraps of the kelp had escaped their bunch and were caught at the top of the cage.

"No, thank you. I would really like to talk with you, if I might."

"Of course!" he said. In his eagerness, he flicked his tail several times and had to grab a hold of the table to bring him back to a seated position. "I assume that after this I will be allowed to go home?"

Yemri had not thought that far ahead. She chided herself for only ever thinking of the move she was currently making and never about all the other moves it would take to complete a full plan. "I am not sure." She decided that was the best truth she could come up with. "I want what is best for you and every Serra. So let us just see what happens right now."

"Sure thing, Ocean Mother."

Yemri pitied him a bit. He was clearly desperate to resume his life, and he was acting with great deference, as though this was a trial and his fate would be sealed by this one conversation. Yemri had only come because of curiosity and to find out how to deal with her own problems. A wave of guilt washed over her, and she hoped he didn't guess the reason.

"I am wondering," she said casually, "how you turned back into a Serra. I have never seen it done before. I do not think anyone has ever done it. Yet you were able to break the enchantment. How?"

"I wouldn't say that I have broken it. No." He drew out the "no" for just a moment, mumbling to himself, before continuing. "I can still feel it inside me, just as I could while I was a Siren, but it's as if it doesn't apply to me anymore."

"It does not… apply?"

"Well, you see, I was not in the first wave of transformation that hit the waters, but my Bondmate was. She was very angry about the Crurals and the things Nephira

278

had done—or rather, had not done—to handle the problem. It was truly the only thing we ever disagreed about. We loved each other very much."

Dorio got lost in his memories for a moment, and Yemri could feel the intense sadness from his loss pushing deeply into her Ku.

"After she transformed, it was only a couple of days until it took me as well. I think the enchantment, from what I know about it, changes the holder of the Ku who does not feel sympathetic towards Serras. My Bondmate changed because she was angry and did not want to live as Serras lived anymore. She agreed with those who wanted vengeance and to live without their Kus. I transformed because I wanted to be with her. I wanted to be a Siren so badly that I no longer wanted to be Serra. And so I was not."

"That is it?" Yemri asked. She realized she didn't know how the curse worked, but also no one had ever explained it.

"I'm not sure I understand you," Dorio responded, and to be honest, Yemri didn't either.

"I mean, you changed into a Siren because you did not want to be a Serra? That is it?"

"The curse, as I'm sure you know, Ocean Mother, changes the bodies of any Ku that does not hold Serra values. My Bondmate didn't hold Serra values when she rebelled against Nephira and our ways. I didn't hold them when I wanted nothing to do with Serras and only wanted to be with her."

Yemri felt his Ku was kind and patient, but she felt foolish that he had to explain it to her. She should understand it all better than this. "So, then, what made you change back?"

"After I found her, we lived together again very happily… only, now we were Sirens. We found that living under Zitja's rule was not much different than Nephira's. She was diplomatic, just, and often kind. Sure, there was the terrorizing of Serras and Crurals, but I did not participate in that. I admit that it was often hard to keep myself from Singing. I did not know that I would be drawn to it so much. The Song has a power that pulls you in. It felt good. It felt right whenever I would sing. But that was not why I was a Siren. I was a Siren because I did not want to be a Serra. And that is really all the curse needed to keep me in its grasp."

"So you changed when you no longer wanted to be a Siren, then?"

His Ku became weighted down with such a profound sadness that it crowded the room to the brim. Yemri felt it so deep within her chest that it became her own sadness. Abruptly, she realized that he had no penumbra at all. She had never seen that before. This buck was an enigma in every way.

"During the fight with the Sentinels, when I was captured, there were a lot of lives lost on both sides. The carnage brought the sharks, as it always does. Both sides had to fear not only the other but also the bloodthirsty sharks. After all we had been through together, it seems so trivial that a confused animal would be what took her from me in the end."

"And so," Yemri clarified, "when you were telling me it was a mistake that you were in prison, what did you mean?"

"It was a mistake that I was in prison, yes, but even more, it was a mistake that I was a Siren. I felt the change coming as I realized I absolutely did not want to be a Siren. I changed right then."

Yemri wanted to say something, but she had asked all the questions she could remember, and she knew that she could not think of the right things to ask on her own. Tope and Nhori had discussed with her at length all the things she should ask, but these questions were the only ones that pertained to changing Zitja back, and that was all her mind could come up with.

"I have other family that I would like to be with for the rest of my days, now that my Bondmate is gone," Dorio said longingly. "I think it will not be long. I feel weak and tired inside. My light is going out."

Yemri nodded. She had heard that many Serras did not live long after their Bondmates died, and going through such a transformation not once, but twice, had to have taken its toll on him. "You may be with your family. I will have it arranged."

"Oh, thank you, Ocean Mother." He sprang from his seat and threw himself at her hands, clutching them tightly. "You will not regret it."

She was about to say something to comfort him when he interrupted her thoughts, frantically trying to seal their agreement with charm.

"Ocean Mother, you are truly as just and fair as you are beautiful." Dorio unwittingly began to undo all the good work he had done for his case. "I have never seen your tail's equal. It is truly remarkable, if I may say."

"You may not," she snapped, and left abruptly.

She swam without purpose, full of irritation and contemplation. His information about retransformation would not help her with Zitja, though she didn't quite know what to do with everything she had learned, either. The curse seemed both so strict and so fluid. Sariah had always said Nephira was reckless when using the KuVis and had not known what she was doing.

It seemed neither did the curse.

When Yemri emerged from Dorio's room, she floated over the balcony and pulled up short. The entrance of the citadel was a grand atrium in which Serras could easily swim to any level of the multi-level building and enter any floor through the open balconies. At the bottom of the atrium were all six balams, most likely waiting to hear what she had discovered. Yemri swam down from the fifth floor, but as she passed her personal and congregation chambers on the third floor, the balams noticed her and swam up to greet her. Yemri and the balams met in the middle, where they accosted her with a flurry of quick sentences and shouted questions.

"What did he say?" Efren asked above the rest, but it was too open of a question, and Yemri was feeling overwhelmed.

"About what?" she responded, agitated. "He said so many things."

"Why did he change back?" Efren amended his question. "How? How did he break the curse?"

"Did you learn how we could break the curse?" Nhori asked.

"Did he tell you anything we can use to defeat the Sirens? Did you learn any of their strategies?" Muleki asked eagerly.

"Strategies?" Yemri responded. She wanted to ask what kind of strategies they expected, but she already felt so stupid for not having an answer.

"What are their plans? Their weaknesses?" Muleki prodded further.

"What are we going to do with him now that you have spoken to him?" Freydis asked. "Surely he cannot stay here forever."

"Above all," Nanti added, "Efren's question is the most important. How did he change back?"

"I agree," Nhori jumped in. "We need to know if you learned anything that can be used to change the Sirens back into Serras."

Tope held up his hands and filled his Ku with deliberate calm. "Please, let her answer one question before moving on to another. Just give her time to respond."

Yemri felt smothered and claustrophobic. Though the group tried to wait patiently for her answers, she imagined them crowding closer and closer to her in their anxious curiosity.

"I… I asked him how he changed and… and…" She hadn't really asked any of the questions they were demanding answers for, so she just told them about her conversation with Dorio. About how his situation seemed to only apply to himself and they couldn't force anyone to want to be a Serra, which seemed the only way to change them back. She finished by saying, "And then I told him that he could go home to his other family."

"He most certainly cannot!" Muleki said indignantly. "He is a threat."

At this outburst, Tope calmed the group again and said patiently but pointedly, "Yemri, maybe Muleki and Nhori could interview Dorio? They have a lot of questions and a lot of knowledge about the curse that he might be able to answer."

"Yes." Yemri sighed in relief. "Yes. Maybe they should ask him."

Muleki and Nhori looked at each other for only a moment before they kicked their fins, quickly ascending up the atrium and over the balcony to the fifth floor.

Once they were gone, Tope continued, "Yemri, maybe letting him go home—basically letting him roam the ocean freely—isn't a good idea."

"No. No maybe you are right," Yemri answered, knowing she had given Dorio permission because she was feeling more defeated than agreeable. "Maybe. Maybe Nanti'ouato and..." She looked to her father, who sent an approving tick through his Ku, "and Freydis can come up with a better solution?"

"We would gladly discuss it, Ocean Mother," Freydis said.

"But I do not want him to be a prisoner. That does not seem right. He wants to make amends. He feels like he is dying since being retransformed. He said his Bondmate died, and his light is going out."

Efren looked sharply at Nanti, as though this information was meaningful to them. Then he looked back at Yemri and said, "I am going to join their discussion with Dorio. I was just saying to Nanti that this probably took a toll on him. We wondered if he would survive. I must ask him more questions about it."

"Yes. I am sorry I did not think to ask."

As Efren swam over their heads, Nanti and Freydis made their way down a corridor towards their chambers. Yemri was now alone with Tope, and she breathed out a giant sigh. "I did that all horribly. I should not have gone alone. But I just... Tata, I wanted to learn about fixing the curse. But he did not know about it. We cannot reverse the curse!"

"Yemri, you are trying to be good at this already. You are nine. It will come eventually, but until then give yourself a little leniency. Take the council given to you by the other balams. We will help you."

"I know, but then they do not take me seriously."

"I do not think-" But he didn't get to finish because they were interrupted.

"Yemri!" Pangor called to her Ku from outside the citadel. She could feel him rushing towards her, and she made her way quickly towards the entrance of her great white fortress as Pangor swam inside. He rushed at her with an anxious and excited Ku, his penumbra glowing an exceptionally dark green.

"We have found the Maato."

"Go! Go, get them now!"

"Feleeis," Pangor shouted to the buck still outside the citadel. "We have her order to go."

"Where are they?" Yemri asked, wanting to go as well.

"In the Tipua."

"That is far," Tope jumped in. "When can you be ready?"

"Feleeis was waiting for your command to take one hundred Sentinels right now. I will take another group as soon as they've assembled."

"I'll come with you," Tope exclaimed.

"Then go, Pangor! And bring the dams and pups directly here," Yemri said with excitement, so happy to finally make them free. She could use good news.

"Do you want the bucks taken in and brought under the island?" Pangor asked, "Or killed?"

This was a pivotal moment for Yemri in her reign. What kind of Ocean Mother would she be? She thought about all she had learned from Dorio and what that meant for the evilness that lived among the Serras. She also knew she never seemed to make the right decisions, so she looked to the balam of the Afiti for an answer.

"What do you think?" she asked her father.

He was stoic as he said, "Killed."

Pangor turned and rushed back out of the tall double doors with Tope by his side, much to Yamri's disappointment. Yemri still needed to discuss something with her father, but he was gone before she could say so.

Other Serras often surrounded Yemri, ready to do her bidding, but at the moment she was alone save for her guards, who were close enough to guard her, but not close enough to crowd her. She was in the middle of the white and vast atrium with no one to call upon. She didn't usually send her guards to do her errands, but she had no choice at the moment.

"Tammin." Yemri turned to the bald, poised, and ever-fierce guard.

The dam sprang to Yemri's side. "Can you please find one of the dams who generally help me? Torvi or Gildir, or even Marian will do." Then she pivoted slightly, "Forcer, retrieve my father for me. I think he still has time before they leave for the Maato."

Tammin and Forcer both looked at each other and then at her. Finally, Forcer said, "We cannot leave you unguarded. It is not safe for you."

"I will be fine. I am going to the armory."

Again they looked at each other. "You will still be alone, and the armory is not a particularly safe place." Forcer said, and Yemri was sure he was refraining from asking her why she needed to go to the armory at all.

"Go, please! Send them to find me there."

They swam away quickly, upset and in a hurry to get back to their posts. Yemri made her way towards the far back corner exit of the citadel, under the first floor balcony, down another wide tunnel, and out into the open water. She could see how this area would be very secure for Crurals. The Citadel was the thickest, strongest, most fortified building in Daris. Out the back was a small open courtyard with peat and flowers blooming and swaying in the current. The walls here were thick and tall as well. Yes, the citadel was very well laid out to protect Crurals. For anything swimming, the wall didn't hinder exit or entrance into the space, and this was just another beautiful area to spend an afternoon. She made her way across the courtyard towards the back, where there was a smaller, heavily guarded building, where she knew the Sentinels kept their backup weapons supply.

She had just convinced the guards to let her in—it took more convincing than Yemri was sure Nephira would have needed—and she was treading water in the middle of the large room, taking in the weapon-lined walls, when her father arrived.

"Yemri, what could you possibly need in here? I need to help Muleki and the Sentinels prepare." And then as an afterthought, he added, "You are not thinking of fighting the Maato, are you?"

She was startled but replied calmly, "This is not about that." She looked around the square room. It, of course, was made with the same white, gold, and gray marble that the rest of the city was made from. Though in this room the walls didn't shine nearly as much as the things on them.

The entire wall to her left was lined with long spears made of wood, sharp silver points fashioned to the ends. That would not do. They were too large—or she was too small— and the weight would be more than she could bear.

"I need a weapon," she said firmly, making her way towards the other wall to examine the sword collection it contained. The swords racked along the bottom of the wall were all longer than her arm span, so those would not do. Yemri suddenly recalled hearing that they were all shortened to make them easier to wield through the water. She looked farther up the wall and saw much shorter swords.

"What do you need a weapon for? Nothing." Tope was clearly upset with her, but his anger seemed out of proportion. "If you would not dismiss your guards to run frivolous errands, they would always be able to protect you, and you wouldn't need to arm yourself. Besides, I thought you wanted this Maato situation taken care of. Why did you call me back here when you need me out there?"

There it is.

Yemri answered with irritation, "Father—" but she was interrupted as Torvi and Gildir rushed into the armory.

"You sent for us, Mother?" Torvi asked.

Yemri knew Torvi would be the first to arrive. She was always very helpful. In her early twenties, Torvi felt she had a lot to prove, and after doing the same job for Nephira, she knew the importance of helping the Ocean Mother with tasks and errands. And unlike Gildir, who was about ten years older, Yemri was sure Torvi kept the position because she truly liked it and not just because it was something she was used to.

"Torvi," Yemri addressed her. She couldn't help showing favoritism to the dam with a more eager Ku. "We are going to have a large influx of Serra dams and pups who are in a terrible state. Abused and mistreated, they will arrive damaged and scared. We need enough rooms made available for all of them. I think the tall building towards the back wall is unoccupied."

Though Yemri knew that could be said about most buildings in the city—Nephira hadn't known what to do with the vastness of Daris once it had been gifted to her—Yemri knew this tall building in the back of Daris was large, with many compartments. "Gather a team of graggers and recondition the building. Supply it with comfortable living conditions for them."

As Torvi rushed out of the room, Tope questioned her again. "Yemri, you are being quite hasty. Torvi is barely twenty-years-old; she can't handle a project of this magnitude. It should be overseen by Danda. I'm sure you know this. She is the head gragger in Daris and has renovated most of the buildings."

"I trust Torvi to do a good job. She is very eager to please!" Yemri scanned the sword collection. Some were plain and dull, others ornate and inlaid with gems. She ran her fingers over the ones that caught her eye, still thinking they seemed too large for her.

"That may be true—"

Yemri cut him off. "Gildir, we should have a gathering! Finally the Maato are being brought to justice. The dams will no longer be treated like property and servants. It is cause for a celebration."

"Say no more, Ocean Mother. I can take care of this."

Gildir turned and made her way out of the room while Yemri turned towards the back where the smaller knives and odd weapons were kept.

"A celebration?" Tope questioned. "They are not going to be in the mood for such things when they arrive. They will be upset. They will just have been ripped from their homes and their families. I think it will take time to see this was done for their benefit."

"Nonsense! They are freed. They will be very happy."

Tope breathed deeply and then said, "At the very least, Torvi's and Gildir's duties should be reversed. At least Gildir worked for Nephira for twenty years. She knows the leaders in the community and the way of the city. Torvi is better suited for planning a silly party." He was growing increasingly agitated with her, but Yemri was unrepentant.

"Father." She finally turned to look at him. "I have to make my own decisions. You said to act with authority if I want to be taken seriously."

"I also said you have to take the advice of your balams. In fact, I said that most recently."

"I am! Right this very minute I am taking the advice of Muleki."

Tope didn't say anything, but Yemri could feel his heart pounding in his chest, as if it could pound right through his ribs and beat some sense into her. Finally, he calmed himself enough to reply with civility, "You are still learning, Yemri. I promised Nephira and your mother that I would help you. But you have to let me help you."

Yemri turned back to the wall and scanned the weapons mounted upon it. There were daggers ranging the length of her finger to the length of her forearm. Small, curved blades, heavy metal balls with spikes on the end of a chain, and tiny metal balls all caught her attention.

"You have been helpful," she said, "and I am still learning from you. But I finally know what I need to do, and I'm going to do it. I will be ten next month. I cannot act like a little pup anymore!"

It was clear that Tope would argue with her, but he managed to rein it in and simply ask, voice tense and strained, "Why did you ask for me to come?"

"I do not want to be remembered for my beautiful tail. I need more." In the top corner of the wall, Yemri saw a small gold handle inlaid with rubies. She swam up to the ceiling and examined the blade. It was thicker at the base, and as it narrowed towards the tip, it hooked upwards slightly. The shiny silver blade contrasted with the gold handle, which made the piece stunning. Yemri plucked it off the wall and turned to stare down at her father.

"I am going to kill Zitja right now."

Chapter 16

Santiago

The tournament grounds were remarkable—truly a sight to behold—and it reminded Santi yet again how little of the ocean she had experienced. They were among the first to arrive, thanks to Krell's personal speeding fish wagon. The only others to arrive before them were the ones who had been there for months preparing. Santi was able to gain a unique perspective of the playing grounds before the throng of event-goers arrived.

The entire space was about a square mile suspended in the middle of the Pacific Ocean, hundreds of miles south of Hawaii, on some sort of man-made underwater island. It reminded Santi of Daris, though she knew Daris had been a Crural island, which over time had slowly sunk underwater, abandoned by Crurals and eventually inhabited by Serras. The tournament grounds, on the other hand, had been created specifically for this purpose. She didn't know what caused it to float—because the actual ocean floor was far too deep even for Serras to travel—but Krell had said that the bottom layer was made of large, flat boards fashioned together to create one solid floor. After the floor had been put together, hundreds and hundreds of tons of sand were hauled in and spread on top.

As soon as Santi, Rogan, and Krell had exited Krell's chariot, Santi immediately dropped to the ground and dug into the sand.

"What are you doing?" Rogan asked, looking at her like she was mad.

It only took her a second. About four inches down, she found what she was looking for and popped up. "I just wanted to feel the bottom."

Rogan chuckled at her. He wasn't as impressed as she was, probably because he had been to the tournament plenty of times over the course of his life. But she had never been and was fascinated. They had taken pains to put plants, rocks, and ambiance in general across the whole platform. It looked just like any other ocean floor Santi had seen. Yet it was all created for this weeklong event.

"Do they rebuild this every two years?"

Rogan gave a little negative beat in his Ku as he said, "They have to fix it up. More sand or plants, whatever gets washed away over time, but it took years to build originally. It would be too much work to rebuild again and again."

"Why do they need to build it at all? Surely there is plenty of space for it somewhere else."

Rogan obviously hadn't pondered why the tournament ground had been specially created, and he was quiet for a moment while he thought. Finally, he said, "I know it was originally built because most of the land high enough in the water is occupied with kinships. I think it was easier to build a new space than to cram so many Serras into existing kinships. This was designed specifically for a mass arrival of visitors."

Santi nodded. That made sense. Any time they had traveled to other kinships for large ceremonies or celebrations, the hosting kinship had sometimes struggled to accommodate the crowds. The Auditus Ceremony was a good example: many Serras had to make camp on the Island of Daris, outside the walls, and that ceremony drew a smaller amount of Serras than this tournament would.

In the center of the tournament grounds were five fields set up like the five dots on dice, with one field in the middle and four around the outside. Rogan told her that because so many amateurs entered the tournament, they needed this many fields—and could use more if there had been room enough for them—if they wanted to get through all the games in one day. The amateur event was not a big draw, and many Serras did not even come on the first day, as it was often very boring to watch. After the amateur contest, the intermediate tournament would take one day, also on all five fields. This was mostly a day for the professional teams to scout new players. The games were intense and fascinating as most of the players were trying to prove they had the skills to be a professional.

For the final three days all but the central field were removed to keep the professional games as the centerpieces. Santi looked forward to seeing what that was like. She had always loved watching professional sports growing up—

mostly basketball because it was so fast-paced. She also enjoyed going to baseball games, but that was mostly for the sunshine and food.

The day after they arrived and set up their campsite, they went out to explore the island some more at Santi's request. "Will there be concessions?" she asked eagerly. She knew without him having to ask that he did not know about hot dogs and nachos bursting with their incredible artificial deliciousness. "It's like food that people bring around while you watch the game? They don't have to bring it to you, of course. But, you know, food. Rogan! The food!"

Rogan grabbed her in one massive arm and squeezed her around the neck, squishing her face into his chest as she pretended to struggle for freedom. "Are you getting tired of fresh fish and seaweed?"

Before Amed's death, it had been a joke of theirs that the variety in the underwater diet was lacking. Santi had never been healthier in her entire life, but she would kill to have a cheeseburger and a milkshake.

"Remember all that yummy food the dams made for our Bonding ceremony?" Santi's mouth watered at the thought. "So many new things and flavors." If they weren't floating high above the Dwattle field, she would have stamped her foot in exaggerated emphasis. "I miss fruit! I want some of your mom's mash. Do you think she'll bring some?"

"Maybe we have found your opus. You can be the emissary of new cuisine."

Her eyes went wide. "Done!" She blew him a kiss for his ingenuity.

Suddenly they sensed the convoy of new arrivals, and Rogan's interest shifted. "I hope that is the Daristor group. I have to talk to Amaratizz. She still has not told me who the fourth on our team is, and we should practice together before our match in two days!" He held up a finger to his eye. "Or we could lose in the first round and stop worrying and just enjoy the rest of the tournament."

Santi nodded emphatically. "That sounds like a plan to me." She was excited to play, but more excited to *have played*. The anxiety of their upcoming match was adding to the constant nagging stress caused by Krell's grand finale. They had been able to keep their spirits up only by pretending this was a vacation and not worrying about the end of the tournament. No point in worrying about something they couldn't change or fix.

"I am going to go check," Rogan said, and Santi nodded to let him know she'd be fine. He swam away, and Santi began to make her way towards their temporary shelter. It was basically a tent made from an old parachute that Rogan had gotten from a mercatera before leaving Daris. Rogan said he would normally just sleep on the sand or stay up all night with his friends when he was of Daristor age, but he thought the two of them would be more comfortable in a bivouac—what he called the tent after erecting it.

"Santiago!" The enthusiastic and eager call hit her Ku with a pleasant sizzle. "Santiago, I am so happy to have found you!"

Santiago looked behind her and saw no one. She turned in a full circle, but no one was around. Then she shook her head at herself; she was always thinking about things in such a Crural way. Santi felt the direction of the speaker with her Ku and looked up. Diving down upon her were two Serras. She connected to them and immediately recognized one of the Kus, but the name took a minute to come to her. By the time she remembered, the two had arrived in front of her.

Santi, completely overcome with excitement, threw her arms around one of them and sighed, "Torren!" He looked darker than she remembered. His skin wasn't just tan like her memory suggested but a dark brown that was clearly his natural skin tone. His hair was also much longer than before, hanging in one single braid down his back. She immediately noticed that he looked so much happier. Not that he had been unhappy before, but happiness just seemed to emanate from him now.

After a moment of hesitation, as he recalled the Crural gesture and Santi's fondness for it, he hugged her back with equal fervor.

"I'm glad to see you looking so well." The last time she had seen him felt like a different life. She had met him upon first reentering the water. It was before Santi had found Rogan again, before Sully kidnapped her, before being held by Sirens, before her abuelo died, and Amed, and her and Rogan's Bonding. It had been nearly three years since she'd seen him. So much had changed in such a small amount of time.

She pushed back from the embrace. "I'm sorry, Torren." She placed her hand over his heart. "Amicus," she said politely. "Sometimes I forget myself."

"No!" he exclaimed, taking her hands in his. "I am so glad you did. I have such a fondness for you."

Santi put her hand to her cheek. "That is so sweet." His explanation of the feeling was perfect. "I have such a fondness for you, too, Torren. You were very kind to me at the time I needed it the most. And, in retrospect, you ultimately saved my life."

They shared a warm look. Santi didn't realize just how much she had appreciated his kindness at such a pivotal time. She had not known where to find Rogan or how she would ever go about the nearly impossible task. It was fortunate of her to run into him, but he happened to be with Sully and Caliapi, both of whom were terrible to her—Sully for reasons that led to him kidnaping her, and Caliapi because of jealousy over Rogan. After Sully took Santiago, Torren had been the one to send word to Rogan. Torren truly was her saving grace.

"I am so sorry, Santiago," Torren said as he pulled himself out of the past. "Allow me to introduce you to my Bondmate, Sorrl." Torren indicated the Serra buck next to him, and Santi could feel distinctly this was the source of his newfound happiness. Sorrl was smaller than Toren, yet equally as strong and formidable, with dark skin and eyes, and short white hair. Torren flicked his rust colored tail ever so gently, the tip of his fin nudging Sorrl's green tail in a loving manner. It was a small gesture, but one that reminded her of the special little things Rogan did to her.

Santiago placed her hand on Sorrl's heart and said, "Amicus." He responded, but before either of them could say anything more, Torren nearly jumped at the two of them in his excitement.

"I nearly forgot!" he exclaimed, slinging the bag off his back and digging inside. "I knew you would be here—

298

you are all anyone can talk about." He gave her a significant look, as if she should know what he meant, though she wasn't sure she did. "I brought this for you."

Santi's mouth fell open, and she grabbed the green fabric from his hands and clutched it to her bosom. "My mom's bag! I cannot believe you saved it all this time." She thought she would cry. The bag had been her mother's market bag in Venezuela, and when she came to the States, she'd filled it with her few meager possessions.

Torren was pleased to see her so happy and explained, "We had left without it in the chaos that ensued, but I remembered it and made sure to go back and get it on our way. I know it was not your choice to leave it behind, and I figured you would want it."

Santi shook her head in disbelief and looked at him gratefully. She opened it to see what was inside. What had she felt was important when she first made her way back into the unknown?

"You had some fruit in there that had gone bad, so I got rid of it." He laughed and wrinkled his nose. "But otherwise everything is there."

"Thank you so much!" She saw her waterproof flashlight, probably dead by now; a pocket knife, rusted; ponytail holders, which would really come in handy; an extra swimsuit that she would gladly add to her wardrobe; and other items she was happy to have returned.

"Santiago," Sorrl said as eagerly as Torren, "I am happy to hear the news. I think it's great what you are doing. It will be good for us."

"The news?" Santi chewed on her lip. It seemed like it could be a million different things and possibly nothing. "What thing am I doing?"

"The tournament finale."

Santi began to scowl. Did Sorrl know about Krell's plan? "And what is to happen at the finale?"

The smile instantly vanished from Sorrl's face. "You... You do not know? Surely you know." He looked at Torren, a question in his Ku as to whether or not he was supposed to say anything. "With Zitja?"

Santi felt badly about making him feel uncomfortable, so she sought to ease his worry and answer some questions. "No, yes of course I know about that. Sorrl? Are you a Sentinel, by any chance?"

He was truly confused now. "No, I am not. I am a magister for Daristor in Tipua. Why?"

A teacher. Torren, Santi knew, was a Crural Guardian, so Sorrl did not have inside connections to obtain this information. "I just don't understand how you know about that. I mean, I just found out myself. I guess I just assumed it was a secret. Because it's so gruesome."

He looked a little relieved but concerned at the same time. "News of it has been spreading through the ocean like a tsunami. Though I have to say, not everyone is as enthusiastic about it as we are. I'm afraid many are against it."

"I'm against it!" Santi nearly shouted. "I think it's horrible and disgusting."

The two bucks were completely taken aback. They looked at each other with such intensity she knew they were having a whole conversation in that look, the way so many married couples in the world could communicate.

Both bucks visibly relaxed in their relief. "We are against it, too!" Torren said. "But we wanted to support you."

"We assumed it was your idea," Sorrl said, sending an apologetic tick to Santi. "It is a very Crural thing to do to make a spectacle of killing." Santi scrunched her face at this, and he rushed on to say, "That is, so I assume. I do not know anything of Crurals but what I have heard." He grabbed Torren on the shoulder, gently pleading with him to save him from his *faux pas*.

Santi waved his concern away. "Don't worry, Sorrl. I understand. And I'll even agree. It does seem like a Crural thing to do. It's so vulgar."

The three of them floated a bit awkwardly for a minute before Santi gestured at the tournament grounds about a quarter of a mile away. "I was interested in looking at the fields closer, would you two care to join me?"

They nodded, and the three of them began to make the long trek towards the arenas. Knowing the journey would take a while at Santi's pace, Torren asked conversationally, "How is Rogan doing? I cannot even imagine losing a parent. How are *you* doing, for that matter?"

Santi shook her head side to side. "Oh, I think I'm doing all right. Thank you for asking. I've been more preoccupied by how Rogan is handling it than I have been with my own feelings, I think."

"He is not doing well?" It was a question, but Torren made it more a statement. Of course his friend wasn't doing well.

"He is doing much better now, though I can feel a heaviness in his Ku. He won't talk about it, but I think the hardest part for him is that not only did he lose his father and hero, but all of it happened because of his once-best friend."

"I have never met either of these bucks," Sorrl said, "Rogan or Sully, but what I know of the situation seems very personal. It's almost seemed as if Sully were being vindictive towards Rogan. Deliberate. You know what I mean?"

Santi found herself distracted by Sorrl for just a moment. He and Torren were both rather dark-skinned, but they clearly were not from the same place in the ocean. Sorrl spoke with a slight accent—where she would have said "sich-uashion," Sorrl emphasized the "t." She was again reminded that this was a giant ocean with millions of Serras that she knew nothing about. "How do you mean?" she asked, pulling herself back to his statement.

Santi's silence made Sorrl feel the need to apologize. "I do not mean to be insensitive. It just seems so personal. First, he kidnapped you and put you deliberately into the hands of the Sirens," Sorrl said, aghast. His Ku emanated sympathy for what she had been through. "And then he brought Zitja herself down upon Amed. If I were Rogan, I would wonder why my best friend was out to ruin everything I held dear."

Santi squished her lips together as she thought.

Sorrl rushed on. "I do not mean to sound harsh. It is just my outside observation."

"Oh no," Santi assured him. "I don't think you're being harsh." She shook her head, remembering vividly the last time she had seen Sully, the copper-haired menace. "Sully did say something to that effect before he…" She paused and shivered as she recalled the argument Rogan and Sully had had right before Sully changed into a Siren.

Sully had accused Rogan of abandoning him in his greatest time of need. Rogan had been very hurt by the accusation, and Santi knew that accusation had weighed heavily on Rogan. It was a lot of blame to place on a person. She was ashamed she hadn't realized it before; that had to be part of the reason for Rogan's mood the past few months. She'd remember to bring it up with him later.

"Before Sully what?" Torren prodded, when she failed to continue.

Santi sucked in a deep breath of water. Not many Serras would know. Only she and Rogan witnessed it, and it wasn't as if Sully had any friends left to care where he had been all this time. "Sully changed. He… he was taken by the enchantment, I guess you could say. That is, he's a Siren."

Torren and Sorrl pulled up short in shock. Torren, especially, appeared physically distraught. His shoulders slumped, and he breathed out heavily, as if he had been punched in the gut. Sorrl reached out and gathered his Bondmate into an embrace.

"I always assumed there was still hope for him," Torren said. "We were such good friends once."

After a moment, the three of them made their way down to the field, and Santi stepped down onto the floor. It was made of moss and peat with a thin layer of sand on the bottom. The field was set up with a goal at each end—rocks that had been carved to create a big bowl. Between the two goals, the field of play was scattered with obstacles and hiding places.

"I don't know," Santi said, still taking in her surroundings. "Sully was not the Serra I knew as a child." She stopped surveying the tournament grounds and looked up at the two bucks where they tread water above her. "If I'm being honest, I can't believe it didn't happen sooner. From what I know of how the enchantment works, it seems like his heart had shifted long ago."

"He must have been holding on to something," Sorrl said, letting go of Torren and drifting down to Santi. She was eager to hear whatever he had to say that might enlighten her on the matter. She always loved talking to magisters with their depth of knowledge on subjects she only wished she knew about. "There must have been something he was holding in his heart that kept him from being pulled into the enchantment. Do you remember what happened right before he changed?"

Santi thought hard about the interaction. There was no way she could remember the exact words that were spoken during that intense moment, but the feeling of that moment came back to her immediately, and she knew without a doubt. "I think he was holding out hope for Rogan for something." She remembered the feeling in her Ku that day. It hit her in the gut with shocking clarity. Sully was thoroughly disappointed. "He gave up on something at that moment. I felt it. He wanted Rogan to save him. At least, I think he hoped that there was something Rogan could have done to stop him from changing. And I think he wanted to be forgiven for it all." She wasn't sure why, but something Sully had said before he transformed led her to believe she was right. Sully hadn't been forthcoming about what he wanted or needed from Rogan. He wouldn't have, he was too proud. But Santi knew it was true.

Sorrl's Ku encompassed her in sympathy. "Poor Rogan," he said with compassion. "He must have so much guilt."

"I have thought so, too." Santi's eyes were round with surprise but then she relaxed. It was probably an obvious feeling. Everyone felt guilt when something went wrong. "He must think there should have been something he could have done to stop it." She shook her head. She had felt it in his Ku. Rogan knew. He blamed himself for so much he had done wrong where Sully was concerned. "I wish there was a way for him to make it right."

Torren looked at her, pondering, "Maybe this is the answer to reversing the enchantment. A way to bring Sully back."

Santi started. "Sirens can change back?"

"They have in the past," Sorrl answered.

"What!" Santi was surprised. "How do you know?"

Torren was filled with pride as he said of his Bondmate, "Sorrl is a Serra historian. If you want to know anything about our past, he is the one to ask."

This filled Santi with a delight only Rogan would understand because he was usually at the receiving end of her inquiries. "I am going to ask you so many questions you are going to regret ever meeting me. But first, tell me about the curse. We can reverse it? How? Why hasn't, like, I don't know, the Ocean Mother or someone done it by now?"

"No one can make them change back," Sorrl explained, dashing Santi's hopes. "It is not something anyone can force on another, and honestly, retransformation happens so infrequently most Serras do not even know it is possible. The last one happened dozens of years ago. But what we know from those who have retransformed is that they feel the change, their Ku starts to change, and as they draw back to the Serra way, the enchantment lifts."

Santi nodded.

This could be the key to helping Rogan ease his guilt surrounding Sully. If what she suspected was true, Rogan was carrying around guilt over Sully's transformation. Maybe this was the answer to helping them both. And if she could figure this out, it might be her answer for Zitja, as well.

Chapter 17

Santiago

"Not interested," was what Santi *wanted* to say when the messenger was sent to fetch her for a meeting with Krell. Instead, she bit her tongue and followed. The tournament was to begin in the morning, so she figured Krell was going to give her his version of a pep talk.

A Sentinel raised the flap of Krell's large blue tent and ushered her in kindly. "Thank you," she said pleasantly. It wasn't the Sentinel she was irritated with.

The interior of the tent was almost comically elaborate. A large curtain hung to one side, and it did a fairly sufficient job of hiding Krell's private sleeping area. Plush and cozy, the room was so inviting that Santi wanted to curl up in the soft bedding.

The greater portion of the tent contained a sitting area with cushions and comforts. As if Krell were the cliché of an ancient king, on a small table in the corner sat a bowl of fruit. Apples, grapes, and oranges—things she knew the average Serra had no notion about—sat shining and appetizing. Santi felt the orange was calling her urgently.

Krell was floating in the back of the tent overlooking a table. She couldn't tell what was on that table, but based on the overall décor, she imagined the surface covered with battle plans and tiny action figures that he would move around with sticks while discussing strategy with his generals. It would be totally fitting. Santi wondered where the harem of women was hiding with the giant fan to finish off the scene.

"Santiago," Krell said, not unpleasantly. "Please have a seat. Are you looking forward to the tournament tomorrow?"

If Santi didn't know better, she would have thought Krell was excited. "I am. I think it will be very fun to watch." She plopped—as much as the water allowed—herself onto a blue bean-bag looking cushion right next to the fruit and found it was a very snug little setup.

Krell gave her his version of a smile and agreed. "Watch, yes. But also to win." He made his way over to the seating area and got uncomfortably close.

"Oh, are you playing in the tournament?" She knew he wasn't but she wasn't sure what he was getting at either.

"Oh, no. *You* Santiago." He pointed at her, which she found supremely frustrating for some reason. She wanted to reach up and swat his finger away. "You are going to win the amateur contest tomorrow."

She rolled her eyes. Hard. "I highly doubt I'll win." Rogan was always telling her that Krell was eventually going to catch on to the meaning behind her eye rolls if she wasn't careful, but she rolled with abandon. He was dictating her life at the moment, so she allowed herself these minor insubordinations. It was the only power she had. "Amaratizz is fantastic at the sport, yes. And Rogan is, as well, but I don't think his heart is in it. I am not a great player and haven't played since I was a child. Also, I don't even know who the fourth is yet, and we have never practiced together."

Krell moved to a cushion directly across from her and sank in. It was the most relaxed she had ever seen him. Whatever he was scheming put him in an excellent mood. "Rogan's heart will be in it," Krell crooned. "I assure you." Santi rolled her eyes again. Rogan was right. Krell was going to figure out she was being openly disrespectful to him. "And I have reserved the center arena for you today to practice with your team. You will win tomorrow."

"I still can't guarantee that-"

"You misunderstand me. I am telling you to win. The Serras of the ocean are going to see you as a champion, and then, at the end of the tournament, you will kill Zitja and be their hero. We want you to win favor and be strong in their opinion. We have big plans for you, Santiago. And they don't end with this tournament."

Her stomach dropped. She felt truly sick. "I think they favor me well enough already." Her voice was thin. She didn't exude confidence but still believed what she said, as she groaned, "Serras seem to like me. I don't think any of the rest is necessary." She had no intention of being his puppet for the rest of her life. "And what plans are you talking about? Who is 'we'?" She thought for a minute and figured it wouldn't hurt to add, "Where is Yazi?"

His face brightened at this. "Now you are understanding me! Santiago, if you can pull all this off great things are in store for you."

Santi held her face and Ku rigidly still. Not only was Krell a dangerous buck, he was insane. She had to be careful. "Ok," was all she said.

"Excellent. Now," he pushed himself up from his cushion, "you had better get to the field to practice. Your team should already be there. Do not forget, you *need* to win tomorrow."

She nodded and stood up herself. Krell turned and made his way back to the table. Santi looked at him defiantly, reached out and grabbed the orange from the bowl and stuffed it in her green bag before turning and heading out of the tent.

The center arena might have been reserved for Santi's team to practice, but the mob of Serras swarming it didn't seem to know or care.

"Santiago!" A small, teenage dam she had never seen before called to her upon arrival. "We just want to tell you good luck!" She gestured to the five nearly identical-looking Serras next to her. Santi was struck by the thought that they looked like a boy-band fan club.

"Oh, thank you." She smiled at all six of the pups. Were they still pups if they were teenagers? Santi didn't know the demarcation.

"We came to say that we think you are wonderful," another of the small Serras said. Her blond hair hung loose and flowed gently back and forth with the movement in the water around her.

Santi looked at her skeptically. "Thank you?"

"And what you are doing is so brave," she said with a puckered face. Strangely, her Ku was very calm.

"Good luck at the tournament tomorrow," the original dam said. "And then kill that horrible Zitja!"

The rest of the girls cheered at this.

Santi was stunned. "What!" she exclaimed. At this, an older dam swam up to Santi, an adult version of the small blond dam. She was sleek and composed, loose hair floating around her face and shoulders. Good, Santi thought, someone to get these pups under control. "I am sorry, Santiago," the dam said coolly. "They are excited. They have been wanting to meet you."

"Oh, no, it's fine," Santi waved a hand in the water.

"We know you have to practice. Big day tomorrow!"

"It is, for sure!" Being the daughter of her life-of-the-party mother, Santi knew how to handle a crowd. And, as she looked around, she noticed the crowd was growing several Serras deep all around her, almost trapping her in their desire to talk to her. She looked above and below and breathed a little sigh of relief that, if necessary, she could swim up or down to get away. She could handle the crowd, but being caged in was making her feel squirrely. "Thank you all for your support. It's going to be a fun day tomorrow, isn't it?"

Someone in the back of the crowd shouted, "Especially the big finale!"

The crowd cheered. Santi shivered.

Someone shouted from the side. An older buck kicked himself above the crowd and swam down towards her.

"I think it is disreputable what you are doing. Have you no decency?"

"I'm… I'm so sorry. I…" She didn't want to tell him she agreed with him. It wasn't that she enjoyed the fan club around her, cheering for Zitja's death, but they handily outnumbered Santi and the old buck. She didn't want to upset the group as a whole if they turned angry.

"It is a public display of murder," he heckled.

"No it is not!" came a shout from somewhere. It could have been any one of the crowd. "Santiago is going to free us from the Sirens!" Santi started to push herself below the crowd. Schmoozing a party was one thing; controlling an angry mob was another entirely.

"We need her to do this. She is saving us!" another Serra shouted.

"Celebrated murder." This voice was different than the old buck's. And it was angry.

The shouting became a jumble in her Ku, and she was tempted—no matter how disrespectful—to go HaruKu on them all and run away.

"That is enough." Rogan's sturdy form dropped from above, filling the space she had just inhabited before she began her discreet slide towards the moss. He reached down and gathered her in his arms protectively then placed one hand deliberately on the sword handle above his shoulder. It wasn't exactly threatening, but it did express his point. "Leave her alone." He pulled her in tighter.

So many emotions ran through Santi: desire to flee, gratitude and love for Rogan, Coral's old lessons about Serra manners, and for some reason, a fierce desire to fight everyone. After a moment's thought, she decided slinking away was the only wrong way to handle the situation. She changed her posture from frightened to confident. She shifted so that she fit herself sturdily in Rogan's embrace instead of being protected by it. She spoke to the crowd, filling her Ku with conviction.

"Thank you, um, for sharing your opinions with me. I will take them all into consideration. Now, if you'll excuse us, we have to practice. Have a good evening."

Appeased for the moment, and deterred by Rogan's fiercely protective Ku, the crowd departed. After a few moments, all that was left of the crowd was Rogan at her side, hand still on his blade handle.

They both breathed a shaky sigh, glad that the confrontation hadn't escalated. Rogan took his hand off the hilt and placed it on her cheek, pulling her in for a relieved kiss. The two of them relaxed ever so slightly.

When they finally released each other, they turned towards the playing field. Tizz was waiting calmly, floating in a spot between the ground and the crowd.

Santiago cocked her head at Tizz. "What side of the angry mob were you on, Tizz?"

"Yours of course!" Tizz swooped up to Santi and gathered her into a hug. She pulled back and smooshed Santi's face between her hands. "Such a trouble maker you are!"

Santi disentangled herself from her sister, and the three of them headed towards Torren, who was just arriving on the scene.

"I like to keep things exciting, apparently."

"I am sorry I was not here earlier to help," Torren offered by way of greeting.

"There is not much you could have done," Santi replied. "Except get yourself mixed up in all this. Which I highly advise against."

They all headed to the playing field, dissecting the asinine events of just a moment ago. Rogan and Tizz, in their usual way, made jokes and tried to play it off. Torren was quiet. His Ku was heavy as he considered the implications this conflict presented.

Santi let the jokes wash over her. She wasn't ready to think, she was still reeling from her interaction with Krell right before she was mobbed. She shook her head, remembering that conversation, and said, "They are not even our biggest problem right now."

This quieted everyone, and Santi felt Rogan tense, on his guard again. Her heart fluttered at his protective impulse. He no longer treated her like she couldn't take care of herself—he had grown to trust her ability in the water long ago—but that didn't stop him from wanting to keep her safe at all times. That combination of faith in her abilities and an undying need to keep her from harm was something she could live with. She reached out and clasped his hands both because she loved him and to try to steady him for what she was about to say.

"I think Krell threatened me."

"What!" Rogan's grip on her hand tightened.

"Let's get our team together. We should talk."

Tizz, her face a mask of concern, smiled wryly at Santi. "The team is here."

Santi visibly relaxed. "Torren," she sighed. "Excellent." More than a good dwattle player, she needed someone she could trust. "Tizz was making me anxious with the surprise but I can see why she kept it from me."

Tizz beamed. "I wanted to show you who it was. I thought it would be more fun than just telling you."

"Looks like I am mixed up in all of this after all," Torren said peacefully. "But I am happy to do so."

Santi recounted to the group everything Krell had said about winning and her being viewed favorably among Serras, as well as what he had implied about the possibility of her being Ocean Mother.

"At least that's what he seemed to imply," she finished. "Like I need to win the favor of the Serras so that they would be open to me as an Ocean Mother." She wrung her hands. "He didn't answer me about Yazi, and I'm very concerned about what he is suggesting."

This sobered even Amed's children from their usual jovial nature. "That is not how the Ocean Mother is chosen," Tizz said with great disgust.

Worried but curious, Santi asked, "How is the next one selected?"

Rogan answered. "The current Mother looks for a Serra dam to take her place. But she is not just picked randomly or because someone has performed well in a tournament. She searches her entire reign for the right Serra, looking for the purest Ku."

"Once she is found," Tizz jumped in, "the Ocean Mother will bring the dam to live in Daris to learn from her. Once the current one passes, the new one will take over."

Rogan nodded. "It is very concerning because Yazi is quite elderly, and in her entire time as Mother has not chosen her successor."

"You guys!" Santi said, and then waved her hand when they looked at her oddly. 'Guys' meant nothing to them. "We have to do something. We have to."

"Great," Torren said. "I agree wholeheartedly."

"But what?" Tizz asked.

"First thing we do, I think," Torren answered, "we had better practice so that we can win this tournament tomorrow?"

They all looked at each other, and Santi shrugged. "Yeah, I guess so."

Three hours later, they were tired of playing. Their hearts had never been into it to begin with, but they had improved on their HaruKu communication, which was the biggest challenge in the game. Rogan and Santi said goodnight to Torren and Amaratizz, whose campsites were at other end of the tournament grounds.

"Tomorrow should be a really…" Santi paused in her farewell and thought about all the things the upcoming day held for them. "Interesting day," she finished. Out of habit, she waved goodbye, and her two departing friends looked at her quizzically before turning to leave.

Rogan grabbed her hand. "Shall we go to our bivouac?"

"I guess," Santi said. It was very late and the day had been long and emotionally exhausting, yet… "I'm not tired at all. I feel very tightly wound."

"Same. Seeing Torren again has brought up so many memories of Sully." Rogan said no more, and they drifted towards their campsite in quiet contemplation.

As they approached their bivouac, Santi remembered what she had learned from Torren and Sorrl.

"Rogan, did you know Sirens could change back?" she asked eagerly.

Rogan didn't answer, but his startled Ku told her he had not known. She was about to say more, but she felt a sudden shift in his Ku. Santi followed his line of sight and saw a mass of Serras hovering in front of their tent, waiting for their arrival. Santi felt threatened. She connected to all of their Kus to see if her concern was warranted.

It was.

She felt hostility all around. Santi scanned the area. They had been offered a fantastic, private, ostentatious tent much like Krell's—though not as grand—but Santi had turned it down, preferring not to be so bourgeois. But now, as she took in the scene, the inhabitants of all the other bivouacs gathered around her small tent, waiting for her arrival—Santi wished she had the private campground.

"You filthy Terrasite!" someone finally shouted, breaking open the floodgates of confrontation. "How dare you taint the ocean with your Crural ways!"

Santi had had enough. The entire day had been filled with confrontation and quarrel. She had tried to be diplomatic earlier, thanking the Serras for sharing their opinions, not now. She was too tired.

"Listen," she said firmly but not aggressively. "This is not my choice."

"Everyone has a choice." This came from an old dam who looked to be a hundred years old but was full of fire. "You are choosing to make a public display of murder!"

"STOP!" Santi shouted. A burning anger flared in her chest, making her temperature rise. She had never been so angry before. It was the type of anger one felt when arguing with someone completely unreasonable, someone who would not listen to facts and who didn't make any sense but thought they were completely in the right. "You all want the water to be safe from Sirens. You even support killing them and Zitja. Why are you attacking me for this? Something about which I have no choice?"

The shouts increased all around with no discernable words, just an overall sense of hatred on their minds. A few messages did come through clearly.

"Crural filth!"

"Terrrasite!"

"We should kill *you*!"

Rogan took a few strokes and got between Santi and the mob.

"Hypocrites!" he shouted at them. "You want Zitja and the Siren problem gone, yet you would harass and possibly kill the only one able to do that for you?"

"It is disgusting!" someone shouted.

"It is not her choice," Rogan countered.

The ancient dam, the apparent spokesperson for the group, made her way to the front. "You should sacrifice yourself to the god of the ocean," she said menacingly.

Santi couldn't contain herself any longer. Exasperation replaced fear, and she responded, "And which god would that be? Neptune, Poseidon, or Triton?"

The dam looked sufficiently confused but brushed it off quickly and spat, "Deus."

Santi grunted. "Deus" just meant "God" in Latin, she wanted to tell the woman. Instead, she countered, "Oh excellent! I haven't heard of him before. Whose god is he? Japanese? Polynesian? Ancient Aztec perhaps?" She was being childish, but she didn't care. This day had left her feeling tired down to her bones.

The dam would not be flustered, though it was clear she was growing just as tired of Santi. "Deus is the Serra god."

Santiago cocked her head to the side, her anger temporarily replaced by genuine curiosity. She had never heard of any Serra mythology before.

"Ok, listen!" she said, holding up her hands in placation. She had been thinking about something since her meeting with Krell, and now her decision was firm. Now seemed as good a time as any to tell everyone.

"I'm not going to do it, ok?" she said. She decided not to admit that she couldn't kill Zitja; that was too much to explain at the moment. Besides, they had made her feel extremely defensive, and she didn't feel they deserved more information. "I will not kill Zitja at the end of the tournament."

"No!" came another shout from further in the back. "You have to!"

The old buck made his way through the crowd to face her. He was at least seventy, but spry and healthy. She didn't want to have to get into it with him.

"You have to kill her. Zitja must be stopped."

"What do you people want from me?" She was completely exasperated. Maybe Krell was right and she did not have favor with the Serras.

"Enough of this!" another buck shouted from the crowd. "Just kill Santiago! She is a menace to the ocean."

Rogan, knowing Santi's sais were in the chest in their bivouac, and that neither of them wanted to fight common, innocent Serras—no matter how much they seemed to deserve it—grabbed Santi around the waist and took off towards the tournament fields at top speed. The crowd followed for a while, but the older ones couldn't keep up, and by the time Rogan and Santi reached the fields, the rest of them were starting to lose interest in the pursuit. By the time Rogan and Santi had crossed all of the arenas, the last two bucks who remained in pursuit finally dropped away after shouting something about thinking about her choices. Rogan kept up the pace until they arrived at a big, gray army tent and settled down on the sand.

The tent flaps were flung open, and Sorrl ushered them in. The tent was old, and the metal poles, which had probably rusted away long ago, had been replaced by chords of bamboo tied together. The tent looked unstable, but it provided privacy, which was all an underwater tent was good for anyway. The interior wasn't overly cramped even with the four of them, and they settled on the floor on top of a mound of blankets and pillows.

"I can't do this!" Santi said, still wrapped in Rogan's embrace. "I can't kill Zitja, but what's more is I can't stay here on this tiny island for the next five days while I wait to tell everyone I can't kill her. Someone is going to kill me before I even get the chance to prove it."

"So, do not stay," Torren responded. "Leave the island. Go back home. Attendance at the tournament is not mandatory."

Santi thought about Krell's threats. "It feels pretty mandatory to me."

"Not if you are not here," Sorrl countered.

"It seems… I mean, can we just leave? Can we?"

Sorrl swiped a hand through the water. "You do what you want. No one is required to play. This is a fun event. *Fun*, Santiago! Nothing is going to happen to you for not playing a silly game!"

Santi sighed and leaned back into Rogan, feeling relieved. He reached out and put a comforting hand on her leg, though she could still feel that his body was tense, his mind lost in thought.

"Actually," Rogan said, giving her a little squeeze to show he was on her side as he continued, "that is not true. After the… incident… at the Citadel, we most definitely are required to play, and something bad *will* happen if we do not."

Santi mulled that over. He was right. "Ok. So we play tomorrow, but we have to avoid everyone before and after the games."

Rogan agreed, and Torren immediately offered, "You stay with us. All week. The four of us should be formidable enough to deter any more altercations."

"We will make Amaratizz and my mother stick with us, and maybe some other Sentinels we can round up. We will just spend the week in a large troop."

"My own personal entourage," Santi said, calming a little.

Everyone felt a bit calmer, and they started to relax. Rogan looked at Santi as she nestled in the nook of his shoulder and said, "I am sorry that Serras are acting like this to you. It is a rare thing when we behave so feral. You were sheltered from these types in our small kinship.”

Santi shrugged but burrowed into Rogan's shoulder a little more. “I suppose it was the naivety of being a child that led me to believe absolutely every Serra would be exactly as peaceful and pleasant as, well, as you are all supposed to be, I guess.”

Rogan made an “mmm” sound in agreement. Sorrl said, “I grew up in a small kinship, too. I was shocked when I learned that there are many Serras who border on the values of the Ku-first belief and live in a more unruly manner.”

Santi was going to respond in a Crural way to suggest she understood it all very well, but she suddenly sat up straight, and Rogan's arm fell off her shoulders. “Sorrl!” she exclaimed. “You may know!” He looked interested at her sudden excitement. “Something one of the, um, unruly Serras said to me, it's stuck in my mind. Are you familiar with Deus?”

“Actually, yes!” he said matching her enthusiasm. “He is a legend from the NorMer. The god of the ocean.” He said the last sentence with a little magical wiggle of his fingers.

“Oooooo, fascinating,” Santi said with a gratified ring in her tone. “I love it. Tell me more.”

He sent a feeling of agreement from his Ku. “He is believed to be all powerful.” He laughed. “The torso of a Serra, the tail of an octopus.”

Unexpectedly, Santi burst out laughing, feeling good after such a tense day. “He's a kraken!” She laughed again. “A mighty kraken king. Ha! Crurals have their own mythology about krakens, too." She sobered. "I'm so sorry! I don't mean to offend you. Your beliefs or…"

"No, no," Torren answered for Sorrl. "You have not offended anyone. We do not believe in him. I do not even know the myth. Rogan?" he asked, but Rogan was deep in thought and hadn't been paying attention.

Santi looked at Rogan, feeling mildly concerned. When he didn't respond, Santi decided she'd ask him what he was thinking about when they were alone and turned her attention back to Sorrl. "So, he is not well known, then, if Torren hasn't even heard of him? A dam told me today that I should sacrifice myself to him."

Sorrl grinned wickedly. "Oh, you should try it. Maybe it would solve all our Siren problems."

"Is that so?"

"Oh, sure. There is a sect of Serra who follow his 'teachings,' but what those are, no one really knows. They are very private. Very small. And so inconsequential that their beliefs are ignored. I believe the lore is that Deus is the god that *made* all Serras. It is said he was to be fearsome and unforgiving. Being a Serra was a punishment—a curse—for being greedy and selfish. Seems like a terrible god to believe in."

"Serras were greedy and selfish? Or they were Crurals, turned into Serras, for being greedy and selfish?"

"I believe that is it. They were Crurals, like you. He punished them and turned them into Serras."

Santi shook her head. "And then Nephira turned them into Sirens."

"Yes," Sorrl agreed. "And we have tried to turn the Sirens back, but as of yet, we do not know how. There are a lot of curses and enchantments in this water. Maybe—"

Sorrl cut off as Rogan pushed himself up into the middle of the tent so quickly he startled them.

Everyone stared at him expectantly.

"Rogan?" Santi asked, a bit of excitement welling up in her from the feeling in his Ku. "What are you thinking?"

"Are they coming back?" Sorrl said, not understanding that Rogan's Ku was not threatened but eager.

"No," Santi answered, standing up. "He has an idea."

Finally, Rogan looked down at them from where he floated. Ku strong with conviction, he said, "I want to go get Sully."

Chapter 18

Yemri

To his credit, Tope didn't try to talk her out of killing her aunt. He just followed her under the island with her guards in tow. She assumed it was because he believed this was always the plan and that she just chose an erratic, spontaneous time to carry it out. What he didn't know was that although she had said she'd kill Zitja before, she never truly intended to until she had spoken with Dorio and learned she had no other options. She had ruined the interview in the eyes of the Cor, but for Yemri, she had the answer she needed.

In the tunnel under the island, Yemri swam past the chamber on her right that was still filled with Sirens—where Dorio had been—and she wondered what would happen to them once she killed Zitja. Everyone else assumed that killing Zitja would break the curse, but Yemri had pondered this since talking to Dorio and had decided that the curse being broken at Zitja's death didn't make sense. The curse was in each of the Sirens, or it was in the water itself, she hypothesized, but it didn't lie within Zitja specifically to make or break it. She had not even been the direct target of the curse. Everyone seemed to forget that, but Yemri had heard the story so many times from Sariah's point of view that she could not believe killing Zitja was the answer everyone hoped it would be.

When Yemri arrived at the cell containing her estranged aunt, Zitja swam up to the bars, looked at the dagger in Yemri's hand, and said calmly, "So, you've come to do what others could not?"

"You said I was the only one that could."

"Then we shall see if I'm right."

Yemri stared. Tope, Forcer, and Tammin floated close by, should they be needed.

Yemri clutched the key she had gotten from the guards at the entrance tightly. Zitja would never let Yemri stab her through the bars.

Staring at the Siren Queen from the safety on the outside of the cell, Yemri realized she had gotten herself into a mess. How was she, a small-for-her-age nine-year-old, supposed to kill the greatest threat the ocean had ever known?

She slid the key into the lock and turned. It clicked open, but the gate did not move. Neither did Yemri nor Zitja.

Suddenly, Tope was at her side. He held the gate in place so that it wouldn't open and could quickly be locked if Zitja tried anything. "Yemri, I am afraid I have not been a good father since your mother left us. I do not know what to do. I do not know how to raise you as my child but give you the freedom of an Ocean Mother. All I can do is trust my Ku, and right now I do not care what the Cor wants or thinks is best. Do not go in there. It is not safe."

Yemri placed her hand on her father's heart and spoke quietly, without fear, obstinacy, or regret. "I know."

She put her hand on the gate and pushed it inward as she let herself into the cell. Zitja didn't move from where she was siting next to the gate, and Yemri had to squeeze in to get through the narrow opening. She pushed it shut with a click before her father could follow her inside.

When she and Zitja were face-to-face, Yemri pulled out her dagger. She could have sworn Zitja raised an eyebrow, though looking at her close up, it didn't seem as though she even had eyebrows.

She stared at her aunt hard, focused on the silly detail about eyebrows. She held the dagger at arm's length, knowing she looked like a child who didn't know how to use a weapon.

Which she was. A child.

"You should have asked someone how to use that, tiny seal pup."

"I am not a seal pup," Yemri retorted weakly.

Yemri swam a little closer. Zitja did not move.

She's just playing with me.

Yemri swam closer still. Zitja held steadfast.

"Your mother would be very disappointed in you."

This was the last thing Yemri expected to hear.

"Sariah had her own opportunity to kill me, you know."

Yemri looked into Zitja's face. She had not known her as a Serra. Did she look much the same as she did then? Besides the change in coloring, her face had a tired, wise look to it. Like she had seen everything in the world, learned from it, and had grown weary by it all. She had one arm, but it did not make her look weak. In fact, she looked fiercer because of it.

"My…" Yemri stammered. "My mother would be proud of me." She didn't actually know if that was true. Sariah, in all actuality, would probably not be proud to know her daughter was about to kill her sister.

"I'm sure you are right, seal pup."

Yemri let out a little growl as she raised her dagger overhead. She paused, full of rage, then plunged the sharp blade downward. She felt her hand moving in slow motion, making its way towards Zitja's chest. She stopped when the dagger was at the Siren's breast, pushed the tip so that it punctured a little hole in the woven fabric of Zitja's wrappings, and then stopped. She held the long knife where it was between cloth and skin. Zitja didn't move. Her face challenged Yemri with a hard stare. She dared the slight child to do her worst.

"Where is your penumbra?"

"My what?" Zitja was not expecting this question, and she leaned back so that Yemri's curved blade came out of the cloth with a tiny *pop* that tore the fabric.

Yemri looked at Zitja firmly, studying her face, her torso, her tail. Where there had once been a burnt orangish hue, there was now nothing. Just like Dorio.

With a quick flick of her head, she looked through the bars at Tope. The concern in her eyes made him rush towards the bars and turn the key.

Yemri looked at him and saw no colors. The fear she felt from his Ku should have turned his penumbra from it's usual dark purple to a glowing red—maybe pink or orange. Yemri didn't know the penumbras well enough to predict exact colors.

But what did no penumbra at all mean?

She looked at her guards behind him, just as he turned the key in the lock. No penumbras.

Tope pushed the gate open for Yemri to escape, but Zitja beat him to it. She pushed past both of them, grabbing Yemri's dagger without any effort.

Zitja lunged for Tammin and slashed her along her left cheek, knocking her off balance. Blood poured into the water from the wound. Zitja grabbed Forcer around the neck with her whole arm, cradling his head in the crook of her elbow. She only had one arm, but she worked as if she were an octopus. Using her elbow and forearm to stabilize Forcer's head, Zitja wrapped her tail around his body, brought the blade up, and slashed Yemri's guard from one ear to the next.

It all happened so fast that Yemri was just emerging from the cell as Zitja lunged at her. Tope's decades of training saved her. He grabbed Yemri around the waist, and the two of them tumbled into the cell, out of Zitja's grasp.

But Zitja was never aiming for Yemri. As soon as Tope flung the pair of them out of the way, Zitja grabbed the keys that were still in the lock, turned from the cell, and made her way down the dimly lit corridor.

Yemri and Tope only had a moment to comprehend that their lives weren't in immediate danger before they sprang through the opening of the cell, hot on Zitja's tail.

The Siren Queen was swift, and when she reached the cell full of her fellow Sirens, she lunged at the lock, thrust the key in, and turned. The gate unlatched and swung open just as Tammin and Tope were upon her. Zitja threw the key at the nearest Siren and turned to face the two Serras.

Tope and Forcer lunged at her. Yemri heard the guards at the entrance call out to the other Sentinels above the island before throwing themselves into the fray. The mass of stone around them blocked their ability to call for help with their Kus, however.

Yemri watched, paralyzed with fear and huddling against the wall. The four Serra guards fought against Zitja, and then two Sirens joined in the battle. More and more Sirens flew to Zitja's aid as one Siren after another unlocked their companions from their manacles.

The last of the Sirens had been freed and were fighting hand-to-hand against the Serras when the other Sentinels arrived in the tunnel. The area was cramped with bodies, and Yemri wanted to close her eyes to the horror but couldn't take her eyes off her father. If he were to die, she knew it was her fault. But just as the last of the Sirens emerged from the cell, Yemri saw Zitja call them to halt.

It was the weirdest sight Yemri had seen thus far in her short life. One minute, the Sirens and Serras were churning up the water, and the next minute, half of them had stopped moving entirely. It was as if everyone was dancing, and then half of them forgot the moves and screeched to a halt.

Yemri was still connected to Zitja and heard her command. "Go!"

Without question, without a moment of defiance, without even a last strike at their opponent, the Sirens turned and left the passageway, all except Zitja herself.

As the Sentinels were still grasping that the battle was over, every last Siren escaped.

Yemri was in awe at the absolute power her aunt wielded. She wished to have the same authority.

"Seize her!" Yemri shouted, directing her command at Zitja. But her Sentinels didn't move, which could hardly allow Yemri to call them *her* Sentinels, if she thought about it. They looked towards Zitja, then at Yemri, and only then comprehended that seizing Zitja was not only what Yemri wanted, but was remarkably easy as the Siren Queen made no effort to fight or flee.

The group of them lunged at Zitja and nearly effortlessly apprehended her. They toted her back to her cell and locked her inside once again.

Yemri hovered in front of the bars, looking at her aunt as she had only moments ago—though it felt like hours had passed with all chaos that had since ensued—and contemplated what to do now.

Something within Yemri told her she could learn a lot from her aunt, the feared Zitja, Queen of the Sirens. It made her hesitate. She was drawn to her mother's sister in a way that frightened her. She couldn't kill her right now. She couldn't free her, either. Yemri simply said, "I will kill you later."

She clasped her shaking hands to hide them and turned and made her way back up to the open ocean with a throng of Sentinels and guards on her tail.

Yemri had to be careful. During the monthly meeting of the Cor several weeks after the incident with Zitja, she decided to make her final case and accept the Cor's decision. How she handled her argument would probably require a finesse she did not possess.

It was fine to say what she thought to her father, her tata and protector. But, to the Cor, she couldn't just say, "This is not right! I should not be Ocean Mother and you all know it!" She had to be tactful. She had to make it seem as though she didn't care. That was why she had made her supplication before the meeting officially started to the balams who were already there: Nhori, Muleki, Freydis, and Tope. The other balams had yet to arrive, so she plunged into her agenda while they were still in the Kéntro Agora—the center of activity in Daris where the Nephira statue resided—sitting on benches around the statue.

Yemri was still new to the Cor's proceedings, but she noticed they always met before their meeting and casually discussed things that would be addressed more formally once the meeting had officially started. It was a way to persuade the others to vote in a certain way, Yemri realized.

She felt as if the thin façade of an adult—mature, intelligent—she had been trying to maintain was crumbling around her. And probably had been since the beginning. "Does anyone else think it is strange that I am so young to be the Ocean Mother? It does not make any sense."

No one spoke.

Was her tone light enough? Was her query round-about enough? Were they thinking about why she brought it up, or were they just stunned that she was bringing it up at all?

The Kéntro Agora was a hub of activity. A mercatera had positioned herself off to one edge of the city center, and Serras came from all over Daris to trade with her. Some had even come from outside the city, from nearby kinships—though they were still hundreds of miles away—because they could not wait for a mercatera to come to them and decided to seek the item they needed here at Daris, where trading was always happening. Mothers and fathers played with their pups or went about their business, traveling through the Kéntro Agora on their way to their opus or an errand. If Serras didn't follow strict decorum of politeness, she would have worried about eavesdropping. As it was, she knew they could speak candidly and no one would know of her feelings besides those Yemri wanted to know.

"Yemri," Muleki spoke, and she hoped she had created an ally in him; otherwise he could be a fierce opponent. "You have been in line to be Ocean Mother before your mother's mother's mother was even born. Through our entire history, your line has overseen the care of the ocean."

So he was on to her, at least. Yemri felt this was the nicest way anyone was going to tell her "no, you cannot get out of the job that easily," and she was internally grateful for that, at least.

But she had considered this argument and was ready for it. "Does that make it right? It is clear I am too young. No one thinks I am doing well in this position." And then, as a bold afterthought, she added, "You included, Muleki." She nearly flinched after being so brazen but held her ground. "I… I am too young to do well for my ocean. For the Serras." She lifted up her hands and showed them her palms as a gesture of the absolute nothing she brought to the table to help.

"Yemri, my water lily," Nhori cooed at her in a grandmotherly way that was both supportive and condemning at once. "There have been younger Ocean Mothers. I believe one had the responsibility placed on her when she was four years old. You are not unique in your burden."

Yemri knew this story as well. "That was hundreds of years ago. Even you do not know exactly when that occurred." She felt bad about being harsh to Nhori about her age, but the dam had not been alive that long ago even if she was the oldest living Serra. "That pup ruled at a time before the language, when things were simple. I could easily be Ocean Mother of an entire ocean like OnaKu, but that is not the case. Things are different." She wanted to say one of the bad words she had heard were being conceived but didn't know any. "There are Sirens now!" she said fiercely instead. "I am bad at this. I am a pup still."

Yemri knew their silence was an agreement, but no one dared to admit they wanted an Ocean Mother dismissed. It had never happened. Finally, Tope spoke up. "You are just being hard on yourself, Yemri. In time—"

But he never got to say what would happen in time because a Serra from the courtyard charged at the group. They were not having an official meeting, of course, and there should be no reason for her not to interrupt.

"Ocean Mother Yemri! You can kill Zitja!" She was swimming in hot. A wake was rippling behind her, and her Ku emanated anger and betrayal. "And you are not!?"

Tammin intercepted the dam and held her at bay just an arm span away from Yemri. It did not stop the onslaught of hateful words spilling into the water around them, though. "My family, my whole family was killed by Sirens. I had pups!" she cried while Tammin restrained her by the arms. "My Bondmate, his name was Yord, if you care! He was just taking the pups to visit his mother. It was two kinships away."

Tammin began pulling her away from the balams, and Yemri was tempted to let her deal with the angry dam, but she knew it wasn't Ocean Motherly to ignore her critic.

Yemri pushed herself off the marble bench seat— feeling a pang of loss that Forcer was no longer with them— and made her way to the dam. "What is your name?" she asked kindly.

"They were not being reckless! Two kinships away! My pups! My little pups!"

Yemri reached out to touch her heart, but the dam struggled so hard against Tammin that she stopped. "Please, I am so sorry. What is your name?"

"You are the only one who can kill Zitja, and you do nothing!"

"I am truly sorry for your loss," Yemri said with sincerity. She was. She was truly sorry for every lost life because of Zitja. "She has killed my family members as well. I know your pain."

"And yet you do nothing about it? How can you even call yourself Ocean Mother when you do not protect the ocean?"

The guards were hauling her away, and Yemri followed for a moment before realizing she could never say anything to help ease the grief of this broken mother and Bondmate. She would forever feel empty by the loss of her family. Yemri stopped following. She did not know how word had spread about the blood curse on Zitja, but it was known now, and she would have to kill her aunt. That was clear.

"I am sorry!" was all she could say.

As Yemri's guards were carrying the woman out of sight, the dam shouted one last remark before her Ku disconnected. "You are a selfish Ocean Mother! Nothing more than a beautiful tail with no brains or courage!"

The truth of it hit Yemri in the chest, causing actual pain. No, she didn't feel like she was smart enough for this, and she knew she had no courage. Yemri had thought she had courage. She thought she was brave. But when she came face to face with Zitja the first time, she was not able to follow through. And the second chance had gone just as poorly. Her opportunities for bravery, as of yet, led to nothing.

Before Yemri had even decided what she would do or say next, she felt a Ku touch hers and she dreaded what news was coming. As soon as she returned the connection, Pangor spoke rapidly at her. She felt him swimming towards her hastily as she made her way back towards the stone benches and the rest of the Cor. While she heard the onslaught of disappointing news from him, Nanti'ouato and Efren arrived, a complete Cor to witness her failure.

"The Maato are gone," Pangor informed the group. "They had too much time to prepare after their location was spotted."

Yemri crumpled into her seat and looked at the wiser, older faces of the Cor who surrounded her. Nhori would make a wonderful ocean mother. Nanti'ouato was wise and strong and capable as well. They would know what to do better than she.

When Pangor arrived at the statue of Nephira, he noticed the rest of the Cor and his Ku was slightly abashed at having interrupted in such an assertive manner.

"Please have a seat, Pangor," Muleki offered, "and tell us what you have learned."

"The Maato were in the Tipua when they were spotted." He sat himself down, though he remained stiff and on edge. "The messenger took four days to travel here from the Tipua, and it took my armies about the same amount of time to travel back. In that time, the Maato fled. We do not know where they have gone, but we will start the search again."

As Pangor explained more about the logistics and their deficiencies, Yemri could not get over his lack of penumbra. She couldn't see anyone's at the moment, hadn't since she noticed the absence during her encounter with Zitja, but Pangor's lack of aura stood out to her. His was always so vivid and expressive. She felt as though she were missing a huge part of what helped her understand the world.

Why did I lose the ability to see them?

The Cor broke into conversation and argument. Muleki could only focus on the justice he wanted rained down upon Maatis and the bucks, and Yemri was thankful once again to have him on her side. Tope and Nanti were focused on the plight of the subjugated dams and pups. Others argued points important to them but Yemri wasn't listening to their arguments. She had her own agendas. As always.

"We need a faster way to communicate!" she said, though she wasn't sure if they were listening. "We need a faster way to travel!" The commotion died down a little, and Yemri said, "Tipua is straight east." She pointed towards the Afiti Clan. "We should be able to get there fast. But we need to communicate even faster!"

The meeting never officially began as everyone argued their business right out in the Kéntro Agora. Yemri passed the entirety of it fading in and out of the conversation. No one was listening to her anyway. She would have to do the things she wanted to do on her own if they were going to get done.

She made a mental list while the meeting raged on around her. What did she want to be known for? What did she want to accomplish as Ocean Mother?

First item, she had to handle Zitja. After that—or maybe before, she wasn't sure when she'd have the courage for murder—she wanted to create a passageway to Tipua, invent a faster form of communication, and get rid of the Maato. By the time the meeting was over, she had made a plan, though she couldn't say what the meeting had actually been about. Her own agenda had been set, and she would start to carry it out.

Chapter 19

Yemri

"I will be honest with you because you deserve it, and I think it is not doing either of us any good by not saying it." Tope was looking at her seriously from where they sat in the palanquin.

Yemri felt she would be forever traveling the ocean on this hard seat being pulled along by dolphins. This wasn't her. She didn't fit into this life. "What is it, Father?" Dread started to creep from the corners of her Ku. She just couldn't stand any more bad news.

"I do not want this for you." Tope's Ku was genuine. "Your mother did not want to be Ocean Mother, and she did not want it for you either."

"If I live as long as Nhori, I could not be more shocked."

"The position suited Nephira. She rose to the challenges and adapted with the rough waves. And she truly did improve our ocean. But Sariah never wanted it for herself. She said that it was not who she was. She had fully planned to let Zitja lead and she would provide support."

"It felt wrong to dedicate her life to something only because she was expected to." Yemri added.

"Yes." He looked at her with a new fondness. "That is exactly what she said on several occasions. Did she tell you?"

"No." Yemri felt more forlorn than she had a moment ago. She liked having this in common with her mother, but it didn't change the fact that she had no way out of her situation. "I know it because I feel it. It just feels wrong to me. Doing these things, saying these things, acting a certain way. It is not who I am. But…" She paused to form her idea clearly into words. "I feel as though I will never be able to figure out who I am and what I want when I have to always pretend to be this one specific thing. My path is made for me. It leaves me no time to discover anything about myself. But I do know this."

She paused again and this time when she spoke her voice was heavy with emotion and misery. She was about to say something she had never said and had kept tucked into the deep recesses of her mind. She had never admitted the thoughts even to herself.

"I hate my tail. I hate the way I look. I wish I looked any other way. Why could I not have gotten your brown tail or mother's pink one? But this…" She gestured at the length of her wholly unique, gorgeous, multicolored tail and arm scales. "I did not ask for this. Everyone notices it, and that is all they can focus on. It is all I am known for."

Tope's answer was immediate and perfect. "When they talk about your tail, they steal your power."

He could have told her how lucky she was to be born so beautiful, with rich creamy skin, thick curly hair, and a tail the likes of which had never been seen before, with beauty that promised to come with age. Others would be so happy to have those things and would tell her to appreciate them. But she didn't need that.

She needed the validation of her feelings.

"Thank you," she answered. "They take away from my words every time they mention my scales."

"They are never going to stop remarking on it, whether as a compliment or to deliberately deflect from your position of authority. You have to find a way to not let them take your power from you.

"As for the business of being Ocean Mother, I do not know. I wish I did. Truly. Parents are supposed to know everything. They are supposed to take care of their pups and pave a way for them that is best. But I am at a loss. If it were up to me, I would let you be who you want to be. But it is not for me to decide. I cannot fix the world for you, though I wish I could."

Yemri looked over her shoulder to where Dorio was riding along next to Pangor. Pangor did not trust the former Siren to be alone in the open waters and took it upon himself to watch Yemri's "guest" during the journey.

The decision to have Dorio transferred to OnaKu had been made while Yemri had been tuning out the meeting earlier. She was almost glad for her own stupidity at letting her attention wander because she would have argued the issue. She had promised Dorio he could be reunited with his family. However, when she thought about it, she knew going to the OnaKu was the best option for him. Here, he would have to have an honest and peaceful Ku at all times, and his family was welcome to visit or live with him if they wished. The only problem Yemri had with the idea was that it hadn't been hers and that the Cor had undermined her promise to him.

But she couldn't bring herself to be too angry about it if it meant she got to go back to OnaKu once again.

Tope brought her back to the conversation by saying, "You have a lofty task ahead of you, and a lot to figure out. I am here to help in any way I can, but ultimately it will be up to you to figure out how to fare in the waters of your reign."

When they arrived at the tall weeds that bordered OnaKu, they were met once again by the small elder who had greeted them before, and he explained the rules to those who hadn't visited earlier. Before entering, Yemri felt it her duty to make sure she wasn't bringing tarnish to the kinship she held so dear.

"Dorio, do you understand what this means for you?"

"I do. I am not to leave here and am never to speak again."

"It sounds harsh, but once you see what it is like in there, I do not think you will feel it is a sacrifice."

His Ku was skeptical, but he said, "I will do my best. I am honored that I am allowed to live at all. I know many would rather me dead."

Yemri chewed on her lip but didn't respond as they made their way through the brush. There seemed to be a lot of Serras with murder on their minds lately. It disturbed her to think about how hateful the water was becoming.

Immediately upon entering the boundaries of OnaKu, Yemri was filled with the overwhelming peace she craved. She would have to remember to take this whole-Ku feeling with her and harness it in her soul even when speaking to others.

She let Pangor take over the duties of seeing Dorio settled, as he had been nervous about this solution since its inception. He had spent an hour in deep lecture before even letting Dorio out of Daris for the journey. She would check on her guest and make sure he was settled before she left the kinship, but first, she had her own business to attend to.

Yemri flitted around the kinship, greeting Serras quickly and genially. She could not ask about the one she sought because she did not know how to ask about a Ku she had never felt before. If she wanted to find anyone she already knew, she could simply share the feeling of their Ku and be directed to them. But a Serra she didn't know… she wasn't sure how to relay that message. She would just have to search. It was a task made more difficult by the fact that she couldn't seem to see penumbras, a lack she didn't understand anything about. She would just have to hope she recognized the pup when she saw her.

Hours passed, and she had met with what felt like every Serra in the place except the one she was looking for when Pangor arrived and expressed urgency in his Ku. He was ready to leave. No doubt the commander of the Sentinels, trained for war, protection, and strategy did not feel comfortable for so long in a world of only feelings and emotions. But Yemri would not be bullied by him.

Well, I probably always will be, she admitted to herself.

He was rather intimidating, but right now she wanted to find the Serra she was looking for. She turned to him and swept both of her hands towards the exit in a gesture she hoped meant, "Go ahead and go." She didn't need him to stay, and he didn't need to escort her back. He seemed satisfied and turned to leave, but after only a couple of strokes he turned back to her, expecting her to follow. Yemri waved her hands back and forth to say that she was not going and then pointed to him and swept her hands towards the exit again. He just stared, and suddenly she felt like a giant fool. Why was she adapting a gesturing language when she already had her Ku, which was the point of this kinship in the first place?

It took longer, much longer, than saying, "You go. I am staying," but she finally managed it. She expressed the vibe of Daris to him and filled her whole Ku with the sense of him making the journey. Then she countered it with the feeling of her contented Ku staying in OnaKu, along with Tope. She wondered if Tope would feel the same to Pangor as he did to her. To Pangor, Tope was a superior in the ocean's chain, but to her, he was a kind and wonderful Father.

Her worry was for naught. Pangor seemed happy to be given permission to go and left her behind without argument, which left Yemri free to continue her search. Serras came and went, and every face began turning into a blur.

She was starting to fear that she had actually seen the one she sought but could not recognize her without also seeing her white halo when finally, off in the distance, Yemri saw her. It was her: the short, wide nose, brown skin, and dark hair that flowed down her tail. Even without the aura, Yemri could feel her pure, harmless, and sincere Ku.

She made her way over to the pup and saw that she was, in fact, the same age as Yemri. Or near enough. Their hegira were in the same location in its progression down their bodies—just above the navel, with their arms clear of scales except the patch on the forearms that would remain through adulthood.

Placing her hand on the girl's heart, Yemri connected her Ku and basked in the overpowering feeling of purity and serenity. The pup responded in kind, and Yemri tried to express to her how unique she was.

Yemri was suddenly overcome with a realization like a weight of coral to the chest: this Serra pup knew how to make the right choices. Yemri *felt* it. In fact, since becoming Ocean Mother, this was the first time Yemri actually knew something with absolute certainty. This girl, though she was as young as Yemri and probably had even less oceanly experience than Yemri, could lead the waters better than Yemri. Yemri *knew* it. It had something to do with the purity of her Ku.

Yemri tried to express to her new friend all that she was feeling, but it was so much and so complex that her ideas never manifested themselves in any way this pup could understand.

Tope appeared at their side and made it clear that they needed to leave. Their task had been complete for hours now, and Yemri was wasting valuable time when she had other responsibilities waiting.

She made her goodbyes to her new friend and followed Tope towards the perimeter. On the way, she saw Dorio sitting with an elderly dam whom Yemri knew was his mother and who had moved to OnaKu to be with him. Yemri bid them farewell and felt Dorio's Ku, humble and calm. He would do fine here.

She exited the kinship behind her father, and the water felt colder and harsher on the outside, as if OnaKu was a bubble of protection from not only harsh feelings but also everything that could do harm.

Just as she reached her palanquin, she heard a voice like a song. "Ocean Mother!"

Yemri turned around and saw her new friend approaching quickly. She let go of the seat and made her way over to the pup so they could speak privately.

"Yes, hello!"

"Mother, I was hoping we could speak with our words."

"Of course. I would be happy to. I was not sure you could speak."

"I can." She gave a small giggle. "My father loves to travel the ocean and learn about all the different Serras in it. I go with him so that I learn, too." She paused and then her face lit up with excitement. "I even have a name!"

Yemri didn't understand her excitement. "Does not everyone have a name?"

"No." Her presence was calm and mature yet still held the excitement that comes with youth. Yemri had lost that enthusiasm. "Most of OnaKu has never used the language and does not know how," she continued. "There is no need for names."

"Of course." Yemri felt foolish for not realizing that and remembered Nephira telling her how she was named by her Crural friend from her time in captivity. No one had a name before the language. "What is your name?"

"My father calls me Kalani when we travel."

Of course she would only need a name when she traveled. When she lived in OnaKu without a name, Yemri would describe her Ku as a comfortable heat that brought joy with its warmth. "You were trying to express something to me," Kalani said. "I think you would have gotten there if we had more time. Though I am sorry to confess I am not sure what you wanted."

"Probably because I do not know what I wanted, really," Yemri confessed. "Only that I wanted you to know that you have the most pure Ku and penumbra I have ever seen."

"I am sorry, I do not know all the words. What is a penumbra?"

Yemri tried to remember the other words her father had told her. "It is… it is like a halo of light around your whole body. As if you radiate your feelings in a color." Yemri explained her ability to see them as Kalani's eyes got wider and wider.

"The thing is, I feel like you would do a much better job at all this than I am doing. I wish I could trade places with you. I just feel like you could make better choices than I."

Kalani was very quiet. Yemri was upset with herself for admitting—basically to a stranger—that she didn't want to be Ocean Mother. That was rude of her to burden someone with such knowledge. She had to keep this thought buried deeper because it was going to cause problems for her.

Yemri was just about to try to take it all back, to lighten the mood, when Kalani finally spoke.

"You have a big responsibility, it is true. But think of all the good you can do!" She had a childlike enthusiasm. "With all the opportunity you have, you can truly help the ocean. Make it a wonderful place, keep it safe, expand and grow the changes Nephira brought us! If I had the opportunity…" She trailed off in thought for a moment before finishing, "There is so much good to be done for our fellow Serra!"

What Yemri wanted was to switch places with this Serra here and now. It appeared as if Kalani had more of a desire for the responsibility than Yemri did—or, at least, she seemed up for the challenge. It was also possible, Yemri admitted to herself, that Kalani was just being polite and trying to encourage Yemri.

She nearly slumped in the water at her own rudeness but held herself as regally as she could. Yemri knew Kalani didn't mean it, but she felt chastised. How dare she complain about her privilege and opportunity? "You are right," she conceded.

Suddenly Yemri smiled, something she didn't do naturally or freely lately. "I do have a lot of ideas, and I want to do a lot of good."

Kalani smiled back. "Then you had better get to work!"

Chapter 20

Yemri
Approximately 660 BCE (20 Years later)

"Today is a momentous day for you," Yemri boomed with pride to the over two hundred fourteen-year-olds and their parents. "For you and for the ocean. The Daris Tour program officially begins with you, our first class!"

The crowd around and above Yemri burst into cheers, waving their hands frantically back and forth. "This education opportunity has been a passion of mine for the past fifteen years, and I am happy to see it finally come to fruition." What she did not say was that it shouldn't have taken so long for her to convince the Cor that the youth of the ocean needed to travel said ocean to learn about it. It was the only way for them to grasp their world and gain an understanding and empathy for their fellows. Yet training the Magisters and building the touring system seemed to have been delayed longer than necessary. "Today you will span the waters to learn about our world! And…." She put a lightness in her Ku. "You will all be miles smarter than the rest of us for it."

A chuckle rose up from the Daris Tour group.

"This is just a continuation of the learning Nephira put in motion." Yemri indicated downward to the statue over which she was positioned. Whenever she met with the multitude in this manner, she found that perching herself above the greatest Ocean Mother of all time gave her extra credibility in the eyes of those she addressed, even if that respect was only because of her proximity to her grandmother. "She would be so happy to see the youth of the ocean setting out to learn all they could from their fellow Serra. She always felt there was much to gain by learning about each other."

She began making her way towards the portico, and the Daris Tour pupils followed. The mass of them emerged through the protected archway and tread water over the island floor, awaiting instruction. The parents all huddled nervously close by their pups, unsure about the separation that, before today, would not have happened for a few more years.

"And now," Yemri gestured dramatically to the ocean behind her, "go and learn all you can, take it deep within your hearts, and grow for the benefit of the ocean."

The pups all said their goodbyes to parents and grandparents and eagerly took off with their cohorts. They would travel with their local Magister throughout their journey and then be placed in the care of several different

Magisters in each of the clans. Five groups of forty pups spread out on their various paths to their destinations.

Yemri was so proud that her dream was finally being actualized.

She had met with so much backlash fifteen years ago that she had finally settled on having pups of the ocean simply coming together in Daris. But even that version of Daris Tour had taken seven years to put into practice. And now, finally, it was happening the way she wanted.

I cannot believe it.

Yemri was beaming with pride as the waters around her cleared of Serras. She was nearly alone now and still reeling. Her reign had gotten off to a rocky start and she felt she had had to claw her way through every decision, but now, at almost thirty years old, she was finally getting the hang of it and pushing her agendas through. She had a hard time admitting—even to herself— that the source of her success was advice from the most unlikely source.

But that was a problem to deal with tomorrow. Always tomorrow.

"We are ready to go, Ocean Mother." Torvi had appeared at her side and was gesturing to Yemri's chariot, which sat in the water beyond the island. Torvi had remained Yemri's most faithful and helpful assistant through the years and, in a way, they had grown to be friends.

Torvi held open the fabric that covered the opening of her sterling silver carriage, and Yemri made her way inside. She sat back on the cushion and leaned her head against the padded wall, glad she had remodeled the uncomfortable board she had sat on as a child into this lush chariot. As Torvi settled herself inside and closed and secured the drape, Yemri closed her eyes for a rest. It seemed as though the only time she was able to sleep anymore was while she was being charioted from place to place. Fortunately, it turned out to be just enough sleep to get by.

"Yemri?" She heard Torvi gently touch at her near-sleeping Ku.

Before she opened her eyes, she calmed herself. Torvi would not disturb her rare opportunity to sleep if it wasn't important. She opened her eyes and then sat up eagerly to take the glowing blue nuntium from Torvi. She nearly squealed as she exclaimed, "Serras are using them!"

"It would appear that way," Torvi answered encouragingly.

The nuntium had been one of her favorite accomplishments. For once, it had been surprisingly easy to convince the Cor about their usefulness, but she assumed that was because Nhori was completely behind her on this project. Without Nhori, Yemri wouldn't have been able to make it possible. She didn't know how to make her idea come alive, but Nhori did. Somehow, the ancient dam could wield Vis when she wanted; Yemri wondered if there was more to the mystery that was Nhori, but the elder stayed secretive about it. Nhori saw the nuntium project through to success, and now communication could cross the waters in only a matter of hours, without the need to send a Serra messenger. The only problem was that since its inception a couple of years ago, no one seemed to be interested in the idea of nuntiums. Nor were they using them. It frustrated Yemri, but she didn't know how to get the nuntium system to be taken seriously. She just needed a way to show off the benefits.

Yemri connected with it, and her father's deep, quiet voice filled her Ku. "I look forward to seeing you in a couple days. We will have everything ready for your arrival and kick off the celebration with the Final Swing."

The message ended. Yemri released the jellyfish from its obligation and ushered it out of her carriage.

"Anything important?" Torvi asked. She was always a bit too curious about official business, but Yemri could trust her. As it was, this wasn't an important matter.

"Just Tope. I think he was supporting the nuntium system more than he actually needed to send me a message. Still, it is good to know that they are ready for the Final Swing and the celebration when we arrive."

Torvi pulled her lips up into an awkward smile that looked more like a cringe. The first celebration Yemri had tried to plan twenty years ago for the saved dams of the Maato turned into quite an awful slap in the face. The Maato had moved and couldn't be found, and Yemri had forgotten the instructions she'd given for a celebration in honor of the rescued dams and pups. She and the entire Cor emerged from one of their lengthiest and most heated meetings right into the party when just earlier that day, Yemri had learned the Maato had escaped. To make matters worse, the celebration reminded her she had sent Torvi to renovate an entire building for the anticipated rush of rescued dams and pups who would need shelter. Now there would be no refugees and no need for the shelters.

Torvi's inexperience had turned what was already a mistake into a disaster. She had put graggers in charge who specialized not in restoring old buildings but creating new ones. They and Torvi had decided the apartments designated as temporary shelters for the rescued Maato were too small and could be made larger, so they began knocking down walls and expanding the spaces. A part of one building had collapsed completely when the support structure proved inefficient for the remodeling.

Yemri and Torvi both grew a lot that day, and it took Yemri years to recover from the stain on her reputation as a leader.

Yemri and Torvi shared a tick of remembrance before settling into their seats, and Yemri once again closed her eyes for the journey.

Eventually, she had listened to Tope and put Danda in charge of restoring the building, and they were now constantly bustling with guests and new arrivals to the city. The project itself had turned out to be an important and a raging success, but everyone still seemed to remember its initial failure and the inexperienced Serra put in charge of the job. Fortunately for Torvi's sake, no one remembered just who that inexperienced and under-qualified Serra was anymore. Unfortunately for Yemri, everyone remembered with detail and clarity how miserably Yemri had botched the job.

"I cannot believe this is coming to fruition, Father," Yemri said after greeting him exuberantly. "When you began this project—how long ago was that? —I did not think it would ever work out!"

Tope chuckled genially. His hair was now more gray than black, and Yemri always wondered if it was due more to the stress she caused him than old age. "Nine years, Yemri. Can you believe it?"

Yemri's eyes went wide. At the beginning of the tunnel project, Tope had officially moved from Daris to Afiti to be among the clan for which he was balam. He felt Yemri didn't need him as much, and decided he should oversee the project himself. That was his stated reason, at least. Yemri suspected it was because their relationship was growing more and more tense. They never found the right balance between father and daughter, Balam and Ocean Mother; but the separation had done wonders.

"I did not realize it had been so long." Yemri smiled at her father and placed her hand, for just a moment, on his aging shoulder. "And how is Zyler?"

"I have a little surprise for you." There was a sparkle in Tope's Ku. Instead of answering her question, he said, "I think we are ready to begin the ceremony."

Yemri followed him with Torvi, Tammin, and her new guard Milli, who had taken over as Forcer's replacement after Forcer had been killed at the hands of the Sirens. They arrived at the mouth of a cave that Yemri hadn't laid eyes on since the stone-breaking nine years ago. Then, it had been a solid wall of rock. Now it was a gaping tunnel several Serras wide and tall. It had been made large enough for a caravan to pass through, or—though Yemri and the Sentinels didn't make it public knowledge—for an army of Sentinels to pass through if the need arose.

Yemri beamed in approval and pride. If this tunnel's use was a success, the next tunnel she had in mind to create, which would connect the two halves of the Najilian Clan, should be a much easier sell to the Cor.

Tope addressed the mass of Serras all eagerly anticipating the completion of the tunnel. "Today we complete the biggest—and possibly most important—project the ocean has yet undertaken," he said with much pride.

Yemri was surprised that he thought the tunnel was so important when Tope had been the one to find, reimagine, and restore the city of Daris. "This tunnel will create easy passage between Afiti and Tipua, two meccas of commerce and trade. Not to mention families that will cut their travel time down by days! Let us thank our Ocean Mother for improving our quality of life." The crowd cheered and waved their hands, and Yemri smiled brightly and waved back. She was most certainly not used to praise from her subjects. Over the past twenty years, she had learned how to handle their criticisms and deflect their compliments of her beauty; but actual praise was a rarity even still.

"This is just the beginning of all that is capable in the ocean! May this tunnel stand as a talisman for progress to come.

"Now we bid farewell to the ten graggers who will make the Final Swing and open up the tunnel." Tope gestured to the mouth of the tunnel where ten Serras floated. The crowd cheered and waved their hands frantically—much more exuberantly than they had for Yemri, she noticed, but she didn't have it in her to care.

In the center of the group, holding a giant pick-ax, was Tope's surprise. With shoulders wider than she remembered and biceps the size of her tail, Zyler waved out at the crowd.

Yemri connected to him quickly before he turned into the tunnel and her communication would be blocked by the solid stone, "Zyler! Congratulations!" She knew it was a big honor for him to do the Final Swing.

His response was immediate. "Thank you, big sister." He looked her directly in the eye as he turned. "You are doing a great job." And then he made his way inside.

"See you soon! We will catch up," she quickly added before their connection was lost.

His praise meant more than any of it. He had grown into a good man with a wonderful Bondmate. They couldn't have pups of their own but instead had gathered orphaned pups from anywhere there was a need. They currently cared for six pups under the age of ten. It was a big task, but she had never seen anyone flourish in parenthood the way these two bucks had.

The plan was for ten graggers on this side and ten graggers in Tipua—who were currently having the same celebration on the other side—to go into the tunnel and knock through the final part. They had prepared the tunnel in such a way that it wouldn't take long, and the final push was mostly ceremonial. After the tunnel was completely opened, the graggers from Tipua and Afiti would trade places and emerge from the tunnel to prove its success. The tunnel was not terribly long, so it was only expected to take a couple hours at most. In the meantime, Serras on both ends would begin celebrating.

And Yemri did feel like celebrating. The biggest obstacle in proceeding with her tunnel plan was that the shallow sea was where Anthemoessa and the Siren's lair were located. Obviously Yemri did not want to send any Serras to meet their death just to use her tunnel, but with Zitja in prison for the last twenty years, they were finally getting control of the Siren problem. The clans would always station Sentinels at the tunnel and in the shallow sea to keep travelers safe, but the advantage was that this would create a much shorter route for Serras traveling the ocean.

It would all work out in the end. Yemri knew it.

She found her father in the crowd and told him, Ku full of gratitude, "Thanks for believing in this project."

"It is a good project. A good idea for us. You should be proud."

Yemri beamed. "In twenty-one years as Ocean Mother this feels like a win. A big win."

"The nuntiums are truly great. That you were able to pull it off was a win indeed."

Yemri scoffed. "Nhori pulled it off. But no one uses them!"

"I use them all the time."

"You send me nice, supportive, fatherly messages all the time. Do you use them to conduct business? To send orders? To get in touch with friends?" She pursed her lips in challenge, though her tone was light.

"On that account, I honestly do not remember to use them. Plus, I have many helpers who are happy to deliver messages for me. I worry that if I send instructions with a nuntium, they will not be taken seriously."

"Then you have to make them be taken seriously."

"These are good, Yemri. You just have to help everyone see the value. They will catch on eventually."

"Hmmmmm," she grumbled to herself. How did she make everyone else see the value of nuntiums?

"Ocean Mother?" a small voice said behind her.

She turned and saw a small, nervous pup with her mother. "Yes?" she said kindly, hoping to encourage the pup not to be intimidated.

The pup looked up at her mother, who encouraged her to speak. "My sister, Lolly, went on the Daris Tour." She hesitated a moment and then added, hiding in her dark hair, "I am excited to go, too."

"That is wonderful! It will be a great way to learn."

"Your tail is so beautiful!" The pup said with more enthusiasm than she had said anything thus far. "Everyone always talks about it, but I only saw it for the first time just now."

Yemri had become well practiced in dealing with bucks and dams trying to deflect from important topics and undermine her authority by mentioning her tail. She wasn't quite sure, however, how to take the compliment from a small pup, so she simply said, "Thank you, starfish," before changing the subject. "And where are you most looking forward to visiting on Daris Tour?"

The child's eyes lit up with enthusiasm. "I have never left the Afiti, so I want to see them all. But mostly I always wanted to go to the NorMer Clan. I want to see the cryptids!"

Yemri was glad to see that a small pup who had never left her home clan—probably her own kinship—was eager to travel the ocean. "They are exciting!" Yemri responded with equal enthusiasm. The breeding of cryptids had been another of her projects that, in her opinion, was wildly successful. So far, the balams and Serras were withholding judgment or excitement for fear that increasing the cryptids' numbers could be dangerous. So far they were presenting themselves as gentle—though large—babies with the potential for speed and loyalty unlike any other animal in the water. But the venture was new, the animals large, their ways unknown, and the species had been on the brink of extinction with Serras thinking it best that they die out before Yemri set to breeding them. She had hopes for their uses but it would still be another thirty or so years before the babies reached maturity and could handle a rider. They were a slow growing but hearty creature that could live for hundreds of years. She might not even have the chance in her lifetime to know if her idea proved successful.

"Ocean Mother!" The call was urgent.

She excused herself from the company of the pup and turned to the messenger making his way to her at top speed. "What is it?"

"The Daris Tour group headed for NorMer is missing! They never arrived."

Just as he was speaking he pulled up fast in front of Yemri and she ushered him away from the pup and dam she had just been talking to. They did not need to hear bad news about their family member without having details. "What do you mean they have not arrived? It has only been two days since they left." Yemri was trying to think about how long that journey should take. "Of course they have not arrived."

"No, Mother." He corrected her politely. "Not that they hadn't arrived, but they are missing, they were to meet their Magister outside the boundaries of the Clan for their first lesson this morning. They should have arrived."

"All right." She took a breath. "No need to panic." It wasn't sounding like a problem, yet. "They are a bunch of pups. Maybe they got distracted or sidetracked. Maybe their local Magister did not know the way and there was a set-back."

"This is why," Yemri heard from her other side as Pangor positioned himself alongside her, "I said that the

360

groups should be accompanied by guards." Pangor's tone wasn't smug but he did have an air of confidence in his I-told-you-so moment. "They need supervision of someone who will not get distracted or influenced by the whims of pups."

"Pangor! I do not want the pups to be scared of their ocean. If they traveled with guards it would make them feel as though they are not safe." She took a deep breath and calmed herself. She had long ago stopped letting Pangor get to her. "Maybe there is credit to your idea. Just a couple of guards to hang back in case there is trouble. But they are not in charge of the route or teaching. If the group gets distracted by a learning opportunity, that is fine." She took in a deep breath and held it. "Yes, that could work. But first we have to find this group."

"I will send someone." He said with a spirit of camaraderie, "Maybe I should send escorts for the other groups who have longer to travel. To keep them safe for the rest of the journey."

"That is a good idea, Pangor. Thank you." He turned to leave and she suddenly blurted, "Wait!" When she had his attention again she turned to the buck that had brought the message and said, "Bring me five jellyfish, please."

He looked at her oddly but wasn't in a position to argue as Pangor might have and only left to do her bidding.

Then Yemri said to Pangor, "Send some escorts, that is a good idea. But I will be able to find the NorMer pups quickly." He turned once more and left to follow out her orders.

As the messenger came back holding the heads of five jellyfish, making sure not to touch the bottoms, Yemri thought about gathering the crowd around her to make an announcement.

No, I will wait until the nuntiums have returned.

No need to draw their attention until she was sharing good news.

Pangor arrived at her side, "I have sent out ten Sentinels. Two for each group to find and escort them safely to their destination."

"And I will show you right away that there is nothing to worry about!" She plucked up the first soon-to-be nuntium and connected her Ku. "Hello Daris Tour pups. This is Ocean Mother Yemri. I am sending Sentinels to accompany you through the rest of your journey. Please send this nuntium back and report your progress thus far. May Nephira watch over your journey."

She sent the nuntium to Lolly of the Afiti. She didn't know how Nhori had done it, but a nuntium would find its recipient no matter where in the ocean its destination ended up being. It was truly a marvel… though, she still needed to *know* a recipient. "Torvi!" Yemri suddenly exclaimed. "Please find out the name of one pup in each of the Daris Tour groups."

Once Torvi had retrieved the information and all of the nuntiums were sent, Yemri was nearly giddy waiting for their responses to return. She was about to make her way to the area with food—her stomach was growling for some oysters—when the first nuntium came zooming back towards her.

Yemri's elation knew no bounds. "Pangor!" She said with a smirk. Their relationship had grown into one of playful competition and constant pushing the other to achieve. But in this moment, she was just happy to be right. "Your worry was for naught. Would you like to listen with me before I present it to the crowd?"

He didn't say anything but merely gestured for her to go on. They both connected to the ball of blue radiance and listened to the meek voice.

"Ocean Mother, this is Lolly. Thank you for sending someone to help us. I am afraid we are terribly lost. We were separated from our Magister. Then two of the bucks argued about the path and everyone split up. I do not know where the other group is but… no, actually I do not know where we are either."

The message ended.

Yemri placed her hand over her mouth and listened to it again. She didn't dare look at Pangor.

"We will find them. I will send out more Sentinels. If they have split up, we will need more searching for them." His Ku beat for her in support, without pride. He did not relish in her failure.

"Thank you." She responded, looking up at him. "I think I shall not share this nuntium with the crowd. Please tell your Sentinels to send me a nuntium when they have been found. Not send a messenger. I want the information sooner than that!"

"As you wish." Pangor said gently and turned to leave.

As he was departing another nuntium came speeding her way and stopped in front of her. Yemri released the first jellyfish from its obligation and, with extreme caution in her heart, listened to the new message.

"Ocean Mother." The voice was frantic and chilled Yemri to the center of her stomach. "There were sharks feeding on a wounded seal. We got mixed up in the chaos. We are fine, all of us. But one of the dams now will not come out of the hiding place we found. We still have such a long way before we are in the Najilian that we do not want to waste more time waiting for her. Should we leave her here? Our Magister thinks we should go on as a group and he will wait with the scared pup but a lot of us do not want to go without him. Please tell us because everyone is now arguing about what to do."

Yemri thought she would be sick in the water and took several deep breaths before clearing the message and, as calmly as she could, she put a new message in the jellyfish.

"Please stay together. Help is on the way. They will see you safely to the Najilian. Thank you for being brave and thinking smartly about hiding. Reassure everyone that staying together is the right choice. Nephira be with you."

She sent the nuntium off with a heavy heart. She shook her head as Pangor returned. "You were right." She looked him in the eye and felt his Ku with deliberation. She wanted to feel the reprimand of his admonishment.

"I do not relish in being right when you are wrong, Ocean Mother. Let us just take care of the pups."

There was no arrogance in his Ku. "Thank you," was all she could muster to reply.

Another nuntium sped in followed by another. Yemri's stomach turned over inside her, squeezing her so hard she couldn't breathe. "I do not know if I can listen to them."

"It will be fine. Let us listen together."

Just then Tope joined the pair of them and Yemri cringed. It was one thing for Pangor to see the catastrophe. The two of them spent so much time arguing back and forth that he was used to her failures and successes and took them all in stride. Her father was far away now, and had grown so proud of the Ocean Mother she had become in his absence.

"Shall we all listen together?" She offered the two of them.

The three connected and a pup's voice filled them up. "Ocean Mother! This nuntium is chimba. I will send one to my mother when I reach the Hatu'anu and she will be so happy! We are fine. The trip is long and some of us are tired but everyone is in good spirits and we will arrive in a couple of days."

The message ended and Yemri's guts untwisted. Pangor touched her gently on the shoulder and released her from her daze.

"You did it!" Tope exclaimed. "You should share this message with the crowd. I think this is the opportunity you need to convince everyone of your nuntium system."

Yemri felt like laughing. But it wasn't a laugh for joy, it was a crazed manic laughter building in her stomach to spew insanity, instead of bile. It was nice to hear but he did not know what she had just learned nor did she want to tell him.

"This is a huge success for you." Tope added, not making Yemri feel proud in the slightest.

She reached for the second nuntium that had arrived. Best to hear them both before presenting them to the multitude. Maybe she could share two successes.

Yemri was just about to connect to it when she heard a massive roar the likes of which she had never heard before. She didn't actually even hear it because of her deafness but she felt the rumble so strong in her body she knew it was loud. She looked around and everyone had the same expression she did.

Confusion.

What was that noise and where had it come from? Suddenly the water, sand, and rock began to shake. She was pushed to and fro by the movement surrounding them. Serras began swimming around frantically, trying to get away from the land around and below. When land shook in the past, most often a hot mass of water erupted from it, or heavy boulders would fall. A shaking of the Earth wasn't as devastating to Serras as Yemri imagined it was to the Crurals on land who were at the mercy of the shifting plates. But being so close to land as they were just now, and with so many Serras all in one place, it could be dangerous.

Without warning Tope grabbed Yemri around the waist and flung her as far as he could away from the landmass. In the next instant he was upon her, covering her with his whole body. The earth shook again and Yemri's teeth clattered together. Why would her father push her onto the ground of all places? That was the most dangerous. This was the one time the surface of the water was the safest place to be. She looked out from under his arm as she tried to push herself free.

From the mouth of the tunnel came rubble spilling out into the open water. The earth shuddered again and Yemri could see into the depths of the tunnel as a wall of falling rocks created a perfect seal.

366

"Zyler!" Yemri pushed her father off of her. Not caring about the consequences she made her way into the tunnel. She only went a few Serra-lengths in before she reached the collapse. From sand to ceiling the rocks fitted tightly together, making entry impossible. "Zyler!" She called again though her Ku couldn't reach past the barrier.

Pangor grabbed her roughly by the shoulders and pulled her out. His strength was so overpowering, though she fought to stay, he easily ushered her away. "We will get Graggers to open this up right away, Yemri! But it will not do us any good if you get trapped in the rocks yourself."

"But my brother!"

"We will get him out!" He held her firmly by both shoulders and stared at her hard, his Ku intent and protective. "We will get him out. But you need to be safe."

He let go and swam quickly away. Yemri could only stare dumbfounded. The two nuntiums hovered in front of her. They had followed her into the tunnel and dutifully followed her back out. They would continue to trail her strokes until she released them. They looked the same, little jellyfish glowing blue, perky and unruffled, unaware of the commotion. She picked one, closed her eyes, and listened. The first one she connected to was the one she had already heard. The upbeat voice and good news sounded refreshing yet out of place at the moment. She left it sitting with its message inside while she listened to the other one, just in case. Then she connected to the second.

"Please help us, Ocean Mother!" The voice cracked and strained through the message. "We were attacked by Sirens. Our Magister was killed."

Chapter 21

Santiago

Nothing Rogan might have said could have shocked Torren, Sorrl, and Santiago more. "What do you mean, '*Go get him*'?" Santi asked, surprised but mostly concerned. "He is a Siren now, and he'll surely be… well, wherever the Sirens are?" She looked at Torren for help. She knew the Sirens had been driven from Anthemoessa long ago, even before Sully took her there after he'd kidnapped her, but she did not know where they were now.

"Rogan, surely you do not mean to go find him in Siren Harbor?"

"I do," he said, giving his head a firm nod. "I want to change him back."

"Rogan," Sorrl interjected, "I am afraid it does not work that way. A Siren has to want to change back for themselves. They have to shift their heart to a Serra way of life for a retransformation to happen."

"Besides!" Santi burst in, "I don't know what or where this Siren exile is, but surely they will not just let you waltz right in."

Rogan didn't know what a waltz was, but he got the gist. "Santiago, I want to do this and I feel like I have to." He looked at her seriously, resolution apparent in his body language. She felt lightness and a resolve in his Ku that she hadn't felt since before Amed's death. She knew this was how he wanted to try to make things right.

And she would go with him.

"Please, I have to know you will support me in this." He reached out his hand to her.

She immediately gathered up his hand in hers and held it tightly. "Let's go get 'im."

They pushed themselves up from the floor of the tent, still hand in hand. "I'm sorry, Torren, we are not going to be able to play tomorrow," Rogan said. "Will you please give our apologies to Amaratizz and explain?"

Torren looked as though he might argue, but a slight cue from Sorrl's Ku made him stop. "Sure thing, Rogan. I will let the tournament director know tomorrow. Is there anything else we can do? I can come with you and help." He looked at Sorrl, and Santi knew Sorrl would not object. They had the same implicit trust in their relationship and with each other that Rogan and Santi did.

"No, I do not think that is necessary. We will take our time, be slow and thoughtful, try to get Sully alone…" Rogan paused, seeming at a loss for what they would do next in their plan.

"And then we kidnap him," Santi said, trying to lighten the mood. "Payback!" The idea was enticing for sure. "We will have to hold him captive until we figure out how to make him change back."

They all stared at each other silently. It seemed fake. Santi was sure that she, Torren, and Sorrl were only placating Rogan in his asinine scheme, but she was going to support him no matter what.

An hour later, their weapons were fastened safely in place, and Santi's green bag was slung across her body with the essentials they might need. They set a course directly towards Chile, where they could get caught in the current and have an easier time with their swim northwards. They would have a hard time once they hit the reverse current near Panama, but they didn't have any time constraints, so they could take as long as they needed to get to Siren Harbor.

"Rogan?" Santi asked while they swam at her slow pace. They had decided the object of their excursion was going to be stressful enough so they would not exhaust themselves on the trip. "Why is it called the Siren Harbor? Surely they don't live on the land."

"It is the other meaning of the word harbor," Rogan answered and seemed ready to explain further when three Sentinels unexpectedly impeded their path.

Rogan's grip tightened on Santi's hand, but they did not stop swimming. He adjusted their course so that they could go around the Sentinels.

This spurred the lead guard to address them. He was friendly—almost chatty and nonchalant—but Santi felt his Ku was unyielding.

"Hello Rogan and Santiago," he said genially. "Where are you headed so late at night?" The buck was as large as Rogan and very sturdy. He could be trouble if he wanted to be.

Rogan matched his tone and answered casually, "We decided to head back home instead of watching the tournament."

"But you both are playing tomorrow. Surely you do not want to miss that."

"We withdrew from the tournament."

"You cannot!" the Sentinel in the middle spoke up, a smaller buck but no less sturdy than the first. "You are required to play."

Rogan tensed at this. Santi had told him Krell's plans but did not express to him how ardently he insisted they must play. "No one is required to play in the tournament." Rogan was firm. "You know this."

The first buck spoke up again, still trying to keep things friendly. "Would it not be better to stay for the tournament and leave afterwards? It will be much safer to travel with others." His tone changed ever so slightly, though he still had an air of amiability as he said, "It is very dangerous to be out in these desolate waters alone."

Rogan understood the tone and dropped the pretenses. "Are you threatening us?"

Now that the pretense of friendliness was over, the middle buck spoke up, uninhibited. "There is no threat,

Rogan. The two of you are not allowed to leave until the tournament is over."

Rogan reached up to place a hand on the hilt of his sword. "On whose authority?" he demanded, though Santi knew Rogan was perfectly aware on whose orders the Sentinels were acting.

"Rogan," Santi said. He looked at her and she shook her head. "We are not going to fight more Sentinels."

Rogan let go of his sword. They would have enough fighting in the future with the Sirens and Zitja and Krell. For now, they didn't need to fight every Sentinel that stood in their path.

"Fine," Rogan said, more to the Sentinels than to Santi. They turned to head back to their bivouac, but the Sentinels surrounded them. "You will need to come to Krell's tent. He will hear about this."

They argued with the Sentinels the entire way to the tent, but they already knew protesting was useless. Ten minutes later, they were outside Krell's tent facing a frowning Sentinel.

"Only Santiago is to come inside."

"Absolutely not," Rogan answered before Santi could say anything. They were holding hands, and he held on tighter. "I will accompany Santi wherever she is going."

The Sentinel didn't seem fazed in the slightest. He stayed calm and only said, "She is just going inside. You are just waiting right here. You will practically be together the entire time."

Santi felt Rogan's blood nearly boil with indignation so she jumped in. "It's fine. Rogan. Honestly, it's fine." She put her hands on his shoulders and looked at him while

372

radiating as much calm as she could. "We'll stay connected and you'll hear me. If I need help, I know you'll be inside in a second." She kissed him on the nose. "Besides, Krell almost makes me laugh. He's so bloated with himself I can't ever take him seriously. He just wants you out here so that I'm weaker."

This made Rogan smile. "I have never seen you to be weak because you are without me."

"Because I'm never truly without you." She leaned over and gave him a proper kiss this time. When they broke apart, he gave her a small smile and she went inside.

"Santiago, I thought I was clear with you," Krell admonished her just inside the entrance of the tent, making it clear she was not a guest welcome into his sitting area this time.

"I guess you weren't." Santi did not know how she got the courage to be sassy with him, but he seemed to bring it out in her with the slightest provocation. "It just seems like I should have a choice in the matter, doesn't it?"

"No. No, I do not think so. If you were going to make the right choices, then maybe you could be trusted to make them for yourself."

"How does that even make sense?" Santi demanded. She cut him off before he could answer. "I do not want to be put on display for the entire Serra population to see me try to commit murder. Which, I will remind you, I cannot do."

"You *will* play in this tournament tomorrow, and you *will* kill Zitja and show everyone that they are safe in the ocean, thanks to us."

Santi didn't say anything. So this was what this was about. Credit. But she was starting to understand that Krell wasn't a comic villain. Whatever Krell had in mind was sinister, she was sure. She knew that even if she could kill Zitja, this wouldn't end Krell's ambitions— not at the end of the tournament, and probably not for years to come. "And what if I don't?"

"Then you can share a prison cell with Zitja for the rest of your life. Which I imagine will be short when she kills you in there."

"You can't put me in prison! I won't be breaking any laws by not playing or not killing. This is an overreach of power!"

"I can do what I want." He kicked his tail ever so slightly, but suddenly he was towering over her. His face was ferocious and his Ku was overpowering in its desire to intimidate. His voice was fierce and dangerously quiet. "I make the law here."

For first time, Santi felt truly scared of Krell. A chill washed over her, along with a prickle of goose bumps. Her head felt light and dizzy. She had always thought of him merely as an overgrown man-child who was not getting his way, but now she realized that he would happily and unscrupulously misuse his power.

"Ok," she nodded, showing contrition in her Ku. The sass and eye rolling had to stop. She had to take him seriously as the threat that he was. "We'll play tomorrow. Of course we will. And I will be at the finale to do what you ask."

The next morning, bright and early, Santiago, Rogan, Torren, and Tizz all faced each other in a circle, treading water as they conversed in the massive tent set aside for the

374

competitors. Though they had declared they were having a team meeting to discuss strategy, it was only a ruse to be able to get together and appraise the increasingly precarious situation they found themselves in.

The tent was packed with all the teams preparing for the games, but decorum did not mandate they all be connected via Ku. It was the perfect moment to strategize in secret.

Though the mood was a little gloomy, no one's spirits could be too low in Tizz's presence. She was forever a beacon of positivity and hope.

"At least we can have some fun together today!" she said brightly, "and maybe after the tournament you can go get Sully."

Santi nodded. Though she was distracted with worry about the finale, she decided to make the most of the situation. It was what she had learned growing up: no matter the problem, Celia had always found a way to see a situation in a positive light.

A competitor from one of the other teams approached their group and connected to the four of them. She was a small brunette with a dark violet tail that she kicked gently back and forth. "Amicus," she said timidly, placing a hand on her own heart.

"Amicus," they all responded, returning the gesture.

"I am sorry to interrupt. Before we start, I just wanted to say that I am exceedingly grateful for what you are doing, Santiago."

"Oh!" was all Santi felt she could safely say. What she was doing could refer to a number of things at this point.

"My family was killed by Sirens several years ago, and just knowing that you are going to get rid of all of them at the end of the tournament… Well, it is almost too miraculous to believe."

"That is quite unbelievable," Santi replied, too shocked to close her mouth.

"Anyway, good luck today. I am confident you will win the amateur contest. Thank you for killing Zitja for us. It is wonderful. I hope one day you are Ocean Mother."

And with that, the small dam turned and made her way to her team at the other end of the tent.

Santi's team stared at each other, gaping in disbelief.

"She is seriously misinformed!" Tizz exclaimed, almost laughing.

"Why would anyone," Santi said, exasperated, "want a Crural Ocean Mother? How does that even make sense?" She found herself genuinely angry on behalf of all Serras.

A Crural Ocean Mother? Insane.

Tizz put her hand on Santi's shoulder. "Santiago, you will do the best you can. If what you say is true, then you will stab Zitja just as you have before, and they will see. It is too bad you cannot turn her back into a Serra. Just wield your Crural magic and change her back!" Amaratizz was giggling. "I cannot believe you are going to get rid of *all* the Sirens at the end of the tournament! Then be Ocean Mother! What else, you clever baby seal?"

Santi wasn't sure if Tizz calling her a baby seal was a compliment or a term of endearment, but the other things Tizz had said got her thinking.

"Ok," Santi said.

"Ok what?" Tizz replied, serious again. "Santi, I was just trying to lighten the mood since we have to go play in a bit." She chuckled humorlessly. "I do not mean to put unreasonable expectations on you."

Torren looked from Tizz to Santi with eagerness in his Ku. He could tell what Santi was thinking.

"Yes, I know, Tizz," Santi said thankfully. "I do not mean to think I have some sort of power that others do not—certainly not the power to get rid of all the Sirens at the end of the week! But I am supposed to be the one who can kill Zitja. That expectation has already been placed upon me, whether it's reasonable or not. Maybe will I get rid of Sirens, but in a different way than everyone expects."

"Yes," Torren replied simply. He had guessed where she was headed with this.

"Ok," Rogan also agreed, fully ready to support anything Santi had in mind that might defy Krell. "What do you want to do?"

"Let's go get Sully," Santiago said. "If we can find a way to change him back... Or guide him to transition," she amended, as Torren looked as though he'd correct her. "Then maybe-"

"Then maybe we can figure out the secret to reversing the curse altogether!" Rogan finished eagerly. He flicked his fin lightly against Santi's backside. "Good thinking, Santiago. I was focused only on Sully before, but this could have broader implications!"

"I don't have any great ideas about how to achieve any of this," Santi said. "And if no one has figured it out for thousands of years, I don't suppose we will just magically crack the code this week. But..."

"But it does not matter," Torren interjected. "Something has to be done, and why not us? Sorrl was telling me things he has heard about Yazi; or, I guess, the lack of things he has heard. It is not good. She appears to be missing." He held his hand up in the water as if to remind himself to get back on topic. "Sorrl and I are with you whatever you think is best, Santiago."

"Me, too!" Tizz put in. "And whatever you need from our mother. I am positive Grendor will help, too. Tell us what to do, Santiago, and we will do it."

The three of them looked at her intently, waiting for orders to march into battle. It was a pivotal moment for Santi. She had a huge decision to make: would she foment a daring coup or go with the flow of Krell's plans? Suddenly, the pressure seemed overwhelming.

Amed, what would you do?

"First," she said, and the others leaned in, "we will have to play. That will get Krell off our backs and help us regain his trust so we can have a little freedom for our own agenda. We will just lose the first game and get out of the tournament."

Rogan smiled proudly at her. "That way we are not deliberately defying Krell's orders. Smart!"

"Then," Santi continued, "we will have four days to get Sully and return for the finale. Though," she mused, "after last night, I don't know how we'll get off the island."

"I have an idea for that," Rogan answered, and Santi looked at him appreciatively. She was new to this revolution business and had no idea what she was doing. She needed all the help she could get. "I have been thinking about it since

Krell stopped us last night," Rogan added. "We can make it work.

"Where will we keep Sully once we capture him?" Torren asked. "He will not simply wait calmly while we figure out how to lure him out of the enchantment."

They all looked at each other. "We'll figure something out," Santi said. Maybe they could turn a room in their tiny apartment into a cell. Seemed possible. Maybe.

"And how will we change him back?" Tizz asked with some reservation.

They all looked at each other. Santi shrugged. "I guess we work that out later? Sirens have turned back before. There will be clues there. We just have to find the Serras who know."

Everyone agreed.

"Also," Tizz added in a serious, un-Tizz-like way, "Krell seems to be as big of a threat as Zitja."

"Possibly more so," Torren added. "Zitja is a killer and a heinous leader of an army of killers, but Krell is a devious and sinister threat who has authority amongst Serras."

Santi nodded in agreement. She had truly realized this last night.

"I do not know what we can do," Tizz continued, "but possibly after Sully, we can put our heads together about Krell?"

They all solemnly nodded their heads. Krell was a big problem.

"All right," Santi recapped. "Play, lose, get Sully, decide how to handle the tournament finale, figure out the curse, change all Sirens, then take down Krell. Easy." They all chuckled humorlessly. "One thing at a time, I guess, let's play a game of Dwattle."

"We should go out in the crowd of spectators right now. Look as unsuspicious as possible," said Rogan thoughtfully. "Let Krell's loyal Sentinels see us enjoying ourselves, talking to Serras about how excited we are, and how hopeful we are to win. We lost a lot of trust with Krell last night. We need to do some damage control."

"Brilliant idea!" Santi said, growing more excited as their plans unfolded. She felt proud that they were working to overthrow oppression. "I know just where to start."

Santi and Tizz looked at each other and said simultaneously, "Food."

No more than five minutes later, the two of them tread water amongst the tiered tables of food—at least, that was how Santiago interpreted the surfaces on which the food had been displayed. An array of dishes had been artfully arranged on a circle of shelves that flaunted the delicious bounty. She swam into the middle of the ring of offerings, her mouth watering, and looked around.

Where to start?

Santi first had to inspect every shelf, and she found an order to the layout. One entire shelf seemed to be made up of regular, everyday Serra food: kelp and seaweed, clams, oysters, and shrimp kept in a cage so they wouldn't scamper away. Curious, Santi reached out her Ku to them. Every one of them was at the end of their lives and able to be respectfully eaten. Santi nodded, impressed that even though there was a large amount of them, every single one had been properly identified as ready to be eaten.

At the next shelf, things seemed to get wild as far as Serra foodstuff was concerned, but to Santi, this was home. There was fruit that could only be grown on land: strawberries, nectarines, oranges, and pears. She plucked up another orange right away and put it in her bag. They had always been her favorite, and apparently she had grown a proclivity for stealing them. Although all the food was here for anyone to take and enjoy, she still felt a little mischievous thinking about that orange nestled in her bag right next to the one she *had* stolen from Krell. The fruit had been set on the top tier in little bowls topped with wire netting to keep the more buoyant fruits, like grapes, from floating away. And were those blueberries?

How did they get all this?

The second tier down was laden with a more savory collection of Serra foods, all familiar things to Santi.

Tizz swam up to her and found her studying this shelf very closely.

"What in Nephira's ocean are you doing, Santiago Scout?"

Santi turned and smiled at her sister. Only Tizz and Rogan called her that. She picked up a thin slice of a pinkish substance. "Is this lunchmeat?" She waggled it in the water in front of Tizz's face as the younger girl stared back impassively. "Turkey. Is this turkey?"

"I do not know what that is, you impossible Crural. You would know better than I since you are looking at the Crural array. Serras love Crural food. It is the most exotic thing we can eat!"

Santi felt foolish for not realizing that. She picked up a small white ball and popped it into her mouth, followed by the turkey slice. The rice ball broke apart with the gentle pressure of her teeth, and the saltiness of the turkey filled up her mouth. She chewed happily, enjoying the familiar flavors.

Tizz also picked up a rice ball and threw it in her mouth. After chewing on it madly for a moment, she said, "This has absolutely no flavor." Santi thought that, in situations like this, it was very convenient that they could communicate without having to use their mouths.

"It's subtle," she answered.

"And it is so sticky! Why is it attached to my teeth now?" Amaratizz made a show of swallowing it down and picking the remaining bits out of her teeth.

"Well, it wasn't properly prepared. I imagine that's hard to… well, however it was cooked it…" Santi laughed at the ridiculous face Tizz was pulling. "It's not supposed to be crunchy either."

Santi decided she didn't really care what other wonders from dry land the Serras had figured out how to prepare. She turned away from a green gelatin dessert cut into squares and looked for another shelf with foods that wouldn't be so familiar.

She looked at the tables to her left. If only she had the time and the room in her stomach to try it all!

Then she saw something that made her forget food for a moment.

"Speaking of familiar!" Santi squealed as she dove across from the Crural set-up. Unfortunately, she stopped clumsily and barreled right into her mother, sending them both crashing into Grendor.

Once everyone was righted, and hugs and kisses had passed all around, Celia said, "I should have known the best place to find joo would be at the food."

Santi gestured grandly to her mother and laughed, "And yet here you are, as well!"

Celia only smiled as she held a small balloon-like bag to her lips and pushed a small squeeze of the contents into her mouth. With a smile, she said, "I'm a chubby girl trapped in a skinny girl's body. I can't help it!"

Santi studied the thing her mother held. It looked like a pink ball, squishy and half-empty, with only a small opening in one end. A drawstring kept it closed when not in use. With sudden realization, Santi clapped her hands together. It was Coral's mash! Long ago, Coral had made a mash of any fruit she could obtain through the mercatera—or fruits that Santi had brought from land when she came to visit—and stuffed the paste into bladders for preservation. They were now pretty common food, and Serras all over the ocean were making and trading their own recipes.

Santi was just undoing the ties on a fruit bladder when Celia grabbed her wrist to stop her. "Santee, sweetheart, I don' think joo should be eating that right now. Don' joo have to play soon?"

Santi cocked her head to the side and looked over Celia's shoulder to where Grendor swam behind her, munching on the bounty of food while still paying attention to the conversation. Surely, he would confirm that one could play a little game of dwattle after eating.

"I think I can swim on a full stomach," Santi winked, a Crural gesture her mother would recognize. "It's rather impossible down here to wait an hour after eating to go swimming."

Grendor was interested now; but unaware of the joke Santi was making, he backed up Celia. "You are about to be in front of thousands of Serras all watching you intently. I am not saying you cannot, but just be sure you think it is a good idea."

Santiago Scout Morales Williams stared at them with squinty eyes, feeling as if one of them was going mad.

Finally, Celia understood where the confusion was coming from. As she took another little sip from her pouch, she said, "Santee this is the… um… fermented array." She gestured to the shelves on her right. "Everything on these shelves is intoxicating."

Santi laughed, mouth open, and looked at the shelves. This array *was* much more bountiful than the rest. "Typical," she said, and went to put her balloon back. "You're right. I'd better not before the game."

For the second time, Celia grabbed her wrist. "I'll take that from joo. I don' have to play."

Santi smiled and handed it over just as Celia finished the one in her hand and put it in the waste receptacle. The trash can was a large leather bag whose contents would be fed later to some whales or sharks. Just because Serras didn't want to eat what they considered waste did not mean it wasn't still perfectly edible for other creatures. Santi often wondered what they did with actual garbage, though she had been living underwater for a long time now and had yet to find anything that was truly trash.

"Well, can I just have a little taste of yours?" Santi asked, holding out her hand. "I'm very curious."

"Of course!" Celia handed it over, and as Santi opened the tiny drawstring and held it to her lips, Rogan joined the group and settled at her side.

"Are you sure you want to eat that now?" he asked. "Feel free, but we have to go. It is time to get ready. We play in just a bit."

Santi's stomach dropped. She held the bag hovering just before her lips as she remembered she was not a spectator here to eat and laugh with her mother. She was about to perform—perform and then sneak away, find the Siren lair, kidnap a monster, and then fail at killing Zitja in front of the entire ocean. Fun.

She handed the balloon back to her mom and turned with Rogan to make their way to the tournament grounds. "Enjoy the show, Mommi," Santi called as they left.

"Have a great time! I'll be cheering for joo!"

Santi felt the connection break along with her heart. She was not really looking forward to the next few hours. In fact, she was not looking forward to the rest of this week. Hopefully, they would get through it all and come out in one piece and not end up in prison—or dead.

Chapter 22

Santiago

Their team reassembled in the players' massive tent and faced each other in a circle. "Anyone have questions?" Torren asked. "Concerns? Ideas? Solutions? A way out of this?"

Before anyone could respond, the large tent flap lifted, and a voice filled their Kus. "It is time for your team to take the field."

They all turned to see the tournament director. She was a small dam, but she pulsed with authority and poise, accustomed as she was to directing large numbers of Serras and having them obey her. The four of them followed her obediently as she left the tent.

Before they arrived at the center field—because of course Santi's team would be on the center field—Santiago quickly reminded Rogan, Tizz, and Torren, "Do not make it obvious that we are trying to lose. If they have a big enough lead, score a few points. If Krell finds out we threw the game, I'm sure he'll lock me up tight until the end of the tournament."

They all shared agreement in their Kus and then took off to their positions. "Good luck, everyone," Tizz said, then added quickly, "and let us have some fun!"

Santi and Torren were positioned in the middle of the field, facing their opponents. Rogan and Tizz were towards the back of the field, guarding their goal. Their strategy to appease Krell was to have Santi be the point scorer for their team. That way, she would be in possession of both the dwattle and most of the crowd's attention throughout the game. It would also help their case if they lost because the spectators wouldn't blame Santi if their team didn't score due to her obvious disadvantage of having legs.

They were now HaruKu so that they couldn't communicate, but that did not stop the crowd from calling directly to Santi, a mixture of support and excitement, with only a mild thread of condemnation thrown in.

The spectators were suspended above the arena in hammock-type apparatuses over which they folded their bodies. That way they could relax, eat, and chat amongst themselves—all while looking down on the game. Being situated above the field of play made it so they could see the goings on even when the players were hidden from view of the other team.

Santi worried they might cheer and jeer during the whole game, and she didn't know if she had the fortitude to handle it. She wished she knew how to shut others out from communicating to her Ku, like plugging her ears.

The judge or referee—Santi wasn't sure what she was called because she hadn't been listening—gave each team five dwattles. Santi held them all in her hands. They were heavy copper balls, the size of a plum, smooth and firm. She rubbed her thumb across one in her right hand. This was so much fancier than playing with clamshells or sand-filled seal bladders as they did when they were children.

This was serious.

A wave of nerves rolled through Santiago, but she easily laughed and shook off the anxiety. She glanced at Torren, who was several feet to her left, and smiled widely. If she were allowed to talk, she would have tried to lighten the mood by telling him that, typically when playing sports, the pressure to win made her nervous. It was great that they didn't need to win, so this was going to be fun. But they were HaruKu, and she wasn't good at lightening moods, so she just looked at Torren and smiled like a maniac, giving him a thumbs up. He responded with his own thumbs up, and Santi's eyes went wide in surprise. She laughed again. He was a Crural Guardian. He would know Crural hand gestures, especially one that signified when a person was fine.

Santi smiled and felt a little less tense. This was the easiest part of the next four days. This would be just fine.

Quickly, Santi swam back to Rogan and handed him four of the dwattles. He tucked them away into a little leather pouch he had tied on a strap around his waist. The rules of the game stated that any Serra scoring a point could only have one dwattle on their person at a time. If they scored with two or more in hand—even if they weren't trying to score—all the dwattles they were holding would be taken away. Most teams avoided this penalty by spreading four

388

dwattles amongst the teammates and then leaving the fifth one hidden so the other team couldn't steal it. Since they wanted Santi to make all the points—and by "all" they meant, hopefully, none—they decided Rogan would just hold the extras and Santiago would trek back to retrieve them from him each time she scored.

Suddenly, a horn blasted, and everyone dove for cover. The terrain of this particular arena was of the rocky variety. All five of the fields had been designed with different layouts and obstacles, and Santi would have preferred the weedy one. She did best when hiding among the plants and brush.

Santi dove behind a boulder and clutched the dwattle in her fist. Her goal now was to get from where she was in the middle of the field to the goal at the other end, which was guarded by two Serras. If the other team was smart, they would send one of the guards out to search for Santi and Torren. If they were lazy—or wanted to lose the match like Santi's team—they would keep both guards at the goal.

Santi peered around the boulder. Both Serras stood guard at the goal. Like, right *at* the goal. Unconventional. Santi frowned.

What is their strategy here?

She looked behind her and saw Tizz and Rogan floating within a ten-foot radius of their goal. She looked at Torren and shrugged. Maybe the other team was only using one teammate to score while the other one searched them out. There was no rule on how many players could score or guard or search, and since Santi had only played as a kid for afternoon fun, she wasn't really sure of professional strategies anyway. Maybe watching a professional match would be fun after all, she thought. She could learn a lot. Too bad she wouldn't be able to at this tournament.

Santi waited until the goal guards weren't looking and then kicked out from her hiding spot. Torren emerged from his. They both made their way to a large rock closer to the opponent's goal and wedged themselves behind it. Just then, a player from the other team rounded the same rock and halted in surprise. He looked genuinely stunned to see them there.

All three players put their hands up. Whoever touched the other on their shoulder or hip first would be the victor. Santi thought it was incredibly easy, like touch football. All they needed to do was touch their opponent and then they won the progress they'd made to this spot. The player who got touched would be sent all the way back to their own goal. This did two things: it allowed the winner of the touch-off to continue their progress while also clearing the way of opposition for as long as it took the touch-off loser to make the trip to their goal and back.

The tension that filled her about having a touch battle was nothing compared to what a professional game was like, she imagined. Santi knew that the professionals used more of a tackle-and-wrestle method of choosing who was the winner, and she was again a little disappointed she wouldn't get to see it.

One day…

Santi lowered her hands. Obviously, getting touched right now would be in her favor. A touch would send her all the way back to where Rogan and Tizz floated as lazy goal-keepers and force her to have to travel the length of the entire field—not just the half where she started. It would also give this buck more time to score a goal.

Torren followed her cue and lowered his hands as well.

The buck held up his hands, green arm scales glinting in the light, then flicked his tail and continued on towards the goal, leaving Torren and Santi stunned. They looked at each other, trying to figure out what would happen next. They now had three logical choices. They could chase him down, make the touch, and send him back to his goal; Torren alone could chase after him while Santi went on to score their point; or they could ignore the Serra completely, work together, and get their dwattle down the field.

Torren and Santi looked at each other, but she couldn't tell what Torren was thinking. She was tempted to reach out her Ku, but she squelched the instinct. Instead, she popped out from her hiding spot and made a beeline for the goal. The object of hiding was so that the other team could not easily see and stop an opponent headed to their goal. But when faced with the opportunity to stop Santi, the other player hadn't taken the chance. Now she was even more curious about their strategy.

Are they trying to lose as well?

That didn't make sense. However, Santi reasoned as she darted across the remaining twenty feet, if a team *was* trying to lose the game, they were doing all the right things— just like Santi's team. This was going to be a pathetic game of "who can lose first," if that was the case. She reasoned that if she made a beeline for the goal, they would have to react. They couldn't just *let* her score. They wouldn't.

She continued her forward progress. The game of dwattle was all about hiding, sneaking, and throwing the dwattle from teammate to teammate to confuse and trick the opposition. Heading straight for the goal wasn't a wise strategy, so she continued straight for the goal. The other team would be on her in a second, touch her, and she'd be sent back to her home goal to make the trek again.

Santi was only ten feet from the goal now, and the guards were acting as though they still didn't see her. Even from seven feet away, both of the guards—one to her right and one to her left—were looking away from her as if they were searching the field. Santi groaned. She was making her way past them now, five feet from the goal, two feet. She raised her hand with the dwattle to make a big show of scoring a goal. She could hear the crowd thundering in her ears. The guards couldn't pretend to not see her now, but she also couldn't pretend to miss at this point without raising Krell's suspicions. Everyone in the crowd was watching and waiting, and her path to the rival goal was completely uninhibited. What had started out as a plan to get her sent back to her own goal by being blatantly exposed had instead given her team an easy point.

Santi flicked her wrist and sent the dwattle right into the rock bowl that served as the goal.

The crowd went wild. It felt like her chest and head would explode with the rapturous shouting she heard in her Ku. She couldn't make out any one individual voice, though she knew hundreds of Serras were speaking individual sentences to her.

The two Serras standing guard—a buck and a dam who looked like they were probably brother and sister, with their identical peach tails and confused expressions—looked at Santi as though she were so sneaky to have gotten past them. Santi scowled at them and then—since she knew they wouldn't understand anyway—flipped them off.

The game didn't end with a single point scored, so she turned herself around and made her way back towards her own goal to retrieve another dwattle from Rogan. The field wasn't long—about three hundred feet—so she was back to Rogan in no time, though she wasn't making any sort of haste about it.

She arrived in front of him, held out her hand in shame, and looked at him dejectedly. They had been playing about five minutes and already she had scored a goal in a game they desperately wanted to lose. She was afraid he'd be upset. He probably couldn't see the other end of the field clearly, but if she were here for another dwattle, he would know why.

Rogan fumbled very slowly in his pouch for a new dwattle, looking at her deliberately. He appeared to be berating her for scoring, but that didn't seem likely, as berating wasn't really Rogan's style. But what did his scowl mean? He was trying to communicate something to her. After handing her a new dwattle, he grabbed her hand and pointed to the ground.

She looked down and saw that directly in front of their goal was a dwattle. She was confused for a moment and nearly reached to pick it up. Then she realized the color was wrong. Her team's dwattles were copper, but the one on the ground was silver. She looked up at him in confusion, and he nodded. The only reason for it to be on the ground was if the other team had tried to score and Rogan or Tizz had blocked it. And the fact that the Serra was nowhere in the area must have meant that Rogan or Tizz had sent him back to his goal.

Santi looked up at him and mouthed "why?" Why would they stop the other team from making a goal? Why were Rogan and Tizz actually blocking well?

Santi looked over her shoulder to the opposing goal. It was far enough away that it wasn't clear to her what was happening, but she could see three Serras down there. Their scorer would be getting another dwattle or changing positions with another teammate who was in possession of one. They wouldn't run the risk of trying to get this dwattle from the ground. Santi tried to figure out the strategy of it all.

She knew that if the silver team didn't bring a new dwattle with them down the field they ran the risk of putting in all the effort to get to the goal without being tagged, yet still not scoring. It was very unlikely they would be able to retrieve the dropped dwattle so most teams didn't even risk it as the dropped dwattle could be guarded simply by placing a fin over it to hide it. Any player making an attempt would almost certainly end up getting tagged and sent back to their end of the field. It was bad strategy, and they couldn't know that neither Rogan nor Tizz would put any effort into protecting that dwattle.

There was just no good strategy for the other team to recover their dropped dwattle, which meant most teams never even tried it and the dropped dwattle was out of gameplay. Now the most the Silver team could score was four. Santi had already scored a goal, and her team still had four other dwattles in play.

Santi rolled her eyes and clasped the dwattle in her hand. They would have to lose a dwattle of their own somehow or run the risk of winning this game solely because they had more dwattles to score with than the silver team.

Cool. More pressure.

As she turned away from Rogan to take her place on the field again, she heard a quiet voice through the din of cheering and taunting coming from above. "They are not trying to score." Santi pulled up in surprise and almost turned around, but Rogan's voice stopped her. "Keep going. Do not appear to be listening to me."

Santi kicked her feet slowly forward. She had forgotten that Rogan knew how to communicate HaruKu. "We did not stop him from scoring. He made it look like he missed and then made it look like Tizz had touched him. Santi, they are trying to lose this game, too."

She couldn't respond. She didn't know how without her Ku, and he didn't say anything more. She made her way forward with the dwattle in her hand and found Torren coming towards her. It was clear they were going to be able to win quickly and easily—exactly what they didn't want.

But maybe, maybe they could be really distracting. Really entertaining. She was beginning to get an idea. Two could play at this game, the game of losing. Santi laughed. Might as well have some fun with it.

Santi gestured for Torren to swim away from her to the side of the field. He obliged, and when he was far enough away, she threw the dwattle at him. He caught it in a graceful swoop. Normally, throwing the dwattle was a way to get the dwattle out of one's hands before getting tagged or to get it to a teammate who had a better chance of scoring. Torren and Santi would just be making a show of it, as it was clear there would be no risk of being tagged during this game.

Thankfully, Torren picked up on her game. He threw the dwattle out to his side and smacked it gracefully with his tail, sending the dwattle soaring. It was like throwing a baseball to oneself and batting it away, thought Santi.

It flew nearly out of Santi's reach, but, luckily, she was floating near a large rock. She kicked off of it and propelled herself to the dwattle, swooping low to snatch it before it hit the ground. A cheer rang through her Ku. A dwattle that hit the ground resulted in the catcher being sent—without the orb—back to their goal to make their way up the field again to retrieve it. While a dropped dwattle on the field could be guarded by the opposition, it was less likely to happen, as the opposing team would want to spend more effort guarding their goal.

This could possibly work to their advantage to delay gameplay later, but for now, Santi was in the mood to impress the crowd with nonsense so that at least it didn't *look* like they were trying to lose the game.

With the small ball clutched tightly in her hand, Santi dramatically rolled in the sand, pretending that her dynamic stunt was due to her vast momentum. She righted herself and thrust up her hand holding the dwattle, much to the delight of the crowd.

Santi snuck forward and hid behind a boulder. Torren did the same on the other side of the arena. The field was only 300 feet by 100 feet, which wasn't terribly large. Water resistance, however, created a tough challenge for Santi's swimming, throwing, and general Serra-ing ability. Torren, at the other side of the arena, was roughly as far away from her as the distance from home plate to first base on a baseball field. Santi could probably throw the dwattle that far on land, but she would never have the strength to overcome the water's resistance enough to throw the dwattle to Torren here.

She crouched behind a rock, just for fun. When she sprang out from behind it, she tossed the dwattle in the water to the side and tried to kick at it like Torren had done earlier. She did not connect well with it, and the dwattle bounced off her shin at an angle. Instead of soaring into the air, it shot straight to the ground. Santi growled and clutched her shin, writhing dramatically with the pain.

A cheer rang through the crowd, mingled with some boos. It seemed like a strange reaction for something so miniscule, but she shrugged. The copper dwattle sat nestled in the peat on the ground, shiny and innocent. She looked to where Torren was hiding and held her hands up as if to apologize.

Torren emerged from his spot and was starting to make his way back to their goal when the judge swooped down from her vantage point above the game and stopped him.

Her voice rang out loud and clear for both teams and the spectators to hear. "Because the dwattle never traveled in its intended direction, the fault lies with the sender, not the receiver. The thrower of the dwattle must return to the goal." With that pronouncement, she disconnected her Ku and made her way back to her observation post.

Santi made a silly face and frantically rubbed the pain away from her shin before turning herself promptly around and swimming back towards Rogan and Tizz. When she arrived, she touched their goal and saw a small silver dwattle inside. She looked up at Rogan and smiled and then quickly changed her expression lest anyone catch on that she was happy that the other team had scored. The other team's score must have happened when the crowd cheered and booed simultaneously earlier. She turned around again to make her way out towards her own abandoned dwattle.

Santi arrived back at her previous spot to find Torren waiting for her. Santiago swooped down and retrieved the little nuisance of a dwattle, visibly displeased to see it. The other team wasn't trying to guard it at all.

Torren and Santi were now within scoring range again. They could see both of the guards from their perch in front of the goal, no more than twenty-five feet or so away.

Santi had an idea.

She gestured to Torren to go a little way off in front of the other team's goal. He obliged, and as he did so, one of their two guards followed after him. Santi was pleased. This would look better if they actually appeared to be trying. Then, because it did the guard no good to tag Torren while he didn't have a dwattle in his hand, the three of them just waited for someone else to make the first move.

Suddenly, a massive cheer rang through Santi's Ku, followed again by booing. She couldn't contain her smile this time, knowing that they were officially behind in points. Santi tried to indicate through rough signs and gestures that Torren should pass her back the dwattle as soon as he got it. In a regular game, that would make sense, as he had a guard at his left flank, but she had to be sure he understood that his goal here was not to get tagged. Though that seemed like a good strategy for losing, she could not count on the guard actually doing his job right now.

Torren nodded. She tossed Torren the dwattle, and in the small amount of time it took for him to catch it and throw it back, Santi edged a smidge closer to the goal and got into position about ten feet above and away from it. As the dwattle sailed back in her direction, Santi pushed her bottom towards the ground, and the crowd went wild. It was exactly what she was hoping for. They were falling for the showmanship, and she was glad it covered the truth of her intentions. She flung her upper body down towards the soil as she kicked her legs in a tight arch, the Landry Tuck, a crowd favorite. Her legs connected with the dwattle, sending it flying towards the goal.

The crowd was in a tizzy of excitement as the copper sphere made its way directly towards the goal. Santi turned her torso—still upside down—to watch the dwattle's progress. It hit the rim of the rock structure, ringed the edge of the bowl, and rolled down the sloping edge of the bowl to land just outside of the goal, an utterly irretrievable position. Santi let out the breath she had been holding. That dwattle would be considered out of play now, and both teams now had a maximum score potential of only four.

She wanted to cheer but instead allowed her body to go limp to achieve a show of utter dejection. The Landry Tuck packed a lot of power but not much accuracy; it was better used for passing the dwattle to a teammate who could move to catch it. It was not a great choice for scoring.

Oops, thought Santi smugly.

The judge again descended from her vantage point and addressed the arena. "With five dwattles out of commission, I call this the midpoint of the game, and there will be a short break."

Santi hung in the water, confused, and glanced towards their goal for clarification. Rogan, Tizz, and Torren were huddled together and making their way back towards the participant's tent. When they'd played as a child, they'd played with unlimited dwattles. She thought maybe she should have learned the rules of organized gameplay before playing in a real tournament.

"Come on, Santiago," Rogan called to her gently. "Once half the dwattles are played, there is a break before we continue."

Santi nodded. She knew the game would continue until all the dwattles were played or three hours had passed, whichever came first. She hoped this wouldn't take three hours.

"You know, a break in case you are exhausted from your exertion," Tizz chimed in with feigned innocence.

Santi smirked; she *had* been exerting herself rather well, she thought.

On her way to the tent, she was tackled in an embrace that was both unnecessarily forceful and bursting with love.

"Mommi!" Santi squealed, returning the embrace. "Are you having a good time?" She had forgotten all about the fact that Coral, Celia, Grendor, and others she knew would be in the stands. She was glad now that she had decided to put on a little show for the crowd. She would feel terrible if she made a mockery of the game and blatantly lost.

"Santee," her mother cooed, pushing her daughter to arm's length. "Joo are doing so well!" She gave her a little cheek pinch. "Don' worry about being behind. I know joo'll catch up!" She smiled mischievously before adding, "I never knew joo had such great moves." Celia gave a little seductive

400

bum wiggle to indicate Santi's swimming skills could be put to use other places, and Santi smiled coyly. It was always so much more fun to live in Celia's world than in reality.

At that moment, Amphitrite nudged Santi on the arm and she stroked her turtle friend absently while she tittered at Celia. "I am very mysterious, Mom, it's true." She made her Ku turn serious as she excused herself. "Sorry, I have to go talk with the team. You know, strategize for the second half."

"Ok, yes! Excellent idea," Celia nodded and pulled the turtle along as Santi turned away. "When the game is ober, I saved a leeeeeettle balloon for joo."

Santi put her hand on her lips and blew her mom a kiss before turning and continuing on her way. She felt a pang of regret that she would not be sticking around after the game but would be making her way towards the deadly embrace of the Sirens.

When she entered the tent, she found her three teammates anxiously awaiting her. Without preamble, Rogan filled her in.

"I had to knock those goals in there myself." He was kicking himself side to side, the underwater version of anxiously shifting from foot to foot. "They are not going to make any goals. I was able to make it look like they did it, though. Be smart out there! They are trying valiantly to lose."

"You made those goals for them?"

"Sort of." He lifted one hand, palm up, in a helpless gesture "I made it look like we were in the middle of a struggle, and Amaratizz got in the mix so that it was confusion."

"They threw the dwattle," Tizz said, "but it was not going to go in so, while I looked to be blocking it, Rogan hit it in."

"We were able to pull off that ridiculous stunt twice, but they are not going to let us get away with it again. It was truly asinine what we had to maneuver."

"I feel really terrible," Tizz said, placing a hand on her heart. "Cheating is wrong. But… is it cheating if we are cheating to lose? I do not know."

"I think your Ku is safe from the curses of Nephira," Torren said gently.

"The curses of Nephira" was the closest thing Santi had ever heard to the Serra equivalent of hell. She thought about it and said, "I don't like it, either. It doesn't feel very Serra-like to deceive everyone. But what choice do we really have? The choice even to play the game today was taken away from us."

"I have an idea!" Rogan said abruptly, and Santi nearly swooned with relief.

"Thank Nephira," she replied. "I have used up all my idea power in the last twelve hours."

"Tell us!" Tizz proclaimed, exuding relief in her Ku as well.

Just then they heard the judge in the stands welcoming the participants back on the field for the second and final portion of the game, and all Rogan had time to say was, "Torren, you will trade me places and guard the goal."

The four of them went HaruKu as they took their places on the field. This time, Rogan and Santi were at the middle of the field looking at their opponent's goal as Tizz and Torren hung back to do the best they could not to guard their own goal very well.

The judge called the game to start, and Rogan and Santi dove for hiding places. Santi was under a stone archway not quite large enough to conceal her feet, though they were pulled up to her chest, and Rogan was doing a terrible job of wedging his broad shoulders and long blue tail behind a rock the size of Santi. They were far enough away from each other to throw the dwattle back and forth if need be, but they knew no one was going to come and challenge them.

Rogan threw her a dwattle and gestured for her to throw it back.

Once she did, they both moved up to new hiding places. They repeated this process down the field, tossing the orb back and forth, diving into new hiding places with extra flourish and pizzazz.

Santi dove to catch the dwattle, rolling in the sand before landing like a cat and pouncing into a new hiding spot. She threw the dwattle to Rogan, who caught it while doing a three-sixty spin before swooping into the bowl of another hollowed out rock. Santi laughed. It was nice to see him having fun. He popped his head out of the bowl and waggled his eyebrows at her. Santi took the opportunity to prairie dog her head out of her hiding spot a few times. As he threw the ball back to her, Santi kicked her feet off the moss, caught it high over the ground, and kicked herself back down. On her way back to the ground, she had an idea. Laughing to herself, she landed. Her right knee and left foot landed firmly on the ground, but she punched the peat floor and raised the dwattle high in the air with her left hand, the hero pose she had seen in every superhero movie. She hoped at the very least that it would entertain her mom as much as it did Santi.

After several repeats of their antics, they were close enough now for Santi to make the goal. She assumed the plan was the same as always, which was to look like she would score and then fail. It wasn't a satisfying outcome for the crowd, but it was necessary in order to achieve their long-term goal of getting Sully and hopefully, ultimately, saving the underwater world as they knew it.

One thing at a time.

Santi leapt off the ground, her superhero pose allowing her to very easily spring into action. No wonder superheroes were always landing like that, she thought. She raised the dwattle high in the air, as if she were doing a layup in basketball, while the silver team made lazy waves of their arms as if they were trying to stop Santi from scoring. Before she released the dwattle, however, she caught Rogan signaling frantically to her out of the corner of her eye. At the last moment, she changed course in her throw and sent the dwattle sailing easily into Rogan's outstretched hands.

Rogan caught the dwattle with a flourish and an unnecessary backflip, which made it seem as if Santi's throw had been superhumanly fast. Rogan then torpedoed himself towards the goal and landed the dwattle squarely into the rock bowl.

The crowd went wild.

Santi noticed that although there were plenty of people cheering for the other team, there were not any boos for their goal.

Interesting.

The team headed back to their goal to retrieve their next dwattle. Santi desperately wanted to ask Rogan how actually scoring a goal was a good thing when the judge intercepted them. In her booming voice, which drowned out the chaos from the crowd, she spoke loudly enough to Rogan that the whole arena could hear.

"Please open your pouch."

Rogan looked at her askance. Waves of emotion went through his Ku. He was projecting fear but also… guilt? Santi was confused.

Rogan opened his pouch to reveal two more dwattles. "I…" he stammered. "I forgot!"

The judge collected the two dwattles from him and made her way swiftly to the other end of the field, where she plucked up the dwattle Rogan had just used to score.

"With the loss of these three dwattles and the one now out of commission, Amaratizz's team has no further option to score.

"Joper's team, with a score of 2 to 1, has won this game."

Chapter 23

Yemri

"We seem to be ok." The voice from the nuntium was calm. "The ceiling collapsed but… well, we are still assessing. I can see five or six that are fine, but I cannot see everyone. Oh, there is another one from the other side! Wait!" The voice paused, and everyone leaned in as if that would help to hear with their Kus better. "No." Pause. "No, someone is dead."

The message cut off and the crowd erupted in questions and chaos.

"Who is dead?"

"Who is alive?"

"What about the others?"

"Ocean Mother! What about the rest?"

Yemri took a breath. She had sent the nuntium to the head gragger because she thought that was appropriate. But what about Zyler? She calmed herself before she answered. "We may not be able to get the way cleared quickly." She gestured to the graggers and Sentinels, who were trying to move the debris. "But nuntiums can still reach their targets. Please feel free to contact your loved ones and find out. Together we can determine what it is like in there."

Everyone frantically looked around for one of the limited number of jellyfish. Fights and negotiations broke out all over. Yemri cleared the message in the one she was holding and immediately replaced it with another message.

"Zyler, are you ok? We are working to get you all out of there. Please tell me how you are!"

The nuntium glowed blue and zoomed through the small cracks in the rocks. Yemri waited near the opening, watching for her message to return. Time passed, and nuntiums zoomed in and out of the cracks. Shouts heralded the return of the jellyfish messengers to their senders.

"She is ok! Tany is ok."

"Rolon is injured, but he is alive. We need to get healers!"

A nuntium was quickly sent for a healer.

Some nuntiums were not being returned, and anxious Serras started murmuring.

"What does it mean if it does not come back?"

"He has not answered!"

"We need to get in there!"

Yemri waited quietly while the commotion roiled around her. Tope and Pangor were part of the crew pulling stones away. She kept waiting, watching the hole grow wider.

Waiting for her nuntium to find her.

"You just need to reinforce the tunnel," Zitja said with a stoic look on her face, her typical expression—except when she was angry.

"The endeavor is not a failure, and you shouldn't give up on it."

"I am pretty sure everyone has decided it is a failure," Yemri answered dejectedly. "They will not let me finish it now."

"Who is this 'they,' and why are you going to let them tell you what to do?"

Yemri was sitting in the sand outside Zitja's cell, wearily leaning her head against the wall, eyes closed. Three years ago, someone had told Yemri that she was too casual with Zitja, that she had to present herself with dignity when she was speaking with the ocean's greatest threat. Yemri only laughed. It was far too late for such things. Yemri had been coming to see her aunt like this for years. Her visits had become a familiar part of her schedule—so much so that she often forgot about the threat the Siren Queen posed to the Serra civilization. But that wasn't a problem. Yemri still planned on killing Zitja, but she didn't see why she couldn't keep her locked up for a while longer and continue their discussions.

"The... the Serras. My balams. Everyone." Yemri was defeated. It was obvious she wouldn't be able to proceed with the tunnel when they—everyone—would stop her.

"Yemri." Zitja used her name as chastisement. "We have had this same conversation every day for twenty years. You bore me. You are ultimately in charge. No one tells you what to do."

"It is not every day," Yemri rebutted. "I do not visit you when I am traveling." She was deflecting from the matter at hand, she knew. She sighed. "It is not like that for Serras, and you know it. You may be the Siren Queen, ruling with an iron fist and strong arm, but that is not my way."

"I only have one arm, and it does not have iron at the end of it. I rule by making them believe that what I say is their only option."

Yemri became preoccupied with her thoughts. Every time she had been successful in her endeavors over the years, it had been because she did things the way Zitja suggested. Her aunt's advice had been vital as she matured into the Mother the ocean needed.

Not that anyone sees me as anything but the pup I was when the reign passed to me.

Their conversations began during the time Yemri had attempted to transform Zitja back into a Siren—or to trick Zitja into turning herself back—but Yemri found her plans for the transformation going nowhere. Over the years, however, Yemri had quit trying to regain control over the conversations she had with Zitja. She always gained so much wisdom from her aunt, and she could not let that go. She grew to depend on her aunt's advice, and she didn't think she could hold this position without Zitja's guidance. Every day she would tell her aunt, "I will kill you later." And every day Zitja replied, "I doubt it."

"Yemri!" Zitja snapped her out of her stupor. "You have to do what you want to do. You know what is right. You know what is best. Do it."

"Who is even going to use the tunnel after this?"

"You! You are going to use it, and you are going to make your Sentinels and guards use it. Anyone you are in command of… Oh, excuse me, but you are in command of *everyone*. Make them use it."

"I do not like that."

"Do what you want, Yemri. Stop living your life worried about what others think. Stop making decisions based on what you think everyone else wants or worrying about what they will think of your decisions. What do *you* want?"

Yemri didn't answer. They both knew, even after all this time, that what Yemri wanted was to not be the Ocean Mother.

"Have you recovered your ability to see penumbras?" Zitja nailed her right in the heart with that question.

"You know I have not."

"You have no one to blame for that but yourself."

"You do not know anything about it."

"I know more than you, more than your father. You think Sariah didn't tell me all about them and how they worked? She was my best friend her whole life. I knew her better than anyone."

"Yet you killed her anyway." She wanted to hurt Zitja as she had been hurt.

"You don't know anything about the world you live in." Before Yemri could respond, Zitja spoke again. "I think you have to get back to your responsibilities now, Ocean Mother."

Yemri hated not feeling Zitja's Ku. Had Yemri hurt her feelings? Was the Siren able to have hurt feelings? Was she angry? How did one know what another was thinking or feeling without touching their Ku or seeing their aura?

This interaction bothered Yemri in more ways than Zitja knew. Sariah had known the secrets to the penumbra? What they meant and why Yemri might have lost her ability to see them? It made Yemri angry with her mother for not sharing those details with her, but above all, it made her miss the mother she never really knew.

Yemri pushed herself up from where she had been lounging on the rocky ground and said, "I will kill you later."

As she turned from the gate and started to leave, she heard Ztija's reply.

"I look forward to it."

In two months' time, the tunnel had been cleared out and the HaruVivos had been performed for all four of the Serras lost in the collapse. Some said they were lucky that only four of twenty perished, but for Yemri, the loss of her beloved little brother did not feel so lucky. Today she was meeting with the families of the deceased Serras of the Tipua Clan, who had lost three of the four. Only Zyler had been lost from the Afiti crew.

She waited at the mouth of the tunnel. The walls and ceiling had been fortified with beams of wood and galvanized steel. She had even traveled through it once to prove it was safe. And now here she was, about to meet with the families of those who had lost their lives in this very passageway. She felt a nervous rush surge through her, and she looked back at Pangor and her father. Tope nodded encouragingly, and Yemri took that as a cue to begin the journey. Pangor and Tope followed behind without hesitation.

Praise Nephira for their loyalty.

The rest of the troops, guards, and attendants who had gathered for the memorial made their way through the passageway at a much slower pace. Several ceremony guests had already left days ago to take the long way around, still unable to trust the passageway.

The tunnel was dark. She had to use her Ku to feel the way, which was rather easy. She could feel the throng of Serras behind her and the open space in front of her. All around was thick, dense rock, impenetrable for her Ku.

We need to plant bioluminescents in here.

She breathed in and out to calm her irritation. It would help the tunnel become more popular if it didn't actually *look* like a death trap.

It felt peaceful though, and very silent in her Ku without the motion of water or commotion of plants and animals. It was almost like the channel was trying to deprive her of feeling. There wasn't much for her Ku to be aware of besides those behind her, and they were all rather subdued. The density of the stone almost made her feel HaruKu, as there was literally nothing she could feel beyond the tunnel walls. It made her yearn to go back to OnaKu. She hadn't been there in over fifteen years, but it was still her favorite place. She longed to live out the rest of her days there.

Finally, she saw a little light peeking out ahead, and she kicked her tail faster. Truth be told, she was anxious to get out of the place that had killed her younger brother. She wanted to promote the tunnel and make sure it was used, but she wouldn't ever forgive it for what it had taken from her.

The crowd on the other side was immense. She could feel the grief in the Serra's Kus mingled with anger and disapproval. She greeted the first few Serras she saw, and they were kind, though reserved.

When she turned to acknowledge a statuesque dam to her right, she placed her hand on her own heart, but the stately dam said, "This tunnel was a mistake. Is it truly faster to go the western route from here? Through the tunnel of loss, the shallow sea, the narrow gap, and then down to the Afiti? Is it really better?"

Yemri felt herself get defensive.

Tunnel of Loss. I hope the name does not stick.

She wanted to put this dam in her place. Zitja would not allow herself to be talked to in this manner. But there were many things she didn't tell her aunt about what it was like for her. She couldn't stand the admonishment she'd get if Zitja knew the truth of what the Serras thought about Yemri. Others had spoken to Yemri this way since she began her reign. They had felt comfortable doing so when she was a pup, and now that she was fully grown, she didn't know how to make them stop.

"I am so sorry you feel this way," Yemri responded kindly, though her anger simmered just below the surface. "This route will cut down travel to the Afiti by a fourth compared to taking the southern route. Not to mention its proximity to the NorMer! The clan will no longer seem so remote. But you are welcome not to use it if you do not wish."

"I certainly will not!"

Yemri thought choking the dam the way Zitja would have done was not proper Ocean Mother behavior, so she resorted instead to sympathy. "I am sorry about your loss. I know this is a terrible time for you and your family."

This seemed to deflate the dam's anger—albeit slightly—and she lowered her eyes. "I am sorry for your loss as well. Zyler was very kind to me when I met him." She turned and left, taking with her all of Yemri's energy. She didn't know how she was going to finish this memorial, talk to the Serras who mostly seemed to wish her ill, and mourn her brother when all she wanted to do was deal with her own grief and possibly sit quietly for a few moments.

An older buck with friendly eyes and a welcoming Ku came up beside her, and Yemri relaxed slightly. Maybe they would not all be hostile. Then he said, "Ocean Mother, I have heard of your beauty, and I had to come see it for myself. You are truly a sight to behold."

"You are here for the memorial?"

"I am."

"I am sorry about your loss," Yemri said sincerely. "Do you think this passageway is something you can see yourself using in the future?"

"Oh, oh… The Tunnel of Loss…" He was confused by the turn in conversation. "I do not often leave Tipua. So no, probably not."

The name is taking hold.

She cursed to herself but maintained a friendly, open Ku. "That is a fair reason. I hope that if you do find yourself needing to go to Afiti or NorMer you will see that the tunnel is very safe."

"Yes… That is good, Ocean Mother." He was obviously trying to get away from her now. "Thank you for talking with me."

She turned and let him leave unchallenged. Today was not about her unique tail, her curly hair, or her smooth skin—all things the Serras liked to comment on. She had stopped letting anyone turn her attention in that direction, and she wasn't going to let him today.

As she was about to address the multitude and move things along, she saw a blue blur zip into the crowd from the tunnel, and her heart soared. Since the tunnel collapse, nuntiums had been zooming all over the ocean. She felt conflicted about the circumstances that precipitated their use but was happy about the result, regardless. Now, as she watched the little glowing jellyfish zip through the tunnel, find its recipient, and then be sent back through the tunnel, Yemri couldn't help but smirk. Even the nuntiums knew it was the shortest route to their destination.

Instead of starting the memorial, Yemri made her way to Pangor's side. His face was serious, and she felt his Ku searching her out. "What did it say?" she asked, referring to the nuntium.

"It was Horrus," Pangor said, and Yemri assumed Horrus was one of the generals. She didn't know most of the Sentinels' names, nor who was assigned to which sections of the ocean. She knew she should—Nephira certainly would—but she couldn't be bothered to make it a priority amongst the other things she felt burdened with.

"And?"

"They have found the Maato. They are hiding in the long ices of the NorMer."

Yemri's eyes lit up. Exterminating the Maato had been her first and most passionate goal. "Go get them!"

"I have sent a nuntium to Horrus telling him to monitor their movement, and we will send reinforcements. I am going to take these Sentinels now and send a nuntium for more to join us."

Yemri set her mouth firmly and looked at him with all the authority she had learned to express. "Go through the tunnel. You will be in the NorMer tonight if you do."

"As you wish, Yemri. We will leave now."

She was about to tell him she would meet him at Daris to welcome the dams and pups, but suddenly she was overcome by the urge to finally see her success firsthand. "I will meet you there as soon as I am done here. Then we can bring everyone to Daris together." The dams and pups would be put up in the plethora of shelters in Daris, and the bucks would be put underneath the island. The prison caves had been empty, save for Zitja, for twenty years—forgotten by nearly everyone but Yemri. It was time to fill them up again.

Pangor took off, and dozens of Sentinels followed.

Yemri started the memorial, but she could feel that the Kus of the congregation were against her. She assumed the only reason she hadn't received more backlash was because she, too, had lost a loved one in the Tunnel of Loss.

Even I am calling it that?

Yemri made her speech to the crowd, though she did not fully concentrate on what she was saying. It was a generic speech, sincere and sympathetic, but her attention was elsewhere. Nuntiums were becoming very popular, the tunnel was completed, secure and safe, and now the Maato were going to be brought in. Maybe now, as she was nearing thirty, she would be taken seriously and honored for her accomplishments.

"And so, with the memory of our loved ones," Yemri concluded, "we dedicate this tunnel to them so that every time we pass through it, we will think of their sacrifice for our progress."

She knew it was a bold thing to do, but the passageway would truly make life easier. Tipua often had a difficult time traveling to other parts of the ocean, but this would give them such easier access to Afiti, NorMer, and Daris. She hoped they could see that.

She made her way out of the limelight and found her entourage. "Torvi, Milli, Tammin, we need to leave immediately."

"I do not have a reason to stay longer," Torvi answered just as a Serra couple swam up to Yemri. "So long as you can get away," she finished wryly.

Yemri nodded and turned her attention towards the couple. "Thank you for dedicating the tunnel to our son. That was kind of you," they said, though their Kus radiated no kindness towards Yemri. "My Bondmate," the buck said, gesturing towards the dam, who looked forlorn, nearly curled in upon herself in grief, "has been to the site of his death every day. The Tunnel of Loss will be a mausoleum to his memory."

Excellent! They are using the passage as a death marker, Yemri said to herself sarcastically.

She was irritated but didn't know if she had the right to be or not. It was hard for her to comfort others while she grieved herself. "I assure you it is safe to visit every day, if that is what you need."

At least they are going into the tunnel.

"Thank you, Ocean Mother." Yemri turned to leave, but he continued. "Nephira has truly blessed you with beauty. It was a pleasure to meet you."

"I am sorry for your family," Yemri said and made her way towards the Tunnel of Loss.

Milli and Tammin were on high alert as they closed in on their destination in the NorMer. The water around the Maato hiding place was thick with a sensation of tragedy and turmoil. Yemri felt her stomach tighten, and her chest felt hollow. A battle between Sentinels and Maato bucks raged along the side of the stone structure of the Maato lair.

Was this an abandoned building, a sunken Crural structure, or did the Maato create it?

Sentinels tried to restrain the Maato bucks. Her instructions were to bring in as many as they could alive, that killing was a last resort. She could see that many Maato bucks had chosen to fight to the death rather than surrender, and their bodies littered the battle grounds.

Among the fighting, dams were swimming around in confusion or sitting in the sand, clutching their pups in fear. Yemri had not thought about the fear they might feel, not knowing what would happen to them. She swooped down on one of the dams with two small pups clinging to her. She was thin to the point of frailty, nearly emaciated, her face gaunt.

"It will be all right," Yemri reassured her, placing a gentle hand on her shoulder. "We are here to release you from your captivity."

The dam looked up at Yemri with fear, betrayal burning in her Ku. "They killed my Bondmate! Who will protect us now?" She looked at her offspring, their scales still

418

up to their necks. The twin pups couldn't have been more than a few weeks old.

"We will protect you. We have a shelter for you all ready. I will keep you safe."

The mother placed her twins in the sand before exploding from where she sat, charging at Yemri furiously. "But who will keep us safe from you?" she demanded. The grieving dam struck Yemri twice in the face before Tammin flung her aside. Tammin unsheathed her sword, but Yemri shouted at her to stop. The mother was already scooping up her pups, her attention back on comforting them.

The blow could not have hurt more had the dam stabbed her in the gut with a sword. She had been warned about this. Tope had said that the dams were led to believe every Serra who was not Maato meant them harm and that Yemri was their worst enemy and greatest danger. The brainwashing was a way to keep them dependent so that the dams would willingly stay within the safety of the Maato no matter how horrible their lives were. The evil they knew, Tope had said, was more comfortable to them than the evil they did not. She had been warned, but it still hurt Yemri to the core that she was truly hated by those she was sincerely trying to help. She could only hope the rescued dams would feel her Ku and know of her sincerity.

"You will be safe and taken care of. I promise."

With that, Yemri left the dam to herself and moved on to a dam she saw hanging around the outskirts of the commotion, just staring, her Ku seemingly oblivious. "Are you all right? Are you hurt?"

The dam did not answer, did not look at Yemri, or acknowledge Yemri's Ku's connection.

"Can I help you? Are you hurt?" Yemri repeated, not knowing what else to say. "It will be ok. You are free now."

Finally, the dam connected to Yemri to reply, "Freedom is death. You have killed us."

They are brainwashed.

Yemri had to remind herself that they did not know any better. She conceded she would not be able to convince them now that they were better off. But they would see.

Yemri looked around for any dam who might be happy or grateful to be released from her oppression. She only saw fear. Kicking her tail lightly towards the entrance of the stone edifice, Yemri was determined to remain positive. She would assign Serras in Daris to help them adjust. There were always willing volunteers around the ocean who needed an opus or wanted to serve their fellow Serras. She would create a new opus specifically designed to help those who had experienced remarkable trauma.

Just as she was feeling unsure what to do next, she saw Pangor emerge from the large opening in the gray stone wall. She began to make her way to him, but she paused in astonishment. Following Pangor was an impressive and sturdy-looking buck whom Yemri assumed must be Horrus. He had a commanding air about him that screamed authority. In his hands he held a mass of ropes. The ends of the ropes were looped around the necks of the captured Maato bucks, each rope coiled into multiple loops around multiple necks. Horrus held the ends of three ropes, pulling along behind him twelve Maato bucks from the security of their hideout. The rest of the bucks' bodies were also bound, their wrists tied behind their backs and secured to their tails, rendering them almost completely incapacitated.

Behind Horrus, another Sentinel materialized with his own rope full of Maato bucks. Behind him, another, and then another. Yemri allowed a wave of pride to wash over her as she saw how many of the cruel Maato would be brought to justice, though her excitement was quickly dampened by the dams' behavior.

As the Maato bucks were hauled out, the dams flung themselves at them, screaming about injustice and crying for their release, thrashing against the ropes that held their men bound. Sentinels had to subdue them and prevent them from releasing their Bondmates, brothers, and fathers.

Yemri had not anticipated such strong resistance. It both sickened and saddened her. She was glad that she had decided to come here instead of going straight to Daris to wait for the Sentinels and the Maato, but she would never forget this moment. She could never consider this a win. Her other pet projects—Daris Tour and the tunnel—had also dramatically turned from a win to a loss in one day. Though she comforted herself with the reminder that the Daris Tour pups were all safely delivered to their destinations with only the loss of one magister and that they would always have guards in the future to protect them, she would never live down the initial failures everyone saw in this or the tunnel.

Yemri started as she heard a gut-wrenching scream from the crowd. She followed the anguished Ku until she found the source of the turmoil.

A dam, floating in the water a short distance from Horrus, screamed again as she watched one of the tied-up bucks, who had been thrashing wildly, begin to slowly and horrifyingly turn a ghostly white. At the same time his skin turned pale, his tail turned black.

This cannot be happening!

After his transformation was complete, another's began, then another, and another. The transformations were washing over the Maato bucks with such ferocity, they would all become Sirens in a matter of moments. The Sentinels had to get them out of here. The Maato dams and pups were the only ones who were susceptible to the Song, and Yemri did not trust that the newly minted Sirens would not harm their own kin.

"Get them out of here now!" Yemri yelled to Pangor. "Protect the dams and pups!"

Pangor sent out the commands, and his Sentinels picked up the pace, but it was too late. All around her, dams began writhing in pain. Yemri hung her head in defeat. The most likely outcome was that these bucks would kill their own family members, which was appalling. She knew from her discussions with Zitja that the Song pulled the Sirens in and created an overwhelming compulsion to Sing. But Yemri also knew that the Song was controllable. Most Sirens didn't want to control its power and didn't ever try, but if the desire was strong enough, they could control it. These bucks were choosing to take the dams down with them.

But as Yemri looked around, something wasn't right. The dams—not all, but a handful—were in pain, but not in the way Yemri had seen the Song work. They were in pain the way these bucks had just been.

Sure enough, Yemri looked on in devastation as those few dams began their own transformation.

Was it such a contagious thing?

Were they so entrenched in their captivity that they felt they were beholden to these bucks, whether they were

Serra or Siren? Was this why Dorio had turned into a Siren for his Bondmate so long ago? Had he no choice in the matter? Yemri wished she had been older when he changed back; there was so much that could have been learned from him. Dorio had died very shortly after his retransformation, and Yemri had never thought in all these years to ask the Cor what they learned in their interviews.

Yemri felt ill. Had she made the right choice in releasing these dams? While they were angry and confused now, surely they would come around and see that they were free. Would the ones who didn't transform eventually enjoy freedom?

Is it freedom if it is not wanted?

Pangor and his men struggled to haul away the newly transformed Sirens and eventually made it out into the open water. The dams who had transformed either fought with the Sentinels or fled. Yemri was appalled to see that transformed dams who were mothers gathered their pups and took them along. How would a Serra pup fare being raised by a Siren? It was unprecedented. Sirens didn't reproduce on their own. They increased in numbers only when other Serras were transformed by the curse.

Screaming seemed like the only thing left for Yemri to do. Scream, or run, or hide in a cave with her shame for the rest of her life. Yemri looked around at the aftermath. The Serra dams that remained, some holding pups, fought feebly at the Sentinels tasked with seeing them safely to Daris. Those few who didn't fight back swam distractedly to and fro, confusion plastered on their glassed over faces.

"If you will come with us," Yemri shouted with all the command she could muster—though she knew it came across thin and uncertain, "we will see you safely to your new homes."

The mother of the twin pups who had screamed at Yemri earlier now shouted again, her voice ringing clearly to all who remained, "You have ruined us all! I hope you die a miserable death!"

With all the commotion, no one had noticed that the current was shifting. What had started out as strong currents were quickly becoming a dangerous problem. Rough water was getting stirred up into a frothy mess from the storm overhead. The Maato hideout was located in shallow water, which the Serras generally avoided. It was too rough and dangerous to try to live in such shallow water. The storm overhead was just picking up speed, yet already it was fierce, and the Serras down below were starting to be tossed around.

How did they live like this?

It would be impossible to stay here during the storm, and there would be many deaths if they didn't get themselves deeper. Even someone who wasn't at risk of drowning could perish if beaten too badly by the rough waves. Yemri gave the order to get the remaining dams and pups into deeper water and head to Daris.

"Torvi, I saw an abandoned pup after its mother transformed. Find it and take it to Daris with everyone else."

"Yes! Of course," Torvi replied, her red hair a blur as she streaked away on her mission.

"Milli! See to it that Torvi finds the pup and makes it to Daris safely. I do not want anyone left behind!" Milli followed after Torvi without reply.

"You!" Yemri connected to the Ku of the nearest Sentinel. "Stay behind. Not for long, mind you! We need to leave, but stay and make sure everyone else leaves safely. Be quick, round them all up, but be the last to leave."

"Yes, Ocean Mother," he responded dutifully, without a trace of fear in his Ku at the thought of being the last one to remain. Yemri would remember to thank him later and praise him in front of Pangor.

"Tammin." Yemri turned her attention to the large stone and wood building just as a wooden chunk was ripped from the structure and hurtled through the water in their direction. It was only because she was looking directly at it that she was able to roll out of the way and fling herself safely to the ocean floor.

"Are you all right?" Tammin was by her side in a moment.

"I am completely fine," Yemri said grimly. She flung herself off the ground and looked as wholly unshaken as she could muster. "Who would build a shelter so close to the surface? It makes no sense."

"I think this was Crural-made, Yemri. It looks like the island it is sitting on sank entirely."

Yemri looked around and noted that the island was small, containing just the edifice and surrounding accouterment. It wouldn't be the first time Serras inhabited something the Crurals had lost to the ocean.

Her anger subsided as she realized there was no one to be angry with, and she finished putting her plan into action.

"Tammin, I want you to go inside and make sure no one is hiding. Bucks, dams, pups, whoever is in there, get them out. But be quick! I do not think that flimsy shelter will survive this storm. It looks to be a big one."

"What about you? I cannot leave you alone, and you just sent Milli away."

"I will be fine, Tammin. I am leaving this very minute. Go clear the building and meet me along the way, or I will see you at Daris. I think I shall be fine among this throng of Sentinels."

Tammin looked hesitant, but she eventually conceded, and with a few powerful thrusts of her tail, was swallowed up inside the dilapidated structure. Yemri was alone in the chaos. No one was paying any attention to her as a swirl of activity raged on around them.

When the Maato had begun turning into Sirens, Yemri had made a private decision. She needed to be alone. She had to get away from everything. She was a failure and couldn't bear to deal with everything at this moment. If she could just get away for a few days… Usually, there was no way for her to get even a moment alone, but now the storm made a perfect cover.

Yemri sprang into action, pushing herself as quickly as she could in the opposite direction of the stream of Serras headed for Daris. In just moments, she was swallowed up by the storm, and no one was able to see her. A few minutes more, and no one could reach her with their Kus.

When Yemri was far enough that no one could find her, she slowed her speed. Now was the time to drop down into the depths below the storm, to seek safety in the deeper water. But that wasn't part of her plan, either.

Yemri kicked herself towards the surface, and in only a moment, her head was out in the open air, where she was pelted with rain. She expelled the water from her lungs and tried to breathe in air, but the rain was so heavy and the waves so large that she coughed and choked. She cursed that she could breathe water or air, but not both at once. Finally, she gave up trying to breathe air. As a wave crashed over her, she filled her lungs with water again. She popped above the surface again and held her breath.

Around her was nothing but black water, a roiling black sky, and massive waves cresting in gigantic white peaks.

Where is it?

She looked up in the sky, but it was blackness and gray clouds as far as she could see in all directions. Suddenly, a white streak lit up the sky, glorious and terrifying, but that didn't seem to be the thing she was looking for, though it was beautiful. She ducked under the surface to take a few quick breaths and then shot above the waves once again.

A wave scooped her up and lifted her ten feet into the sky before cresting and crashing back down. Her stomach churned from the flow of the water. As it lifted her up and pulled her down again, she vomited.

She kicked herself under the water and dove a few feet until the ocean began to calm. She breathed in and out heavily and tried to clear the foul taste from her mouth.

Where is it?

She tried to maintain some semblance of composure. The water was still rough at that depth, so she kicked herself lower until the push and pull of the current subsided. She breathed again.

She had decided recently that seeing one of those colorful sky arcs was something she wanted to do. It had taken a while to come to that conclusion. Having people tell her about them her whole life had made her feel oddly resistant to seeing one, as if never having seen one left her somehow victorious over their inquiries. She didn't know what she was winning, but for years it felt like she had, if only so she could be contrarian.

Then something in her shifted. It was the same feeling she had when she'd decided that Zitja had been right all along. She had to take control, make people listen, and do what she wanted to do. She had always been curious about the colorful phenomenon, but by avoiding it simply because other people told her she should see it, that didn't make her win.

No one was winning.

Yemri took in a deep breath and threw herself towards the surface. She broke through with so much momentum she almost caught air, though the heavy rain made it seem as if the sky held as much water in it as the ocean did.

Yemri looked straight up. The thing she was looking for should be in the sky. Everyone always said they only appeared because of a storm. She had been above water plenty of times in the sunshine or at night and had never seen one before, but she'd never surfaced during a storm. There was so much rain and so many dark clouds that she wondered how anyone would see any colors if they were here. She was looking up into the blackness, the rain falling in heavy sheets against her face and arms, giant waves tossing her up and down, back and forth. She thought she was going to be sick again when she spotted a large mass of wood being pitched around in the ocean several feet away.

At first Yemri thought it was just harmless driftwood. But as the beam whipped across the surface, chased and pushed by the wind, Yemri realized the storm was just as dangerous as she had warned everyone it was. There was a reason she told them to flee from storms. What was she doing up here? Just proving a point? And to whom?

The wood floated closer, and Yemri realized the mass wasn't driftwood but several smooth planks of wood all fashioned tightly together. It was the hull of a ship, and a rather large one by the looks of it. She spotted another large piece of the ship, and in the water—swelling a dozen feet in the air—was a huge sheet of white canvas.

There had been a shipwreck close by. Yemri expelled the water she had been holding in her lungs and gulped in rainy sea air.

I should help the Crurals, she thought.

Surely they would all die in this storm that was also very likely to do her in, and she wasn't at risk of drowning. She could not see where the ship had been, but at that moment, a wooden beam hurtled towards her on a rogue wave. Yemri had just a moment as the wave dipped down for her to propel herself over the log, fling herself through the air, and land gracelessly on the other side. She'd had enough. She wasn't going to see the colorful arch, and she couldn't help the Crurals even if she could find them. It was time to head for safety in the depths.

Just as she was bending at the waist to dive under the waves, she was struck on the head. It left her dazed and seeing blurry. Yemri was now completely surrounded by massive ship fragments on every side. When she was struck on her left side by another strong mass of wood, this one broke skin and bruised a rib. She screamed out, blinded by pain, but she still knew she needed to get under.

Yemri thrust herself downward just as a swell pushed her up higher and higher—so high that she simply couldn't get under the surface. She kicked and kicked as the wave pushed her high into the sky. Finally it broke. The wave crashed in on itself, and Yemri was flung into the debris. She hit the ship's sturdy mast and her tail landed amongst ropes and became entangled. Her arm was surely broken, but she couldn't be sure as the adrenaline coursed through her. She was struggling to free herself from the ropes as another wave crashed on top of her, raining down more pieces of the ship. She could not free herself from the ropes and was being pelted by heavy wooden objects.

A moment later, a mast the size of a building swung through the water, hitting her on the head. Everything turned bright white. Then everything went black.

Chapter 24

Santiago

Santi floated, staring at Rogan, as a wave of groans, boos, and a few cheers swept through the crowd. Rogan connected to the team and said, head and shoulders hanging in shame, "I am so sorry, everyone."

Santi swam up to Rogan and placed a hand on his shoulder. "It is ok. I love you anyway."

He looked up just enough for her to see his tiny smile, and she winked at him.

After that, the crowd of spectators overwhelmed them, offering condolences. They were jostled about by well-wishers, though there was also the occasional accusation. The accusers seemed less concerned about the outcome of the game and more concerned about Santi's part in the demoralizing upcoming event of killing Zitja.

Celia, Grendor, and Coral were there offering words of encouragement and reassuring them that they were still winners in their eyes. Grendor was quiet, though not accusatory; he knew Krell's wishes but didn't necessarily support them himself.

Finally, Rogan was able to pull Santiago away from the crowd and into the safety of the participants' tent. As soon as they entered the tent, the two goal guards from the other team accosted them. The one Santi knew was named Joper spoke aggressively. "You were supposed to win! Why did you do that? We were working so hard to let you win, and it was like you were not even trying."

"What?" Santi exclaimed.

"We were told to lose. Threatened even! But you cannot possibly be that bad." He looked at them in confusion.

"Listen." Rogan put his hands up in a supplicating gesture. "We did not ask to win. We did not even want to play." This revelation seemed to ease the animosity of the other two players. "We figured if we had to do something we did not want to do... well, then we might as well have someone who wants to play progress through the tournament."

Joper and his sister looked at each other before the small dam spoke. "I worry we will get in trouble."

"Don't worry about that," Santi said. "We'll support you!"

"Now go," Rogan added. "Prepare for your next game! And have fun playing a real game against an opponent that will be a tough challenge." He smiled at them.

The two shared something between their Kus before the buck asked, "And you are sure you will swear we tried our best to lose?"

"Yes, of course!" Santi said emphatically. "We are just very, very bad at this sport!"

"Ok then." They both smiled and made their way back to the other two members of their team.

Tizz and Torren, who had been listening discretely to the conversation, now joined Santi and Rogan.

"I cannot believe Krell took it so far," Torren said in awe. "He really wanted you to win, Santi."

"Yeah, he wants me to be some sort of hero." She let out a sigh and scrunched up her lips. "He has big plans for me. I worry that confessing to Joper's team that we wanted to lose will come back to bite us. But they deserved to know."

"Come on," Rogan urged. "We had better leave the island before Krell comes to find us himself."

"Concerns? Ideas? Solutions? A way out of this?" Santi asked, stealing Torren's line from only hours ago. She thought asking for input was something Amed would do, and she wished she had Amed's talent for clear-headed strategies right now. One thing she didn't want was for anyone to feel like they were being forced to help her.

"No one has to do this who doesn't want to," she reiterated.

The entire scheme was a result of their joint brainstorming and Rogan's original idea; Santi hoped there wouldn't come a point in the plan when they couldn't find a solution to any problem they ran into.

When no one seemed to have more to say, she continued. "Sorrl and Torren, are you sure you're comfortable with this arrangement?"

"It was my idea," Sorrl said, nodding his head, his short white hair staying perfectly in place. "It is for the best. You need Torren's help, and I cannot leave my students unchaperoned."

"Grendor and Celia, we'll meet you in thirty minutes, ten miles south of the tournament grounds." The two of them didn't respond as they took off to do their jobs. Celia was almost too eager to be the distraction—a role she was born to play—while Grendor played the thief. He was less enthusiastic but felt the cause was justified. Santi also suspected Grendor was at the end of his patience after having to submit to Krell's overreach of authority and was just as eager as the rest of them to put a stop to his power-hungry ways.

Coral's Ku was heavy and worried. "Amaratizz, you are old enough to make your own decisions. You are smart, and brave, and strong-"

"Mother," Tizz said with great care and comfort. "I will be ok."

"I worry. Of course I worry."

"Rogan and Santi will take care of me," she said. "They always have."

Tizz was sixteen now. She was not trained in fighting, but she was a much better swimmer than Santi, and naturally agile. She and Santi were probably evenly matched in the "take care of" department, but Santi's heart swelled at the confidence.

"We will, Coral," Santi reassured her.

"I know, Santiago. I think I wish I could go with you, but it is not my place." Coral had never been the one for adventure; she left that to Amed and their children, who had an abundance of passion for adventure. "You will need me here to keep Krell at bay. I still have a modicum of sway over many of his Sentinels. I can keep them off you while you are gone."

They all said goodbye to each other after they checked and rechecked that their bags were full of food and supplies and their weapons were secure. Tizz had fastened her father's khert—a large arrowhead shaped blade that sat atop a brass-knuckle type hilt—to her hip, though she had never practiced with it and had admitted she would rather not do any fighting. She took after her mother, choosing peace and negotiation over violence. It was the main reason both Coral and Amaratizz were so willing to help retrieve Sully: it had the makings of a great experiment for peace. Could their family figure out how to reverse the curse on Sully? And possibly the rest of the Serras?

Forty minutes later, Rogan, Santiago, Amaratizz, and Torren were huddled ten miles off the southernmost point of the tournament grounds, treading anxiously and expecting something to go wrong.

"I can't believe we haven't run into any opposition yet," Santi remarked. "They were very adamant that I not leave. And after our little stunt…."

Tizz laughed and said, "I am sure they are scouring the tournament island for you."

"There should not really be anyone guarding the waters in this direction," Rogan reassured Santi. "Why would you head south? Your home—and generally everything in the ocean you would want to visit—is north and east of the tournament."

"Which is exactly why we went south," Torren added. "And it seems to be working. I do hope Grendor was successful and we can leave soon. "

"Won't it take longer?" Santi asked with a laugh. "You know, heading the wrong direction first?" She squeezed her hands into fists anxiously as she stretched her Ku's awareness into the surrounding water.

What is taking them so long?

"Not that I don't think it's a good idea, and obviously it's more important that we get away from the tournament grounds and Krell, but I really have to be back for the last day. Being on the run from Krell is not the kind of future I want to have."

Tizz laughed at this comment. "Santi the runaway!"

"More like a fugitive." She rolled her eyes. "How fun."

"I am not familiar with that word," Amaratizz replied. "A Crural concept, no doubt. I say embrace it!"

"I don't know about that. I think it would be better just to get back by the end of the week. Then we can focus on Sully and the curse instead of running from Krell forever."

"Do not forget about not killing Zitja," Tizz added, trying to keep the mood light. "You still have that fun challenge to look forward to."

Santi was strung tight as a bow and her Ku was so on edge that Tizz sobered and asked gently, "Have you decided what you will do?"

Santi nodded and breathed out her tension. It was amazing how much more relaxed she felt now that she had made up her mind. "Whatever Krell decides for this grand finale, I'm just going to use it to explain to everyone that I can't kill her. I'll convince them that reversing the curse is our best option, and if we work together, we can make it happen. It's all I can do. But more importantly, I will show them I'm not Krell's puppet. That is why we must make it back for the end. I have to use this opportunity to make my opinion known."

"Do not worry," Rogan said comfortingly. "Once we get into the current I told you about—the one that will take us almost directly to the Panama tunnel—we will be able to make up the time we lose now by going in the wrong direction."

Santi thought about the implications of using the current. She knew Sully had used it to cross the Atlantic when he kidnapped her, but she had been tied beneath a whale and hadn't been able to really feel the benefits—not that she had been paying attention to that aspect of the journey. She was suddenly struck by an important thought.

"Why did Sully take me to the Mediterranean? You said that the Caribbean is the new home of the Sirens, where we are headed now. What if Sully is actually over in Europe? We'll never find him."

"I wondered that too," Torren added. "I guess we can never know for sure. Rogan?"

Rogan's ready answer made it clear he had thought this through. "I assume it was so that it would be harder for us to find him. Long ago, the Sirens made their home at a place called Anthemoessa, in the shallow sea, which you call

437

the Mediterranean. That is where Sully took you. They were driven from there and made to reside in the Siren Harbor before my father was Sentinel Commander. But my father," a pang ripped across Rogan's Ku so intensely that his three traveling companions felt the sorrow and heartache as strongly as if it were their own. Rogan paused then started again. "Amed knew they would not take you to Siren Harbor. They would not risk their lair being found out. Kidnapping you was a trap for my father, so they wanted to take you somewhere he was sure to find you."

"He told me," Tizz added, " that they went to Anthemoessa because of its cave system and because it's difficult to reach deep inside the shallow sea. The Sirens knew it would be harder to get Santi out of there, making it a better location to trap Father. I thought he would have explained that part?" She touched each of their Kus deliberately, searching for the acknowledgment that they knew this aspect of the kidnapping. When she found none, she continued.

"We were traveling near Siren Harbor when he explained it to me. It started because he was warning me about the dangerous waters, and he was cautioning me to be safe, but the conversation led to Santi's kidnapping. It is how I learned so much information that will help us today! Have any of you been there? Or know about it?" Again, she waited and searched their Kus, but when no one answered in the affirmative, she gave a little scoff. "Well, it is a good thing you brought me then. I am going to be very valuable."

That lightened the mood somewhat, and Santi matched Tizz's tone. "It seems as if everyone has a quarter of the information and ideas needed to pull this off, so together we have all the information we need. Perfect!"

The light mood was washed away as Santi one again fretted about Celia and Grendor. "How long has it been? Surely too long?"

"Almost an hour," Torren answered reluctantly.

It left Santi wondering how they all seemed to know the passing of time without watches or the sun for guidance, but she was too nervous to get to the bottom of it now. Celia and Grendor were worryingly late. If they didn't arrive soon, the rest of them would have to go back to the island. They couldn't possibly execute this convoluted plan without success on Grendor and Celia's part.

Minutes ticked by. They all waited silently, too worried for conversation at the moment.

And then they felt something. Coming upon them very quickly was a swarm of... something. Santi tried to connect, but it was all moving too fast. Her companions, however, had been waiting for this. A moment later, Grendor was pulling up beside them with a team of Krell's marlins.

"Well done!" Rogan exclaimed, and all of them felt relieved. "Remarkable! We needed you to steal Krell's speedfish for this to work, but I did not dare to believe you could."

"The credit goes to Celia," Grendor replied. Santi couldn't help but be pleased by the way Grendor's Ku emitted overwhelming pride when he mentioned Celia. "She kept Krell distracted with a whirl of questions and—I could not believe it—admonishment about not 'taking care of her baby.'" Grendor didn't mimic Celia's accent, but Santi could hear her mother clearly in those words. She imagined Celia drilling Krell—currently the most powerful and influential Serra buck in the ocean—with a string of questions about the rest of the tournament and demands to know "how could joo put so much pressure on my babee?" It made Santi smile.

Grendor passed the marlins' reins off to Rogan, and the four of them each grabbed hold of a cord. They had decided that leaving the old Beetle behind would be faster, and instead they all tied themselves to the team of marlins, looking like some strange combination of fish/sled-dog/water-skiing situation. Santi wasn't sure this would work over the long distance they had to travel.

A moment later, they were off. Santi closed her eyes against the rush of water pushing against her body. When she opened her eyes again, she looked at the rope she held, which was tied around her waist and then attached to Rogan, who rode in front of her. She was sure he was taking the brunt of the force of the water with his own body, just as Torren did for little Tizz next to them. She shook her head.

I hope this works.

They had been traveling for a couple hours, finally turning east towards the main current. The current was supposed to take them to Panama with greater speed, but she didn't think she could take any more of the onslaught of water. The pressure didn't hurt, but it was exhausting, and the constant pressure left every nerve feeling a little raw. She didn't think she could take the greater pressure once they entered the current.

When they came within yards of the great current, Santiago was surprised she could see it ahead of them, ever so slightly. The water in the current rippled with the rush of movement. Had she not known to look for it, she would not have noticed the subtle change.

She was suddenly filled with nervous anticipation. Their group turned slightly so that they pulled up parallel to the current before thrusting themselves into it. Santi couldn't have prepared for the feeling that engulfed her. It was as if she was both sucked into the current and pushed forward by it, and she stumbled slightly. If she hadn't been secured to the team of fish, she might have tumbled bottom over top. The sensation of being both pushed and pulled at the same time was bizarre. What was even more bizarre was that the pressure she was expecting was all but nonexistent. It was as if the current alleviated the force from the pull of the fish. However it worked, Santi was grateful for the reprieve.

"Chimba!" she said, and laughed.

They carried on for hours. Santi grew tired from the monotony of the journey. She adjusted the rope around her waist. She couldn't help but notice the irony of heading for Sully while being tied to another fish, though technically a whale was not a fish. She still felt the whole thing was terribly poignant.

As the sun began to set, Santi realized they had been traveling over ten hours, and maybe closer to twelve. She wasn't very good at judging time underwater. Her eyes were heavy, and her arms and legs felt like lead. She didn't know how she could possibly keep this up for another day and a half. That was when she actually took notice of Rogan in front of her. He had been there all along, but she had been riding along in a sleepy daze. Only now did she realize that he was not awake. In fact, he was folded over on himself, sleeping as soundly as any man she had ever seen sleeping on an airplane: uncomfortable but still oblivious to the world. She looked to her right and saw that Torren and Tizz were doing the same, though Tizz had sprawled herself out on the rope in front of her. She had her arms folded across the cord, head resting on her arms, and her tail streaming behind her. It seemed Santi was the only one who felt an obligation to remain conscious.

With this newfound permission to slip into oblivion, Santi copied Tizz's posture and fell instantly asleep.

Santi awoke to Rogan untying the marlins, and she watched as they swam away. The current was still pushing them all along, but they had slowed remarkably. Santi cocked her head at him but didn't ask.

Rogan knew what she wanted and replied, "Torren is gathering a new set of marlins. Luckily, they are plentiful in this area, so we think we can get more than eight. And with a bunch of fresh, well-rested fish who have not already traveled a thousand miles, we'll get there even more quickly." Santi broke into a sarcastic wide-mouthed grin. "I know! Arriving at the Siren's lair even faster! Exciting, right?"

Torren arrived, herding over a dozen frisky marlins like sheep.

"There are four for each of us," he said.

Rogan and Tizz took the ropes in their hands and moved towards the swarm to begin their own wrangling. Santi gave a little shrug and also made her way into the chaos. She began winding her rope as she saw the other three doing, each had their ropes neatly in hand. Marlins swirled around, brushing her feet every once in a while and catching a fin on her hair. The fact that Torren was able to make them all come with him raised so many questions in her mind, but for now she chalked it up to the marvel that was the ocean in general.

She paused in the water, still winding the rope. The marlins never stopped their harried movement. That, combined with the rush of the current, left Santi feeling overwhelmed. She looked at the others for a clue as to what to do.

Rogan had one of the massive fish in a tight embrace around the middle as he slipped a rope loop around its head and secured it snuggly, just below the gills. When that was done, he turned and caught another and repeated the process. Torren was just working on roping his first one. Though the marlins had all followed him to their group, it still looked like he was having a small struggle getting them roped up. Santi took a deep breath and felt a tiny surge of anxiety. These fish were more than twice as large as Rogan, who was already formidable, and even Rogan had to manhandle them.

She looked over at Amaratizz and shook her head incredulously. The lightweight dam was gently fitting a loop over the head of her third marlin—a fish three times her size—while it sat motionlessly in the water. Her fourth fish was waiting patiently for its turn to be tied up. Santi's face crinkled in disbelief.

Ok! she told herself, squaring her shoulders and plunging into the task. Rope finally wound in her hands, she held a loop in her fist and reached out to grab the first fish that passed by. It slipped through her hands easily. She tried again with the same results.

"Fish in water are slippery little jerks, huh?" she mumbled under her breath. A marlin swam in an erratic circle next to her, and as it came around, she threw the rope, trying to lasso it. She was not discouraged when that tactic failed only because she didn't have high hopes for her cowgirl skills.

Santi scowled and redoubled her efforts on the next marlin that came close. She lunged at it, arms stretched wide, and landed on the fish. She wrapped her arms around the head, legs around the body, and held on. Riding it like a sloppy bull rider and feeling a little more satisfied with her burgeoning cowgirl skills, she successfully wrangled the giant fish. Santi pulled the open loop of the rope over its head, tugging it downward to sit just below the gills, as she had seen everyone else do. Only then did she let go, unfurl the cord, and tread in the water while holding it like a leash. She nodded, looking proudly at her accomplishment.

Pleased with her efforts, Santi glanced up to see her companions looking at her, completely flabbergasted, their Kus filled with stifled amusement.

"Well," Tizz said, smiling brightly, "that is one way to do it."

The three of them came over, and with barely any effort at all, collected the last three giant fish and hooked them up to Santi's rope for her. Tizz easily slipped the next loop of rope over the head of a marlin and ushered it into line in front of the one Santi had laboriously wrestled. The bucks added their catches to the line, and Santi tied the reins around her waist. Her own four-fish sled team!

"Ummm, yes," Santi said trying to be stoic. "Thanks."

"Not that I would not love to see that again," Rogan said. "There is just no time."

Santi felt Torren connect to the school of marlins as a whole and instruct them to go. The mass of them shot off at a speed far faster than the previous group had been able to accomplish. Santi held on to the rope in front of her to try to remain steady and let her feet dangle behind her. There was no point in even trying to kick her legs; the effort would be completely unhelpful.

"You guys used your Kus to get the marlins in your ropes, didn't you?" She didn't need them to answer. She knew they had. "Duh. As if I haven't been doing that with Amphitrite since I was a child." She silently reproached herself.

When will I remember to do things like a Serra and not try to wrestle my way through everything like a Crural?

"What I don't understand though, Tizz, is how you did that so peacefully. The stupid fish were basically lined up to get in your ropes."

"I do not know," Amaratizz said thoughtfully. "I have always had a way with animals. Most things actually. Things just come easy for me when I apply my Ku."

"That doesn't really help me, I guess, but I'll definitely apply my Ku harder."

"Santi," Rogan offered, leaning over and gently placing his hand on the small of her back, bursting with love and pride, "you are doing great."

"Thank you," she said. And she meant it. She felt like she was trying very hard, and it was nice to be acknowledged.

"Ok, everyone had better wake up now!" Torren's voice said with some urgency, and Santi's eyes snapped open. She woke more quickly than she ever had before.

"Sirens?" She asked, pushing out her Ku and looking around frantically.

Rogan and Tizz were blinking themselves awake, and Santi felt a pang of guilt at being the only one who didn't have to take a shift keeping the school on course. She had made sure over the last two days to take turns staying awake with each of them, but as she was the only one who did not know to direct the fish on the right path—nor did she know the right path—she was at liberty to sleep as she wished.

"No, nothing like that." He chuckled at Santi's panic. "We are coming upon the Panama Passageway, so everyone is going to need to be awake and make sure their group gets into it and maneuvers though it without incident."

Santi eyed the path that lay before her and was again filled with panic, a panic composed less of fear than worry. Until now, she had only had to minimally guide her marlins. They naturally followed whoever was leading the group, and right now that was Torren, who was currently charging head-on into a solid land mass.

The Panama Passageway was the point at which they were going to cross from the Pacific Ocean to the Caribbean, at the juncture of the north and south American landmasses. It was one of only two Serra-made tunnels that cut through landmasses. The other was in the Mediterranean, and it was called the Lost Tunnel. She wasn't sure why it was named that because everyone knew of its existence, but she was sure there was some story there. The Panama Passageway's name made sense though. What the name did not do was inform her about where the opening was and how they would travel through.

"It is a small passage, so I think we should go in single-file. And probably slowly."

Before Torren had finished speaking, Tizz was bellowing, "I will go first!"

Rogan, sensing Santi's apprehension through her Ku, reassured her calmly, "It is not dangerous, and it is very short. Just follow behind me and take as much time as you need. Or I can go behind you to make sure you are ok."

Santi grabbed the rope in front of her that would now serve as reins. "I think I'd rather follow you." She nodded and smiled hesitantly.

"Just remember, my love, those fish are stupid and clumsy, but even they will not swim headfirst into the walls."

This made Santi laugh at her white-knuckle grip on the reins, and she relaxed her shoulders. She told herself she was ready, but her stomach flipped as Amaratizz let out a little hoot and dove into the nearly imperceptible tunnel mouth carved into the rock, full speed.

Torren followed Amaratizz, albeit with less reckless enthusiasm. Rogan slowed down significantly, and Santi followed his lead, pulling on the ropes in front of her, feeling for the first time just how much strength the marlins contained in their powerful bodies. Hours ago, when she had directed them out of the current to make their way towards the passageway, she could feel the difference in the water's resistance, but until that moment, she had not fully appreciated the marlins' strength. Now, as she guided them, it took all her strength to pull the ropes, straining her biceps and pushing her feet out in front of her, wishing she had something to press against for resistance. She couldn't stop the big fish—didn't know how she would actually get them to stop when it was time—but she was able to slow them enough so that when Rogan disappeared into the tunnel, she felt better about negotiating her way inside.

Use my Ku.

She shook her head at her forgetfulness and connected to the marlins. It wasn't like connecting to other Serras, or even to Amphitrite. These fish were all instinct and habit. They wouldn't follow her words or suggestions, but she tried to instill in them a sense of slowing. It might be working—she couldn't tell—but she continued to strain with her arms nonetheless.

The land mass loomed closer and closer, endless and solid. Eyes focused on the small opening through which the others had disappeared, Santi continued to pull back with both arms to slow the fish, pulling harder with her right arm to line them up with the tunnel opening. The fish made the shift to the right. She eased up and breathed a sigh of relief as she and the marlins slipped easily into the tunnel.

She was immediately blanketed in darkness, and her panic resumed. How would she keep them from running into walls if she couldn't see anything? Santi reined in the fish harder, and they slowed slightly. Finally, after what seemed like hours, she saw a bright glow up ahead, and the tightness in her chest eased. If she headed straight for the light, they would be fine.

She lined up the team of fish and let them pick up speed. In no time at all, they were basked in the glow of hundreds of green luminescent orbs set in nooks all around the perimeter of the cavern. Seeing how vastly large the tunnel was allowed her to breathe another sign of relief. She could have stood on Rogan's shoulders and still not reached the rough sides of the tunnel, so it was definitely large enough for her team of marlins to traverse without incident. Then they passed the last of the luminescent lamps, and the tunnel gradually grew dark again.

"Santiago?" Rogan's voice was reassuring but worried. "I can feel you getting farther behind me. Is everything ok?"

She couldn't feel his Ku. It wasn't because of the mass of earth around her, as she could feel straight ahead if she tried, but because she had been so focused on her task she had forgotten to expand her Ku. She did so now so that she could reconnect. "I'm just a little nervous. Go ahead, I'm coming!"

Again, Santi reined in the team. She let Rogan's Ku go. She couldn't hold on to it while managing the team. She was too uneasy. She did not like speed while they were in the dark. What if the tunnel curved? What if there was a stalagmite to cause injury? She would rather a collision happen at a slower pace.

Just as she was getting used to the dark again, she saw another green glow up ahead and eased up on the reins, allowing the marlins to pick up a little speed. They made their way into another portion of lighted tunnel and then back out, into darkness. Santi chewed her lip, wishing the entire tunnel was lit. She was beginning to think her anxiety could not handle driving the team through the tunnel any longer when she saw light up ahead once more. This time, however, the light had a yellowish tint to it, and she knew it was sunlight. "We're almost done!" she cheered to her marlins, feeling like they had become comrades through the perilous journey.

"Santi?" She heard Rogan's voice touch her Ku.

"Yes!" she answered, far more exuberantly than necessary.

"We did not think you were coming out!" He was both relieved and bewildered.

Santi made her way out of the tunnel and saw Tizz, Torren, and Rogan all waiting with their teams. Once she was back in open water, she realized she had been moving at a snail's pace. The narrowness of the tunnel, combined with the blinding darkness, had made her feel like she had been recklessly speeding. Now she could see that her marlins were crawling along about as slowly as Santi swam herself.

"We have been waiting nearly ten minutes." Rogan detached himself from his team and made his way towards her. "I was about to go back in to get you because I could not connect with you through the solid rocks. But I was afraid we would collide…but that was when I assumed you were going faster and would be out at any moment." He came over to her, reined her team to a stop, and placed his hands on hers. He shook her hands free of the cord. Only then did Santi realize how securely her hands were clamped onto the rope, her muscles tensed like solid marble from finger to shoulder.

She let Rogan shake her hands free, and she tried to shake out her arms. Everything was tense. She looked up at Rogan's face with embarrassment but found nothing but acceptance and concern in his eyes. Maybe a hint of humor. He massaged her biceps and shoulders, and she felt herself relaxing. Her entire back had been pulled tight with the strain, and she felt it all ease up.

"It is intense in there," he said, giving her a squeeze on her shoulders and a kiss on the cheek.

"Apparently," she answered, looking towards Tizz and Torren, who were making themselves appear busy. "Thanks." She kissed him quickly and took a deep breath. "So how much longer, do you think?"

"A couple more hours and we will let the fish go, and then we will swim the rest of the way in."

Everyone got back in formation with Rogan leading this time, and they were off; headed, uninhibited, towards Siren Harbor.

"Amaratizz," Rogan said. Santi thrilled at the confident authority in his Ku. It reminded her of listening to Amed direct his men, and it also reminded her that she didn't know all the sides of Rogan yet. While she'd been on land, Rogan had been learning from his father. It made her rage at Krell once again for taking that away from him. She vowed that the two of them would not rest until Krell was taken down and things were restored to the way Amed had left them.

Rogan continued. "Now is a good time to tell us everything you know about Siren Harbor. The more we know, the better prepared we can be, and the better our plan will be." He paused, and Santi felt him wrestle with himself. Finally, he said, "I am sorry we have not discussed this before. My thoughts were too focused on how I was going to make Sully change back. I should have readied us better before now."

"Do not worry, brother. We still have a couple hours, and everything I know will not fill that time."

"Rogan," Torren added gently. "You are going to have quite a chore on your hands to change him back, so the more time you spend thinking about that, the better."

When no one spoke, Tizz took that as her cue. "As we previously discussed, 'harbor' does not signify a geographical location where the Sirens built their home after being run out of Anthemoessa. It better describes the express purpose of the area. There is no actual land or harbor, but the area has been so secured by the Sirens that it is a safe harbor, out of reach from the Sentinels."

"How can that be?" Santi couldn't help herself. "How can they have created a place that is safe for them? Why don't the Sentinels go in there at full force and remove them or kill them or take them captive?"

Tizz answered her question as if she had been waiting for it. "That is the clever part. My father said the area their lair is hidden in is completely void of obstacles and hiding places—and, really, from any advantageous landscape in general. The terrain is full of flat plateaus and deep chasms, but it is relatively open ocean with nothing above or around except Crural ships and sea animals. He did know that the only way into their lair is one opening in the ocean floor that leads to caverns. One way in, one way out."

"Very clever," Rogan said. "That was probably why they did not return to Anthemoessa when they were chased out. My father said the battle to remove the Sirens from the islands was expected to rage for years, but once they were finally driven out, they never tried to come back."

"The problem is the chasms I mentioned before," Tizz said seriously. "The harbor includes some of the deepest parts in the entire ocean. Even Serras do not swim down that far."

"Can Sirens swim deeper than Serras?" Santi asked, genuinely interested. Rogan's team pulled alongside hers so that the two of them were next to each other, nearly touching. She had always been able to follow Rogan to whatever depth he had swum, but were Sirens made of sturdier stuff? She looked at him questioningly, but his Ku expressed no hint of insight.

Amaratizz made a small throaty noise and said lightly, "I absolutely do not have that information." She grew serious again. "But that might not even be the worst part. The area the Sirens have secured as their 'harbor' is massive. We cannot possibly search the entire expanse of ocean floor there—even if we ignore the deepest parts—looking for one small opening to their hideout."

The group was silent. Santi had always been creeped out by the extremely deep parts of the ocean, and she gave an involuntary shudder. Rogan reached out and held her upper arm in his massive hand, stroking her skin with his thumb for reassurance. "Ok," Rogan said resolutely. "Let us come up with a solution to find the entrance before we swim into the harbor at all."

Tizz made a sound of agreement before adding, "So we just have to find this tiny entrance in a huge region, even though it will be guarded, and it's practically impossible to make it in. Then we can find Sully. And then we have to get out of there again with a kidnapped Siren on our hands. Anyone have any ideas for all of that?"

Chapter 25

Yemri

When Yemri became aware again—her head fuzzy and entire body aching immensely—she thought she had gone blind… or worse.

Is this death?

The average Serra didn't have a belief about what lay beyond the HariVivo, only that they joined the froth and became effervescence. Maybe this was it. Eternal blackness. And cold.

She was slowly realizing just how cold she was.

Yemri tried to warm herself, to use her Ku and her mind to combat the frigid feeling on her skin. This was the first time in memory she had not been able to do so. Even while traveling in the NorMer without extra coverings, she hadn't been this cold. She tried to swim, but each stroke of her tail sent shooting pain to the right side of her body. Every swipe of her arm hurt her neck, shoulders, and head tremendously. She stopped. Surely after death, one would not be in pain. It didn't seem fair.

Off in the distance, she saw a tiny green light.

Well that is something, at least.

It was the only thing she could see anywhere. It wasn't far, and at least it was something to focus on until she understood where she was.

The green speck grew brighter but not much bigger, and suddenly it was right in front of her. She could have reached out and touched it. She could now see that the tiny green speck was attached to a feeler coming from the head of the most hideous ocean animal Yemri had ever seen—huge teeth, a round, plump body, and fins that looked useless. Yemri put the pieces together and knew she was not dead.

She was too deep.

The storm hadn't killed her, but the depth might. Her breath came quicker and more panicked. She tried to grab on to the fish, to use its tiny bit of light to help guide her, but it bit her firmly. She screamed and shook her hand vigorously. Finally it let go, and she clutched her hand to her chest.

She kicked her tail backwards, then stopped. She didn't know where to go. The biggest danger at this depth was not knowing which direction was up. She needed to get higher, out of danger, out of the cold, and find some way to orient herself home. But where was up?

Yemri reached out her Ku and felt nothing, even at the extent of her reach. Because of her duties as Ocean Mother, she had learned from a young age to expand her Ku for miles in order to connect to thousands of Serras. That she couldn't feel anything in all that distance was truly troubling.

She assessed what other means of orientation she had with her.

Her hair had come out of its ties. Hair was usually a helpful guide to find the surface, as it often lifted upwards—if only ever so slightly—but it was floating around her in all directions. Not helpful. She held her arms out to the sides and closed her eyes. She didn't feel as though any part of her was being pulled any specific way. She kicked her body in a ninety-degree turn and reassessed. Still her hair floated outward in all directions, and she couldn't feel any sort of pull. She turned again. She was now facing the opposite direction from when she started, but she still felt the same. In shallower waters, you could sense the pull of gravity. There was no such pull this deep.

What I need are bubbles.

But at these depths, there wouldn't be a pocket of air anywhere. Nothing was magically going to release a stream of air for her to follow to the surface. Down here, nothing had contained air for years, if ever. She looked around. She couldn't see anything. There was no amount of time that would allow her eyes to adjust to such darkness. Even if there were bubbles, she wouldn't see them.

An idea struck her. She pulled the string of pearls from her neck and released them into the water. She only waited a moment for fear of losing them in the dark and ruining her experiment. She reached out to find them, but they were in the same place. She waited a little longer, her hands just hovering around them. Pearls should sink, but they held steadfast in their position. Her own necklace betrayed her, keeping the depth's secrets.

She retied them around her neck and took a wild guess. Swimming in any direction was better than staying put and perishing from the cold—or being eaten. With that thought, she kicked her fin a little faster and bore the pain she felt with each stroke.

She wished she hadn't entertained the thought of being eaten. Down here, that was the biggest threat. The dangers of the depth were worse than sharks and Sirens, worse than Crurals, or getting caught in a fishing net. These were the depths that Serras, Crurals, sharks, and Sirens alike avoided. The depths hid massive fish, beasts, and creatures, all hungry and hoping for a rare meal in a place where everything was a hard-fought battle for survival.

She didn't stand a chance.

Just then, Yemri spotted another speck of green, larger than the last but moving swiftly in the distance. This time she stayed clear of it. Many of the creatures down here had some sort of bioluminescent function to make it easier to see, and most of them were the predators. She had been lucky before that the fish she found was so small, yet she hadn't even left that encounter unscathed.

She swam in the opposite direction of the little green light and only hoped the fish wasn't headed towards the surface. She couldn't tolerate going much lower, she was sure.

Yemri reached out her Ku to the little glowing light. Maybe she could get a sense of where it was going, get her bearings from there.

Nothing.

She then remembered the little fish that had bit her earlier hadn't had a Ku either. Did they not have them down here? Did these fish and creatures not use them? Yemri assumed it was a safety measure. The depths were dangerous, and staying alive was the only goal. A Ku could be a dangerous way to become dinner. But learning that nothing down here used a Ku made Yemri more nervous. There could be beasts all around and she wouldn't know. At any moment, *she* could be dinner.

Yemri continued to swim, though she wasn't sure if she was swimming in a straight line. She was just steering clear of any lights or obvious entities she noticed. There was no way for her to know if she was making progress towards the surface, but she figured if she swam in one direction long enough without reaching the surface or becoming incapacitated with cold, then she would change direction and try again. She tried to keep her mind from dwelling on the fact that she could very well be swimming in a circle and not know it.

Suddenly, she bumped into something with her left shoulder. She froze. It was soft and forgiving, but nothing attacked her, so she decided to reach out and touch it. When she raised her arm, however, she realized she had misjudged the distance and hit it harder than she had before. This caused the beast to go on the defense. Blue fear signals triggered down the length of its long body, designed to frighten her off. A light traveling the length of the creature to show just how long it was, how much she should fear it. The streaking light repeated, starting at the head and making its way towards the tail again, and a third time.

As the long eel-like animal lit up a fourth time, another, more massive beast, appeared, a light revealing its face. Yemri assumed this was to see its meal more clearly.

458

The two animals faced each other, one large and round, with a glowing face, the other long and sleek, pulses of light still traveling down its length.

The round beast lunged, devouring the eel in one massive gulp. Yemri froze in paralyzing fear. But as she watched, stunned, the beast with the glowing face was then bitten in half from behind, directly opposite Yemri. There was no light to give away what the other beast was, making it look as though the glowing face was whole one moment and half disappeared the next.

Yemri pushed herself backwards with all her might, away from the sudden and violent carnage. She watched as the glowing remains floated for a moment longer before they, too, were swallowed. Yemri thanked Nephira that she had initially run into the animal lowest in the food chain and not the more massive animal. It had been just a body length away from her!

She continued pushing herself away but could not stop shivering. It wasn't the cold that made her shiver, however. Her blood pulsed through her body so quickly she felt hot. Too hot. Nearly faint. She momentarily hoped she was swimming deeper, if only to cool off from the unbearable heat consuming her body.

No, she was not shivering from the temperature. Not anymore. She was shaking from the thought that all around her were hundreds of creatures. Hungry, sharp-toothed creatures looking for an easy meal. How she didn't bump into more of them, she wasn't sure, but they were clearly here, all around. At any moment she could run into the wrong one, and that would be the end of her.

Somehow, she managed to keep swimming, reminding herself that holding still could just as easily mean death. Forward movement was the only way out.

Yemri swam on, remarkably unscathed, for hours. She was tired and weak from lack of nourishment. She thought she might have lost about a day, possibly more, depending on how long she had been unconscious. How long did it take to fall completely lifelessly into the depths? Hours? Days? As if in agreement, her stomach let out a gurgle, and she froze in panic. Her ears had been deafened in childhood, but she knew such things could be quite noisy.

Could the creatures down here hear? Even though she had been deaf for twenty years, this depth felt quieter than deafness. Before, she could hear loud rumbles or, once in a while, the highest pitch of a dolphin. But this… The quiet was eerie. The quiet was deadly. It was a quieter silence than she had ever heard. It pulsed through her.

The implications were swirling around in her fatigued brain when she ran, face first, into a smooth, hard surface. She grabbed her nose with one hand and touched the object with the other.

This darkness will be the death of me, one way or another.

She was angry.

She was tired and hungry like she'd never been before, but now she was also angry. She'd had enough of all this, and she could not believe that she couldn't get herself out of it. Most of all, Yemri was realizing things about herself that she didn't particularly like. With no one at her command, no one to advise her, and no one spouting opinions she could ignore, Yemri realized this was the first time she was truly alone and without any of the usual methods by which she made her choices. In any other circumstance, she would be very pleased by this.

Now Yemri was struck with the reality that she had never truly made a decision on her own.

As her nose began to feel better—luckily it was not another thing to add to the list of body parts that were hurting or possibly broken—Yemri used both hands to feel the smooth surface in front of her. It felt like the polished surface of the buildings in Daris. She moved her hands side to side and couldn't feel the end of it. As she slid along beside it, it began to curve slightly, and Yemri guessed it was rounded in some way. She wondered whether it could guide her to the surface, though she felt nothing in its shape or size to indicate which direction she might be traveling.

Was this a stone cylinder she could not penetrate? She pounded a fist on it and was rewarded with a sore hand and nothing else. How large was this? Was shelter inside? Who had smoothed this so finely that she couldn't feel any imperfections? And why was this edifice in the depths?

She banged on it again. If it was shelter, she wanted inside.

After hammering her fists on it a few more times, it suddenly began to light the waters around it with a soft blueish purple. Yemri kicked herself away. She had learned to fear the light down here, and she worried what this new brightness might attract.

The light grew stronger and stronger. Yemri looked around in fear of what the glow would illuminate around her.

Nothing.

Impossible. Every time she had seen a glow in the distance, it lit up many evils around it, ready to eat and be eaten. That there was nothing in the vicinity of the light as far as she could see was remarkable.

Then she saw through the stone, though she now realized the substance was not stone, as she had originally thought. No, she could see right through it.

Yemri had never seen a substance like it before. It was smooth, clear, and radiant. Had she not thoroughly felt its firmness only moments ago, she would not have believed there was even a wall because it would have looked like glowing light. But it wasn't just light. There was a barrier between her and the light.

And there was something inside.

Yemri saw a face, and it was wearing an expression of pure rage. What was even more shocking was that the head of the creature was as large as her body. On his head—for the face was that of a man—was a golden crown so large that it could have contained a regular-sized kinship in its circumference. His body was massive, muscular, and firm. His posture was defensive. Below his torso, where his tail should be—or legs if he were a Crural, which he clearly wasn't—was not one Serra tail, but many. Yemri tried to count them as they shifted through the water inside the barrier. She thought there seven, maybe eight or nine. She sucked in a startled breath, and her bowels churned in her gut.

Those were not tails. They were tentacles.

Each tentacle was as large as a whale, smooth and strong where they attached to the giant's torso, and lined with enormous suction cups like an octopus along their length.

Yemri turned to flee, but a voice spoke to her, and she found herself turning around to face the giant creature.

The words were spoken in a language she had never heard before, but the voice was deep and commanding, and she froze despite not knowing the meaning. The giant said something else and then went quiet.

Yemri stared at the mythical creature and he stared back. Neither spoke. Neither moved. The giant man with the squid body was so large she couldn't see the whole of him in one glance. Yemri was starting to feel very light-headed. She didn't trust her senses or her judgment. Exhaustion, hunger, and fear overwhelmed her, leaving her feeling on the verge of blacking out entirely.

The monster made an awful sound, deep and booming, that rolled through Yemri's body and turned her guts. She didn't know if it could get out of the transparent encasement in which he was, apparently, trapped, but she decided she'd better leave before she found out.

The beast made a bizarre gurgling noise as she kicked her tail to make a hasty retreat. When she was a few strokes away the beast boomed at her, "Why have you awakened me?"

Yemri froze. She turned only her head to look at it.

"Latin, I see," he said. "Come closer so I may look at you."

Yemri certainly was not going to move closer. She was still poised to get away, but her curiosity was piqued, and she stayed where she was. She also didn't want to admit it outright, but she suspected she was not frozen by fear or curiosity but rather a force beyond her control.

"I said come closer!" he shouted, and suddenly Yemri's body turned of its own accord to face the enclosure, and she was being pulled towards the giant by what she could only assume was her very Ku itself. Her arms and tail trailed behind her as her chest led the way, dragged against her will. Finally, she felt his hold on her release as she was deposited in front of his massive face.

"Do you speak?"

She was too frightened to utter a peep.

"I know you understand Latin. You did not understand Norse or Ænglisc, which means you learned from Nephira how to speak and not from the humans. You are also dark skinned, so I presume you are Afiti or Tipua because Najilian is far from here, though it is possible. However, a tail like yours means you have been blessed by a deity. Maybe me, though I do not remember it. Of course it could very well be a fluke."

Yemri was completely shaken to her core. How did he know so much? How did he know her grandmother? The clans? How had he guessed things so accurately? It was not possible.

"Who…who are you?"

"She speaks!" he said. He seemed weary… or as if he was contemplating something she couldn't possibly comprehend. "I am who I am, though I have been called many things."

"Then… what are you?"

"I am what I am, though-"

"You are many things?" she interrupted, finishing his sentence. Twenty years of Zitja's influence had honed her impatience with nonsense.

464

"Oh, very clever! I enjoy a sharp wit."

She didn't feel clever or sharp. She felt tired. Excessively tired and hungry and impatient with being told riddles to her questions instead of answers, all while she was held against her will. "What shall I call you then?"

"I have been called Lir, Yu Qiang, Ceto, Kraken, Poseidon, King Titan, Neptune, God, Nu, Njord... Shall I go on? I can."

Spare me.

Feeling bold—from exhaustion, she assumed—she replied, "What do you prefer to be called?"

"For you, Deus."

"That is a very grand and fitting name, I would suppose." Yemri steeled herself. She probably shouldn't be so flippant, but something about days of extreme danger, exhaustion, and hunger left her a bit punchy. Besides, she was irritated by his riddles, and he seemed to enjoy bantering. "Then, Deus, how did you get down here? Are you a prisoner?"

"In a way, are we not all prisoners?"

This wise creature of fables was tiring Yemri in her weakened state. She did not care for riddles and axioms meant for pups' stories. But, though she felt impatient with this godlike, arrogant creature, his question struck her as poignant, a question she had frequently entertained in her heart of hearts.

"Yes, I suppose we are all a prisoner to something," she answered.

"More true for those such a you and me. Is that not right, granddaughter of Nephira?"

"You know who I am?"

"Yes. My prolonged slumber has made me sluggish, but I am catching up on the events of the world that I've missed since I went to sleep."

"How long ago was that?"

"How long since the Serras were created?"

Yemri couldn't tell if this was an answer or another riddle.

Before she could think of a response, he asked, "Why have you awakened me? What do you need?"

"What… what do I need?" Yemri repeated dumbly, and she assumed that admitting she had only accidentally awakened him would not be wise. Despite his initial crankiness, he seemed to be a pleasant being… for now, anyway.

"I am at your service, Ocean Mother."

Of all the beings who had called her Ocean Mother, she had never before felt more respected for the title, but she also felt foolish. There was magnificent respect radiating from him for her position, but, truly, he must be above such a feeling. It was like being addressed by the king of the world. Surely, they could not be equals. And if this really was a god as he said others had called him….

"I do not need anything that you can help me with, I am sure." Even as she said it, she felt the burden of her entire life both press down on her and release from her at the same time. It was as though she was being reminded of her failures, triumphs, responsibilities, and mistakes, yet also forgiven for them.

"Hmmm." The sound of his disbelief rumbled in her heart. "Everyone has a need." He waited quietly.

"What I need…" she started, and then couldn't think of how to finish. She had never taken time to think about what she needed. No one had ever asked. "What I need is to make the right choices for my Serras. To stop being such a failure. To *know*. I need to know…" But she did not even know what she needed to know.

"And what would do that?"

What would do that? Such an odd phrasing. "Tell me how to stop being a failure."

"First, you have to tell me what makes you a failure."

Had she been standing, she would have fallen. Had she known how to cry, she would have started. "Everyone says that I am."

"And do you think you are?"

"Yes."

"Why?"

"Because I have not done anything right. I have not done things the way they should be done."

"And what is it you should have done?"

The questions were draining. It was more introspection than she had ever done. Maybe that was where she had failed most. "I guess…" She was starting to feel whiny, and she hated herself for it. It was like she was nine again, trying to get a grip on the very water as it rushed right past her. She took a deep breath and tried to think about what he was asking. "I guess…" She breathed again and made her voice strong, removed the doubt from her Ku and told the truth as she saw it. "Things have not worked out flawlessly or without error. I have made too many mistakes in my time as Ocean Mother."

"And that is what made you a failure?"

She only had to think a moment before she nearly shouted, "No!" She was angry now, though she wasn't angry with him. She might have been angry with herself, or the others in the ocean, but mostly she was angry for never having pondered any of these questions before. "I did succeed in doing the things I set out to do. I have been good to my Serras, and I have made the ocean better than it was before. At least, I believe it is. It is only that I did not do everything without mistakes… without trial and error. But that does not mean it was not done well."

She thought about the tunnel and the nuntiums, resurrecting parts of Daris that had still been in ruin after Nephira's death. She thought about keeping Zitja out of the water for twenty years and how keeping Zitja prisoner reduced the threat of the Sirens. Yemri thought about ridding the ocean of the Maato and freeing the dams and pups. Maybe that had truly been a failure, but if even one enslaved dam was free who had wanted to be… and all those innocent pups… she had done right by them at least.

"No, I am not a failure. I have only failed myself by never allowing myself to take pride in my work. Always second-guessing and doubting. I never allowed myself to make a decision, see it through, and be satisfied in what I had done."

"So then." That was his whole sentence.

"So then… I want the right person to be in charge. I want to help the ocean in small and silent ways. I want to be true to myself." She felt a change in her then. Freedom. Yemri knew many things about herself in that moment that she might have known a long time ago had she only allowed herself some time and space for introspection.

468

"You are right," Deus said with a reassurance that no one had ever given her before. "I cannot help you with those things."

"It is ok. You have already helped. I know what to do now. Which way is the surface?"

He pointed directly at her.

"If this is a metaphor about how all I need is inside me, that is not helpful. You have already helped me figure-"

He cut her off. "No, Ocean Mother, the surface is behind you. My prison is on the ocean floor."

The ocean floor?

She shivered involuntarily. Surely this wasn't the very bottom of the ocean! It might take a whole day to get to the surface, and she was already so very tired.

Suddenly, despite her trepidation, worry, and fatigue, she was filled with gratitude for Deus and the enlightenment she received. "Thank you," she said. "You have truly helped me today." And then a thought occurred to her. "You are a prisoner? Why?"

"Not all who have encountered my resolutions to problems are happy with the result."

"So... you were imprisoned because someone was angry with you?"

"I would assume that is the reason anyone is imprisoned."

She thought for a moment and then asked, "Can I help you get out?"

"You can. But only if I am helping you. Otherwise, here I stay."

Yemri thought. It seemed unfair to leave him in prison after all he had done for her. "There is one thing you could do for me that I cannot seem to do myself."

"Anything."

"Can you get rid of the Sirens?"

"I possibly can."

"Possibly?"

"Well, it is a tricky thing, wiping out an entire species. Shall I kill them? Hmmm." His voice rumbled in her chest again. "Transform them into something else? Imprison them like myself? Hmmm. And do they deserve it? I possibly can, but there are many variables."

"Can you transform them back?"

"I possibly can."

Yemri bit at her lips. Was it worth it? She could quite possibly be a hero. She could bring Deus to the Serras and show them she was going to make them safe forever. The possibility of that outweighed her concern. "Yes, let us do it. I want you to handle the Sirens."

"I will do that for you, Ocean Mother."

"Ok. How do I get you out of there?"

"You simply need to release me."

Yemri frowned. Even his imminent liberation from his prison didn't get her a straightforward answer. She looked around for a lock or lever or something on which to press. Nothing. Finally, she said hesitantly, "I release you."

The clear encasement slowly vanished, and Deus spread out his long tentacles as if truly stretching for the first time in centuries. As they unfurled, Yemri wondered if she had made a mistake. This beast who thought himself a god was nearly as large as Daris. He had been imprisoned for a reason; maybe she should not have let him out.

"Ok, let us go," she said in a wobbly voice.

"I will take care of it," was all he said before he shot through the water away from her at such speed that, although he glowed a faint blue, she lost sight of him in a moment.

"What about me?" She waited for a response, but he was gone.

I hope I have not made another mistake.

For all her resolve, she was still questioning her choices. Epiphanies came easily, but true change took time, she thought.

She sat in the water for a while, waiting to see what might happen. Finally, the adrenaline from her surprise and terror dwindled, and she began to feel very cold again. The only way for her to get home was to swim up. So she began her ascent.

Yemri swam for hours in what she hoped was the right direction before she felt the water begin to noticeably warm up. She knew she was swimming slowly; she was so tired and near starved. But with the realization that she was going in the right direction, and now that her appendages were not so numb, she picked up her pace as much as she could. Her wounds even felt better. It shouldn't be too long now before she was out of the utter darkness. Then, eventually, she could reach depths where sea life was again in abundance and she could find something to eat. That thought alone spurred her to swim faster than she had been.

After the water got warmer, she had no idea how long she swam when she began feeling tempted to sleep. At this moment, she felt like she'd never slept in her life. She very much wanted to crawl into a cave and sleep for a week. But here in the open ocean, with nothing to ground herself to, and no landmarks anywhere, she could very possibly sink back down and have to start her ascent again when she awoke.

When she judged she had ascended high enough, she decided to push out her Ku. She had to know if anything was around. She didn't care what she found, she would eat it. Ku or not, predator or not, she would simply take a bite out of anything as it swam by at this moment.

Yemri opened up her Ku and expanded it as far as she could. There was nothing with a Ku in the vicinity, though she was high enough now that she was confident the waters were empty simply because they were sparsely populated, and not because of an abundance of creatures without Kus.

She hoped.

Finally, she felt something, like a beacon. High overhead was a large ular surrounded by an entire community of fish and animals that used the whale for food and safety. Yemri aimed straight for the feast above her. The water lightened slightly as she rose, and by the time she reached the whale, she was warm, surrounded by bright light, lively Kus, and all the food she could eat.

Yemri stuffed herself with as many fish as she could without being wasteful. What she really wanted was to eat until she put herself in a coma and then sleep on the back of the whale, ending up wherever the whale ended up. But that was not the Serra way. Eating to excess was greedy. Extra lives did not need to be lost just because she felt so hungry.

Yemri ran her tiny hand along the underside of the ular. "Thank you, friend." And then she pushed herself

472

beyond him and up towards the surface. It wasn't far now, and in less than a quarter of an hour, she was there.

The actual surface wasn't originally her destination, but after being so deep and cold for so long, she thought a little sunshine on her face might be nice. She broke through the surface and expelled all the water from her lungs. When she lay back and opened her eyes to the sky, what she saw made her breath catch in her throat. She was filled with a powerful emotion she couldn't identify, a confusing combination of delirious happiness and deep troubling sadness.

Maybe it was the exhaustion. Maybe it was because her journey had come full circle. Whatever the cause, her emotion caught in her chest. There it was: the thing that had gotten her into this mess in the first place. In the distance, containing all the colors of her tail, was a giant arc of color expanding across the blue sky.

It was breathtaking.

For the first time in her life, she didn't think being beautiful was a bad thing. Beauty could bring people joy, and maybe that was enough to change her regard for her unusual tail. The sight above was glorious to behold, and she wished she could float on her back in the sunshine and marvel at it all day.

Yemri squared her shoulders. Her conversation with Deus had been enlightening. The sight of this natural phenomenon was motivating. She had to find her way back to Daris. There were changes to be made.

Chapter 26

Santiago

"We are going to have to go HaruKu," Rogan said as they all sat huddled in a patch of dense drift weeds and Crural litter that created a thick and sufficient hiding place. Rogan and Tizz sat on the ground, and Torren sat on a piece of scrap metal. Santi was sitting on a big square object that she couldn't identify, but it seemed as suitable a seat as anything else.

"Luckily, we have all that dwattle practice to rely on," Tizz joked to ease the tension, but it came off as stiff. Her heart wasn't in it due to the circumstances, and Santi was surprisingly glad to see that Tizz's ever-positive attitude did have a realistic side to it. Being only a mile from the noted Siren Harbor *should* take the joking nature out of anyone.

They had decided that their best bet for finding the entrance was to wait for a Siren to show up and follow it.

Unfortunately, while they had run across quite a few Sirens before getting to the actual harbor, the Sirens had all been swimming in different directions. The four decided to sit and reevaluate their plan while the coast was clear before they were found out and apprehended—or worse.

"We are going to need to watch for a pattern in their movement," Torren said attentively. "We have seen…what? Seven Sirens going different directions? If we wait just a little while, we will see enough of them going in the right direction to at least get us closer to the harbor, maybe even to follow one of them into the lair."

The group sent agreement through their Kus but said nothing. They had been fortunate that the Sirens they had seen were swimming high enough above them that they hadn't been overheard, but hiding so close to the harbor left them all feeling subdued and anxious. For the past few hours, they had spoken only when necessary.

"I think," Santi added, trying her hand at strategy and leadership, "if problems arise, or we get separated or stopped or… well, just anything…if we need to create a diversion or, you know, well, things that come up in these kinds of movies."

She frowned at herself. Only Rogan would have a vague understanding of what a movie was, and either way, she wasn't doing a good job with her attempt at confident leadership. She hadn't made any sense whatsoever.

She squared her shoulders and spoke more confidently. "I think Rogan needs to carry on no matter what. Of all of us, he'll be the best hope of getting Sully to come with him—willingly or unwillingly—and the rest of us can support him or cause a distraction. Whatever he needs."

They all agreed with her silently. Finally, Rogan responded. "Santiago is correct. Everyone do whatever you can or whatever you have to, and I will find Sully and bring him out." Their Kus were in agreement, and they felt bolstered by their mediocre plan—and terrified by it as well.

In a stroke of leadership genius—or sheer obviousness—Santi added, "We will meet up here if we get separated."

Everyone absorbed the implications of what it could mean if they got separated and sat silently watching and feeling the water around them for any approaching Sirens. Santi felt Rogan, Torren, and then Tizz close off their Kus. Feeling for Sirens was sporadic and unreliable, so having their Kus open presented a serious disadvantage in that it could give away their position. Santi closed hers off, as well, and sat in the overwhelming silence that was three thousand feet below the surface of the water. She drummed her fingers against the box on which she sat—some sort of rusty metal object now covered in grime and moss— and grew steadily more anxious. She needed to be back for the tournament finale in three days.

It wasn't that she was afraid of missing the finale. It might be nice to take her chance to show Krell that she was right and he was wrong. It was just that there was so much to worry about right now: Sully, the Sirens, Zitja, and finding out what happened to Yazi. Adding having Krell hunting her to the list was one more thing she didn't want to worry about.

Santi took in her surroundings as much to look for errant Sirens as to clear her mind of Krell. The area was littered with Crural junk. Not all of it was garbage, but some was. Most of it was Crural objects and furniture that was unlikely to have been deliberately thrown into the ocean. Off to her left was half of a four-post bed, a small nightstand or table, and an antique sewing machine. Santi cocked her head to one side. It looked like a fancy woman's bedroom had just found its way to the bottom of the ocean.

Squinting her eyes, she looked further. About a tenth of a mile away in a dip in the ocean floor, an old ship was nestled. There was no evidence that it had belonged to pirates, but she decided it was a pirate ship, just for fun. It looked mostly intact, and the dip in the ocean floor allowed it to sit almost straight up in the water. It was majestic and horribly creepy.

Santi kept scanning the ocean floor. They just needed to find a few Sirens going in the same direction, and they could follow one of them wherever the rest were hiding.

Just then a cruise ship passed overhead, casting a massive shadow over them. The cruise ship reminded her that Crurals also traversed these waters, and it immediately dawned on Santi what she was sitting on. She jumped up when she realized she had been sitting on the black box of a downed airplane. She shuddered. This portion of ocean between Florida and Puerto Rico was heavily traveled and known to be a place of tragedy for ships and planes. The other three looked at her odd reaction quizzically.

Before she could explain, Sirens began shooting towards the surface like fireworks.

Santi looked to the left of the surfacing Sirens, aghast, and then instantly dropped into the weeds to hide. She pointed. The other three were already gaping with shock and horror, and all of them hunkered further down into the concealing weeds.

They were much closer to the very spot they were looking for than they had realized. Dangerously close.

One after the other, dozens upon dozens of Sirens broke free of their underground sanctuary and skyrocketed towards the massive ship overhead.

Santi watched in awe. They were practiced. They were deliberate. They were out for blood. Santi nestled closer to the box, leaning her left side against it with her legs curled in the sand beneath her. A group of half a dozen Sirens swam the few hundred feet to the old pirate ship and picked up the long chain from the end of the anchor. Santi's eyes were wide, and she felt paralyzed with fear and curiosity. Another group of Sirens was collecting a swarm of sharks that had wandered into the area. The implications horrified Santi.

Sirens were much smarter than everyone gave them credit for. They weren't just unthinking, destructive animals.

This is... Santi didn't know how to explain the teamwork that was going on between Siren and shark.

They're... It's like... an arrangement.

No one could hear her because they were all HaruKu, but she strongly suspected that the other three had guessed what the Sirens were up to.

The Sirens were working on attaching the end of the anchor chain to the twenty or so sharks when Rogan whispered hoarsely, "Now!"

No one but Rogan moved. Santi, Tizz, and Torren were all distracted, watching the cruise ship massacre unfold.

Finally, Santi realized Rogan was gone. She spotted him creeping along the ocean floor, using his hands more than his tail as he hugged the ground as much as possible.

Santi made eye contact with Torren and Tizz, and they followed Rogan—Santi first, and then Tizz and Torren.

They were completely exposed. Santi felt horribly vulnerable, absolutely at the mercy of whatever came across them first.

The entrance to the lair was close, and they arrived quickly and peered inside, scared and nervous. Nearly a thousand feet overhead, more than two hundred Sirens swarmed in a buzz of activity, but diving into the Siren lair seemed equally as dangerous. The cavern they were peering into was crudely made. Santi could tell that it was not a naturally occurring cavern, but no effort had been taken to make it look beautiful. A few feet inside, it became a black abyss. They could see nothing through the darkness, and with Kus closed tightly, they couldn't feel anything, either.

Rogan looked at them stoically and decisively before grabbing the rim of the hollow and propelling himself downward, into the lair. Tizz followed immediately, and Santi shook her head. Fearless, always. If she had dared to speak, she would have told Tizz, "You're my hero." Instead, she took a deep breath and followed Tizz into the gloom.

Darkness engulfed her. Santi had to shake off the panic that threatened to push her into a tearful retreat. When she couldn't push the fear aside, she tried to ignore it, thinking of her sixteen-year-old hero. It did not remove the fear that tightened her stomach into a solid knot.

With no light to see by, Santi could only rely on her sense of touch as she continued to dive. The wider mouth narrowed sharply into a much smaller tunnel, and her heartbeat raced. There could be danger anywhere, and at any moment her life could be over. She wouldn't even see it coming. Santi allowed tears of terror to stream from her eyes and get lost in the water around her. Tears, she conceded, were all she could do to release the fear that consumed her. Better to cry than to turn around and flee. She could live with that.

As her eyes slowly adjusted to the dimness, she was able to make some sense of their surroundings. What was at first total blackness lightened to gray, and the edges of things began taking shape. Soon the bottom of the cave appeared, and the tunnel they were in was put in perspective. They had traveled directly down and were now near the bottom of the cavern. They paused in what felt like a giant silo of rock large enough for several Serras to line up end-to-end. They had swum past two passageways that led off the main tunnel, one in front of Santi and the other behind her and higher up. A third passageway opened at the floor of the silo-like shaft to Santi's left. Rogan pointed to Torren and then to the tunnel behind Santi. Torren, without hesitation or complaint, turned to the opening and swam through, quickly swallowed by the darkness. Santi's stomach flipped over, realization making it churn. Rogan meant for them to split up and find Sully—or whatever else was down here—on their own. Rogan pointed towards the lower tunnel, the one at the floor of the main cavern, and touched his chest. Then he pointed to the first tunnel they had passed, high above their heads, and directed Santi and Tizz to go together.

Amaratizz grabbed Santi's hand, and Santi felt a wave of relief that she would not have to be alone. Rogan quickly pushed himself forward and kissed Santi quickly but earnestly on the lips. Santi returned the kiss fervently and pushed away the thought that it could be their last. They placed their hands tenderly on each other's chests and gazed deeply into each other's eyes, trying to say all they could without their Kus.

Without pausing further, the two girls kicked upwards towards their designated tunnel. Santi looked over her shoulder just in time to see the end of Rogan's stalwart blue tail swallowed up by the passageway below. She turned and focused on her task.

As they plunged into the tunnel, Santi's panic increased. She had been so worried about what would happen if they couldn't find Sully, but what if they did? Either option was going to be a hard-fought battle for their lives, and although hundreds of Sirens were in the water above them, how many were left down in these caves? And what happened when the Sirens finished with the cruise ship? She squeezed Tizz's hand harder. Her shoulder blades tightened, and her arms were so stiff she could barely swim. They were in it now. Nothing left to do but continue.

The tunnel they were assigned was like a massive hallway, with openings spaced along each side. Each opening was lit, but the tunnel itself was dim, so they kept to the top of the passageway, where it was darker and the shadows hid them.

Santi and Tizz timidly crept up to the first passageway that opened on the left and peered under the top of the round entranceway, their bodies pressed against the ceiling. It didn't take them long to realize where they were. Santi's stomach flipped over once more.

Fixed all around the room from floor to ceiling were tall wooden pillars. Attached to the pillars were hammocks strung up seemingly at random so that they crisscrossed each other in a chaotic maze of white ropes and sleeping nets. Santi imagined it must be like negotiating an obstacle course every time a Siren wanted to find his or her bed.

The room wasn't very large, but it was large enough to hold about eighty sleeping Sirens. It was a relief to find the room completely empty. Fighting Sirens in here would be like getting caught like a fly in a web.

Santi pushed herself away from the opening, the rough rock scraping her fingers. She and Tizz needed to check every room. Knowing they had a plan eased Santi's worry a bit. Swimming around blindly in the tunnels of the Sirens' lair was nearly the most frightening thing she'd ever experienced, but now she knew what to do: search every cavern. At least that was something. They had a purpose, and she breathed easier knowing there was a long hallway ahead of them and many rooms to check.

The next room was on the right, so Santi kicked off the wall to the entrance. A quick peek revealed that there were Sirens in this one, and Santi and Tizz immediately pulled their heads back. After a tense, breathless moment, they carefully peeked around the door again.

This chamber was not full. More of the hammocks were empty than occupied. The two scanned them all quickly. With their white skin and black tails, Sirens looked very similar to each other. But there were still differences. Sirens maintained their original hair color, along with their body shapes. Many of them also wore jewelry or distinctive pieces of clothing. Though Sully now shared many traits with the Sirens, Santi knew they would recognize him when they found him.

He was not in this cavern. They moved on.

In the next chamber, a solitary Siren was occupied with... a book? Santi stared, surprised, from her vantage point above the entryway. The Siren was holding a soggy, leather-bound book with surprisingly strong pages. And she was most certainly reading while lounging in her hammock, tail kicking herself in a gentle rocking motion. She tenderly turned a page.

Santi was completely taken aback. No Serra she knew of besides Wayne could read. She knew it was common with the Thaeds because they studied Crurals so intently and knew everything about them, but this... She was flabbergasted. Had this Siren been a Thaed once? How had she obtained this book and how was it still holding up?

She watched the Siren dam read for so long, flipping pages delicately so as to not tear the fragile paper that Tizz had to pull aggressively on her arm to get her to move.

Santi looked up at Amaratizz almost in confusion. She had nearly forgotten their purpose. Sirens, she reminded herself, were not only killing machines with no thought or soul but also individuals with their own purposes and interests. She was suddenly assaulted with memories of the conflict she had felt at her Bonding ceremony about killing the beautiful Siren adorned with the green gems.

She followed Tizz from room to room, crawling along the ceiling to scope them out. Every cavity contained at least a few sleeping Sirens, but one was absolutely chock-full. Every hammock was occupied, and not all of the Sirens were sleeping. They had to look a long time, ducking away several times to muster their courage. Sully was not in this chamber, either.

The hallway eventually split in two, each branch lined with more chambers. Santi threw her head back in a sigh that she would have liked to turn into a full-blown tantrum. Instead, she righted herself, took a deep breath, and she and Tizz split up to look down the hallways.

Alone now, Santiago checked the first room she came upon. Without Tizz by her side, she felt terrified—but more determined. Brave Amaratizz had rubbed off on her, and now she had to prove that she could do this herself. She had been working so hard to be this Heir everyone wanted, and she had felt proud and confident at one point, but in the five months since Amed's death and Krell taking over—not only as Commander but somehow as leader of the entire ocean—Santi was back to feeling like a helpless Crural. She shook her head.

No.

She could do this.

And that's when she saw him. In the third room she looked into, she spotted a copper head of hair, a strong, sturdy jaw, and a stark gold band hugging a strong bicep. She pushed herself back up against the ceiling so forcefully she hit her head. That gold band brought back a memory so strong that it hit her in her gut like a punch. So much nostalgia was held in that little piece of jewelry. The wonderful day—just months before the attack on Rogan's kinship that had forced Santi out of the water for six years—came back to her and replayed fondly in her mind.

~

"But your hair is so fantastic!" Santi sighed mournfully as she watched as Sully's curly copper locks were shorn. The thick and flowing locks that streamed down his back—though his hair was usually braided—were now only about three inches long.

"Maybe you could keep some of it?"

"What part would he keep?" Maeve laughed at her, setting down the knife and picking up a straight razor.

"I am just so tired of it getting in the way and getting caught on things," Sully answered. He had been set on shaving his head for a while now, but his mom was more attached to his hair than he was and kept putting off the haircut. It took a great deal of arguing, but he had finally convinced his mother to cut off his hair, and now and Santi watched in disbelief.

"It's just so unique!" Santi lamented. As a twelve-year-old girl who didn't know how to do her own hair, she was sorrowful. "I mean, I get it, my hair is so thick and heavy. But in the water, you don't really have to worry about it being heavy!"

"That is not true, and you know it!" Sully retorted. "It slows me down."

"I know," Santi sighed. Apparently, she was just as attached to his hair as Maeve. "Rogan, help me out! He should keep some of it."

They were outside Sully's shelter so that any errant hairs could float away. Maeve didn't want to have it floating around their home for weeks, getting tangled in everything. She and Rogan were there to collect the discarded hair and deliver it to Coral, who had an idea for an art project that Santiago was curious to see.

"Oh, sure," Rogan answered. "He could keep half of it. Just shave off one side."

"Wait!" Santi shouted exuberantly as Maeve wielded the razor. "You could give him a mohawk!"

Sully, Rogan, and Maeve all looked at her. Maeve paused, blade in hand, intrigued.

Santi gestured excitedly while the bundle of copper hair in her hand floated around with her movement. "It's where you shave off all the hair except for a strip down the middle." She lifted the long strands of Sully's shorn hair, placed a hand at each end, then held it on top of her head from forehead to neck to show what a mohawk would look like. "I think that would be much lighter and less of a problem for you. Then we can still see your fabulous hair."

Rogan cocked his head at Santi. "His hair is…fabulous?"

"It is!" she insisted. "Like you don't know! It, like, glows in the sun."

"It does," Maeve agreed. "When he was a little boy, I used to call him my fire pup."

Santi's eyes went wide. "How do you know what fire is?"

"Oh, I love Crurals. I spent a lot of time with them when I was younger. My kinship was very friendly with the village above us."

"Like how I'm very friendly with the kinship below me!"

Maeve gave Santi a sassy smile and a wink. "Just like that. Ok, so we do a…hock? What was that you called it?"

"A mohawk!"

"Shall we, Sully?"

He nodded, and Maeve took the razor to the side of his head. As she shaved, Rogan and Santi collected the hair and put it in a pouch for Coral. After a few clarifying questions to Santi about the details, Maeve deemed the haircut done, and Sully ran his hands all over his head.

Immediately, Rogan shouted, "I want one, too!"

Santi dove into their shelter, kicked her feet off their tiled floors, and propelled herself down the hall to Maeve's room, where Santi had once seen a handheld mirror. Against the wall on the other side of her fuchsia bed was an object that looked like a dresser but with tall legs and one only drawer in the middle. It was carved wood and inlaid with shining shells on the top. On the surface of the table was a brush, a few different strings of pearls, and clamshells that Santi knew were filled with bright colored pastes.

On the wall above the dressing table hung a small round mirror with a handle. Santi snatched it off the hook and brought it out to Sully, who used it to inspect his new hairdo.

"Chimba!" he said with enthusiasm. "Great idea, Santi!"

Maeve was already working on shaving the sides of Rogan's hair. "Now you just need some tattoos and piercings," she said.

Santi, becoming accustomed to Maeve knowing about Crural life, added, "Yeah, a little gold hoop would go great with your red mohawk."

"What are those?" Sully asked.

"Well, a tattoo is ink that stays permanently on your skin," Maeve said, "though I do not actually know how they do it. And a piercing is just that: a piece of jewelry that pierces your skin."

"Yes!" Sully said. "I want them."

Santi felt like she needed to explain further. "Sully," she said, "a tattoo is made by little needles that push ink into your skin. You have to get stabbed over and over again."

Sully turned white. "I do not want that!"

"I do!" Rogan said. "I can handle the pain."

"Ho-kay," Santi said, laughing. "How are you going to get that done?"

"I do not know." He mulled it over. "But I could do it."

Brushing Rogan's machismo aside, Sully asked, "And what is a piercing? A gold hoop would be cool."

"We can do that. I bet Coral has the supplies to make a gold hoop," Maeve mused. "Where do you want it, fire pup?" She smiled at using his old nick-name.

"I want it through my left arm!"

Santi and Maeve both laughed so hard that Sully looked like he might actually cry. His bottom lip was pushed out so far Santiago and Maeve both immediately tried to stifle their guffaws, and Maeve said, "Oh no! That is not how it works."

"Your arm is too big!" Santi added. "Most people pierce their ears. Some do their nose or their belly button or their tongue. You can pierce your eyebrow, even. But it has to be a small amount of skin. You can't go through muscle and bone!"

Maeve finished shaving Rogan's head then, and he grabbed the mirror to check out his new look. "I could put the tattoos right on the sides of my mow hock."

"And I want a piercing on my arm!" Sully said petulantly. The laughter had clearly hurt his pride.

~

Santi hadn't thought about that memory in a long time. After that day, Maeve had given Sully a gold band that wound around his left bicep, and he had worn it unfailingly ever since.

The memory rekindled her fondness for her old friend. He was always so full of heart and adventure. It also reminded her just how important Sully had been to her, not just to Rogan. She was glad they were doing this, looking for him and trying to help him change back to being a Serra. She was angry with him for the kidnapping and torture—she would never forget it, and it would always make up who she was—but now… It had been years now, and it was a memory that she could mix with ones like the mohawk to create an overall picture of who he was as a Serra.

Santi had loved Maeve dearly, as well; the thought that Crurals had tortured and killed her left Santi feeling devastated. She could understand Sully's need for revenge. Wasn't her death much like Amed's, and weren't she, Rogan, and Tizz also trying to retaliate in their own way? She didn't understand why Sully had to kidnap Santi to seek that revenge, but maybe that was another mystery they could unravel.

Rogan never did get a tattoo, but Santi thought it might be sexy and wondered how they could make it happen. She'd need Crurals for a tattoo, and perhaps because Maeve had been so comfortable with Crurals was the reason she had been taken and killed. She hadn't had enough fear of them. *Of us*, Santi reminded herself. Sometimes she forgot she was actually a Crural.

She suddenly realized she was still pressed up against the ceiling, frozen in indecision and lost in thought. Sully was in that room. So close, yet so far from her ability to retrieve him.

There were about forty other Sirens in the cavern. Luckily it wasn't one of the full rooms, but there were enough hammocks filled with bodies to create a real problem for her.

She backed silently out of the room and searched the main hall until she found Tizz peering into one of the other rooms. When she placed her hand on Tizz's arm, her little sister jumped and sprang into a stance of self-defense. Fortunately, she made no noise, and Santi immediately backed off, putting up both hands to show Tizz she wasn't a threat and silently apologizing for startling her friend.

Santi tugged on Tizz's arm, smiling, and jerked her head towards the other hall. Tizz's eyebrows rose so high they nearly got lost in her yellow-blond hair. The two of them made to the main hallway, but Amaratizz stopped Santi from going further. She shook her head at Santiago.

"No," she mouthed. Santi understood. They had done their job in finding Sully, but they couldn't get him out on their own. They had to find Rogan and Torren.

They made their way along the ceiling of the tunnel, and when they reentered the main chamber and saw it was also empty, they allowed themselves to breathe fully for the first time since entering the cavern. They had made it down and back without incident. It was almost too good to be true.

The two lowered themselves to the sand, silently in agreement that finding Rogan was the best idea. As they were creeping towards the tunnel into which he had disappeared, they suddenly sensed a commotion happening above them. They shrank back into the corner where the wall met the floor and huddled in the shadows.

Above them was a mass of bodies erupting from the tunnel Torren had gone into. Santi felt herself wanting to look away and had to resist the childish thought that if she couldn't see the Sirens, they couldn't see her. But she couldn't tear her eyes away, her body tensed to flee.

That's when Santi noticed the legs.

Nearly a dozen legs attached to some very frightened humans, were kicking frantically out of the passageway. It took her a moment to register what she was seeing, and then she untangled herself from Tizz and kicked herself off the floor. She swam quickly, not wanting to miss her chance, and grabbed Torren by both shoulders. He looked shaken and worried but focused. Following behind him were five Crurals looking starved and panicked. The fear in their eyes told her they had experienced terrible things.

Tizz followed behind, and the three of them stared at each other, trying to speak without using their Kus. In that moment, Santi vowed she would learn how to communicate HaruKu.

Torren was sure of himself, however, and he pointed at Tizz and then traced a circle with his hand to indicate the prisoners, and finally he pointed towards the sky.

Tizz gave a curt nod, opened her arms to metaphorically gather up all the cowering Crurals, and smiled her kindest Amaratizz smile. Santi knew with that dazzling, peace-making smile that she was destined for greatness. In the face of her worst fears, in the dungeons of the most fearsome monsters, Tizz was concerned about making others feel safe. She gathered them all together and led them towards the exit above.

If Santi knew which god to believe in, she would have prayed to him or her that Amaratizz could take those Crurals away from here safely, navigating their way through the hundreds of Sirens that were swarming the cruise ship far above.

Torren and Santi were focused on Tizz and the fleeing Crurals when movement from below caught their attention. Rogan exploded from the bottom tunnel at full speed, both swords drawn, looking over his shoulder at the tunnel behind him.

Without hesitation, Torren unlatched the ax from his side and dove down to meet Rogan while Santi pulled her sais from her thigh holsters and followed. The three of them floated in the middle of the silo near the floor, poised and ready. Three Sirens burst from the tunnel in hot pursuit.

Good. At least we aren't outnumbered.

Santi lunged forward first. She wanted the smallest Siren, a dam about her size, before she got left with the other massive, brutish buck or the just-as-large dam.

The little one spotted Santi and arced her blade through the water, swinging it towards Santiago's head. Santi crossed her sais above her and caught the blade between them without even a thought, her body effortlessly flowing through the forms she had practiced for so long. She retaliated with a quick three-part strike—right, left, right—that forced her opponent backward, her confidence surging. She might still be a slow swimmer, but a slow fighter she was not.

Santi continued to fight—striking, defending, striking, striking, and striking again—purely on instinct. It was all muscle memory, swift, and graceful.

The fighting moved them back and forth, up and down through the corridor. This was taking far too long, Santi thought. She worried that something might be wrong with Rogan or Torren. Were they still fighting? Were they injured? She allowed herself a moment to flick her eyes around, but the momentary loss of focus allowed the Siren to strike a blow to Santi's ribs just below the top of her swimsuit, cutting a long gash in her skin. The cut wasn't deep or fatal, but it was bleeding, and the pain helped her to refocus.

Santi lashed back quickly, running the dam through three times, once in the left shoulder and once in the right before plunging her sai into the dam's belly. Santi pulled back and hoped the dam would have enough self-preservation to flee. She didn't want to kill her. In that moment, the memory of Sully and how he came to be a Siren combined with the memory of the Siren reading in her hammock made her hesitate from delivering a killing blow. Santi didn't know this dam's life, and she didn't know how she came to be a Siren, and she was conflicted. The Siren looked young—about Santi's age—and because Sirens didn't age past their point of transformation, Santi knew something had happened to this dam in her prime to cause her to transform.

The dam, obviously in great pain, glared at Santi with utter hatred. Santi came back to reality. Even if she felt sorry for the dam, Santi realized that letting this Siren go was a foolish decision that could bring about their deaths. What if the dam went to fetch others? What if she only feigned fleeing but came back and stabbed Santi in the back? Letting the dam live was not acceptable because there were no good outcomes. Santi had been trained to fight for a reason, and it wasn't so she could start to feel bad for Sirens and ponder their life stories.

Santi lunged at the dam and sank her sai into its heart. The Siren gaped at her, and a quick succession of emotions crossed her face: anger, betrayal, pain, rage. Her eyes rolled back into her head and her face went still. As the dam floated towards the floor, Santi turned to help her friends.

Torren was on the floor, bleeding and writhing in pain. He did not look like he had long left. Rogan was fighting both of the other Sirens at once. From her vantage point above them, Santi watched the combat to see who had hold of Torren. That would be her next target.

It was the buck. He was fighting against Rogan with only half his attention while his mouth was open in gruesome Song. Santi dove straight down at him, wondering only for a moment if it was considered poor form for her to attack an opponent from above—stabbing him in the back—but then she figured all was fair if it meant his life or Torren's.

She used her momentum to slice her sai down into the buck's neck. The buck froze, and Santi could clearly see that, although he was strong and capable, he was very old. Santi pulled her sai from his neck, and he pressed his hand to the wound that was flooding the water around them with blood.

When it was clear to Santiago that he was no longer a threat to her or Torren, she looked to the last remaining Siren, but the dam was laying on the floor of the cavern, pierced through the heart.

Santi made her way over to where Rogan was helping Torren right himself. Torren was desperately weakened but looked as though he was ready to finish what they started. Rogan shook his head and must have spoken to him HaruKu because Torren shook his head vigorously back and forth several times before slumping his shoulders and kicking his wide azure tail towards the surface.

As soon as he was out of sight, Santi pointed towards the tunnel she and Tizz had been assigned to and nodded vigorously.

"You found him?" Rogan asked.

Santi nodded again.

"Where is Amaratizz? Is she all right?"

Santi could hear the panic seeping through his words even though his face was relatively passive and she couldn't feel his Ku. To reassure him, she gave a big thumbs up and smiled even wider than before and pointed towards the opening above them. He immediately relaxed.

"You really found him?" It was almost a whisper. Santi didn't bother responding because he was looking over his shoulder towards the tunnel behind them. He turned to her, and she nodded once, sharply. He grabbed her hand, and they made their way towards Sully.

When they were situated in the doorway to the room in which Sully was sleeping, Santi could almost feel Rogan's defeat. Sully was right there, but he was surrounded by forty or so Sirens in a tangle of nets.

Rogan kicked himself inside. Santi took a deep breath and began to follow, but Rogan turned and put up a hand. She could see regret in his eyes but didn't understand why until he said, "I am sorry," and pointed to her legs. After a little inner struggle, she pushed her feelings of hurt and inadequacy aside and nodded in agreement. She would be far too clumsy in there. Rogan was a sleek and graceful swimmer. His tail was wide, strong, and vast, but he could wield it with grace and elegance. She could not. Just to propel herself forward, she had to kick wildly.

Before he turned back to the task at hand, he began unbuckling the straps on his chest. Santi was about to protest as he thrust the swords at her to hold—he would need them if things went poorly!—but she realized he would never make it through the maze of hammocks with them on his back. She clutched them to her chest and pushed herself out of the room and into the tunnel.

She poised herself at the archway, helpless, plastered to the side of the wall with only her head peeking around. Santiago felt the rough rock against the fingers she had scraped earlier, felt the cut at her side; she focused on the small pains of her body to avoid the pain in her heart as she watched Rogan make his way inside.

Rogan set a direct path for Sully against the far wall, floating smoothly and slowly, not rushing, and being careful with every stroke. He came upon the first crossing of hammocks in his path and pushed his arms out in front of him like a diver. He easily slipped through the narrow gap in the ropes with his arms, shoulders, and torso. As the top of his tail started to pass through the opening, he did something with his fin she had never seen before. The end of his fin was wider than his wingspan; the width of his fin gave him his strength, speed, and power. It was over six feet wide and just as deep blue as the rest of his tail. It wasn't thin or translucent like some others, but sturdy and opaque. As he shifted through the small opening in the ropes, Rogan somehow folded his fin together, decreasing the width and making him completely aerodynamic. The length of his whole body was usually around eight feet long, but with his body tightened into this sleek line, he was probably eleven feet long. The added length didn't seem to hinder him.

Rogan had to use the gaps between the hammocks to make his way to Sully. He was impressively agile, though Santi held her breath as he slid carefully through the tight spots. Rogan slipped his entire body right by a sleeping Siren before deftly turning and tucking himself up, easily avoiding both the head of that Siren and the next tangle of hammocks being used by two other Sirens.

Santi let out her breath, relieved.

But now that he was in the mix of the Siren and hammock trap, getting out would be all the harder.

Luckily for them, every hammock did not hold a Siren, but there were still enough that every pillar held one or two. Santi could only watch on in tense anxiety as he made his way towards the back of the room. At one point several bags hung from hooks on a column, blocking the gaps he had been sliding through thus far, obstructing the only path he could take. Santi shivered, he literally looked like he was trapped in a net.

They both held their breath as one Siren within arms reach rolled in his hammock, his tail slipping over the edge slightly, and his arm hung over the other side. The Siren remained asleep but his arm now obstructed Rogan even further. Impossible.

Rogan turned and looked back at her as if to say, 'here goes nothing' before he flattened himself out horizontally, parallel to the Siren who had just made himself more comfortable; as if Rogan was going to sleep in the water right above the Siren. She saw her Bondmate take a noticeable deep breath, then blow it out making himself as small as possible. Completely flat and level with the sleeper, he barrel rolled between the two hammocks, gliding right through the narrow space, only inches away from Sirens on the top and bottom. When he made it through and righted himself, he looked visibly shaken, as if he didn't think that would work and still didn't think he had pulled it off.

After pulling himself together, Rogan realized he wasn't far from Sully now, though how he was going to get him out after getting himself in seemed suddenly, absolutely impossible. He wove his way through the remaining lines of hammocks so smoothly that in no time at all he was treading water in front of Sully's sleeping form. Had there been bells attached to every single hammock, Rogan wouldn't have tripped a single one. There were no indications that the Sirens even knew that he had entered the room.

That was all about to change. As soon as Rogan woke Sully, Santi was sure things would get difficult very quickly.

Rogan looked over his shoulder at Santiago. Though the look on his face was indiscernible, though they were HaruKu, they were connected through their Binding. This was the first time she truly felt that bond, and she knew he meant to tell her, *"However this goes, I love you."* Suddenly her heart ached. He had been so important to her when he was her childhood best friend and then later when Sully had abducted her. But now… Now Rogan was the most important thing in her life. Despite the difficulties they'd experienced after Amed's death, she loved him so much she was struck with actual pain. It hit her right in the space above her stomach and under her heart, that space that held the heaviest of emotions. It ached for him now.

As they looked at each other now, for what might be the last time, Santi was determined. She would be better for him. They would be the unstoppable team she knew they could be. She placed her hand on her heart, and he copied the gesture before turning back to his old friend.

Rogan slowly reached out his hand, and Santi wasn't sure if he was going to try to wake Sully or cover his mouth or just yank him up and try to pull him out—ignoring all the possible alarms and tripwires in their path.

But suddenly it didn't matter. Santi spotted a Siren stirring in his hammock in the other corner of the room. Santi pushed herself back behind the stone archway and pressed her back against the wall.

What do I do? What do I do?

She peeked back inside just as the Siren noticed Rogan. The Siren was clearly alarmed but didn't move. He opened his ugly mouth wide, teeth bared. Santi could see his larynx vibrating. It would only be a moment before he realized his Song didn't work on Rogan, and that moment was all the time she had.

She quickly connected her Ku to Rogan's. It didn't matter at this point if they were found out because they were about to be dead in a moment anyway.

"Rogan! They see us! Just grab him and go!"

With that, Santi turned and swam as quickly as she could down the hallway. She couldn't wait to see what happened or to help Rogan. She had to hope he wouldn't need his swords because she had to take them with her. An idea had formed in her mind, but she would never be able to keep up with Rogan—followed by a horde of Sirens—so she had to get a head start. She only hoped she could make it there in time, and that Rogan could get Sully out before all the Sirens were upon them.

Santi kicked frantically, making her way past room after room. Finally, she reached the main hallway. She kicked off the wall to propel herself more quickly down the hallway. She was yards away from the main chamber when she started feeling banging and thumping in the water behind her. The vibrations seemed to echo off the rocks and through the water, so it was hard to pinpoint exactly where the commotion was coming from. She looked over her shoulder but didn't see anything yet.

Finally, she made it to the first cavern before the main silo chamber, and she pushed herself inside. It was still empty. She breathed a sigh of relief and dropped Rogan's swords to the ground. She would need her hands, and he could gather them himself. Without stopping to enjoy her reprieve, Santi stuck her head out of the doorway to look back down the hallway.

The hall was empty.

Santi began ringing her hands. The vibrations had stopped. Everything was eerily quiet. She waited.

She looked around the empty room to verify that it was empty and that no Sirens were lurking, about to get her. There was nothing but columns of hammocks crisscrossing the room. She looked back into the hall. Nothing. She took in a deep breath and held it. Having a lungful of water felt heavy and safe. She felt comforted by it, though it was only a shallow security. She looked over her shoulder towards the main silo. Luckily, whatever the bulk of the Sirens were doing to that poor cruise ship was taking a long time. They hadn't yet returned.

Santiago looked back down the hallway. Nothing. She was making herself dizzy constantly checking every hallway and corner for Sirens or Rogan.

Where is he?

She resisted the urge to open her Ku again. She had only risked it when they were already spotted, but for this part she would need to be undetectable to the Sirens. No one understood quite how a Siren's Ku worked—if they had one at all—but it had been proven that a closed Ku around Sirens always provided an advantage.

She stared intently down the hall and finally let out her breath. She leapt into the hallway so he would see her. Rogan was shooting down the corridor, Sully wrapped in a death grip around his torso, and no one was behind them. Exactly what Santi needed for her half-cocked idea to work.

Santi signaled wildly for Rogan to follow her, and she flung herself back into the room. A second later, Rogan appeared. The two of them pushed themselves up against the wall.

Sully struggled wildly. "What are you doing?" he yelled at them, his voice feeling like a low grumble in Santi's Ku.

Santi jumped on his back and wrapped her arms tightly around his neck. He began to fight even more fiercely, but the combination of Santi on his back and Rogan holding his arms at his side was overpowering.

While they struggled with him, Santi saw the Sirens stream down the hallway towards the main chamber and up towards the opening to the ocean above. She couldn't believe her plan had worked! Rogan and Santi pushed themselves and Sully further into the back of the room and close to the wall. With any luck, the Sirens would think they had escaped the cavern and search for them outside.

I hope Tizz and Torren are safely away.

Santi squeezed tighter and held on while Sully struggled. She was doing it wrong. She was merely cutting off his air supply—though not effectively—which would take forever. She needed to be stopping the blood flow. Santi readjusted herself so that her forearm and bicep hit his arteries. While she pressed his neck with all her might, Rogan wrangled Sully's arms behind his back and tied them together.

"Stop this!" Sully said directly and clearly into their Kus. But in just a moment more, Santi was gratified in her efforts. Sully began to slump, and in a few seconds he was unconscious. In the movies, this maneuver would render the victim unconscious for as long as the movie needed him to be incapacitated. In real life, however, Sully would wake up almost as soon as she let go; but if she held on too long, he would die.

She risked communicating with Rogan again, quickly, and said, "Go. I'll catch up." Then she disconnected her Ku and untangled her arms. Rogan lifted Sully over his broad shoulder and fled from the room. Santi gathered up his swords from the ground and followed as closely behind as she could, but she was soon left in their wake. As Rogan and Sully ascended, they were engulfed in the darkness of the cavern mouth. Sully began to rouse and fight back before they vanished from her sight. She kicked her feet as hard as she could and hoped for two things: that Rogan could manage to get Sully out, and that she could get herself out, too.

Chapter 27

Santiago

The massacre above was grotesque. The Sirens had managed to scuttle the cruise ship—rip a massive hole in the side—and were pulling passengers from the wreckage, killing and capturing as they went. Santi was appalled and nauseated, but at least the Sirens were distracted.

She emerged from the opening carefully, stayed low to the ground, and didn't run into any trouble during the quick journey back to the meeting spot. Stealthily, she navigated her way into the weeds and found the black box that had been her seat. Heightened adrenalin left Santi feeling giddy, and she congratulated herself on her part in successfully finding and retrieving Sully. She felt an almost crazed sense of happiness, and she wondered when it would wear off.

To her relief, Tizz was there too, watching Rogan and Torren tie Sully's tail to his hands, which were secured behind his back. They had all made it back, a little banged up and injured, but alive and well.

A repulsive surge of guilt suddenly overwhelmed Santi at the thought that the hundreds of Crurals dying above made the perfect cover for their group to capture Sully and leave unharmed.

Tizz looked up and sighed, "Santiago! You made it! I was going to go get you, but Rogan made me stay."

Santi nestled herself down beside Rogan, who had finished with Sully, who now lay helplessly on the ground. They embraced. Rogan slid a massive hand up her neck and into her hair. He kissed her as if they'd just escaped the end of the world.

When they broke apart, Rogan kept his hand on the back of her neck, his thumb stroking the soft hairs at her nape. "I was about to go back and get you myself, but I knew you would make it," he said.

She wrinkled her nose at him and then turned, his arm around her shoulder keeping her close, and the four of them stared at Sully. Sully, thoroughly trussed, lay on the ground, thrashing futilely and glaring at them. No one else moved. No one spoke. They were all too tired and stunned that they had actually managed to get Sully out of a Siren's lair.

Finally, Sully asked the question that was already going through the others' minds. "What is your plan here?"

Rogan looked at Sully intently, and Sully struggled in his bonds but met his gaze. Santi felt Rogan's Ku wrestling with something. She looked between the two of them. So much history, so much hurt. Rogan was probably trying to figure out just what to say to Sully to make the curse release him. Finally, Rogan looked away, apparently deciding to say nothing, and turned back to the group.

The silence was intense. Their team had done the unthinkable, but what now? Everyone waited to be told what to do.

"Well, Santiago?" Torren asked expectantly.

"What?" She looked up at him surprised.

"Tell us what to do now," Tizz said. "Because we sure do not know what to do with him."

"Huh." Santi laughed. In books and movies, the leader always knew they were the leader. "I guess I assumed Rogan would tell us what to do now."

She looked at Rogan, and he laughed and shook his head. "Not me! I mean, yes, I wanted to do this, but you're the one who came up with this plan."

" But you…" She paused and sighed. Then she shook her head as she said, "This is breaking into Sentinel headquarters all over again." When he looked at her with confusion, she continued. "We're always hyping each other up to do crazy things without even knowing how it ends."

"Oh yes," Tizz piped up. "You two have always been like that."

They all stared at each other, and Santi felt a new determination. "We have to take him to Daris," she said with conviction. "We'll have to keep him there for a time until we can change him back… or find somewhere else to put him." She figured they could throw Sully into the extra room in her and Rogan's shelter and barricade him in somehow. Was that even possible? She wasn't great at thinking two steps ahead, but one step she could do. And that step was to get to Daris as quickly as possible.

Sully had stopped struggling. He lay on the sand, and Santi couldn't tell whether he was defeated or plotting his next move, though she could tell he was listening intently to their conversation about his fate.

"Will we put him in the prison cell?" Tizz asked, "because I do not think the Sentinels will let us remain in control over what happens to him if we put him there."

"We will not be able to get him inside the enchantment anyway," Rogan reminded them.

"No," Santi said, feeling stupid for forgetting the enchantment. Of course they couldn't put him in their shelter.

It came to her quickly, as if the idea had just been waiting for her to snatch it up. "I have a place we can keep him. It's outside the walls. I only saw it once, but I think it'll work."

Without further discussion, the group put complete trust in Santiago's idea. They closed their Kus, and Rogan and Torren picked Sully up between them. Giving themselves a wide berth around the opening of the Siren den and away from the cruise ship carnage, they traveled across the ocean floor quietly and calmly, their Kus closed tightly. When, finally, the ocean floor dropped away and there was nothing but the depths of the ocean beneath them, they picked up their pace until they could find dolphins or another way to hasten the journey.

When they felt safe enough to open their Kus, the first thing Torren said was, "It feels very wrong for me to be a Crural Guardian and not help those passengers aboard the ship."

Santi could tell that, like her, he had been wrestling with the guilt the entire time, and she wanted to ease his concern. "There was nothing you could do, though. Us against all of them? We stood no chance. But you did free those five that were prisoners, and that isn't nothing."

Torren was silent for a moment before he finally said, "I do not know if I should have done that, either."

"Why not?" Amaratizz was genuinely flabbergasted. "I was able to get them away from the Sirens and leave them very close to land. They will be all right."

"Yes, but...." Torren paused, thinking. "We have never found Crurals who have been captured by Sirens before, so there is no protocol. But it seems like they should have been debriefed in some way. They are just going to go back to their homes and share the terrible experience they have suffered. We will all be found out."

"Maybe," Santi responded, "but I can assure you that while Crurals love to hear wild tales like these, they don't really believe them. Sure, their names and stories will go viral, and they'll have hordes of fans, but it will die down quickly. There is literally too much on the internet for everyone's attention to stay on them for long." She knew most of the words she had just said were nonsense to the Serras, but they didn't seem to care. Her confident tone was reassuring enough. She had a sudden thought. "The only problem is that if anyone comes down to investigate the story, I imagine the Sirens will get to them before they find any Serras." Now she was torn, too.

The four of them were quiet for a moment until Rogan lifted his head suddenly. "Dolphins!" he proclaimed, and he and Torren left Sully in the custody of Santi and Tizz.

"Wait here. We will return with them in a minute. We have to hurry to Daris."

The two bucks swam away, and Santi turned to Tizz as they held Sully between them. "I don't see why they're bothering. It's going to take, what? About another two days to get to Daris? That's the last day of the tournament. Then four days back to the tournament grounds. We might as well run away into hiding now."

Sully suddenly took advantage of their momentary distraction and thrashed around so hard that he managed to shake himself free from their grasp. What he could not do, however, was get free from the ropes that bound him, and instead of escaping, he merely began to sink into the abyss below.

Tizz looked at Santi and giggled. "Maybe we should let the unknown eat him."

Santi smirked and nodded, but then said, "Rogan really wants him. But we do have a little time to let him get scared down there."

The two girls waited until they couldn't see Sully in the darkness of the depths before they plunged into the blackness themselves, guided only by their Kus. When they found him, they plucked him up. Santi grabbed him tightly by the arm and said fiercely, "Rogan is trying to help you. Just let him."

"Is it help if the person doesn't want it?" Sully asked, though he wasn't as hostile as she expected. It sounded like a genuine question. His voice was the same as she remembered, not from the kidnapping and the altercations they'd had since, but the voice from his childhood, the voice with smooth edges and everlasting patience.

"I guess this is forced help or, like, an unwanted favor." Santi truly hoped it worked. Initially, she had been doing all this for Rogan, but along the way her motivations had changed. She had hated Sully—and Rogan had too, to some extent—but this was what Rogan wanted—to make peace with the loss of Amed. And now Santi wanted it, too. Santi wanted the real Sully back more and more. She was as determined as Rogan to see what they could do for their old friend. "Just shut up and hold still," she said firmly, with a threatening squeeze to his arm.

When they emerged from the darkness, they could see Rogan and Torren above them, waiting, with the dolphins already in ropes and harnesses.

Rogan gave her a funny look. He had, of course, heard everything that had transpired; the dolphins were not so far away that they lost their connection. "Let him fall for a bit, did you?"

"He is just so slippery," Tizz said wryly.

Rogan and Santi shared a smile and a warmth in their Kus. She felt Rogan's ever-present love for her consume her heart. Santi was glad that no matter what happened going forward, Rogan was back to his old self, and they were going to come out the other side stronger than ever.

A day and a half later, they were letting the dolphins go far enough outside Daris that they could overlook the entire island. Sully had been remarkably cooperative though not at all agreeable. Just because he didn't fight them the entire trip did not mean he had been easy to deal with. He was dead weight with only the occasional struggle, but he was adamantly resistant to any of Rogan's attempts to talk to him. Sully even resorted to putting Tizz or Torren under his Song when Rogan pressed him too much, though Santi found it curious that Sully didn't really try to hurt them permanently. Sometimes he would only use the Song that left them paralyzed but unhurt, just to send a message. It also made her realize that he hadn't called down any of his Siren friends to help him. Maybe their former friendship still had a hold on his emotions, she mused. Whatever it was that kept Sully's deadly Song at bay, it made Santiago even more curious about Sully's complexity. She hoped Rogan could pull it all off. She wanted to know what was happening in Sully's stupid Siren brain. And then she'd probably punch him for all the trouble he'd caused.

Eventually, Rogan grew resigned to traveling quietly and quit trying to goad Sully into talking. He'd wait until they were alone to try to reach him.

The island loomed in the distance. Santi was stunned again. It was just as beautiful and breathtaking as the first time she'd seen it. It was shining white and gold, lit brightly in the dark blue of the water around it. "How does the city glow like that?" Santi asked, but when no one answered, she figured it was just as magical to them as it was to her.

Movement at the back of the city caught her eye then. A small battle was taking place just outside the wall, where a hundred or more Sirens were locked in combat with Sentinels. The Sentinels easily outnumbered them.

"Maybe we should stay away from the city right now," Tizz said. "Those Sirens are probably here for Sully, and if they see us with him…"

"They couldn't possibly be here for Sully already," Rogan answered, thinking like a soldier. "Even if they knew where we were headed, they certainly could not have beaten us here."

"It's ok," Santi added. "The place we're taking Sully is near the front of the city on the other side. We can just swing wide around the island and avoid any notice at all."

They followed her lead, swinging to the left to give the island a wide berth. They hadn't been swimming long when Torren stopped, pulling Sully and Rogan to a standstill.

"Look." Torren gestured with his chin towards the entrance arch to the city. Rogan, Santi, and Tizz looked. They were far enough away that they had to squint, but it was clear that three Sirens, their black tails stark against the brilliance of the city, were trying desperately to push their way through the enchanted barrier that protected the city. One was ramming himself again and again against the barrier, though he made no progress. The other two were meticulously groping along the opening of the archway and above the walls, trying to find a weak spot.

"How is no one noticing them doing this?" Santi asked incredulously right before realization struck. "Oh! The others in the back are a distraction! This isn't about Sully. It isn't even about the battle behind Daris."

They all tread quietly, staring. They didn't want to risk passing too closely and have Sully call out to them. "Why are they trying to break into Daris now? They have known for thousands of years that they cannot get inside."

"You have something of ours," Sully responded, suddenly breaking his days-long silence.

The four of them sent silent questioning ticks through their Kus before Rogan finally said, "Zitja."

Of course.

"Somehow, she managed to get inside, and now they think they can, too," Rogan continued. "And maybe they can." He said the last part quietly, more to himself. "Either way, they want to get her back."

"But she isn't there anymore." Santi said, and Sully looked up at her so quickly she knew she had made a mistake in revealing that information. She shrugged it off. "Whatever. They aren't going to find her is my point."

"So what do we do now?" Amaratizz asked. "We cannot go around and risk them seeing us. That leaves above, below, or through. None of which are possible."

Santi nodded. Above would make them clearly visible to the Sirens and all the Serras below in Daris. Santi didn't know how deeply the island extended into the water below, but if it was like any other island, it would go all the way to Earth's core. She was sure it was impossible to swim below.

"We will have to go through," Rogan answered Tizz. "Well, through the under."

Santi raised her eyebrows at him. "You sound crazy."

Tizz and Torren looked at Rogan with wide eyes. Even Sully's interest was piqued.

"We had better blindfold Sully," Rogan added decisively. "The caves and tunnels below Daris are meant to be a secret."

Santi smiled. She loved learning the mysterious parts of the ocean. She went over to Torren's bag and pulled out the ropes that had been used to harness the dolphins. Handing the coil of rope to Amaratizz, she made her way back to Sully and promptly dropped the bag over his head before tying the strap in a knot under his chin. He squirmed and wiggled, but Rogan and Torren gripped him firmly on either side. Santi turned to Rogan with a big smile and said, "Let's see these caves!"

Rogan directed them down to where the water got dark and then guided them further still. Santi couldn't see anything and relied solely on feeling Rogan's Ku to take her in the right direction. After diving a considerable distance, they swam towards the island.

"How do you know about this?" Amaratizz asked, but then immediately answered for herself. "This is another Sentinel secret. Nephira, I should change my opus goal."

"You do not want to be a Sentinel," Rogan answered, and Santi couldn't tell if he just knew Tizz—even Santi knew Tizz's soft heart had no business being a Sentinel—or if he was projecting some of his recently acquired bitterness into his statement.

"I know," Tizz verified. "But I sure do want to know all the stuff that is kept secret from the rest of us. Does mother know these things? Are you allowed to tell Santi?"

"Until now, I have not been allowed to know literally anything," Santi answered, and was surprised at the anger she felt.

Suddenly Rogan stopped, and Santi ran into him. The arm that wasn't holding Sully wrapped around her shoulders, and Rogan hugged her tightly. She relaxed, her anger wiped away. She hadn't been angry with Rogan anyway. He kept the secrets he had to. Her anger was directed at Krell for keeping her in the dark about everything that was planned for her.

Torren, holding onto Sully on his other side, stopped as well, and Tizz came up behind them. "We are here." Rogan said.

"Will Sully be able to get in?" Santi asked, unsure of the enchantment's reach.

"Yes." Rogan let go of her shoulder and moved slightly forward. "The caves do not have access to the city above, which means the tunnels do not pose a threat, so this area is not under the same enchantment."

Then he remembered something. "Also, our Kus will not reach far—just around our immediate vicinity. The caves and tunnels are thick and probably have their own sort of ancient Vis, so do not get separated."

"Rogan," Santi said hesitantly, "is there anything we need to worry about under here? Anything… dangerous?"

His Ku lightened and he eased the tension he was projecting, though only a little. "Oh no, not at all. But if any Sentinels happen to be down here, we will have a problem. The three of you should not be here. And bringing a Siren… Well, I am sure I do not have to tell you that is clearly not allowed."

He moved forward, groping at the rocky mass slightly, then led them all further to the left. Abruptly, Santi felt his Ku become disconnected. Immediately after, Torren's presence also disappeared from her awareness.

She kicked forward quickly. If they were disappearing inside the cave, she would have to follow closely behind or risk never finding the entrance at all. Amaratizz was a bit slower than the bucks and Santi swam right at her tail. As soon as Tizz entered the tunnel, Santi lost her Ku for a moment. She kicked her feet frantically and felt herself enter the narrow tunnel.

Once she was within the boundaries of the deep rock cavern, she felt three faint Kus ahead of her, but absolutely no awareness of Sully. She hurried so that she was just behind the other four.

After just a few feet, the tunnel opened up into a wide, long chamber lit with rods of luminescents. Santi had only ever seen the bioluminescent bacteria trapped in small orbs before, but these almost looked like fluorescent light tubes running the length of the floor beneath her. The small orbs wouldn't be sufficient to light up the massive passageway, she reasoned.

"We've been spending a lot of time in caves and tunnels lately," Santi remarked.

"This one will be markedly less dangerous than the other ones we have been in recently," Rogan said, giving Sully a rough shake as if to illustrate his point. "But if we see anyone, just hide. And if you are caught, tell them you are lost. Whatever you do, do not say you are with me. We will all be in far greater trouble if you say I brought you here than if you claim to have stumbled in here yourself."

"You got it, brother," Tizz saluted. "Tell them you led us straight here and have them take you away."

Rogan's Ku was light but annoyed. "I preferred it when you are off at Daristor and I was the one making the jokes."

They swam on silently. Rogan's warning had made them far more aware of the seriousness of their situation. They were not clear of repercussions just yet—not until they made it back to the tournament grounds in time for her grand show. Santi's heart sank. The finale was today, and they couldn't possibly make it back in time. Even with marlins pulling them, the trip would take nearly three days.

"Rogan, tonight is—"

They all froze. At the end of the long tunnel, two Sentinels had just rounded the corner. Everyone scattered so effectively that no two people went in the same direction. Santi flung herself into the nearest opening, a cavern off the right side of the main chamber. It was completely dark. Even the entrance was so hidden in shadow that it was almost impossible to see anything as she huddled just inside the opening. Santi saw Tizz swim up to a crevice in the ceiling, and Torren took off somewhere with Sully. Rogan, Santi assumed, was making himself look like he belonged in order to create a distraction.

Santi breathed in and out slowly. Her heart was beating so hard she was sure the Sentinels—no matter how thick the cave walls were—could feel it. She peaked out of the opening. The glowing rods lit up almost the entire cave—everything, Santi noted with relief, but the couple inches at the top of the cave where Tizz was plastered to the ceiling. Santi saw the tip of her tail peaking into the light for a moment before Tizz tucked her tail all the way up to the ceiling and disappeared into the darkness.

Santi couldn't see anything else from her hiding place, so she stayed put. Best to give Rogan more time to usher the Sentinels elsewhere. The room she was in was so dark that she couldn't see her hand in front of her face. Bioluminescent bacteria were efficient at lighting up a single room, but the light was very localized and didn't reach through doorways and around corners like the light of an incandescent bulb or the sun would.

Unexpectedly, she remembered being in a dark room in the Sirens' lair, and she felt the same panic run through her. She realized that she had no idea where she was or what else might be in this room of indeterminate size. She could feel the panic overpowering her senses, and she struggled to calm herself.

Santi pushed out her Ku. If she couldn't see what was around her, she would have to feel it.

She was instantly filled with regret.

The cavern was massive. She wasn't able to reach the far wall with her Ku before her ability faltered. But all around her, she could sense entities sharing the room with her—a half dozen, at least, possibly more, though she didn't pause to count. In her surprise and fear, she was ready to fling herself out into the main chamber, even if it meant getting thrown in prison. She grabbed hold of the rocky entrance to the cavern, about to swing herself out when she was struck firmly in the chest.

Here it is, she thought, *time to fight.*

She slid her arm down her thigh until she found the sai in its holster. Right before she unsheathed it, she connected her Ku—intending for the connection to be brief— to see what she was up against.

Her hand froze on the hilt.

"Nessy?"

The beast bumped against her chest again, and Santi wrapped her arms around its head. "Nessy! I can't believe…" She stopped herself. How could she even be surprised to find her mythical friend underneath a mythical city in the middle of the Atlantic, surrounded by mermaids? A Loch Ness Monster fit right in.

"Honestly, Nessy, I shouldn't be surprised by anything as long as I live after the nonsense I've been through," she whispered to the cryptid affectionately.

"Santiago!" Rogan popped up so suddenly on her left side it felt like he was shouting.

She swore and jumped so hard that she bumped into Nessy and the wall.

"Rogan! Why?"

"What do you mean, why?"

"I don't know," She sighed. "Why are you yelling? I am really frickin' on edge at the moment."

"'Frickin,' huh? That is new." His Ku was far too light for how tightly strung she felt. "Come on, we are fine."

They traveled down the corridor together until they met up with Amaratizz and Torren, who were holding Sully between them.

The rest of the trip was easy as they emerged from beneath the city. They were rounding the side of the island and ascending into the sunlight above when Santi finally felt safe in asking, "How did you dissuade the Sentinels?"

"Oh, I just told them I was on duty and the premises were secure. There was really no reason for them not to trust me."

"So Krell isn't searching for us? All Sentinels aren't on high alert for us? We aren't about to be ambushed and killed for our treason?" She felt that her Ku was a little shrill.

Rogan answered with a shake of his head. "I worry that your only experience lately has been with Krell's bucks. I promise you, the rest of the Sentinels are not like that. It is true he has a powerful few in his pocket at Daris, but that will not be the truth for the most part."

"In his pocket!" Santi laughed, feeling light and carefree now that the end of this adventure was literally in sight—off in the distance she saw where she intended to leave Sully while they went back to the tournament. "Rogan, you've never had a pocket in your life."

He smiled at her. They were all feeling carefree. They had pulled it off. Well, they'd managed to kidnap Sully, at least, which was no small feat. Dealing with the rest was another matter.

As they made their way across the top of the island, Santi was happy to see that they were far enough away from the archway to their right and the fighting at the back of Daris on their left that they would be able to go about their business without being noticed by either group of Sirens.

"Where are we going, Santiago?" Torren asked.

"It's almost directly head of us, a little to the left, towards the back of the city. I saw an empty cage just sitting on the sand. I think it'll be perfect."

"There is an empty cage?" Torren asked incredulously.

"I know. It's silly, and I don't know what it's actually for, but it was just empty."

It took Santi only a moment to locate it, right where she had seen it last, "See? He'll fit perfectly!" She didn't want to let on how relieved she was that the cage was still where she'd seen it before.

"Santiago!" Amaratizz laughed. "This is not empty."

Santi looked at it. Had something been placed in the cage since she was last here? She peered inside the tight mesh weave of the walls of the cage and looked up at Tizz skeptically. Nothing was inside except for some of the spikey little pom-poms she'd seen before. She gave Amaratizz a side-eye. "Tizz?" She gestured towards the cage. "Are you talking about those pink… whatever they are?"

The younger girl laughed outright. "Those pink 'whatevers' are urchins. Red sea urchins. They eat the kelp. That is how the *horps* keep the area around the city clear of vegetation that would obstruct visibility. The urchins are kept in the cages so they clear specific spots."

"Okaaaaaaay." Santi drew the word out as she thought. "So then, what is a horp, and can we put Sully in there or not?"

Rogan cut in. "Yes. Torren, open it. We will put Sully in the cage." But he paused in a way that told Torren he had more to say. Finally Rogan added, "better shake out the urchins first, they could sting him rather badly." Rogan still sounded as though maybe he might like Sully to receive a few stings but finally he proceeded, "this is a good idea, but it is very vulnerable. He will be found soon."

Torren opened the cage, shook the urchins free, and they wrestled Sully inside of it. He resisted, but his bonds made it easy enough for them to shove him inside.

Once Sully was secured, Rogan relaxed fully for the first time since leaving the tournament grounds. He turned to Santi, smile wide and genuine joy in his Ku, all irritation and anxiety gone. "The horps are the opus in charge of maintaining the city. They keep it clean and clear of debris—both Serra and Crural debris—and maintain the landscape. They also find a majority of our bioluminescent bacteria to supply the mercateras." He turned to the group, "We can put Sully under the island. There used to be prison cells down there, but they have rusted shut long ago, which is why I did not mention them before. But with this cage, we can tuck him into one of the many unused tunnels and he will not be found for a very long time."

He then directed his attention to Tizz and Torren. "I have to get Santiago back to the tournament immediately. They may already know we are gone, but if we are back in time for the finale, I don't think there will be ramifications for her absence. I do not feel comfortable leaving Sully here without a guard."

Before he could ask further, Torren spoke up. "I will stay. I can hide his cage away somewhere and then make sure he is undisturbed. Get Santiago back in time, and tell Sorrl where I am."

Rogan gave him a thankful nod and turned to Santi and Tizz. "Let us go. We have to get back immediately. It should only take a few hours."

Santi smiled so hard she might break her jaw. "Nessy!"

Chapter 28

Nhori

"Milli!" Nhori grabbed her by the upper arm. "Where is Yemri?"

"She is with Tammin." The young guard was kind but irritated at being accosted so.

"No, Milli, she is not." Nhori was angry. She had watched over Yemri since she was a tiny pup while also trying not to intrude on her role as Ocean Mother, but it seemed that her guards didn't take their job as seriously as she did.

"Please, Nhori." Milli was holding a small pup in her arms. "Three days ago, we lost dozens of Serras to the curse. Everything was chaos, there was a storm, we-"

"Milli, you listen to me. Your job is Yemri. Nothing else."

"Yemri sent me to save this pup. I did as she asked. I am sure she is here. Please," she looked down at where Nhori's hand was grasped firmly around her. "If you will just let me go, I will deposit this pup with a healer and go find Yemri immediately." She eased her defensive tone and looked Nhori in the eye for the first time. "I am concerned about her, too, and your news that Tammin is not with her worries me more than you know. But she is a grown dam who is capable of taking care of herself. We all fled the area, but everyone made their way here." When Nhori still looked worried, she added, "There are more coming behind me. She will be with them."

"She was so much easier to watch over when she was small and meek."

Milli looked at her. That wasn't necessarily true, but there was nothing they could do about it now. Nhori let go of Milli's arm, and the guard swam away in search of a healer. Nhori clutched her hands together. Nephira had asked her to protect and guide Yemri. If only Nephira knew what a difficult task it was. Yemri was both weak in conviction and strong willed, foolish, and determined. A trying combination.

Nhori closed her eyes and sighed, then opened them and looked at the flood of refugees and prisoners coming towards the island.

This dam is making me old. She laughed at herself. *And I am already extremely old.*

Shaking her head and speaking to the water around her, Nhori grumbled, "Yemri makes keeping my promise to you very difficult. You know this, Nephira."

There was time to continue waiting outside Daris' walls. Nhori didn't have anywhere to be, so she tried to convince herself that it was not yet time to worry; Yemri wasn't really late in returning and nothing was truly amiss. But she had a feeling in her Ku that something was wrong. Her intuition was always right because it was more than intuition. She was one with the water in a way only one other had ever been. Nhori would wait a little longer before trying anything drastic. But only just a little.

In the far distance, she felt Pangor and many Sentinels. She breathed a small sigh of relief as she allowed herself to assume Yemri must be with them, though she didn't feel her. As the swarm came into view, Nhori could see they were towing in at least a hundred Sirens and was chilled with the reminder that she couldn't feel their Kus. She was probably the most powerful Serra in the ocean—unless there were others hiding their capabilities, just like she was—but if she couldn't feel a Siren's Ku, it truthfully must not exist. The implications were frightening.

Nhori swam up to Pangor and tried to keep the panic out of her Ku. He would take it all in stride, ever level-headed. "Pangor! Where is Yemri? She did not arrive with her guards, and I do not see her with you." She breathed. "I know she is capable, but I fear something is wrong."

To his credit, he took her worry seriously. Yemri might vex him constantly, but Nhori had his utmost respect. "The Serras of the Maato began transforming." He gestured behind him, and Nhori pushed backwards in shock. She had not realized these were not just any Sirens captured from the ocean; they were former Maato! "In addition, the Maato lair was very close to the surface, where there was a funnel storm. It wreaked havoc on our mission and sent everyone scrambling. I am sure she is behind us."

"A funnel storm! No!"

Pangor was not unsympathetic, but he was preoccupied, "Nhori, if you will excuse me, I have to see to these prisoners."

"Of course. Of course." She ushered him away with a sweep of her hands. She was also very distracted. A funnel storm could be very dangerous, especially if they were close to the surface, as he had said. Someone should have made sure Yemri got away. A strong enough funnel could have picked her up and taken her a great distance. The whole ordeal would surely kill her.

It was finally time to be drastic.

Nhori made her way inside the city and headed for the citadel. If she was going to do this, she'd need to lie down. It would take all her energy and could possibly leave her too weak to move, so she might as well already be on her sleeping cushion before she began.

"Nhori?" A young buck Nhori dimly recalled was named Rane was at her side. "Pangor sent me to ask you about the… um, the secret prison. Are you aware of it?"

"Yes, of course."

He looked visibly relieved as he rushed on. "Oh good. Well, you see, the main chamber is now full. He wondered if you thought we should put them in with Zitja? He did not think that was a good idea and thought you might have a better suggestion."

"No, that most certainly is not a good idea. In fact, I can name several bad ideas that have just taken place. Tell Pangor to take the overflow Sirens to Nephira's old stronghold in Afiti, into the tombs there. And also tell him not to send messenger pups with confidential information in the future."

The young buck looked sufficiently chastised, though it was not his fault. Nhori didn't care about his feelings, however. "Yes, of course, Nhori," he said meekly and swam off to relay her messages.

Nhori made her way to her rooms.

Nhori had told Yemri and Pangor that putting their enemies underneath the city was a very dangerous thing to do. It left their city vulnerable to anyone that would do them harm. What was to stop Sirens from tunneling upwards to avoid the protective enchantment? Nothing but a few guards. And what if a mass of Sirens escaped knowing full well the details of the underwater entrance location? The city would surely be doomed.

Twenty years ago, Zitja had freed the other Sirens that were imprisoned with her, and Nhori had had to handle their memories before it became dangerous. She had already done so for Zitja. The young Siren was not pleased to be cursed yet again, but Nhori had no choice. Once Zitja left the caves—Nhori prayed that day never happened—Zitja would have no memory of the underground tunnels and caverns. She would never be able to find the place again even if she tried.

It always struck Nhori as devious when she had to take matters into her own hands without bothering to seek approval from Yemri, but it had to be done, regardless of how Yemri might feel. Just as Nhori had made the Crurals forget about the Serra's existence after Nephira had been rescued, and she had made the Sirens forget about the tunnels under Daris, she would do all in her power to keep safe everything they held dear. But she couldn't possibly keep up with every errand pup sent flitting around the city with valuable information.

Nhori closed the heavy door to her chambers, which she typically left open. She usually didn't feel the need to cut herself off from those who needed her, but in this moment, she needed absolute privacy. This was not the first time cleaning up after Yemri had to be done. Nhori was always fixing the pup's mistakes…

Though, she is not a pup anymore, is she?

Nhori wanted to find her. She loved her. But she was very exhausted by her. No one had helped Tope raise Yemri after Sariah had been killed, and he had swum difficult waters when his very young daughter had become the Ocean Mother. Nhori knew they had all failed Yemri and that the young dam was still struggling to figure out her place.

The fact that no one seemed concerned about Yemri's disappearance was alarming to Nhori. Though, she did admit, they were all very preoccupied and had every reason to believe that she was just behind them, traveling with another guard or another group. It was only because Nhori was in tune with the ocean's Ku that she was so alarmed. She often wondered if anyone remembered that the ocean even had a Ku.

With a heavy sigh, the elder dam lay back on her sleeping nest. Nhori was unique. She was not merely a Serra, though she had chosen to live as one of them instead of the alternative, so she tried to keep things in perspective. She remained in touch with the Vis more than everyone else because of who she was. Still, they should not all have forgotten so easily. It hadn't even been forty years since

Nephira's return from captivity. They could have kept a better grasp on it if they had tried.

Nhori rested on her back. Her tail—tired and frayed with age and use—lay across the maroon cushion, the fin hanging off the end and over the sides. Nhori felt tired already and hadn't even begun. She didn't know how many more decades she had left in her. Certainly, there was not enough strength in her to live another century.

Her Ku was already encompassing all of Daris, which was commonplace for her; now she pushed it out farther. She felt the Sentinels taking more and more Sirens under the island, their Kus vanishing as they entered the tunnels in the dense land mass below. As she felt them disappear, she hoped Yemri wasn't somewhere she couldn't reach.

She pushed her Ku out beyond Daris, then farther and farther. In moments, she felt the boundaries of the Afiti, followed by the Najilian on the other side of the Atlantis. She expanded her Ku in a wider radius. By the time she was aware of the Nhori clan and the NorMer, she was feeling noticeably weaker. She closed her eyes and felt any tension she had been holding in her body drift away in an eerily death-like limpness as she continued to push her Ku. Nhori felt around the landmasses and through the small seas and giant rivers.

Where could she be?

Nhori refused to admit the possibility of Yemri's death. She had protected the pup from everything within her power since the pup was born. As Yemri grew, she had protected her from Pangor's wrath on so many occasions she couldn't count. Nhori had even saved Yemri's life when they had been traveling through the ocean and Sirens nearly attacked their caravan. She had done all she could to keep the dam alive and well. She would not lose her to a funnel storm and irresponsible guards.

Nhori would not rest until she found Yemri. Feeling her energy draining away, she slowly gathered up Vis from the surrounding areas in which she was searching. But Nhori wasn't as strong as she had been when she first placed the enchantment on Daris, gathering up Vis and easily bending it at her will. She was weak and tired now. Centuries of life—though she would never admit it—were taking their toll.

Nhori pushed and found the Hatu'anu, down at the southern-most landmass, and then up to the northern. Yemri was nowhere to be found.

She cannot be dead. She just cannot be.

When her awareness covered the entirety of the ocean, feeling every Serra, fish, and animal in the water, Nhori realized there were only three options: Yemri had transformed into a Siren, she was on land, or she was dead.

Nhori would not entertain the first or last option, so she gathered her strength and pushed her Ku out still farther. She began shaking with the effort, and suddenly, she was devastatingly cold. Wishing she had the strength to reach for a coverlet, Nhori took a deep breath and pushed her awareness onto the lands that touched the ocean.

There was nothing, and her strength was gone. She gave one last involuntary shudder, and everything went black.

"Nhori."

She was being shaken gently, but the voice was urgent and frantic. She did not want to open her eyes, but she did want the disturbance to stop.

"Nhori. Nhori, please!" There was a short pause and then, "I can feel her Ku. She is awake."

And then from the other side came a much gentler but deep, "Nhori?" It was Tope. Now she surely didn't want to awaken. There was nothing but bad news to deliver.

"Nhori," the dam's voice was back, still urgent, but the shaking had stopped at least. "We have tried to wake you for two days."

Two days?

Using her Ku had never taken so much out of her before. As if to confirm, her stomach gave a sickening roll that left her feeling nauseated. She didn't open her eyes, but she finally connected to Yemri's annoying little aide, Torvi. "Torvi, find me something to eat, would you?"

"Of course, Nhori." And she left the room immediately.

Finally, Nhori opened her eyes and looked sideways at Tope. Nephira was the only Serra who knew what Nhori truly was, and to a small extent, Sariah. She assumed Sariah had told Tope some of it, though none of them knew just how powerful she had once been. She could see in Tope's eyes he knew she had done something, though he could not figure out what.

"Is she dead?" he asked, his heart trying to be strong. Yemri was the last of his family. The buck did not deserve this.

"I could not find her in the entire ocean. I am sorry. It does not mean she is dead, exactly…"

"It just means that if she were still alive in the ocean, you would know it."

They sat silently until Torvi arrived with a basket of mussels, clams, and scallops. Nhori ate it all up and sent Torvi out for more. Once they were alone again, she leaned her head back against the wall behind her sleeping cushion and closed her eyes, still feeling remarkably drained but on the mend.

"Two days?" she asked, and Tope confirmed with his Ku. "I fear we will have to proceed as though the worst has happened." Tope confirmed again. "Yemri was the last in a centuries-long line of Ocean Mothers."

Yemri had never shown interest in Bonding or bearing children, and Nhori felt it wasn't her place to push either of these matters. What did she know of Yemri's heart's desires? And thus, they were now left with no progeny. "This development is unprecedented. I do not know where we go from here."

"Nor do I. We are going to have to call in the other balams and discuss how to proceed."

It was Nhori's turn to confirm thoughtfully. "In the meantime, we have some things to do."

"You want to clear out under the island?" Tope asked. Nhori's Ku was clear on this without her saying anything. "And close down the Tunnel of Loss?"

"I have come around on the tunnel, though it needs to be fortified more thoroughly, and we need guards placed there. That tunnel leads straight to Anthemoessa. It is not a safe route."

Out of respect for the possibly-dead, Nhori did not mention how absurd she thought its location was. Although it was very convenient for the Serras, it was also very convenient for the Sirens. Funneling Serras straight to the Siren's lair was asinine. But that did not need to be said again.

By the time Torvi had returned with a second round of food and she had eaten her fill, Nhori was feeling much better. She pushed herself up from her nest and sighed, "Let us get to work."

Nhori pulled Vis from the water around her and stole a little extra from Tope and Torvi—they were strong and wouldn't notice—and by the time they were making their way towards the portico, Nhori was feeling better, ready to tackle the matters at hand.

"Pangor." She reached out to his Ku as soon as she located him in Daris. "Meet me outside the city. We have to clear the catacombs."

"So, she is dead then."

She simply said, "Hurry."

She felt something brewing but could not tell what it was. Maybe the Sirens were finnally coming for Zitja, maybe a storm was threatening on the surface. Without expanding her Ku, she did not know, but she felt it best to reserve her strength for whatever it was.

Pangor arrived at her side, and Tope continued along at her other side. Torvi had followed behind meekly, unsure about what was going on but eager to help, and everywhere Sentinels and Serras were going about their business.

Why are there so many Serras outside the city?

She wanted to shout at them to seek shelter, to get inside the enchantment, but she had no idea why she was frightened. There was no reason.

"Pangor, did you take the overflow Sirens to Nephira's stronghold?"

"They are on their way there now."

"Good. Take them all there. If for some reason they do not all make it, shame…"

Pangor commanded nearby Sentinels to clear the tunnels and cells under Daris. He shouted other orders and sent a messenger ahead to tell those at the stronghold to expect more.

"You know, you really should use the nuntiums. They are much more efficient."

Pangor looked at her, cocked his head, and then said, "Someone find me a scyphozoa." Pangor had a habit of being extra pompous when he was ordered around. Nhori pursed her lips. She wasn't impressed by his use of the official name for jellyfish, but he had learned that such extravagances intimidated Yemri.

He swam away, and Nhori gave a smug look to Tope. "And now we had better…" But she trailed off as a wave of fear washed over her.

"Nhori?" Tope asked.

"He is coming."

"Who is coming?"

She turned back towards the city and looked at it in a panic. What could she do now? "Torvi! Get Pangor back." There was nothing they could do for the city. He was coming, and he would destroy them all.

"But Nhori," Torvi said with a meek voice, "you just sent him into the catacombs to get the Sirens." She was scared. She did not want to go down there.

She should not even know about it.

"Go, Torvi. Go!"

Torvi left without further word.

"Whatever you need from me, Nhori, I am here for you," Tope said.

"You know what I will need," Nhori answered, though she wasn't sure if he did.

Her doubt was assuaged when he said, "I do, and you are welcome to it."

She did not respond because just a heartbeat later, she felt *him* coming.

Memories assaulted her as the feeling of his Ku raged inside her, just as it had centuries ago. They had been friends long ago. Possibly, they would have spent immortality together, but Deus had his own ideas about how the world should work and took it upon himself to decide what was best.

They were gods of old: he for the ocean, she for the beings in it. She wasn't his wife, as the mortal legends had told. He wanted to control her, control everything. She would not have it. The two of them, along with the gods of the skies, land, animals, the elements, war, passion, forgiveness, and more had nurtured the world in the beginning. But, over time, they were needed less and less, and so they disappeared from activity on the planet. Some died, others chose an earthly existence—like Nhori—though they were nearly immortal. Deus, on the other hand, did not want to lose his former glory and had to be imprisoned for the safety of everyone in the world. He had already done enough damage when the earth broke apart.

But he was free now, and it was up to Nhori alone to handle him.

Nhori floated at the ready. She did not think she would be strong enough to kill him. She only hoped she could stop him.

She steeled herself.

At the same time, Pangor and a line of Sirens in chains came filing out of the tombs. At the rear was Zitja.

Pangor thought it a good idea to take her out with the rest of them?

Nhori didn't think that was wise, given the circumstances, but how could Pangor have known? She had to be quick. In another heartbeat, Deus would be upon them.

Nhori connected to every being in the vicinity. She pulled the Vis out of the plants, the rocks, the fish and animals; lastly, she connected to the Ku of the Ocean. She turned to face her challenge.

Tope pushed himself back in the water, overcome with terror upon seeing Deus. "What is that??"

He should *be terrified,* thought Nhori.

"DEUS!" Nhori shouted, her voice filling up the water around them. Because of the strength of her connection, everyone heard her and felt her power.

No one moved.

Floating before them was the torso of a man larger than two porticos. He had the lower body of an octopus—an octopus so large that could pull the island of Daris from its perch and fling it into the depths.

"How are you out of your confinement?"

"Your Ocean Mother asked for my help."

No! Nhori groaned inwardly. *She could not possibly be so foolish.*

"We do not want it," Nhori boomed at him while breathing a small sigh for Yemri's life. The dam was alive; foolish, but alive. The reason Nhori hadn't been able to find her was because she was too deep. A Ku could not penetrate those depths; evil resided down that far. Now it appeared that the evil had escaped the depths.

Pangor, duty-bound to protect the water and its inhabitants from those that would do harm, made his way towards the front of the island. His Sentinels—more afraid and curious than anything else—followed along behind, towing the ropes full of Sirens with them. Some Sirens stared, mouths agape. Others knew this was a threat even larger than themselves and froze in the water, towed limply along by their ropes.

"The Sirens are doing you harm." Deus lifted a giant tentacle and took a massive swipe through the water, sending Siren and Sentinel soaring so far that they disappeared from her Ku. Many of them had surely died on impact with his mighty appendage.

Tope looked at her with an expression that begged to understand what was happening. "Are they dead?" Dozens of good Sentinels had been caught in the sweep of his suctioned arm. "Where are they? Who is he? What do we do?"

Tope was beginning to sound frantic, and she could feel Pangor's Ku was joining him in turmoil. She addressed them both. "This is Deus. He was once a god and thinks he is still." She directed the last part at Deus, hoping he would understand that his powers and authority were no longer wanted or needed in the world.

But he responded, "Nhori, your mortal existence has left you frail and old. A pity, to be sure. I can feel it. You will die if you do not join me once again. I can restore you."

Nhori did not respond to him but addressed Tope and Pangor further. "He does not reason the way we do. If he is here to help us, we are surely all doomed. He has been imprisoned in the depths for centuries. It seems Yemri has released him."

"She is alive?" Tope asked. Overwhelmed by all he had learned, he was only able to focus on the news of his daughter.

"It would seem," Nhori answered, "though *we* may not be in a few more minutes."

Pangor was shouting commands to the remaining Sentinels, and Nhori added to it. "Release the Sirens from their chains."

"Nhori?" Pangor questioned.

"Even they will understand who the true enemy is here."

The kingly beast lifted another tentacle, slapped it to the outer wall of the protected city, and flung it to the side, like plucking a plant from the sand. "There are evil Kus inside your city as well, Nhori. Serras' Kus are turning sour. You are losing control. I will clean them out for you."

The abrupt destruction of the perimeter wall had roused Serras from their homes and startled them where they swam. Most fled deeper into the city, but many, overcome by curiosity or stupidity, swam through the broken barrier and out to the commotion. Whether they thought they could help or were just too stunned for self-preservation, they joined the tumult on the island, surely to meet their own doom.

"No, Deus!" Nhori said firmly. "Go back where you came from."

"Where did I come from, old friend?" He was lifting another giant suction-cupped tentacle, but before it could land on its target, Siren and Sentinel both charged at him. Several went at his face and torso, others to his raised limb, hacking at it with swords, knives, and axes. Nhori watched, aghast, as a dozen Sentinels and twice as many Sirens worked to cut off the appendage that broke the wall. Nhori knew they shouldn't waste their time on Deus's arms. They would do more good focusing on his face and torso.

Nhori was about to tell Pangor to organize them at Deus' head when, with another mighty swipe through the water, Deus shook off dozens of Serras and Sirens like they were shrimp. He raised a boulder-sized hand to his face and swiped away any that were trying to attack him.

"This is not going to work," Tope said as he unsheathed his sword.

"Stop," Nhori said. She had assumed they would fight him together with their swords and spears and courage, but now she knew they would have to fight him another way. "Find me Zitja, quickly."

"Zitja?" he asked, but did not wait for clarification before maneuvering through the chaos of swiping tendrils and swinging weapons.

"Deus!" Nhori shouted again, pulling Vis from the water. If she reached too far for the power, it would take strength that she very much needed to preserve, so she had to take from what was right near her. And it wasn't enough. "You will go back to your prison."

He made a tsk, tsk sound. "You have allowed evil to take over the ocean," he said. "I am disgusted for you." He paused as if to locate Nhori so that he could chastise her directly, as if he could not possibly find her miniscule form in the commotion, though Nhori knew Deus knew exactly where she was. He made a deliberate show of saying, "I am embarrassed by you. I am here to fix your mistakes."

"These are not my mistake,." Nhori responded, kicking herself up in the water slowly. The highest point of the city was only halfway up his chest. She swam up beyond that. "These are not mistakes. This is how mortal beings learn and grow. We will fix things ourselves."

"Nhori," Deus scoffed. "You do not need to trouble yourself with the problems of mortals and fish-people. You are better than they."

"No. No, Deus, I am not. I am them. And they are me. Some of us choose to watch out for our fellows."

She was still rising in the water. She was just reaching his face when Tope and Zitja arrived at her side. Deus took another swipe at the crumbling wall and demolished the entire side of Daris. The Siren Queen, unchained and obliging, put her only hand on Nhori's shoulder and whispered, "Do it."

Nhori did have time to question how Zitja knew—or what Zitja knew—of Deus, but Nhori had underestimated Zitja's wisdom as a youth, and she would not do that again. Nhori pulled from Zitja and Tope all the Vis she could harvest from them and still leave them alive. She filled up her own body so full of surging power that it was coming off of her in waves. Around the ocean, Sirens and Serras alike could look at her and see her glowing with the power she was absorbing. Zitja alone contained so much Vis from her enchantment that Nhori felt as if she were as young as she was back when she and Deus ruled together.

Nhori spoke firmly. "I bind you once more to your prison. You will not try to help or harm these waters!" Tope grabbed on to her other shoulder to support her as she swayed with the power she now held inside her. Then, in a breath, she thrust the KuVis through the water and hit Deus in the chest.

The mighty being was pushed back through the water. "Nhori, you know you cannot undo this without me," he threatened.

"Then we will leave it done," she said as she continued to push him more firmly with the KuVis radiating from her. She pushed so far that he was out of sight a moment later, and soon after, he no longer posed an immediate threat. He was still able to do harm to the ocean, however.

Reaching deep within herself, Nhori pushed him yet farther away. She was shaking and felt faint. Her arms and tail tingled and lost feeling. Her sight went next. Nhori took a long pull of energy from Zitja and Tope until she could take no more and pushed it out at Deus. She could feel him fighting her, thrashing against her power and clawing through the water, tearing down any stones or lands in his way. "You will do no more harm to Serras or Crurals," she commanded as she siphoned off the last of Tope's Vis and pulled more from Zitja.

Fighting from afar she wrestled Deus into his glass prison and with the final wisps of her strength draining, she knew this would be her last great endeavor.

Nhori sealed him back up securely in the coffin-like encasement. She used the end of her waning strength to make sure he was secured.

She said as the world went black around her, "You will do no more harm." Then as her body sank lifeless through the water Pangor gathered her into his arms.

Chapter 29

Yemri

Yemri felt something was wrong long before she arrived at Daris. "Kalani," Yemri asked nervously, "how long do you think it took us to get from OnaKu?"

"I believe the journey took about a week, since we did not have a travel aid."

Yemri looked at her friend with wide eyes. She was nervous and suddenly wracked with guilt at being gone for so long, but seeing Kalani's bright white penumbra eased her concern. "I am sure it took me longer to get to you from where I was before getting to OnaKu," she said. What she did not admit was how long it took her to orient herself after her encounter with Deus. She should probably be better at traversing the ocean, but while she had been swimming around lost, she realized she had always been escorted through the ocean and had never actually had to navigate herself.

As they arrived at Daris, Yemri felt sick. It had been over a month since the incident with the Maato and the storm. The journey had taken too long. Clearly, she had missed a lot.

The western wall of Daris was nothing but rubble and debris.

"What happened here?" Yemri asked, aghast. "What could possibly have done this? How will we repair this?" She was overwhelmed.

"This is quite a disaster," Kalani answered calmly while she took it in. "But look, repairs are already being made." She gestured to the signs that showed repair efforts were underway; surviving square stones were stacked on the island, ready to be put back in place, and the rest of the rubble was being sorted and assessed for usefulness. "We are resilient, Yemri. We will fix this."

Yemri uncoiled her tense muscles. Kalani had just confirmed for Yemri that she was making the right decision.

For once.

As they made their way through the portico, Freydis was entering as well and spotted Yemri. She swooped down on Yemri and placed her hand on her heart. "I was so happy to receive your nuntium! Ocean Mother, praise Nephira you are alive! We were all so worried!" Her penumbra glowed bright yellow, and her Ku confirmed her sincerity.

Yemri returned the gesture by placing her hand over Freydis's heart—noticing her own yellow penumbra and glad to be able to see it again—with a genuine earnestness she didn't realize she felt. "Thank you so much for your concern."

Freydis and Muleki had been the only ones to actually answer the nuntium that she had sent to all the balams, though she assumed they would all follow her instructions to meet her at Daris. She had found it odd that Nhori didn't answer and rather hurtful that her father hadn't, but at the moment, she had bigger concerns. "I want to address some issues right away. Do you think everyone else is here? Muleki said he would be here, and I assume Nhori took over in my absence." Nhori had always taken over for Nephira, so it made sense that she would help everyone during this time of uncertainty.

The way Freydis's Ku vibrated at her was confusing. The waves of pity and regret seemed out of place. Yemri was about to ask about it when Nanti'ouato and Efren arrived. Nanti looked haggard and tired beyond her age.

"Yemri," she cooed and placed her hands on either side of the younger dam's face. "I am so extremely sorry."

Yemri cocked her head and looked at Nanti with puzzlement. Nanti's Ku was radiating devastation far out of proportion for Yemri's absence. "No, no Nanti'ouato. Do not worry. I am fine, I promise."

Nanti looked at Freydis and then at Efren. Their auras had suddenly gone dark green.

"What?" Yemri asked, panic beginning to mount. "What has happened?"

Just then, Muleki arrived from the interior of the city, and Yemri began to put it together. "What has happened to Nhori?"

Nanti, who still had a supportive hand on Yemri's shoulder, answered reluctantly, "It is best just to tell you everything. It is not only Nhori. She and your father are both dead."

Yemri gasped violently. Her hands clutched at her chest, and she pushed herself backwards through the water.

"No! No, it cannot be!"

The emotional anguish was suddenly an actual, physical pain. Her head throbbed fiercely, and her stomach felt like it would cave in. She wanted to flee from the news, but Nanti continued. "Zitja escaped, and Sirens have overtaken the tunnel between the Afiti and Tipua. I am sorry. I know this is a lot to absorb all at once."

Yemri was sure Nanti was still talking, but she could not hear her. Her father was dead. Nhori, the mother figure she had grown up with, was dead. Zitja had escaped.

Yemri interrupted whatever Muleki was saying to her and blurted, "Zitja killed them?!" It was a question, but she was sure it was the truth.

Again, the four balams—four remaining balams of six—shared a look and an unspoken tick in their Kus.

"What?" Yemri nearly shouted. She was frantic. "Tell me what happened here! What happened to the wall? How did my father and Nhori die? Tell me, please!"

No one answered her for a moment, but before Yemri became any more frantic, Efren, the one she with whom she had the least personal relationship, answered her. "There was some sort of… monster. It was a massive beast, larger than the entire city of Daris. It had the lower body of an octopus and a giant crown on his head. I do not know. No one has ever seen the likes of it before."

Yemri took several ragged breaths that caught sharply in her throat. She felt shaky and was sure she'd pass out at any moment. She did not hear anything Efren said as he explained what happened with Deus.

I did this.

These deaths and this destruction, this was on her head.

She looked at Kalani, who was glowing bright white as she listened intently to the story Efren told. Yemri forced herself to listen.

"Nhori, it would seem, still knew how to harness KuVis. She sent him away and locked him back up. But he was too strong for her to handle alone. She had to take power from those around her. It would seem it took all her life-force to imprison him, and the effort killed your father as well."

Muleki added to the story. "I spoke with Pangor afterwards. He saw it all. Somehow, Nhori used energy from Tope and Zitja to conquer this… creature."

"So Zitja is dead as well?" Yemri exclaimed.

"No," Muleki responded with an air of disbelief, "though she was significantly weakened to the point her Sirens had to carry her away."

An eerie calm washed over Yemri. A scary, dark calmness. It consumed her. She was void of feeling and emotion. Such intensity emanated from her that the balams were frightened by Yemri's energy. Finally, she spoke. "Shall we go inside and begin this meeting?"

No one spoke. Her Ku was mysterious, tinged with a frenetic energy.

What was left of the Cor, along with Kalani and any guards in attendance, followed her inside silently. Freydis,

Nanti'ouato, Efren, and Muleki sat in a circle on their cushions without uttering a word. As Kalani sat down, Yemri could tell the others were curious, but no one dared ask who she was. Once everyone was seated, they looked at Yemri expectantly, worry and anxiety filling the room. She turned to her guest and spoke.

"This is Kalani of OnaKu, from the Najilian."

There was a murmuring of welcome, but everyone kept their questions to themselves for the time being.

When they were quiet, Yemri made her revelation. "She will be taking over as Ocean Mother."

Yemri expected an eruption of commotion and disapproval. She had prepared for every argument.

She was met with silence.

Since no one said anything, she began with some of the arguments she had prepared.

"Kalani is right for this position in a way I never was. As my last official order, I am removing the birthright aspect of Ocean Mother. It will now be passed on to the dam who is best suited for reign. I have chosen Kalani because of her pureness of spirit. She will be right for the ocean, and she will choose her predecessor and train her. There is too much left to chance when the rulership is bequeathed by legacy and tradition. Since the introduction of language and the loss of our powerful Ku connection, we run the risk—for the first time in our history—of putting the Ocean Mother at risk of corruption and persuasion.

"A pure Ku will not run that risk."

Still, everyone was silent. Yemri was tempted to scream at them to speak, to answer. She wanted them to argue or ask questions. Even a mutter would be preferable to the silence. Anything.

"I have done the best I could, but I was never suited for this. It has taken me a long time to come to terms with the fact that it is completely fine not to be a leader, not to be the one in charge. It is tempting to think that when you are in charge, you are the most important. But being in charge is not the most vital role. There is importance in every one of us, no matter what calling we find ourselves in. And that is why I will continue to do good works... just not as the head of this ocean."

"Yemri," It was Freydis, calm and gentle. "This... this is a good thing that you do."

Muleki spoke with reverence. "It takes a wise person to know when they are not the best suited for the job. You are choosing your people over pride."

"You have made a good choice," Efren said.

Yemri was confused. "That is not what you told me when I was a child. No one would let me quit then." She found herself feeling angry with them. All this hardship and unnecessary loss, so many mistakes! She could have been done with the responsibility long ago.

"I'm afraid," Nanti'ouato said with a gentle Ku, "that sometimes we do not like to think that pups know what is best for them. We think our age gives us wisdom about the young ones that they cannot possibly know about themselves. But there is incredible wisdom to be found in the youth, as well. We should have listened when you said you were not suited for it, but we assumed you would grow into it." She sighed with true regret. "But there was nowhere for you to grow with the circumstances you were put under. And for that, I am ashamed."

For the second time in her chaotic life, Yemri could not have been more shocked. She had no reply.

"What will you do now?" Freydis asked, genuine concern pouring into Yemri's Ku.

It would be a lie if Yemri were to say her feelings were not a little hurt. She had imagined resistance, if not for love for her, then for keeping with tradition—or possibly out of some sense of loyalty. Were they so happy to see her gone? Was she as much a failure in their eyes that she was in her own?

But she was also glad the news was received well. At least it made things easier. "I plan to live in OnaKu. I think it is necessary for me, and I will be a better person because of it. I still plan to do good for all Serras, but I think I can do a much better job on a smaller scale."

"We genuinely wish you the very best, Yemri," Muleki said. They had had their disagreements in the past, and quite possibly he wished she could have resigned twenty years ago, but right now he was full of love for her. "Your heart has always been in the right place."

"That is probably the only thing about me that has ever been in the right place," Yemri quipped. She sighed. She was looking forward to being in OnaKu again where she could mourn the loss of her entire family for the first time in her life. Duty had never let her dwell in sadness for any period of time, never allowed her to mend her soul after such tragic losses.

She was ready to heal, but first she needed to grieve.

5 Years Later

Yemri sat with a small pup on her lap, braiding the child's peach-colored hair while sneaking in tiny hugging squeezes. The ocean moved gently all around her, making the tiny hairs float to and fro.

Yemri's Ku was bursting with love and joy. She had found happiness within herself in a way she had never been able to before. She was finally feeling ready to leave OnaKu for the first time since arriving so that she could set out and spread her joy to others and do service for her fellows.

She was just finishing the last of a rather elaborate tangle of braids when a dam appeared at her side. The dam was stouter than the average Serra, with a cherub face and thick hands, which she placed over Yemri's hands. She was emitting so much love from her Ku that Yemri instantly felt affection for the dark-haired Serra.

The dam gestured towards the entrance to OnaKu, and Yemri understood that the dam was new to the kinship and would rather speak with words. A wave of panic washed over Yemri. Would she remember words after so much time in silence? But the dam's Ku was earnest, and Yemri obliged.

She pushed herself off the sandy floor where she had been seated and passed the pup back to her mother. Yemri gave the tiny Serra one last little pat on the head and followed the plump dam out of the boundaries of the kinship.

Yemri passed through the tall weeds and nodded to the ancient guard, who smiled in return. She hesitated for just one moment as a twinge of fear gripped her stomach before she pushed herself out into the open water.

"Ocean Mother!" the dam said, placing her hand on Yemri's heart. "It was so hard to find you. Everyone kept your secret well." Then, without warning, the dam pulled Yemri in for a fervent embrace.

Yemri froze, resisting, until she realized that the dam meant no harm. The gesture began to feel rather pleasant, but she was still grateful when she was released.

"I am not the Ocean Mother," Yemri responded.

"You will always be Ocean Mother to me, Mother Yemri. I am forever thankful to you for all you did for me."

"I am sorry… um?"

"Getdrid, if you please."

"I am sorry, Getdrid, but I do not know that I have done anything for you to be thankful for." Yemri remembered her many failures as Ocean Mother, but she felt no more guilt or remorse. It had taken her a long time to forgive herself for her mistakes, but she was finally at peace.

"Oh, but you did. I was born and raised in the Maato. I was a slave my entire life."

Yemri put a hand to her mouth. "I thought… I thought…"

"You thought we all hated you."

Yemri assented in her Ku.

"We did. I did, for sure. That was the only world I knew, and you tore it apart. You might remember me? I am ashamed now of my behavior back then. I attacked you. I had twin pups, and it was only out of fear for them that I behaved in that way. Please forgive me."

"Oh, Getdrid, you do not even need to ask forgiveness." She took Getdrid by the shoulders and squeezed before letting go and saying sincerely, "You did nothing wrong. I swarmed into your home and tore away everything you knew. There could have been a better way."

"I do not know if that is true. Those bucks were horrible and needed to be dealt with, probably only in the way that you did. Yemri." She grabbed both of Yemri's hands and held them tightly. "From the time I was small I was worked to the bone, nearly starved, and treated more disgustingly than you can imagine."

She laughed. "Look at me now!" Getdrid let go of Yemri's hands and held her arms wide, gesturing to her whole body. "Look how healthy I am! Am I not the roundest Serra you have ever seen? My children are healthy, no one is overworked, and we all eat as much as we could ever want or need." She was bursting with pride, and Yemri smiled— probably the most genuine smile she had given in her entire life.

"I will return soon to my family in the Afiti, but I had to make this journey. I needed you to know. Yemri, I had to thank you. You saved me. You saved my pups. They will never have to live the horror I was raised in."

Yemri and Getdrid spent hours talking on the borders outside OnaKu. Finally, Getdrid said, "I must be going. It is a long journey."

Yemri responded, "I will come with you. I would like to see my friends again, and I have been away so long."

Getdrid's Ku was hesitant.

Yemri could not understand the emotion she felt when Getdrid had been so open and loving only a moment before. She continued speaking to try to ease the discomfort, to get a feel for what could be wrong. "Daris is in between here and Afiti. I can go with you, and then you can continue on alone. Unless…" Getdrid still appeared extremely nervous. Yemri assumed she was trying not to hurt Yemri's feelings, so she helped her out by adding, "Unless you would rather I did not join you. That is completely fine."

"Oh, it is not that!" Getdrid seemed to deflate as she realized the emotion she was emitting. "It is only that I fear for you, Mother. The Serras of the ocean…"

When it was clear she was uncomfortable saying more, Yemri tried to help. "What? They do not like Kalani? They are angry with me for abdicating? Things are terrible?"

"No, no nothing like that. Things in the ocean are good. They love Kalani. It is worse than this for you, I fear."

"Go on," Yemri encouraged.

"They do not think kindly of you. I hate to tell you this. I worry that if you reemerge that you will not like how you are regarded. Your Ku is at peace here. I can feel it. I would hate for that to be ruined for you."

"They hate me," Yemri said without emotion.

Getdrid sent an affirmative tick of her Ku but didn't dare to say it.

Yemri thought for only a moment before she settled on her feelings about the news. She almost laughed. Then she sighed and said, "Getdrid, this is something I am well acquainted with. They did not like me as Ocean Mother, so why should they like me now? I do not mind their hatred anymore. I have learned who I am during my silent contemplation, and what they do or say cannot penetrate my peace of mind."

"In that case, I would be happy for the company," Getdrid said.

Yemri looked at the dam. Her bright yellow penumbra shone as a reminder that, although she was outside the safety of OnaKu, she could still do right by her fellow Serras… and herself. Their words could still hurt Yemri, but they would no longer influence or change her. It was only after her encounter with Deus that her ability to see penumbras had returned. It had taken her a while to understand it, but she realized that meeting with him had changed something in her. For all he had ruined at Daris—and the loss of Nhori and Tope—he had fixed something inside Yemri. He taught her to question things in a way she never had before. She had never been her authentic self, always going along with others or fighting against them. Once she had cleared her mind and heart of all the buzzing that was constantly filling it, when she finally decided to be her genuine self, it was only then that she saw penumbras again. And now she never again allow others' opinions to threaten the peace in her Ku.

Chapter 30

Santiago

Santi sat in her private section with Rogan to watch the finale, but she couldn't focus enough to know what was happening. Her mind and her attention were drawn to other things. And just because Krell had called their section private didn't mean that it actually was.

Their first visitor had been a clearly angry Amphitrite. Santi had never felt such an emotion from her giant turtle friend, but it was clear she was upset at having been left behind. Santi made a thousand apologies, and Amphitrite was placated enough to sit beside Santi now as she half-watched the game.

When the game was finished, a never-ending stream of Serras had come to talk to her for one reason or another, which, combined with her general distraction due to upcoming events, left her not noticing the goings on of the game at all.

"I was really curious about this game on a professional level, too," Santi said to Rogan when they had a moment alone.

"Huh? Oh," Rogan answered, distracted for all of the same reasons as Santi. "The tournament is every two years. We can watch the next one, Santiago." He squeezed her hand, which he had held tightly since their return to the tournament grounds. He didn't look at her now, but she knew he wasn't really seeing the game either.

Just then, another opinionated Serra floated up to their "private" seats and smiled timidly. "Santiago," the young dam said nervously, nearly bowing at the hip. "I just want to say it is amazing what you are doing. Honestly," the dam was brightening now and seemed to be gaining confidence, "it is so amazing to think that when this match is over, all our problems will be over!"

Santi raised her head to look the dam in the eye. The dam was older than Santi—which wasn't hard, she told herself, as she was only twenty-one and feeling younger every minute—but this dam held a weight in her heart of someone twice her age. Santi shook her head as she replied, "Nothing I can do will be an end to anyone's problems." She felt an obligation to comfort this dam, but she didn't know what to say. But, like everyone else, this dam hadn't come to hear the truth. Santi assumed this sad creature was here for the same reason all her supporters came to talk to her. "I am so sorry for any loss you have experienced because of the Sirens, but Zitja's death—whenever it comes—will not take that sorrow away from you."

This gave the Serra pause before a grin broke across her face and she reached out and grabbed Santi's free hand. "You are so humble. It has truly been such a special experience for me to meet you. Thank you, Santiago. May Nephira bless you." And with that, she turned and left.

Rogan turned towards Santi and they shared a meaningful look, the kind of look that communicated everything even without a Ku connection. Santi closed her eyes and slumped against Rogan's chest. He placed his hand on her head and held her close, still not letting go of her other hand.

When they had returned from their escapades in the middle of the penultimate Dwattle match, Krell had been livid at not having seen them since their defeat in their own Dwattle match. There wasn't much he could do to them, however, when they said they were just avoiding the tumult of the crowds and had resurfaced exactly when he told them to. He merely ushered them to this viewing platform that was supposedly signifying their honored-guest status.

Santi and Rogan had decided it signified their spectacle status and put them in plain view of the Dwattle spectators, giving the crowd two events to anticipate.

As if to validate her suspicion, Santi was roused from her reverie by another connection followed by a much bolder greeting.

"I hope you will be able to live with yourself once you have done the unthinkable."

Santi didn't want to look up, but she didn't want to be rude. By "the unthinkable," this Serra probably meant killing…which Santi had just done a few days ago in the lair of the Sirens. She breathed in deeply to muster her courage for the confrontation. She'd been raised in the Coral School of Manners and the Celia School of Entertaining a Crowd. She often thought of her two mothers when dealing with the impossible situations she found herself in as of late.

She sat up and opened her eyes. The Serra before her was a dam of nearly identical appearance as the last. Same middle-aged lines on her face, same slight frame, and even the same light pink tail. The only difference was the look on her face and the feeling in her Ku. She was angry and wanted Santi to hear all about it.

Santi sighed and was about to answer when the dam continued. "May Nephira curse you for taking another's life in such a despicable manner." She turned and closed her Ku as she swam away, not giving Santi a chance to respond without yelling towards her back—which Santi had no desire to do.

Rogan looked at her and gave her his usual charming smile. "Nephira is going to be very busy blessing and cursing you so much."

This made Santi smile and look at him with appreciation. "What am I going to do?" Her question was honest and earnest. "I mean, I know what I'm going to do, and I think I know what I'll say, but I do not think it will make a difference. What am I going to do when they see that I have not fixed everything all at once?"

Rogan turned to her and clasped her other hand. He looked at her with his dark eyes that comforted her as much as his words. "Santiago, I have loved you for a very long time, and I have known you only a small time longer than that. If there is one thing I know about you, it is that you always make the right choices. You are a good person. No matter what the Serra Ocean thinks is right, you will make the right choice."

She breathed out hard, pushing water through her nose and clearing her lungs. She leaned in and wrapped her arms around his waist so that her head could rest on his chest again. She was very tired. All the adrenaline she had felt from their success with Sully and the ride here on Nessy had evaporated quite quickly, leaving her utterly drained. "I appreciate your confidence in my ability to make the right decision." She looked up into his eyes. "I just wish you could tell me what that was."

"I know."

She felt his Ku as closely as she could, but even if he had an idea of what she should do, he wasn't going to tell her. He was too good. He was too selfless a person to put his opinions onto her. He would support and love her no matter what, but he knew that for her to feel right about her upcoming choices, they had to be her own.

Santi startled as another Serra approached, only this time she jumped off her cushion to greet him. Santi met Wayne in the water above her viewing platform and gave him a firm handshake.

"Wayne! It is so good to see you!" She wrapped him in a hug and was alarmed to feel how frail he seemed. She had just seen him at their Bonding, but he appeared so much older since then. He had to be in his late eighties by now and had lived through several Siren attacks on his kinship. It was a wonder he was even able to make the journey to the tournament.

"Santiago! I would not miss this for anything. I heard you were playing, and I had to see it. Shame you lost, but you did spectacularly." He placed a hand on her cheek and smiled widely before his expression became serious. "I am sorry for the thing you have to do next. I would not wish such a choice on anyone."

"The choice?" Santi asked. So far everyone had had opinions about it, but no one had been concerned with her choice in the matter.

He made a small humming sound. "Yes, the choice is the worst part. Everyone is talking about what you should do, why they know best, how you are horrible or wonderful." He made the "mmm" sound again, as if he were agreeing with himself. "No one is worried about what this choice will do to you, dear sunshine."

Santi sighed contently. When she was a child, adult Serras were always calling her starfish, but Wayne asked what a Crural would call children. She gave him many options, and he thought "sunshine" was the best pet name. He'd called her that often, though he hadn't done so since she was small.

"Well, I've decided what I'll do. I just know that no one will be happy with it. Maybe you know what I should do instead?"

Wayne grabbed both of her hands in his tiny ones and said, full of compassion, "That is not something I can tell you. But you know," he mused a little before finishing confidently, "you have always been a good pup. You always kept those two troublemakers in line." He gestured to Rogan, and she knew he meant a young Sully, as well. "I know you will make the right choice now."

When Santi didn't reply, Wayne added thoughtfully, "Santiago, it is hard to do what is right, but so long as you can live with your actions, you will be able to sleep at night. Do the right thing. Then stand by it."

"The thing I want to do though…" She thought about their goal to learn about reversing the curse with Sully, then to try to expand that to the rest of the Sirens. "It is probably impossible. And no one is going to believe me when I tell them."

"I have read a lot of Crural books and magazines, and I can tell you that I know for certain we have something in common, Crurals and Serras, and that is that none of us listen to words. It is a shame, really, but no one wants to hear the truth. They have to see it to believe it."

Santi thought about this but wasn't quite sure how it applied to her. How would she show them that she wanted to undo what Nephira had done? Especially since no one had been able to do it since? She looked at him calmly but said nothing.

"You have to show them that you will do whatever you say you will do. Be a woman of action, Santiago, and they will trust you."

Just then the announcer broke in. "And with that score, Team Howiz wins this years' tournoi de jeux!"

The crowd erupted in cheers, and Santi thought she would promptly pass out. Her stomach dropped so far in her body she felt faint and nauseated.

"I guess it is your turn now," Wayne said.

Santiago's head felt too light. She looked at Wayne fondly. He had always been such a character, always so full of fun and life. She had never experienced this serious side of Wayne. "I appreciate this more than you know, Wayne. Thank you."

"Always."

Suddenly, she had a marvelous idea. "Wayne!" She turned over her shoulder and pointed. "In that section you will find a Crural woman named Celia. She is my mother. Sit next to her. She will be the best example of a Crural you have ever experienced!"

Wayne's eyes went wide, and he pinched her cheek. "I did not get to meet your mother when she was down for your Bonding. It will be my pleasure." And with that, he took off, albeit painfully slowly, towards the section where Celia was sitting.

Rogan came down and held her hand, squeezing it firmly, as a Sentinel suddenly appeared over her left shoulder. She looked up. "It's time."

"If you will follow me, Santiago," he said, not unkindly, but not with warmth either.

She and Rogan pushed themselves up off their seats and over the small balcony in which they had been sitting. They followed closely behind the stoic, ironclad Sentinel. What he was prepared for with so much armor and weaponry, Santi wasn't sure, but she knew it wasn't a good sign that he was outfitted so thoroughly.

She didn't let go of Rogan's hand. If anything, she needed him to guide her because she couldn't seem to make her legs work properly. She could not kill Zitja, this was proven. But she also did not want to be put on display and forced to do something that—were she able to do it—she did not want to do in such a manner. She was fervently on the side of the Serras who berated her for making a spectacle of killing. She would have to convince them of the truth. She didn't have experience swaying a crowd, but she had been practicing in her head how she might convince them that she was determined to reverse the curse.

They arrived at the blue tent just outside the arena for the athletes. After the game finished, the players had not been allowed back inside, so Santi and Rogan sat alone save for their one guard. They waited.

They seemed to wait forever, the pressure and suspense pressing on Santi's chest. Her breathing became shallow and quick.

"Santiago." Rogan gave her a small shake. "You are going to hyperventilate."

"Can you do that under water?"

He cocked his head at her in what she thought was a very Crural gesture. "Can you exhale too much without inhaling enough, even under water? Is that what you are asking? Because yes, my love, you can."

She took one long, deep breath slowly, then let it out again slowly and felt better. Her head was clearer, anyway. "Rogan, I don't want to do this. What do I do?"

He looked at her sincerely. Santi knew he would not tell her what to do, but he took the request seriously anyway. "When you get out there." He paused, as if that was the end of the whole sentence. Both of his hands were on her shoulders firmly but gently. He kissed her softly on her lips then pulled away. Finally, he spoke. "Give them Hell."

She broke down crying.

It was both exactly what she needed to hear and also a very dear thing for him to say. It was very Crural. He only knew of Hell as the place or concept because of listening to her over the years. She allowed herself a few more tearful moments, and then she straightened, shook her head, and shook off the self-pity. She squared her shoulders and gave Rogan one of her customary firm nods. Then the corner of her mouth turned up slightly.

"What do you even know about Hell?"

"Only what you have told me. It sounds awful. I figured if there was anything they deserve, that is it."

Santi was just about to smile, truly smile for the first time since their return to the tournament grounds, when another Sentinel, just as armed as the first, burst into the tent and announced, "They are ready for you, Santiago." He turned to Rogan. "And if you will follow him," he gestured to a Sentinel just outside the flap of the tent, "he will take you to your seat."

"I cannot go with Santiago?" Rogan asked, genuinely concerned.

"Of course not," was the only response Rogan received.

"It's fine, Rogan. I'm fine." Santi reached out and gave him a small squeeze on his wrist. "I can do this. I am going to give them Hell."

Rogan leaned over, held her fingers and then ran his massive hands up her arms, and caressed her shoulders and neck. With his other hand, his thumb holding her chin, he kissed her passionately, as if it were the first time they'd kissed and the last all at once. She wrapped her arms around his waist and then slid them up his wide back. She felt strengthened, whole. She felt as if his love and support made all things possible. Even this.

Especially this.

When they broke apart, he still held her by the neck and chin. He didn't need to say anything. His look and his Ku told her, *"You got this."* Though Santi knew he would never use such poor Crural grammar.

In the same motion that the Sentinel used to usher Rogan out, he handed Santi her bundle of sais and leather holsters. She scowled momentarily.

When they returned from their Sully adventure, they had gone straight to their bivouac and stashed their weapons, changed, and tidied up. They wanted to make sure they looked presentable for the upcoming event and the company they would have to associate with. That this Sentinel had her sais meant someone had retrieved them from her personal space, and that did not sit well with her.

Nevertheless, she began buckling the leather straps around her thigh just under her sealskin loincloth. She had chosen the most Serra-like costume she could find for this moment, casting aside her usual swimsuit in favor of a more primitive animal skin cloth. Her lower half was covered by sealskin that fully concealed her front and back. She was not interested in exposing her backside the way most Serras wore their loin coverings—Santi not having scales to cover the skin back there. The straps of the loin coverings wrapped around her waist and stomach in a crisscross pattern before tying in the back. On the top, she wore large clamshells.

Coral had been skeptical when Santi asked her to make them for this event, saying it would be uncomfortable and that Serras did not typically wear shells in such a manner. Santi acknowledged everything Coral had told her, and she agreed, but felt this was the right way for her to make a statement, if only to herself. Clamshells were such a cliché thing for mermaids to wear in all the movies and pictures Santi had ever seen that, although she had never seen an actual Serra wear shells on their chest, she felt it encapsulated the irony.

Ok, so this is not the most *Serra outfit I could find,* she admitted to herself.

Maybe she wasn't wearing what Serras really wore, but she was wearing what Crurals thought Serras would wear, since Serras were expecting her to do something they believed Crurals would do. It felt poetic.

They deserved the Hell she was going to give them.

She finished with the last buckle on her holster, righted herself, and straightened the pearls and flowers that hung around her neck. Then, almost unconsciously, she hooked her right foot behind her and stroked the simul around her left ankle for strength.

"I'm ready."

When she popped out of the tent behind her guide, she felt thousands upon thousands of Kus connect to her, almost pushing her back with the near physical strength of it.

How courteous. She clenched and unclenched her teeth several times. *They waited until I was in sight before they began their berating.*

She hadn't felt their hatred, jeers, and taunting in the tent, she realized. It was another Serra courtesy that she knew Crurals would not abide by if they had the chance. Surely, if Crurals had Kus, they would use them to harass anyone they wanted to so long as they were in Ku's reach, whether visible or not. Crurals loved trolling people anonymously. Luckily, Serras were a more respectable breed.

As it was, now that she was in sight, the rebukes and criticisms poured over her. She knew the supporters were in there too; their voices were just quieter, less pronounced with their lack of angry fuel. She tried to tune it all out, push it to the background as if she were hearing it with her ears in a crowded stadium. She focused on the din less and her purpose more. As if she'd turned down the volume on a radio, the taunting became a buzzing hum, individual voices now indistinguishable.

"That's better," she said out loud to herself with her actual mouth and voice. There was no one to talk to, so it felt nice to talk to herself like she used to.

I'll have to remember that, she thought, and then out loud finished, "It feels better to be passive aggressive sometimes." She laughed. She had never used her voice and lips to make words under water before. "Bring back a little of the old me, hmmm?"

She smiled and looked around.

"Maybe I've finally cracked under the pressure. Going a little cuckoo." She decided this talking to herself thing wasn't the best and refocused on following her guard across the playing field.

They swam towards the center of the arena, and Santi noticed they had already brought out Zitja. Zitja was tied to a post planted in the ground. It was all becoming very real.

And very repulsive.

When Santi arrived in the middle of the arena, she took in the scene. The Dwattle field had been cleared of all objects and obstacles so that the crowd's view was completely unobstructed. The field was now just plush green moss. Santi was tempted to swim the ten feet towards the ground and throw herself on it in a fit of tantrum. Above her were all the Serras who had watched the game, leaning over their hammocks. Almost the entire island of spectators had been there for the last game—what was the point of coming all this way only to miss it? But even more Serras had crowded in who hadn't been there before. The lucky ones at the top got to enjoy the view from above without swimming. Around the sides of the arena, Serras were stacked on top of each other, treading water in place to watch. That was the "standing room only" section, Santi thought. Looming before her, growing closer with every stroke she took, was the Siren Queen. The post in the ground rose high overhead, and Zitja was tied in the middle of it. Her mouth was stuffed with fabric, and another white cloth was tied around her mouth and neck so that she couldn't Sing. Zitja's pale white arm was pulled backwards around the pole, and her stump was tied at the elbow. Her coal black tail was stretched down the pole, where her fin was wrapped in more rope.

The Siren Queen, the murderous and savage scourge of the ocean, had been rendered completely harmless.

"It is despicable!" a voice broke through the crowd Santi had been tuning out.

Her guide brought her face to face with Zitja and went away, leaving her to wonder if this was it, this was the moment, and they were both on display.

As she was wondering if it was time to get to murdering, the crowd suddenly hushed, and a powerful voice broke through the hum.

"Serras of the ocean have been waiting for this very moment since the day they were born." Santi looked around for the voice and spotted Krell floating down from above the crowd. He descended majestically towards Santi and Zitja, as if he was the main event. "Our ancestors hoped for this day their entire lives, and the lives of their ancestors before them.

Yet we are the lucky few who get to have our greatest wishes come true."

"Unbelievable," Santi said. She wished she could make snarky comments to Rogan, but singling him out with her Ku now would be unforgivably rude, even if she did not care at this moment.

"Friends! We have done it! My Sentinels have captured the beast, and our Heir will vanquish her!"

Santi tuned out Krell, along with the noisome crowd. She knew that the entire arena would know if she closed off her Ku tight, and that would be suspicious—though she wasn't sure if she cared at the moment—but she applied the skills she had just discovered and, with Ku open, she let it all turn into static, Krell's speech included. The more he droned on about his accomplishments, the more she studied the crowd and deliberately avoided hearing anything he said.

Looking at the faces in the horde, it was hard to make out anyone in particular, but when she tried, she could see the frowns. Every single one of the faces she looked upon was either typically unreadable or remarkably frowning. It was an odd thing, Santi mused, for an expressionless people to all share the same expression. She felt unsettled.

She was snapped out of her reverie when Krell gestured behind her with both his hands. Santi looked up into the private seating area where she had been only moments before and was shocked to see Ocean Mother Yazi. Santi focused her eyes on the frail old dam and her ears on Krell.

He was in the middle of his long monologue, but Santi understood well enough what he had been saying when she heard, "…is so proud to be alive to see this. I have it on good authority that Yazi has given Santiago her blessing just

570

this morning from her private tent, and she looks forward to working with Santiago in the future. Our ocean and home…"

Santi tuned him back out quickly, like turning down the volume on the radio. She could not stand to hear more lies. Yazi's blessing in her tent? That certainly didn't happen. Santi was seething. How was Krell not a Siren? He seemed to have all the criteria of those who were engulfed in the curse.

To her growing list of impossible tasks, Santi now added taking Krell down. She would see the end of him one way or another.

Abruptly, he looked at her and Santi froze. Had he somehow heard what she was thinking? Had she said it to him through her Ku? No, she wasn't connected to him. He looked at her expectantly, and she realized she had missed what he had said, but his Ku made it clear. It was time. Kill Zitja. Be the puppet I want you to be. Follow the plans and path I have set before you. Be the next Ocean Mother.

Santi looked at him squarely. She deliberately did not look at Zitja. She connected to all the Kus she could—a fraction of the Kus in the crowd—and the throng was silenced. They waited anxiously to hear what she would say. Those she could not connect to found someone in the crowd to connect to for a relay of the message. When she spoke, it would only take a moment for her words to travel through the mass of Serras.

She felt Krell's Ku startle. The plan was not for her to speak—he probably preferred that she never would again— but she was ready to say what she came to say. Krell glared fiercely at her and sent a fierce tick to her Ku, threatening her not to say anything.

She blatantly ignored him as she faced the multitude. "Serras, I thank you for honoring me with your support." Not necessarily true, she thought to herself, but she couldn't very well have said, "You've all been jerks lately," so she kept on lying. "It is my pleasure to be here before you, to do all that I can for the ocean." There was a surge of hands waving through the water, and her mind was filled with their cheers.

Time to get to the truth.

"I must tell you that I have discovered I cannot kill Zitja." The commotion around her abruptly halted, and the water got eerily silent. She rushed on before things turned hostile. "Zitja cannot be killed. She is truly immortal. But do not fear. I-" but before she could explain her plan, her rousing speech that she hoped would leave them encouraged, the crowd began murmuring and shouting, and Krell swooped down upon her.

He put a finger right in her face and told her, "You will kill her now or I will kill you."

"Krell!" she screamed. "I can't. I told you!"

Audience members were vaulting from their hammocks now, many trying to flood the arena. The Sentinels had to hold them at bay. They shouted at her so fiercely she could not tune it out.

"Kill her!"

"Save us!"

"Coward!"

"Terrasite!"

"Filthy Crural!"

"How dare you?"

Krell put both of his hands on her shoulders and pushed her at Zitja. "Kill her now."

Santi looked at the Siren Queen. They had put her crown back on her head. It had not been in the cell with her, but for some reason they wanted it on now. It was beautiful, made of coral, pearls, and starfish. It looked elegant and regal nestled on Zitja's head of black hair. Santi could feel Krell's dangerous Ku, the spectators churning in her mind; but through it all, Zitja spoke.

"Go ahead, little Crural. Show them."

Santi thought about what Wayne had said about needing to show people the truth and what Rogan had said about giving them Hell.

"Fine!" she shouted and shook off Krell's hold on her shoulders. "Fine!" she said again, even louder, to the crowd. Everyone was quiet again. Her supporters and critics. Everyone wanted to know what would happen.

She reached her hand around the hilt of her sai and slowly pulled it from its holster. For a moment, she was tempted to run Krell through the heart and be done with the whole thing, but she knew he would feel her intentions immediately, so she stopped her mind from even entertaining the idea. Killing him would not solve her problems. It might delay them, but nothing would be resolved. And then she would surely spend the rest of her life in the dungeons below Nephira's Stronghold.

All her attention was on Zitja.

Raising her sai overhead, Santi kicked her feet swiftly towards her goal and then swiftly, gracefully, and precisely, Santiago stabbed Zitja through the heart just as she'd done before. Santi could almost feel the tension in the crowd. They were on the edge of their proverbial seats. Were Santi's words true? Could she really not kill Zitja? What would happen in the next few moments would change their lives forever, whether that would be the end of the Sirens or the end of hope. They all waited to find out.

Santi slid the sai out of Zitja's body, and the two looked at each other. The skin closed around the wound on the Siren's chest as if she had never been stabbed at all, and Zitja's one good arm came free of the bindings. Santi had sliced through a rope with one of the side tines without realizing it. Zitja reached up and pulled the cloth from around her mouth and spit out the rest.

The Siren Queen opened her mouth and the arena broke into chaos.

At first glance, it looked like Zitja's Song was affecting one in every ten Serras, and Santi tore her eyes away from the crowd to look in horror at Zitja. That's when she realized the Siren's mouth was closed. She was not Singing. Instead, her eyes scanned the crowd, and she appeared just as confused and bewildered as Santi was.

Suddenly, Rogan was at her side. "They are changing!"

"Who is changing?"

To answer, Rogan gestured all around. Santi brought her hand up to mouth and felt dizzy. Serras of all ages, genders, and beliefs towards Santi's killing of Zitja were writhing in the water; when they stopped their harried thrashing, they revealed their change.

The curse had taken hold.

Even worse, Zitja had escaped the rest of her bonds and snuck away, rallying the new Sirens to her. Sentinels were flooding the area, and common Serras were taking up arms. The chaos that surrounded them was going to get a lot worse and a lot more deadly.

Rogan reached to grab the hilts of his swords. "Come on, Santiago! They will need our help!"

"No." Santi put her hand on his forearm before he could unsheathe his swords. "*This* is not our fight."

He looked at her and searched her Ku for understanding. Hands still poised above his weapons, his biceps twitching to fight, he paused but did not seem ready to relent.

"Our fight is bigger. Maybe we succeed here but suppose we don't. Rogan, we have to fix this. All of it." She gestured to everything around them, the chaos and fighting, but she meant beyond just the arena. "We have to stop Krell and Zitja. We have to save Yazi. We have to return Sully to himself, and we have to reverse the curse. This, right now, will not fix anything."

Rogan let go of his swords. "First we have to find our family," he said.

Santi nodded once, and he pulled her along to the section where Celia was, a vulnerable Crural.

When they arrived, Santi and Rogan saw that Grendor had gathered Celia up in one arm as he held his sword in the other, fighting off any who would do them harm as he untangled them both from the crowd.

Grendor saw Santi and without pausing told her, "I will meet you in Daris. Your mother will be safe."

"I know," she responded as she felt them make their way to the edge of the island. She held them in her Ku as she turned just in time to see a newly transformed Siren lash out erratically, screaming and lunging for Wayne.

"No!" Santi shouted as she let go of Rogan's hand, grabbed her sai, and lunged at the Siren. She hit him in the face with a firm fist, stabbing with her sai. But the Siren dodged at the last moment, and her sai connected only with its shoulder. The Siren had a small knife, which it stabbed towards Wayne. Santi pulled her sai out of its shoulder quickly and plunged it into the heart of the Siren. She felt no qualms about killing someone who would do her loved ones harm. Wayne was right; once she made a choice she stood by it. And if killing Zitja would end all Sirens, she would kill the Siren Queen a thousand times.

The Siren hung limply in the water and began floating toward the floor. Relieved, she looked to her old friend, but the relief was fleeting. She gathered Wayne in her arms, the Siren's knife protruding from his chest and said, "I'm sorry Wayne. I'm so, so sorry." She had failed him.

He closed his eyes. He was already so weak that his life force was fading quickly. He whispered, "You did really great, sunshine."

"No, Wayne." Santi was frantic. "Hold on! I'll get you a healer."

But Wayne's light was too dim to hold on any longer.

She clutched his lifeless body to her chest, his tail hanging limply, and cried out loud with her voice. "NO!"

She only uttered one sob before Rogan grabbed her around the waist and she let go of Wayne. He began floating to the moss below as she turned, still shocked, and looked at her Bondmate. "Rogan, Wayne." Another sob escaped her body. "Wayne." She couldn't believe it. The Serra she had known since she was ten years old and who had loved her as much as her own abuelo was gone in just a moment. She would never see him again. Never bring him a Crural object for him to misuse.

"Shhhh, I am sorry, my love." Rogan ushered her under the bedlam. "My mother and Amaratizz are safe. We must leave now." As if to illustrate his point, a grappling pair of Siren and Serra careened so hard into Rogan and Santi that they were separated, and she was flung to the mossy floor.

Santi wanted a moment. She wanted to grieve Wayne. She thought she would just curl up in the peat and cry. He was the first Serra she had met besides Rogan, and he had always been such a dear friend.

Rogan came down to her, and she knew she couldn't wallow. She kicked herself off the floor and met him in his descent. When they rejoined, he grabbed her around the waist to haul her away. "Why?" she said to no one. "Why is this happening?"

"I do not know," Rogan answered. "But we will go to Daris and find out what to do next."

"What about Amphitrite? We have to find her!" Santi had concern for everyone she cared about. She could not let anyone else succumb to the fate Wayne just suffered.

"She will make her own way." But when he saw that Santi was still searching, frantic, he added, "Santiago, she will be fine. She will outlive us all, and you know it."

She nodded. The green turtle was cunning and quick. She would be fine. And they had to leave quickly.

Daris was the smartest place to go. Grendor would know what to do. But then she realized that Grendor had to take orders from Krell. This snapped her out of her grief. "No!" Santi said fiercely. She untangled herself from Rogan and looked at him as the fighting and chaos raged around him. "If we go to Daris, Krell will be the one making the decisions about how to handle this."

"But you have an idea," Rogan guessed, feeling her Ku and getting hyped up with her. "What you said before about fixing all of this?"

"Yes. We are going to take care of this. We can't let Krell decide how it's handled. He will make the wrong choice. Maybe I will, too, but it will be mine to make."

"Where are we going?"

"We have to go to the NorMer Clan. We'll find answers there."

She had been thinking about going there for a while. Ever since Merrek had told her that the NorMer were holding valuable secrets and Sorrl had afterwards confirmed the old woman's ramblings about Deus, she knew answers would be found there. Rogan held her tightly as he towed her swiftly away from the tournament island.

It took days to shake off the horrific feelings that lingered after the tournament, And it took nearly two emotionally overwrought weeks, when nuntiums arrived from Cora, Tizz, and Celia to let Rogan and Santi know they were all right, before Santi felt her heart unclench. She and Rogan were not quick in their journey—traveling at tail-speed or visping occasionally under an ular, with frequent stops for rest and food—but when they finally arrived in the NorMer three weeks later, it seemed news traveled faster than they had, and chaos traveled even quicker.

As soon as they breached the boundaries of the NorMer Clan, they were accosted by a small group of Serras who ushered them into a cavern and told them to wait. One of them said, "You are safe here, but do not leave," before he vanished back through the cave opening.

Three hours later, Santi was pacing the rocky floor of the cavern, preferring the feel of ground beneath her feet while she was so agitated. "We've been here forever, and we don't even know what we're waiting for."

Rogan wasn't calm, either, but he could see the state Santi was in and chose to let her play the role of nervous worrier so that he could be her counterpart. "I am sure there is nothing to worry about. He said we were safe, and in the time we have been here, we *have* been safe!" His voice rose at the end of the sentence, energetic and quick to bring levity to his words.

"But that was so long ago. Why-" But she didn't finish. She felt commotion on the outskirts of the cave and she stopped pacing. As always, the thick rocks blocked her Ku, and it wasn't until someone arrived just at the opening to their cavern that she felt their presence.

A solid-looking buck in his middle years entered the cave as though he owned it and everyone inside. Santi took his confidence as a threat to their freedom and put her hands on the sais at her thighs.

From behind her, Rogan burst forward and placed his hand on the older buck's chest, "Amicus, El E'tajari." Santi scowled at the unfamiliar name, but she let her hands relax on the hilts of her sais. The buck whose name Santi heard only as a string of letters jammed together returned Rogan's gesture, and it became obvious they knew each other well.

"Santi, this is my father's dear friend, El E'tajari. They knew each other their entire lives."

"Amicus," she said, placing her hand on the older buck's chest. He did look a lot like those from the Tipua. Like Rogan and Amed, El E'tajari had dark skin and hair, and was built just as broadly and impressively; but where Rogan and Amed's eyes were a brown so dark it was nearly black, El E'tajari's eyes were a light violet. "It is nice to meet you Ellee..." She faltered, and Rogan jumped in graciously.

"El Ee-Ta-har-ee." He smiled. "And this is my Bondmate, Santiago."

"Santiago! Amed boasted of your strength and cunning. It is truly an honor to meet you."

"And you," Santi said honestly. It was so nice to meet people who knew Amed, though her fondness for her honorary father did not quench her curiosity or anxiety. "But what I don't understand is why we are meeting you in this cave and why we had to wait for so long. And why I get the feeling you are not about to let us leave any time soon."

"As to the wait, I can answer quickly. You were waiting on me, and for that I apologize. We did not know where in the ocean you would turn up, but we have been on high alert for you. I told them to summon me as soon as you were found. I was in Daris when I received the nuntium and got here as soon as I could get a cryptid."

To Santi's relief, Rogan was finally becoming as suspicious as Santi was. His Ku took on a firm formality as he asked, "El E'tajari. What is going on?"

El E'tajari gestured for them to sit and, when neither Rogan nor Santi made any indication that they would relax for the discussion, he continued as they hovered in the water in the center of the cavern.

"About ten percent of the Serra population changed into Sirens." Rogan and Santi both gasped, and Santi nearly toppled backwards in shock. Ten percent equaled hundreds of thousands of Serras. "After the events at the tournament, word spread about what happened, and that seemed to cause more transformations throughout all the clans of the ocean. In the three weeks since the tournament, our contacts have reported that those who changed were on both sides of the argument about the public killing of Zitja. Many who felt you should kill her seemed to have transformed when you proved that you couldn't; others who were against it appear to have transformed because you tried. That is only speculation, and we might never know the true cause of the transformation. One thing is clear, however..." He paused so long that Santi already knew what he was going to say before he said it.

"I can take it," she said.

"We have found that the second cursing—which is what they are calling the wave of transformations three weeks ago—is being blamed on you, Santiago. It seems to be an almost universal belief across the whole ocean."

"This is not her fault!" Rogan jumped in vehemently.

"I know that," El E'tajari reassured him, putting a hand on Rogan's shoulder to steady the younger buck. "And others know that. You have many supporters throughout the ocean, Santiago. Those who have met you and know your Ku are fond of you and trust you completely. It seems you have made an impression on everyone you have met." He smiled widely. "That is to be commended. However, the amount of Serras one can meet in a lifetime are merely a handful compared to the entire world of beings, and thus, it has become dangerous for you out there. I thank Nephira my people found you first."

Santi let out breath she had been holding throughout his explanation and grabbed Rogan's hand for support. "I have so many questions I don't know where to begin… But I guess I'll start with the most important: where is the Byblio of Nephira?"

It was not a question either of them had been expecting, and both Rogan and El E'tajari looked utterly confused.

Rogan spoke up and asked the question she probably should have. "So, what do we do now?"

"Santiago," El E'tajari answered, taking her absurd question seriously. "I do not know of that which you speak, but I will have a scholar and magister friend of mine come and visit who might be able to answer your questions. As to what you do now, you wait. We will take care of you here until it is safe for you to emerge."

"No!" Rogan and Santi said together. When they realized they both felt the same way about their forced seclusion, they shared an agreement between their Kus. Rogan said, "If you do not mind, El E'tajari, we are not the type to sit idly by while others handle problems."

"Of course not," the elder Serra answered, his bright violet eyes sincerely apologetic for the circumstance in which they found themselves.

Before he could provide another excuse to keep them there, Santi broke in. "With all respect imaginable, El," she said, testing the shortening of his name with a look—when he did not object, she went on—"I have a purpose in this ocean. My abuela did not diligently work her life towards

582

something for me to hide in a cave. And yet here I am. I know I am the key to fixing this."

"I commend your dedication, Santiago, I do," El E'tajari answered with as much respect towards her as she had shown to him, even though she suspected he thought she was a raving lunatic at the moment, "but you do not understand. Not only is nearly every Serra in the water angry with you, but Krell has put an order out for you to be seized and brought to him. You are to be punished. I fear he means death."

"All the time with this guy." Santi rolled her neck, cracking it in three places. Somehow, she could never take Krell seriously and always found him more annoying than threatening. "I should have killed him when I had the chance."

"Did you ever really have the chance?" Rogan said almost snidely. "You would never have been able to kill him."

Santi was immediately defensive. She could have! She had been working hard. It might have been possible for her to best him in combat.

After a moment, she admitted to herself that that wasn't true. The best she could do was sneak a deadly blow on him… if she could get past his personal guards. She blew water firmly out her nose and shook her head. "You're right," she said. Why couldn't Rogan just keep to the jokes? She squeezed his hand. "I appreciate you being realistic."

"El," she said, turning her attention to the emerald-tailed buck before her. "We appreciate the hospitality and offer for protection, but we cannot stay. Let everyone else fight the battle at hand. Rogan and I have a thousand-year-old curse to reverse."

El E'tajari looked between the pair of young Bondmates, and Santi knew he was having a hard time letting them make such a decision when he was in a position to protect Amed's offspring. Finally, his shoulders relaxed as he conceded. "I will send my magister friend to you to start you on your search for that which you desire. Please stay here, safe, until you know where you will head to next. I will try to help you in any way I can. Though I cannot always be with you for fear Krell will suspect my absence, I will lead you in the direction of supportive Serras when I can."

"Thank you, El." Santi pushed herself forward and wrapped her arms around his shoulders in a friendly embrace. "Amed would be grateful to you for taking care of us. And for letting us make our own mistakes," she added.

She pushed herself back and the three of them said goodbye. "Please be safe," El E'tajari said as he turned his violet eyes towards the open water and left them alone.

The two young lovers turned and faced each other. Holding both of her hands in his, Rogan asked, "Do you think we can do this?"

She responded, unsure of everything ahead of them save for one thing. "I think that as a team, we can do anything."

Treading Waves

Glossary

Amicus – A word to show love and/or respect in greeting or leave taking

Artisan – Artist; An Opus

Aucupium *[awk-you-pee-um]* – eavesdropping via Ku

Auditus *[odd-it-us]* - Deafness caused via eardrum piercing. Auditus inducts the newest members to the Sentinels

Bab – Casual term of endearment and respect from the NorMer Clan

Balam *[ball-um]* - An elected official who represents the clan and protects them

Binding - The joining of Kus who have chosen each other

Bondmate – How two beings that have entwined their Kus to another are referred

Buck – male Serra

Byblio [Bib-lee-oh] – *A mystery that we have not yet learned

Cantor – An artisan that produces music; an Opus

Chimba – Cool, awesome.

Cor [Core] – Counsel made up of the balams of the clans (also referred to as "the Ocean Mother's Heart)

Consecration – Declaring the name of a one-year-old pup to family and friends

Courier – Transports Serras to and from destinations

Crural *[crur-awl]* – Humans

Crural Guardian – Protectors of Crurals, helps save lives during shipwrecks and oceanic disasters

Cryptid *[crip-tid]* – Ancient water beasts that can be ridden for fast travel

Dam – female Serra

Daris *[dare-iss]* – Serras' only main city

Demis [Dem-ee] – Serras with Crural blood in them

Daristor [Dare-iss-tour] - Youth aged 13-16 that tour the ocean in a group to learn about the ocean and various opuses

Deus *[day-us]* – Ancient and legendary god trapped at the bottom of the ocean

Dumke *[doom-key]* – People who take care of animals and plants in the ocean

Dwattle – A game Serras play similar; the name of the small round object used in gameplay

Gragger – Architect or builder

Haru [har-oo] – Prefaced before a word to signify "without"

Haruvivo *[har-oo-viv-oh]* – The death rites releasing a Serra into the ocean

Healer – doctors/midwife

Hegira *[hee-gear-uh]* – The migration of scales Serra pups experience; as they age, more skin is exposed along their body

Horp – City maintenance, landscape, and sanitation workers

Iskar *[iz-car]* – A knitting type needle

Keda *[kay-duh]* – A game/sport similar to surfing

Kinship - Tribe/community of Serras

Ku *[coo]*- Essence of the heart, used to communicate to others, power of all life

KuCores – Underwater animals, typically mammals, that have kus

KuVis- Strength/power within found in all animals, flora, fauna, and the ocean

Lourier – Actor; an opus

Magister – A professor in Daristor

Mercatura *[merk-uh-tour-ah]* – Traveling salesman

Mossup – Derogatory term for a female

Nurturer – Teacher for Serras age 1 – 12

Nuntium *[none-tee-um]* – A message sent using the ku of jellyfish

Ocean Mother – Leader of all the Serras; used to be a hereditary position but now is passed down to a dam chosen by the current Ocean Mother.

Opus [Oh-puss]– Career

Peace Maker – Conflict resolution specialists
Penumbra – A colorful aura that very few Serras can see around others
Pup – Serra child
Sentinels – Protector of the ocean against any threat
Simul [Si-mule]– Bejeweled matching strands wrapped around both parties to signify bonding
Thaed *[thay-ad]* – Study and research humans; anthropologists
Terrasite – Offensive slang referring to humans or Serras with human blood
Tournoi de Jeux [French for "Games Tournament"] — Dwattle championship tournament that occurs once every 2 years
Troag *[troge]*– Center of Daris
Ular [Oo-lar] – Used when referring to a whale that is working for Serras in some manner
Visping – Traveling under an Ular to utilize the protection, food, and current draft the animal provides

Names Pronunciation Guide

Amaratizz - A-marr-uh-tizz
Amed – Ah- med
Amphitrite - Am-fih-tryt
El E'tajari – El Ee-tah-har-ee
Phinell – Fin-el
Maato – Mat-oh
Maatis – Mat-iss
Nhori – Nore-ee
Santi – Sahn-tee
Zitja - Zeet-juh

Acknowledgements

A self-published book is anything but published by oneself. I have so many people to thank that it would be selfish-publishing of me to end this book without doing so.

My most heartfelt gratitude goes to my husband, Dan. I spent months at a time doing nothing but writing and grumbling while he brought in coffee and sustenance when I was too busy to leave my desk. He was a champ through it all and picked up my slack. I am forever thankful to Dan for his patience and support. I'm happy to be on his team in life.

Next, my beta readers and their endless tolerance of my neurosis and perfectionism, they are the true heroes here: Celestie has been with me from the beginning and is only getting harder and harder on me. She is forever steering me clear of phrasing that sounds "scaterwhompous" and keeping me in line when I ramble on and on. Kristine has the most acute mind for timelines and accuracy. Without her my stories would be riddled with timeline flaws and inaccuracies. She has also been extremely valuable when I absolutely cannot get a sentence or phrasing to work and I feel she needs credit for writing entire sentences in this book. Corrie is on a quest to eradicate anything "barfy" or unrealistic and will let me know every instance in which a character has acted in a way that makes them unlikable. Erin brought value to this book by hating it the first time she read it. Every comment about her loathing for Rogan and Santi only pushed me to evaluate their characters and make them better. Kristie, with her meticulous librarian ways, makes me see how terribly I'm explaining scenes and is forceful in her desire to eliminate all passive voice from existence. This book also picked up a new beta reader, Sara, whose eye for precision and dedication to exactness cannot be matched. It is because of her I was finally able to include the much demanded glossary, and the credit is all hers.

Cassandra and Becky put the finishing touches on all my books to make then polished and presentable to the world. I could not call this story a book without them!

And lastly, endless thanks go to my family, friends, and the fans of the Siren Anthology. The outpouring of support and love through it all has been phenomenal and rendered me speechless on many occasions. My success is because of you.

I get to take pride in saying, "I wrote a book," but for all of these wonderful people, I hope they take pride in the role they played. For without them, this book is could not exist.

Born and raised in Utah, Savannah moved to New York in 2010 to pursue her dream of writing. *Treading Waves* is Savannah's third novel and book three in the *Siren Anthology*.

When not writing Savannah is often thinking about imaginary places, playing roller derby as Fancy Nasty, and eating more Cheetos than she should. Savannah lives in New Jersey with her endlessly patient husband Dan, cat Poe, and puppy FLOTUS.

S.R. Atkinson